D0302288

To Steal Her Love

Matti Joensuu is one of the Nordic countries' leading crime writers and a former investigator at the Helsinki Police Department. *Priest of Evil* (Arcadia) was shortlisted for the 2006 Glass Key Award for Scandinavian Crime Novel of the Year. His works have been translated into thirteen languages.

David Hackston studied Scandinavian languages and literature at University College London. He has worked extensively from both Finnish and Swedish, and his published translations include works of prose, poetry, drama and non-fiction. In 2007 he was awarded the Finnish State Prize for Literary Translation.

Matti Joensuu

*To Steal
Her Love*

Translated from the Finnish by David Hackston

Arcadia Books Ltd
15-16 Nassau Street
London W1W 7AB

www.arcadiabooks.co.uk

First published in the United Kingdom by Arcadia Books 2008
Originally published by Otava as *Harjunpää ja rakkauden nälkä* 1993
Copyright © Matti Joensuu 1993

The English translation from the Finnish
Copyright © David Hackston 2008

FILI, the Finnish Literature Information Centre, has supported the translation of this book.

Matti Joensuu has asserted his moral right to be identified as the author of this work in
accordance with the Copyright, Designs and Patents Act, 1988.

All rights reserved. No part of this publication may be reproduced in any form or by any means
without the written permission of the publishers.

A catalogue record for this book is available from the British Library.

ISBN 978-1-905147-74-8

Typeset in Bembo by Basement Press, London
Printed in Finland by WS Bookwell

Arcadia Books supports English PEN, the fellowship of writers who work together to promote
literature and its understanding. English PEN upholds writers' freedoms in Britain and around
the world, challenging political and cultural limits on free expression. To find out more, visit
www.englishpen.org or contact
English PEN, 6-8 Amwell Street, London EC1R 1UQ

Arcadia Books distributors are as follows:

in the UK and elsewhere in Europe:
Turnaround Publishers Services
Unit 3, Olympia Trading Estate
Coburg Road
London N22 6TZ

in the US and Canada:
Independent Publishers Group
814 N. Franklin Street
Chicago, IL 60610

in Australia:
Tower Books
PO Box 213
Brookvale, NSW 2100

in New Zealand:
Addenda
PO Box 78224
Grey Lynn
Auckland

in South Africa:
Quartet Sales and Marketing
PO Box 1218
Northcliffe
Johannesburg 2115

Arcadia Books is the *Sunday Times* Small Publisher of the Yea

Tweety

The night emitted a faint sound, or perhaps it was a smell, imperceptibly wafting out of the darkness, something soothing like the smell of boats and wet jetty planks, and though Tweety couldn't quite put his finger on it, he could feel the effect it had on him. It triggered something inside him, opened a hatch long clamped shut at the bottom of his mind, and in a flash he realised that his powers were intact after all.

The power fizzed within him. Particularly around his groin and calves, but more than anywhere else it nested in his chest, residing there like something alive, a cat maybe, or a bird, a silver, gleaming bird spreading its wings in a coat of arms, and there was no doubt: it thrilled him. More than what he had felt in Brownie's flat, or the emotions Little Foal's corsets had stirred within him; more than the redhead on Temppelikatu with the black-seamed nylon tights and a pussy shaved as smooth as porcelain. But still he pretended nothing had happened. He stood on the spot, just as before, trying his best not to think about it.

But Tweety knew what he was doing. You couldn't think about the power; it was forbidden, like laughing was forbidden too. And it wasn't just any old Tom, Dick or Harry who'd said so; it was God himself. Best not think about that either.

Besides, just thinking about the power frightened the hell out of him. As chilling as when he was little, when the willy-eaters started grinding their teeth in the dark, when you're suddenly sure a cancer is lurking in your bones or that you'll catch AIDS if you don't manage to cross the road before the lights turn red. He imagined Reino dying, Mother Gold too, that he'd killed them somehow, accidentally, without meaning to. And this was more than just spite, it was punishment for thinking about the power, for the fact that the power existed, that he existed. And when all this flooded his mind at once: farewell, power. After that the most stunning woman in the world could have staggered past, stone drunk, her arse and tits almost bare, ready and waiting, but trying anything would have been pointless.

Tweety waited a moment longer. And when nothing started gnawing away at him he glanced around casually, briefly scanned the street in both directions, then let his eyes linger on the other side of the road where the word *Nightclub* glowed in red lettering. But nothing important happened yet. Only the night danced, its skirt billowing across the sky, and he caught the smell of the bay at Töölönlahti, the faint smell of August, that hazy, dreamy smell that always arose when the swallows flocked during the day.

'Summer is dying,' he whispered solemnly, as though he were standing at an open grave, and after a short silence he gently touched the front of his jacket, almost as though he were crossing himself, right by the pocket where the pouch and the knife he had meticulously sharpened earlier that evening lay biding their time. The movement was entirely unintentional, but there was something startling about it, as though within him stirred a barely controllable urge to send someone to the bosom of the earth.

He wasn't really thinking anything like that; he was thinking that his time would soon be up. His internal clock told him so, it never got fast or slow. He was thinking about how he could walk through doors, and above all about how he was invisible. In that, at least, he was right, as few people would ever have noticed him, though he wasn't even trying to hide but stood leaning against the wall in his regular spot beneath the archway where so far everything had always begun well. He stood perfectly still – at this, he was a master – and his clothes were carefully chosen and grey. They were even the same shade as the granite of the surrounding masonry, and at first glance he looked undeniably like a part of the building, a pillar or something only dogs would notice before leaving a puddle at its foot.

But Tweety wasn't waiting for dogs. He was waiting for a woman. It didn't matter that he didn't yet know which woman, what kind of woman, but somewhere deep inside he sensed that tonight she might be blonde, a bit like Wheatlocks, maybe even a bit chubby, the kind of woman with supple, bouncing breasts and a sprightly, round behind. And if she had a figure like that, she might be wearing a bodysuit or a camisole

– and he loved them. He could just see how it fitted around her: clinging tight against her body, like a second skin. Its straps would be like silk threads, decorated with a small rosette or a flower. And he knew it would have lace cups to hold her breasts like a pair of tender hands.

'Jesus,' he sighed and was about to drift off, but he didn't have time. The nightclub's door jolted once, twice, but then the person coming out hesitated; perhaps they were waiting for someone. They kept their hand on the handle and held the door ajar letting yellow light spill out into the street like liquid that wouldn't disappear no matter how much the darkness tried to lap it up. Sounds darted from inside. They were nothing but pounding echoes, but you could tell what it was like in there: dim lamps and expensive drinks, leather and hardwood furnishings, women dressed in silk, threads of perfume streaming through the air like vines. Though all this he knew already; he had sniffed the clothes of many people who had come out of that door.

Tweety looked around: there were no taxis in sight. That was a good sign, it filled him with warmth, and in a flash he was certain that the person about to step outside would be The One.

But it was a man that came out. Arsehole. He was fairly drunk and stumbled out of the door sideways, as though the building itself had popped out a lump of shit. His suit was appropriately brown, too, but in every other respect he looked like the kind of man whose life consisted of nothing but Rolex watches and BMWs. He stood there holding the door open, and a moment later a woman appeared, blonde, and something surged inside Tweety, so much that he had to lower his gaze. He glanced at his shoes long enough to say their names out loud – the left was Pessi and the right Moses – and only then did his throat feel loose enough that he dared take another look at the woman.

By God, she was stunning! His own age, perhaps in her thirties. Strangely she was both slim and well built, like a doll. Her face was beauti-ful in a doll-like way, almost symmetrical, and her dark-red mouth glowed like a berry ready to be eaten. And her hair… It was almost white and covered her forehead like a curtain, but around the ears it went wild and gushed in curls down over her shoulders.

She certainly had good taste: her blazer was like cream, beneath it she wore a jumper that looked like it was made of silk, and inside that there appeared to be just the right amount of life. It almost certainly had lacy frills, then there was the smell of perfume and skin and armpits warm from dancing. But best of all was her skirt: a very short skirt, green and dazzling like a jewel. It didn't even try to cover her bottom, and it was just the kind of bottom a woman should have: one that you notice, then immediately want to know what it feels like to the touch.

They didn't hang around. They headed right in the direction of Töölönkatu, side by side, though with enough distance between them to indicate that this was clearly the first time they had met. You could see this on them too; you could smell it. The man suddenly turned frisky, moved closer to the woman and wrapped his arm around her waist in a familiar, possessive gesture. He might even have given her a shifty squeeze; the woman stumbled, then giggled immediately afterwards. She had a nice giggle, like the sound of a hare bounding away with a little bell around its neck.

Tweety continued to stand where he was. He never starting moving straight away; not even this time, though he was certain they hadn't spotted him. In any case, he still had to christen them.

'And your name shall be Silkybum,' he whispered and stared at Silkybum's buttocks, and they were certainly worth looking at. They swung pleasingly beneath her skirt as if they were laughing together. They had reason enough to laugh: they knew from experience exactly what kind of fun awaited them.

'And you can be the Corpse,' he continued, almost a snarl, and cast a glance somewhere between the man's shoulder blades. He didn't really know why a name like this sprang to mind; he normally christened the men Pig or Swine. The name Corpse startled him slightly, like seeing a flag at half mast, but it was too late to change it now. Once the Corpse, always the Corpse, and this Corpse was strolling towards the corner of the park with his arm around Silkybum, and turning left.

Tweety shook his head, dispelling the unpleasant thought, then listened to the night once again, but this time he listened with action ears, pointed ears with hairy edges, like those of a troll or a sharp-toothed beast. A car hummed along Mannerheimintie, only its lights visible, and somewhere in Kallio an ambulance howled, moaning like a suffering dragon being dragged along the street. But the night was still charged and promising, like the opening bars of *Thus Spake Zarathustra*. But this time it was the strains of *Carmina Burana* that began ringing in his head, and he pushed himself away from the wall.

Pessi and Moses flashed silently across the pavement; Tweety's step was quick and relaxed. But this was just for show; he was ready to stop at any moment, to break into a run, to stagger around like a drunk or sink like a shadow behind the cars. He wasn't even aware that he could do this for everything was stored on a mysterious disk in his mind so that, in any given situation, the right programme would start running by itself.

He came to the corner. Silkybum and the Corpse had passed the hotel and were walking straight ahead. They seemed unhurried, in a way that suggested they didn't have far to go, and more than likely they were going to Silkybum's flat, because both outside the nightclub and at the corner of the park she had gestured almost imperceptibly to show the way. Seeing them again, he noted that the Corpse was actually quite stocky, but he didn't give the matter another thought. He generally never paid any attention to the men involved until it was time to take care of them. And in that, too, he was a true master.

Perhaps he didn't want to think of the Corpse because he himself was rather short and slender, petite even, right down to his gaunt face and thin fingers, worn away by hard work. Only his head didn't fit the pattern. It was as though it belonged to someone else, like the bird in *Tweety and Sylvester* where his nickname came from. It was also because, ever since he was a child, he had wanted to be a bird. His real name was Asko, but he had never liked it. Even before he had gone to school the other children had worked out how to put the letters S and P in front of it.

They walked single file through the night, a fair distance between them, but every now and then Tweety caught Silkybum's scent in the air, the thrilling smell of sweet perfume, the sour smell of the wine she had drunk that evening. At moments like this he wanted to speed up and close the gap between them, just enough to hear the hiss of her nylon-covered thighs as they brushed against one another. But he let go of the thought and was content with the knowledge that he would be able to stroke them naked later on. It occurred to him how magnificent it would have been to be her corset; he would have spread across her skin, caressing her all over, all at once, though of course it would have felt strange that his face was suddenly elastic and his lips were a row of jutting hooks. But it would have been worth it – unless she decided to throw the whole thing in the washing machine when she got home.

The air was thick with the smell of grass and mud and earthworms. Hesperia Park was just ahead of them. But Silkybum and the Corpse walked past it, carried on along the pavement, crossed the road, and turned right at the end of the hedgerow, and Tweety could sense that they were almost home; it all but radiated from Silkybum. She was getting ready for something; she'd changed the rhythm of her footsteps and even started swaying a little, and she'd just checked that she still had her handbag. Her keys were probably in there. Tweety sped along beside the row of hawthorns.

He stopped when the hedges came to an end, and now his eyes were nothing but two watchful slits. All he could see was Silkybum, then she suddenly disappeared round the corner. It had to be Vänrikki Stoolinkatu, the one that rose up a steep hill. Tweety darted between the cars and, as though it had a will of its own, his right hand kept slipping into his jacket pocket. The bottom of his pocket was full of small pieces of tightly rolled-up paper, like small birds' eggs, and he selected the second one that came to his fingers – he wasn't sure whether he could trust the first one, it might have been nothing but a scaredy cat – then with practised fingers he began rolling it tighter still.

Tweety leaned against the wall, held his free hand against the stonework and peered round the corner; skilfully, in such a way that he seemed to grow with the wall just enough to see what he wanted. He had guessed right: they had stopped halfway up the hill and were now standing barely twenty metres away from him. The Corpse his hands on his hips and Silkybum was rummaging through her bag, gutting it like a fish. There was a jangle of keys and they both burst out laughing.

Silkybum went up the stone steps, the Corpse close behind her, exuding both power and a certain rubberiness, and Tweety realised that they were far drunker than he had guessed. But that was a good thing: the Corpse would last one session at the most, and after that they would have no difficulty falling asleep, and they would sleep very soundly indeed.

The door opened and they stepped inside, or rather the corridor sucked them in, and in a flash Tweety was on the move. With his legs moving like a sewing machine needle he sprinted up the hill, the hand holding the ball of paper outstretched and ready. Magically he could see that there were no other people walking about, no beady eyes, and he could see that the door had already started to close. But he didn't panic.

He was less than ten metres away and, besides, he knew the doors in this house. They were stiff, as slow as mating whales, and the pumps in their mechanisms often held them ajar for a full few minutes.

Pessi reached the step first, followed swiftly by Moses, and with his free hand Tweety grabbed hold of the door handle; it was a thick copper tube and reminded him of a horse's penis. He didn't stop the door altogether, he just slowed it down a little. The fingers of his right hand fumbled for the latch, finally located the cold metallic plate and immediately started pressing the paper egg into its angular nest.

Tweety loosened his grip on the handle. As the door stood ajar he caught a glimpse of Silkybum and the Corpse; they were waiting for the lift, standing with their backs to him. The Corpse had his hand beneath Silkybum's blazer and was fondling her neck. Then the door swung shut. Tweety tried to control his panting as he gasped for breath; he wanted to hear what the lock had to say. And it said 'click', but the 'clack' that should have followed didn't sound, and the warm joy of success flooded into his chest.

'The damn lamp's broken!' he snarled almost immediately, as though he were afraid of his sudden happiness. The words themselves startled him; he wasn't even sure what they meant, but still they bubbled out of his mouth from time to time, often just as his excitement was about to culminate. But now wasn't the time for culmination or relief, it was the time for fingers tickling in his stomach and for being on his guard. Tweety looked around, this time without waving his arms about. He carefully scrutinised the street, the cars and the houses, and the windows in particular, but he couldn't see any lights, not even the old lady who often couldn't get to sleep and who snuck about peering out at the street so that she wouldn't have to face death so frightfully alone.

He crossed the street and hoped that Silkybum lived on that side of the building, but didn't turn round to look up at the windows just yet, it would have been too soon, and he imagined the lift arriving and the Corpse holding open the accordion door. CHILDREN UNDER TWELVE MUST BE ACCOM AN ED... read the defaced instructions. And now Silkybum was extending the key towards the lock, and perhaps she was annoyed that the smell of next-door's meat gravy made the entire stairwell smell like sweaty armpits.

Tweety stopped by the wall of the house opposite and turned around. Silkybum's house was imposing; five stories high with large, recently replaced windows that gleamed with darkness. He tilted his head; he imagined them walking into the hallway and he sensed that a light would flicker on somewhere very soon, unless her flat really did face on to the courtyard. Still, that wouldn't be a problem; he could get into the courtyard through the stairwell. Another option would have been to make his way up to the floor where the lift had stopped, and after that it wouldn't be hard to work out where she lived by listening behind the doors.

A light came on! It was on the third floor, the window on the far right; something inside him registered this immediately. Already he began envisaging the landing, and he knew that Silkybum's door would be the last on the left after coming out of the lift. The light shining through from the hallway was pale at first, but soon afterwards a lamp was switched on in the living room. It was one of those rice paper globes that women seemed to like so much, and he had often wondered how a thing like that would blaze if he were to hold a flame to its lower rim as a leaving gift.

A figure came to the window and pulled down the blinds. Tweety sensed that it was Silkybum; there was something so graceful about the figure and, after all, it was her flat. The Corpse was probably taking off the fabric excrement he was wearing, but Tweety didn't want to think about him any more. Neither did he want to stand around loitering for too long; someone might ask him what he was doing or at the very least notice him standing there. Besides, he knew from experience that waiting was bad for him; the power might drain away between his toes, and at the moment he set off he didn't want to be Asko again, the man who forced his way into his skin and took over his body for days at a time, who stole his clothes and used them as if they were his own, leaving him nothing but rags.

Tweety started walking up the hill. He stared fixedly at the pavement, but in fact he was looking inside himself, examining all that he could uncover in his mind. His mind was an unusual one. Like old sailing ships it had a bridge and a deck and innumerable levels in between which were so dimly lit that you had to carry a lantern at all times. The lowest decks were so far down that the faint smell of formic acid hung in the air and all around came the sound of rustling and whispering, and on Sundays you could hear music that sounded like the insects' harmonica orchestra.

On the first deck, a naked woman sat in a glass chair, but Tweety didn't pay her the slightest attention; he couldn't very well crawl around outside. He knew exactly what he wanted. After a day at work, he wanted to come home to Wheatlocks.

'Hello, my love,' said Wheatlocks as she greeted him at the door; she must have heard his Mercedes pull up in the drive.

'Hello, love.'

'Looks like you've had quite a day,' she continued. Her voice was comforting, and when she spoke it was as though she gave him permission to be tired, to be himself.

'You're not wrong. They faxed the spring collection through from Brussels, but Weckman had forgotten the high heels, of course.'

'He's such a dimwit.'

'Sometimes I'd really love to give him the boot, but he's got an unbelievable eye when it comes to fashion. It's as if he can smell next season's colours.'

'My love,' said Wheatlocks once again and moved closer to him, and that meant to hell with Weckman and his shoes. What a magnificent woman, fair-haired, poised and, above all, intelligent. She was his wife. And just then the smell of roast beef and garlic potatoes came wafting in from the flat behind them, while from the living room streamed the soft, relaxing tones of Herbie Mann's flute.

'My love,' she sighed and wrapped her arms around him, and there she remained, tight against him, soft and warm, then she laid her head against his neck and tasted it with tiny kisses. She loved him. And not only because she needed him, benefited from him, spent his money. This was LOVE, like a warm power surging into him through her fingers, and it made him feel good and he knew that life had a meaning after all.

'My love,' she ran her fingers down his back, and only then did he realise she was wearing a silk dressing gown that he had brought her from London. It slid open by itself, and he moved his hand to her waist, and her skin felt like velvet. His fingers searched further – and beneath the dressing gown she was wearing a black bra, stitched with yearning like a poem, and a pair of panties, so small they could have fitted in a matchbox, and thin, lace-edged suspenders.

'My love,' she whispered, gently unzipping his trousers, then they started moving towards the bedroom. Wheatlocks went first, her buttocks tightly pressed against his groin, and with his right hand he caressed her breasts, their raisin tips, while his left hand slid downwards along her smooth belly, down beneath her knicker elastic; between his fingers there was cotton grass, then suddenly honey too.

'My love,' Wheatlocks uttered. 'First from behind, then the missionary position, then sitting in the armchair and over the desk and…' He didn't say anything. His hands spoke on his behalf; he lifted up her dressing gown and pulled down her little panties, Wheatlocks sighed and bent over, and there in front of him were her white hips and her buttocks, and his cock was like a copper door-handle.

Tweety turned on to Vänrikki Stoolinkatu; he came from Hesperiankatu just as before, only this time from a different direction. The first thing he did was look up; Silkybum's window was dark, just as it should be. They'd had well over an hour.

He headed straight towards the main door, his steps now calm as though he were walking home. Just before he reached the door, he unzipped his coat and put his hand into his inside pocket, and the first thing he felt was the handle of his knife. He fingered it for a moment, long enough to locate the silver skull he had pressed into the wood, the eye sockets, the teeth, and only then did he check that the pouch was there too. And there it was, like a second heart. It was a thin purse made of chamois leather, and when he moved it a soft metallic jangling sound came from inside, as though it contained a collection of brass tacks and an animal slowly gnawing away at them.

He stood on the front step, grabbed the handle, pulled, and the door opened. Of course it opened, he'd never doubted it. He scooped the paper egg from the latch, slipped it back into his pocket and stepped inside, and *Carmina Burana* began ringing in his head once again, the part where the women's voices are at their loudest. He stood on the doormat, perfectly still, listening to it, listening as the door pulled itself shut. The blue wedge of streetlight on the floor became narrower and narrower, then it disappeared altogether and the lock said 'click–clack', and everything was just as it should be.

Tweety didn't switch the lights on; he never switched the lights on. He allowed his eyes to accustom themselves to the darkness in peace and tried to imagine what position Silkybum was sleeping in. He had an inkling that she might be lying on her front, her hands beneath her head and her legs slightly apart. Perhaps her camisole was on the floor, now nothing but an empty shell, but it would still carry her scent, and perhaps he'd be able to hold it as he came, low and silent, lying along the skirting board like a giant boa constrictor.

Mustikkamaa

Harjunpää had got a stone in his shoe back on the footpath, and he wondered whether to stop and take it out, but by now it had stopped chafing his foot and he decided to let it be and quickened his step in the hope of maybe getting home sooner, but above all so that he could keep up with the woman in front of him, and to his slight amazement he found that he almost envied her. She was ploughing ahead energetically, amusingly even, in a way that made him think of a bird, a sandpiper or some other quick-footed wader, and he got the nagging feeling that, in comparison, he was like a tractor, an old green Zetor that had trouble getting started.

The woman talked incessantly, explaining what she had discovered again and again. Maybe it was something about her voice. In one way it was beautiful, like the sound of a woodwind instrument, but too refined, and perhaps it was this that made her seem somehow dishonest – not like the people he normally dealt with. The only person this woman was deceiving was herself, and she had a right to do so if she so wished. Harjunpää hadn't been listening to her for a while, but mumbled politely every now and then. 'Yes.'

On top of that, he hoped that the woman was wrong, that it wasn't a body after all but a sunken log or a stone – surely he might at least be afforded this much good luck after all the pain, the crying and the crawling about under trains of the previous night. But the main reason for his sullenness was that it was very early on a Sunday (it was ten to six in the morning; he had checked as he got out of the Lada), and his twelve-hour night shift was almost behind him, or rather it was inside him along with the fatigue, and together they weighed him down like a chest filled with lead and the multicoloured glass found at crash sites.

'Or what do you think?'

'Yes, sorry?'

'I said, what do you think?' the woman repeated and stopped in her tracks, and for a brief moment Harjunpää thought of answering her honestly: he was thinking of the man run over by a freight train in the early hours, and in particular he was thinking of the man's left hand, which they hadn't been able to find anywhere, and the furore that would erupt in the media should it be dislodged from the undercarriage somewhere further north: GRUESOME DISCOVERY AT PROVINCIAL TRAIN STATION!

'Pardon? I didn't hear.'

'I can see that. And to be perfectly frank, I don't think you're taking this very seriously – or me, for that matter.'

'I'm sorry… It's been quite a night. Three deaths, one manslaughter and a man run over by a train. And now this. And on top of that, a woman was raped and my partner had to go out there by himself. He's only been in the force a few months.'

'Well!' the woman exclaimed, more to her Great Dane than to Harjunpää. She yanked on the lead and the dog cowered in surprise, and Harjunpää admitted to himself that he didn't like the woman; he hadn't liked her from the start, though he couldn't say why. She was in her fifties and, just like her speech, there was something very prim about her, her old jogging suit notwithstanding. On her wrist she wore an intricately braided golden chain and her perfume was one of those familiar, expensive fragrances. As her address she had given the rather exclusive Granfeltintie. Perhaps Harjunpää was truly envious of her, or maybe it was because you simply can't like everybody.

'I did say who I am, yes? My name is Helen Ekstam-Luukkanen.'

'Yes, madam, I've written it down.'

'And my husband is Risto-Matti Luukkanen.'

'Yes,' Harjunpää muttered, keeping his expression impassive, though he realised that the woman was expecting a reaction of some sort, at the very least a raising of the eyebrows. She gave him a flimsy smile and set off again. The path soon became narrower, nothing but a furrow running between the twigs and tussocks. Spiders' webs sparkled in the air, heavy with the scent of dew and moss and the mushroom season. The name Risto-Matti Luukkanen didn't mean anything to Harjunpää. It only served to remind him that the name of the assistant in the hardware store in Kirkkonummi was one Taisto Luukkanen, and this reminded him that the roof of his daughter Valpuri's rabbit hutch had broken after Pipsa had used it as a trampoline and he had promised to buy some new wire mesh a week ago.

'I asked you whether you believe he drowned here.'

'Let's take a look at him first… Still, they can drift for miles, you know. If it isn't a stone, that is.'

'This is not a stone. My morning jog has taken me past this spot for seven years. Those three to the left are stones, but this is a body, I could tell straight away.'

'Yes.'

'My first husband said "yes" all the time, and after a while it became quite unbearable.'

'Yes… absolutely,' Harjunpää corrected himself and took a firmer grip on his bag. The handle had been repaired with iron wire and now it had started rubbing against his thumb as if it too had something against him. Be a stone, he thought, just please be a stone! Then he caught the murky, clay smell of the sea, and behind the gnarled pine trees gleamed its motionless, placid surface.

They reached the rocky shore. Red and glistening, it stretched out in both directions, and in front of them it sloped beautifully, round and steep, into the sea. Directly across the sound lay the island of Sompasaari with its colourful skyline of tanks and containers, on the right loomed the bridge to Kulosaari and to the left was Korkeasaari, and behind everything else, its contours softened by the fog, lay the entire city and its familiar spires. The sea felt far away, at an exceptionally low tide, and in the half-light it looked improbably green, almost toxic, as if it wanted to suck everything into its folds and keep it there until its bones had rotted away. On the Mustikkamaa side of the bay a woolly mist drifted aimlessly above the water's surface.

'Over there,' said the woman and pointed her finger. 'More to the right.'

All Harjunpää could see were two ducks paddling calmly towards Korkeasaari, blissfully unaware of anything else. But then he saw what the woman meant: about ten metres from the shore a couple of large boulders jutted out from beneath the surface, four of them altogether, and he stared at them for a moment, in particular the one towards which the woman was gesticulating.

He looked more closely, and there was no doubt that it was different; the others made ripples as the water gently ebbed and flowed, but this one bobbed along with the water, heavily and awkwardly, and Harjunpää began to accept that the woman had been right all along, and with that the taste of the previous night rose up in his mouth. A moment later and he was certain; he'd seen the same thing so many times before. It was a human body, floating in a position typical for drowning victims: face in the water, limbs dangling towards the bottom, only the shoulders barely visible.

'Damn it.'

'Excuse me?'

'It is a body. You win… you were right.'

'I told you so! I've walked past this spot every morning for a good many years, and this is the place I do my stretches and look out at the sea, and this morning there were suddenly four stones. Hang on a minute, I thought to myself, stones don't just multiply by themselves, and that's when I climbed up this hillside to…'

'You did the right thing,' Harjunpää thanked her, and now he really wanted to get rid of her, partly because in a childish way he felt as though she had beaten him, but mostly because he knew that he would soon have so much to do that he wouldn't have the time or the inclination to be especially polite to anyone. Aside from that he didn't like her enthusiasm for the matter; she was too keen, so much so that in other circumstances he might have suspected all kinds of things, and he had met hundreds of people who had made similar discoveries. 'Thank you very much. And if we need any more information I'll call you. Have a very good day.'

He turned, perhaps a little too casually, and began tottering down the embankment, and the exertion that lay ahead finally hit him. Fatigue almost overwhelmed him, it heaved inside him and he thought of how wonderful it would be to curl up in the nearest rocky hollow lain with hay and forget about everything. The matter was far more complicated than that; his policeman's soul was somehow broken, but he didn't dare think about that now, because otherwise he might not have been able to keep on going. And if he had said it out loud, someone would have commented, 'You don't have to be here, you know.' But he did. And that made it all the more diabolical.

Almost without noticing, his thoughts had turned to work, and he already knew that he would have to photograph the body as soon as possible, drowned bodies can blacken in as little as twenty minutes; that he would have to take a sample of the water in a film container; that he'd have to get Mononen on the job, and of all the other things he had to do. He still wasn't sure how he was going to get the body on to dry land, and a moment later he was certain that the nearest emergency station and rescue pole were at least a kilometre away. Typical. The fact that he was alone didn't help matters either, but he couldn't help that. He couldn't help the fact that the superintendents had been watching American police dramas and come to the conclusion that the 'initial patrol principle' was always a good thing, and because of this the number of detective inspectors had been cut, as they were deemed as useless as paper machines, and night shifts now ran on a skeleton staff of four men.

'Or what do you make of it?'

'What?'

'Do you think he's been murdered? I can sense it. No, I'm certain of it, just as I was certain it was a body.'

'If you'd be so kind as to wait back up there…' said Harjunpää. He could feel himself getting irritated; he hadn't noticed that the woman and her dog had followed him. Of course, homicide was one option among many, but he hadn't wanted to think the worst straight off. Already he was envisaging himself undressing the body amid the smell of death at the coroner's office and discovering a knife wound between the shoulder blades, and he imagined the extra hours this would incur and realised that he wouldn't get home until around six in the evening.

'Quite frankly, your attitude is… Don't forget, I'm the one that found him.'

'I haven't forgotten. And I'm the one that's going to examine him. Now, please, go back up the hill.'

Something hard flashed across the woman's eyes, or perhaps he had only imagined that too, but at any rate she raised her chin almost threateningly and didn't make any indication that she was leaving.

'Are you ordering me about?'

'I'm not ordering anybody… But this is now a police investigation, and that means that bystanders have no business being here.'

The woman pursed her lips tightly. The dog sat down on the rocks. It looked like a good-natured fool; its tongue dangled from the side of its mouth like a lump of meat. Harjunpää turned round without taking another look at either of them, but as he walked down to the shore, he said: 'In any case, it could be a terrible sight. Boat propellers sometimes tear bodies to shreds leaving the guts hanging out...'

Between the rocks was a narrow strip of water, the ground a mixture of sand and gravel. Harjunpää jumped down on to the sand with his bag and suddenly felt a chill. The fog had slowly drifted closer to the shore and now he was almost inside it, like being in a grey pocket, the rest of the world somewhere else. The sun could barely be seen. He quickly glanced around: the ground was littered with horsetails, algae and shells, all manner of small objects and a single slipper eaten away by the water, but as far as he could see there was nothing obviously linked to the body.

Then he looked out towards the body – and there was no doubt that it was a body. Its back was covered in dark material, so wet it was almost black. Though it was impossible to make any reliable observations, it looked like a brown flannel shirt. For one reason or another Harjunpää had an inkling that the body was no longer fresh, then he realised why: it was clearly not floating on its own, its back was buoyed up by the accumulation of gases inside, but was partly resting on a jagged rock just visible beneath the surface. Maybe it had been brought in by the waves of the previous day or a current of some sort had drawn it into the bay. It turned slowly and tilted in the water, almost ghostlike, as though a giant slimy fist had risen up from the bottom, grabbed hold of it and pulled, and it was surely only a matter of minutes before it disappeared again.

He opened his bag and pulled the hand radio up to his mouth. 'Control, this is Harjunpää from Violent Crimes,' he stated. If good fortune were on his side, for once, a police boat would be on patrol nearby, and with any luck it would be on site in a matter of minutes.

'Control. Violent Crimes to A 5.'

He would at least ask for the nearest patrol car to be sent out and for them to bring the first rescue pole they could find. Calling out divers from the fire service would take too long. 'Control, do you copy?' The Criminal Investigation department's own call centre had been discontinued and they didn't have anyone from their division stationed with the emergency services either. Someone had to be there, though it was still so early in the morning that there may only have been two men on duty, and if that were the case, both of them would of course be on the telephone.

'Control. Violent Crimes to A 2-3.'

'How are you going to get him out of there?'

Harjunpää spun around; the woman was standing exactly where she had been before. She was actually rather beautiful. The dog had pulled its tongue back inside its mouth. Harjunpää knelt down, put the radio back in his bag and glanced at the body. It was moving more quickly now; he could only see half of its shoulders, and when he stood up again it all seemed perfectly clear.

'I'll have to go and get it,' he growled, unzipped his coat and let it fall to the ground. Then he removed his revolver from the holster on his waist, put that in the bag too, then began untying his shoes – and only then did it occur to him that he would have to take his trousers off too. He looked up at the woman, almost pained.

'Imagine if it were your father,' he said, and this time he wasn't being sarcastic; he truly wanted her to understand. 'Or your husband Risto-Matti. You wouldn't want there to be people standing around watching.'

The woman didn't say anything; she swung around, in a way that suddenly made Harjunpää feel sorry for her, then she was on her way, climbing back up the rocks with jogger's legs, and with that she was gone, the fog thick between them. Somewhere in the distance he heard the dog yelp.

Harjunpää didn't hang about; he undressed quickly leaving only his boxer shorts, rummaged in his bag for a pair of rubber gloves and pulled them on to his hands. The water was bitterly cold; his skin quickly tightened into goosebumps. He suddenly felt squeamish, as though a warning light had started flashing, then he remembered why. In a similar situation years ago he had stood on a broken bottle and it had cut his foot – badly. After that he'd been on crutches for a long time. That must have been it. He began to slide his feet along the bottom, very carefully, so as not to hit them on anything. Sludge started bubbling up to the surface and the air was filled with a rotten, gaseous smell, and still his feeling of nausea hadn't passed.

The water already reached well up his thighs, and was becoming deeper more quickly than he had guessed. He was trembling all over, so much that it almost hurt. He stopped and looked at the rest of the journey. He still had about half way to go. He sized up the stones, assessing how he could use them for support, and it was then that he realised they weren't natural stones after all. They were great concrete blocks covered in algae, a piece of rusted iron jutted out of the one closest to him, and he couldn't think of any explanation other than that there must have been a jetty here once – a couple of hefty mooring rings had been bored into the rocks on the shore.

Hesitantly he peered over at the body, almost as if he were afraid his eyes would scare it and it would try to run away. It had rolled over on to its side, and now he could see that it didn't have a head; through the shirt collar splayed nothing but greyish shreds of skin. Something light dangled amongst them, probably a vertebra. The back of the head seemed still intact, or perhaps it was nothing but a loose piece of scalp flapping in the water, limp as the matted grey hairs attached to it.

'Jesus Christ,' Harjunpää gasped. That same water was now swirling around his groin, and for a brief moment he almost wanted to turn back, he even made a move towards the shore, then he bit his lip, muttered a stream of curses and carried on. Walking became easier; the slippery stones came to an end and there was something smooth beneath the balls of his feet, a beam of some sort. He waded forwards, careful not to step to the side. The beam was somehow disconnected from the sea floor, angled so that the water seemed to rise more slowly, though it was already up to his waist. Out of the fog flew a giant seagull that began encircling him.

Now I can reach it, he thought, and stretched out his arm; he was less than a metre away from the body. He decided simply to clench his fist, filling it with shirt and water, and pull; there was no way it could tear without the body coming with it. He couldn't quite comprehend what happened, it all seemed like a hallucination; the surface of the water began to rise as though extra water had suddenly flooded in, and it ran up his chest like a cold hoop, streaming around his shoulders and neck. Instinctively he gasped for breath as the water splashed in his eyes, and a moment later they were engulfed with the sea.

He was under the surface; everything was blurred and green and his ears were filled with a rushing silence. The beam had broken beneath him, this much he understood as he sank further. The surface was merely a disappearing silver film. Something scraped against his shin, first on one side then the other. It felt as though something were falling on top of him, and his leg became wedged between two stones and he couldn't get it out.

He yanked again, but he was stuck fast, and he was suddenly consumed with a blind panic: he was so utterly alone, so utterly small.

His chest started to burn and a shimmering stream of bubbles escaped from his mouth: God help me, I want to live! Somehow he understood that he needed to crouch down first, to sink even further, but it felt so unnatural. He wanted to go upwards, he wanted to reach the surface. Suddenly his leg came free! And he started rising upwards, but so slowly, so agonisingly slowly, and above him he could see a dark blob, and he knew what it was. It was sinking towards him, right towards his face. He stretched out his arms and his hands were filled with something slimy and soft. Then he reached the surface.

'Help!' he shouted, or at least he thought he was shouting. His mouth filled with water and he spluttered: 'Help!'

But it was useless, there was no one to hear him. The only person who had been there, he had shooed away. Then he realised how close the shore was and he knew he would get through this; he wasn't in any immediate danger, there would be someone to take care of him. He began paddling, a strange one-armed doggy-paddle. With his other arm he held on to the body, dragging it behind him though for a moment he felt that he no longer had the strength.

Then his feet struck the stones on the bottom. He stood up and waded forwards through the spray of water, and now he took hold of the body with both hands, dragging it like a sack and paying no attention to all the things he should have watched out for. The body must have been in the sea for years; it was only a torso. As well as its head, it was also missing its arms and legs. The joints still showed, however, which was a comfort in itself; the body hadn't been dismembered, the limbs had simply fallen off by themselves as decomposition had progressed.

'You bloody nearly killed me...'

He heaved the torso into the shallower water on the shore. Its only item of clothing was the torn, checked flannel shirt, and upon seeing it Harjunpää felt inexplicably sad. He had an inkling that the body was that of an old man who had once pottered about with a cap on his head, stopping every now and then to reach into his pocket for a silver, turnip-shaped pocket watch ticking with time gone by.

He slumped on to the gravel, and suddenly he wasn't sure what he should do next. He peeled the rubber gloves from his hands, then looked at his leg. It was bright red with blood, but he realised that it couldn't have been too serious; he couldn't feel any pain and he could still walk. It must have been scratched; the bleeding looked more profuse because his skin was wet.

But he was still at a loss. Perhaps that was why there was so much space inside him that he was filled with a powerful, unexpected sense of melancholy. He remembered a time when he was so small that he could barely see over the table; he used to think the pickled cucumbers were hedgehogs. He missed Pipsa, his youngest daughter, and Valpuri, and strangely enough, Valpuri's rabbit too. And finally he realised that he was grieving for Onerva, grieving as though she had passed away. He had been grieving for some time, but had somehow managed to suppress it. Finally he gave in; he slumped on to the sand, rested his head against his knees, and he was so cold that he began whimpering.

'Hello! You there!'

Harjunpää's legs were bare, his feet were covered in sand and the sand was mixed with dried algae and a small broken shell. He stared at them and only slowly realised that the voice was addressing him. He stood up stiffly. His mind was already perfectly calm.

On the rocks above stood a man. He wasn't a very big man, but he exuded power, Harjunpää could sense it. It was in his eyes too, along with a flash of disparagement and a small amount of hatred. From the man's eyes Harjunpää realised what he must have looked like in his wet underpants, hair stuck to his forehead in clumps, his legs bloody, his skin covered in goosebumps and blotches of green slime.

'My name is Risto-Matti Luukkanen.'

'Yes,' Harjunpää mumbled and vaguely remembered having seen the man somewhere before, on the news or in one of those magazines in which the glitterati posed with champagne glasses and explained at length how they had grown apart from their partners or grown back together again, and it dawned on him that Luukkanen was some kind of local politician or the director of a large company. Helen stood further back. She looked much smaller now, almost stunted; the dog wasn't with them. Perhaps Risto-Matti only ever walked one of them at a time.

'You have taken it upon yourself to insult my wife in a most uncouth manner,' Luukkanen began. Harjunpää knew this tone of voice and knew

what was coming, but he wasn't sure whether he was under any obligation to listen to it. He settled for a shrug of the shoulders.

'Do you know Assistant Chief Constable Kontio?'

'No... I do know Chief Inspector Kontio.'

'Sir, you are shameless.'

Harjunpää shrugged again. The fog had thinned and the sun warmed
him, and it felt good. A bee buzzed somewhere close by. He felt alive.

Tapanila

To the south of the central train line, nicely tucked away from the newly-built apartment blocks in the quiet suburb of Tapanila, ran Tasankotie, and beside that lay a dense birch forest. At least, that's what it looked like to the average passer-by, as the thick willows by the side of the road hid everything else from view.

In fact, three narrow dirt tracks spaced a couple of hundred metres apart wound their way through the birches, and each of them led to a dead end. If anyone were to walk along one of these tracks, they would see that the forest was divided into distinct plots of land, and that about a dozen of them had been built upon. The houses weren't very big, and many of them looked as though their building plans had existed solely in the minds of the builders themselves. But one thing any passer-by would notice straight away: the inhabitants loved those ramshackle houses. Everything was kept in good order, a gleaming patch on a tin roof, a set of gates newly painted, paths raked and tidy, flowers and berry plants and fruit trees all around.

But there were other kinds of plots too, the kind that had been cut off for years behind overgrown hedgerows, and if anyone were to start clearing the land they would discover ramshackle sheds and collapsed wells, battered old cars and abandoned refrigerators – things that seemed to live forever though the inhabitants had first changed then disappeared altogether.

Then there were a number of plots that looked overgrown at first glance, but where the buildings were still standing, and if you stopped to look for a moment: there was an old lady's corset and a pair of woollen socks hanging on the clothes line; over there a thin trail of smoke rose from the chimney; and on the steps of a dilapidated yellow cottage a chubby-cheeked cat lay preening its tail in slow, satisfied motions.

It was obvious that people lived there and fought for their very existence, the bane of the local council, which had long had its eyes on the area for development. To realise its plans, the council had denied applications for planning permission and cut back on local amenities and now, as its final trump card, it maintained the vague threat of compulsory purchase. But the little devils just carried on living there, and in the winter cleared the road of snow by themselves.

One of these indeterminate plots was Joutsentie 3. The plot contained four buildings in all; the middle one was the biggest. It was an odd-looking cottage, split into two sections, and with a sagging felt roof beneath which there appeared to be some sort of attic room. Twenty or so metres away stood a building painted red; it had once been a sauna, but now curtains hung in the windows and a geranium plant stood on the bench by the front door. An implausibly large television antenna jutted from the roof of the third shack and the surrounding land was scattered with toys. The fourth building was clearly some sort of workshop; in front of it stood old cars and a digger roughly taken to pieces with a blowtorch. Behind the other buildings was a caravan jacked up on a trestle, and up to its door wound a path that betrayed a permanent resident.

The plot was surrounded by an ominous spruce hedge, and other plants grew wherever there was enough space: giant birch trees, raspberry bushes, nettles, willowherb. On the western edge of the plot a vegetable patch and a potato field had been carefully hoed.

At Joutsentie 3 lived the Leinonen family. The Leinonens weren't very popular because they were 'newcomers' – the other local families had lived in the same houses for two or even three generations – and on top of this they were a strange, messy bunch that made the whole area susceptible to the ambitions of eager, small-time bureaucrats.

Tweety was the youngest son of Old Mrs Leinonen.

He had been getting ready to wake up for some time, drifting in no-man's-land; he was still downtown collecting small baskets made of folded squared paper from the street. He didn't know what he was supposed to do with them, but he knew that they were very important. At the same time he was listening to a conversation in the other room, though he didn't really want to. The man's words were a dark red colour, almost black, and the woman's were bright turquoise.

'… go and talk to him anyway. This is a big break for us and everyone's got to pull their weight.'

'I can't. He'll just patronise me again.'

'You're imagining things. He is your brother, mind. And what does it matter how he talks to you? Just as long as he keeps them off our back. And he can do it. He knows people – said as much himself last midsummer.'

'But what if he knows we're up to something?'

'He won't. Listen, I'll say this, though you know fine well. He's got business dealings that wouldn't last the light of day. What was it he said once? He loses over ten million a year and the insurance company pays it all back…'

The red voice belonged to Reino, Tweety's oldest brother. Reino's bed creaked as he sat up; there came a rustling as he took out a cigarette and a hiss as he lit a match. There was a note of irritation in his voice, but his girlfriend Bamse hadn't noticed; she was a bit slow.

'So what? Act as if me and Lasse have finally got ourselves a proper job but that it'll go tits up if the pigs keep sticking their noses in. Act serious, like you're in a bit of a panic.'

'I could do that, I suppose… But what if Lasse's wrong?'

'I've thought about that too, what if it's all just talk. But I think I agree with him.'

'But… is there any point getting ourselves involved in this at all?'

'Too right there is, we've got to. They haven't got anything on us. Think of it as a family business, we're the only ones that know about it. That Valkeakoski gave them what for when they couldn't come up with enough evidence. And this time it's definitely Lampinen. I've already seen him twice in a week, and that's hardly a coincidence. He's had it in for me since I said in court I'd seen him hanging around me for weeks on end, but that I'd just thought he was some poof who'd got the hots for me…'

Reino gave a dry cackle. Tweety still didn't open his eyes. He wanted to explore what was inside him, but he couldn't quite make it out, and lay listening to what the day had to say for itself. Birch branches caressed the roof, Toby was scuttling around in his cage, and every now and then, Tweety heard a chink from outside as the rake struck a stone – Sisko was out in the vegetable patch – and somewhere at the back of their plot a pop resounded, followed immediately by a metallic clang: Lasse was out doing target practice with his air rifle.

He was crazy about that rifle. He was even crazier about his Smith & Wesson, and he had good reason to be: it was a .357 Magnum Special, one hundred per cent rustproof steel and with a barrel like an elephant's trunk, but he couldn't use that one for practice unless they went down to the pit, because it was an illegal firearm. Still, he always carried it with him. Reino had recently lost his temper with him in the pub when he'd started fingering it under his jacket. He could well shoot someone one day, accidentally at least. He was good-natured at heart – he was probably the best natured of all three brothers – but he was jittery in a bad way.

Downstairs they were still talking about what they referred to as the Chancellor – they didn't want anyone to use the wrong term by mistake, or for Lasse's wife or Mother Gold to get wind of what was going on. But Tweety didn't want to sit around listening to their conversation; it irritated him that Reino couldn't just decide that it was going to happen *now*. He just wished it was all over.

Tweety pulled the blanket from over his face. His world lay in front of him: an attic room with a sagging roof, barely big enough to fit anything more than a bed, a table, a chair and a chest of drawers with brass lion's paws for feet. At the other end of the room there was a hatch in the floor with a set of almost vertical steps leading downstairs. The other way out was through the window and down a ladder propped beneath it. Through the square window he could see a section of the path and the red cottage in the yard. The room was in a chronic state of disarray.

Its walls were papered in lumpy cardboard covered with paintings, most of which were very small and painted on whatever sawn-up piece of hardboard had been available. But they all used striking colours, depicting wild landscapes that could only exist in the furthest reaches of the mind. If an expert had seen them he might have fallen silent for a good few moments. So far only the people at home had laid eyes on them, and that was enough for Tweety. 'You're a sick man,' Reino had commented, the edge of his nose twitching.

Tweety reached down and opened the door of the wire-mesh cage, and Toby scuttled along his arm and into the bed. Tweety picked up a chocolate drop, placed it between his lips and waited. Toby sniffed him from head to toe, turned, snatched the chocolate drop, then darted inside his shirt to munch on it. Toby was a black-and-white rat. And he was smart, too: at the table he would hide in Tweety's sleeve and snatch only the most delicious bits of food from his plate. Apart from that, Toby was the only creature in the world that really understood him. They didn't need words.

'He must be around here somewhere, I just can't think where,' said Reino. He'd lowered his voice, but Tweety guessed that they were talking about him. It was pointless trying to whisper; the house was so ramshackle that you could almost hear people breathe.

'What if he's gone and got himself a woman?'

'No chance. He's the last person who'd understand women. Born a sissy, that one.'

'Maybe I think of him a bit differently… Anyway, none of our business really.'

'I'm just worried he doesn't play about so much he loses the plot entirely. Then where will we be?'

Bamse yawned and Tweety could tell she was stretching too; he'd once peeped through the hatch. She stretched so that her breasts stood out, and this she did because she was up for it. She was always up for it; that's probably why Reino had picked her. Then the bed downstairs gave a creak and Tweety yanked the duvet up over his ears.

Born a sissy. He thought about this, and he could feel a fever rising inside him. Reino had told Bamse to say that he and Lasse had got themselves jobs, but he hadn't mentioned Tweety at all. And now he was banging her downstairs so that the bed creaked. Tweety couldn't understand what she saw in him. Reino was a short, stocky slob who smelled of sweat, smacked his chops when he was eating and farted whenever he pleased. He was just like Dad.

Tweety groaned and turned on to his side, and Toby nimbly darted out from underneath him. Reino had taken Dad's place in the house; he treated Tweety in the same way too, as though he were nothing but a dogsbody. But with the Chancellor, for once they were at his mercy: without him, their blowtorches would be useless – they wouldn't even get into the bank. He'd been stringing them along all the while. He could have easily told them the sequences to the various locks, but instead he'd said he didn't know anything about those sort of locks, because if he'd done that they would have made themselves a set of keys, and after that Reino and Lasse would have done the gig on their own and the idea of splitting the money into three would never have been mentioned again.

He raised his head, but they were still at it and he couldn't bear listening to it. He pressed his hands over his ears. He wanted to live downtown! He wanted to be by himself, he wanted a life of his own! He fucking hated Reino sometimes! He hated him the way he had hated Dad. And he hated Dad because he couldn't even do them the favour of dying so that he really was dead, and Tweety was constantly worried that one day he'd come back, stroll in through the door and say hello. That's what he'd done when he was released from prison. He'd killed a man called Ryynänen, but they weren't allowed to talk about that. Tweety had been very young back then, but he still remembered: Dad turned up, said hello, and yanked Tweety away from where he lay next to their mother, and from then on his bed had always been on the floor.

Still, he wasn't coming back. He and Heikki Ahola had gone off to try out their salmon lines – it would be four years ago come November – and the following day Heikki's boat had been found off the tip of Katajanokka, then a week later his body washed up in the same place. But nobody had ever found so much as Dad's fur cap.

All of a sudden the Corpse and Silkybum entered his mind, though he'd been trying to forget them. Them, and the entire evening's events.

He'd been right about the door and that they were both sleeping heavily; in the stairwell he'd been able to hear their breathing, thick with drink. Inside the flat, a small one-bedroom place, he'd had no difficulty getting his bearings because light from the street had shone in through the blinds, so much so that he hadn't even had to resort to the bathroom-light trick.

Taking care of the Corpse had been simple. He was sleeping on his stomach. First Tweety had pulled the sheet over his head, then tucked the edges under the mattress, and when the Corpse had started tossing and turning Tweety gently laid his hand on his neck and he had calmed down; in his drunken slumber he must have thought it was Silkybum's hand. Finally Tweety had covered him with a blanket as well, paying particular attention to his head, and there he'd lain, wrapped in a cotton coffin, hearing nothing, seeing nothing, breathing his own breath. His sleep became heavier with every moment and soon he lay perfectly still as though he were unconscious.

Silkybum was covered with nothing but a sheet. But her sleep had become restless while Tweety was burying the Corpse, almost as though she had sensed something or felt ill from the wine. She didn't seem to like the Corpse, or perhaps she couldn't accept that she had brought the man back home, as she had shoved Tweety's hand away as soon as he'd laid it on her body.

Then suddenly she was awake. Tweety was lying on the floor barely twenty centimetres away, and if she'd got up for the toilet she would have stepped on him. He followed her as she sighed and looked for a more comfortable position, and it took her half an hour to get back to sleep. But then the Corpse had turned and Tweety had had to bury him again. Time went on and just as he was about to get down to it with Silkybum she sat bolt upright, saw what was going on and screamed, and he watched as the blanket billowed in the darkness like a black sail as the Corpse jumped up. Then he was gone. It had been such a botch-job that he didn't want to think about it any more.

Tweety felt suddenly agitated, as though a wire taut inside him had snapped. He tried to make himself believe that it was because of last night and what Reino had said, but it wasn't. It was something else. Then he twigged: he'd heard something, and he knew immediately what it was. He pulled the blankets from over him and crouched down by the window. Mother Gold had come outside; her door had given a creak. He couldn't stand that sound, but he didn't understand why. He didn't understand the cottage either; it made him feel extremely tense, as though the whole dive might cave in on him or burst into flames. It must have been because someone had died in there once, and somehow he could sense it. Mother Gold was upset that he never popped in, but he couldn't.

Toby darted back into his cage as though he was scared too, and Tweety went back to bed, closed his eyes and tried to find those paper baskets again, but it was no use. There he was, lying between sticky sheets that smelled of his body, and now there were even more wires inside him and he could feel them tearing at his bones, his flesh and guts, leaving blood and pus dripping and stinking all around.

He sighed, his skin was damp with sweat, and then he realised what it was: he had dropped his wallet in Silkybum's hallway. That must have been the dark object on the floor, right next to Silkybum's shoes; he'd even heard a clap as it hit the floor. But he didn't have time to think of the matter further: a car pulled into the yard. And he knew it was going to be a police car, a blue-and-white Saab, both its doors opening at once and two big men in uniform stepping out, handcuffs dangling from their belts.

Tweety darted back to the window and pressed his forehead against the window so hard that it gave a crack. There was no police car; there was nothing else either, he'd been mistaken. Perhaps someone had pulled up in next door's yard. Mother Gold was hobbling along the path; she was coming to visit them just as she did every Sunday, but Tweety didn't stay around watching her. He bounded over to the chair and started rummaging with trembling hands through the pile of clothes, looking for his trousers. He found them. The wallet was in his pocket. And in addition to being buttoned up, the pocket was securely fastened with a safety pin.

'Jesus,' he sighed and slumped into the chair. His heart was beating inside him and he couldn't think. He made out the sound of a door being opened in the distance and Reino saying something equally far away; Mother Gold started on about how much she missed their father, the way she always did, then commented on how they hadn't made the bed. The water pump outside gave a squeal. Bamse had started making the coffee.

Tweety collapsed on his bed, pulled up the covers and thought of the mat at Lasse's door. It was a worn old jute doormat. He thought of it in the rain, when it was wet, waiting for everyone to wipe the mud from their feet on it, and he felt sorry for it. He felt just like that mat. He felt like Asko, and Asko's world was like a pigeon drawn with a blunt pencil, a pigeon run over by a car, its feathers blown about by the laughing wind.

He pretended to be asleep; he knew that Bamse would come and wake him up. He often mixed her up with Wheatlocks. She was so much closer than Wheatlocks and far more real, and she'd just said that she viewed him in a different way. Maybe she'd take him if something ever happened to Reino; or maybe one morning she'd sit down on the edge of his bed, caress him and say that Reino was a good-for-nothing, that he's all talk, that he'd be out in the evening and that she wanted Tweety for herself.

The lock creaked as Bamse pushed the door open.

'Get up, Tweety!' she shouted; her voice was shrill and white as a little pebble. 'And clean out that rat, it stinks in here!'

Grandpa and Järvi

'Timo!' shouted Elisa from the other end of the corridor. Harjunpää couldn't work out quite what she was doing in the Violent Crimes department, and he couldn't go and ask her because he was in a hurry. He had to inform the chief superintendent that there was nothing wrong with the motor in the police-station lift after all – it was the repair men that were to blame. They'd caused the system to short-circuit, either on purpose or out of sheer stupidity, but still demanded their wages and it was costing the department so much of the annual budget that case after case was being left uninvestigated. He walked in without knocking. Tanttu was standing in his greasy overalls with his back to the door. There were other men in the room too, everyone on the departmental board, and then Harjunpää noticed: a lift motor was lying on Tanttu's desk, and Harjunpää couldn't say what he'd come to say. Tanttu cast him a dissatisfied look, but he'd been wrong: the chief superintendent proceeded to open up a zinc coffin containing a man's body. It had been roughly patched together after autopsy, the stitches like splinters in his skin. The man was already partially mummified or dried up with embalming fluid – then all of a sudden he started to blink, sat up and looked at himself in horror – what had been done to him and what he had become – and he started to cry, demanding to know who had pronounced him dead and on what grounds, and everyone stared at Harjunpää: he was the only officer from Violent Crimes working that shift and he'd been on the scene. A marching band struck up with the 'Narva March'.

'Timo,' said Elisa and laid her hand on his ankle, and Harjunpää realised where he was: at home on his napping mattress beneath the

31

benches in the sauna – it always was the most peaceful spot in the house – but still something was bothering him. All he could hear was a rushing sound, as though he were tipsy and had sunk beneath the surface.

'You've still got your earplugs in,' said Elisa, at least her mouth moved as though that was what she was saying, and Harjunpää pulled the small foam cylinders from his ears and the world surrounded him once again: the radio played softly, someone was jumping with a skipping rope, and from outside came the hum of a lawnmower. People loved them. Or rather, people hated grass: it refused to stay in check.

'Morning,' Harjunpää mumbled and slowly began to realise that everything wasn't as it should be. He couldn't have slept for more than an hour, he could feel it, and aside from that Elisa would normally have lain down beside him, rested a while, and sometimes they would start caressing one another and let things progress from there… and it was the most beautiful thing there was: to give your love and yourself to someone else, and to receive it back in equal measure. At moments like that he understood more clearly than ever that the whole world could march over them, but there would still be someone he trusted, someone who trusted him in return and who would never abandon him in times of hardship.

'Grandpa?' Harjunpää asked, and the restlessness he had just slept off was suddenly once again in his mind. 'What's he…?'

'It's OK, Timo. He and Pipsa have gone strawberry-picking. But someone rang from work. Valpuri answered and she had her headphones on while she spoke to him… Anyway, you've got to go and report to a DCI Järvi.'

'Now?'

'Straight away, they said. The caller didn't say who he was, that's why Valpuri believed he really was a policeman.'

'Oh dear…'

Harjunpää couldn't even begin to understand. It was extremely rare for the unit to telephone anyone who'd just been on night shift, let alone call them back into work. It could only mean that something serious had happened, a plane crash or something else of that magnitude; either that or someone had made a monumental blunder.

He didn't understand why he had to report to Järvi either. Järvi wasn't in Violent Crimes; he was the head of Special Branch. Harjunpää's mouth felt suddenly sticky. He slowly began to crawl out from beneath the sauna benches, and the events of the previous night all began careering through his mind: the manslaughter, the bodies, the suicide victim under the train, then he remembered Luukkanen and his promise of repercussions – but that would have been utterly nonsensical, even though he had been asked to report to Järvi. In any case, Luukkanen had only mentioned Kontio.

'We were supposed to go to the Söderholms,' said Elisa, and Harjunpää thought he could detect a note of disapproval in her voice, though he knew it wasn't aimed at him but at the weighty boot pressing against the neck of all small-time officers.

'If you could call them… or take the little ones. Pauliina can look after Grandpa while you're gone.'

'I've already called them, and we're going next week. Come down and eat, there's scrambled eggs and coffee.'

Harjunpää leaned against the sauna door; he was restless, full of frantic orders, but he didn't have a spark of energy. His face expressionless, he stared at the clothes hanging on the line and the three flannel shirts among them: one blue, one green and one red. The red one had faded in countless washes and now it was an indeterminate shade of brown. The shirts belonged to his father. The air carried the faint smell of his father's pipe smoke. Harjunpää rubbed his forehead, as though he wanted to be rid of thoughts that weren't true, then he turned on the shower and the water stung his shins, though he had dabbed the grazes with Betadine.

'How's he been today?' asked Harjunpää and spooned scrambled egg into his mouth, more to please Elisa than anything. His stomach was still asleep and his thoughts had carried him somewhere else entirely, driven by an almost imperceptible desire to escape something. Järvi's telephone had been continually engaged, as had the phone in the coffee room – that could mean something, or it could just be pure coincidence – and the switchboard at the Public Order Division had only been able to say that a Combat unit had been called out, and that came under Järvi's jurisdiction.

'Well, he's… He was rubbing his chest a bit this morning and took a couple of nitrate tablets. Maybe he's just having a bit of a blurry day.'

'Yes,' Harjunpää muttered when he couldn't think of anything else to say, and he hoped Elisa wouldn't ask him about Social Services and the forms – he'd had such a busy week and on top of that he'd been at a loss with all the paperwork, as with the matter as a whole.

It had been almost a month. A police car from the Kirkkonummi precinct had pulled up outside their house, all the kids in the neighbourhood running behind it. Arponen had got out of the car and come inside scratching his brow.

'Evening all. There's a man out there in the car – he's a bit senile. You know, demented. The thing is, he claims to be your father.'

'Get off… My parents live in Käpylä. I spoke to them a few hours ago on the phone.'

'This is a Georg Johannes Harjunpää. And the Register of Births and Deaths seems to confirm his story. He says he was married again and that he and his wife had some sort of prenuptial agreement, and now that she's passed away, her children have come and sent him packing. Seems he's screwed everything else up too, no pension to speak of, you name it…'

'Let's take a look at him,' Harjunpää had said finally; his tongue felt dry and a chill ran through him, and the calm he had tried to build up within him had been shaken. His parents had divorced when he was five years old and he had thought of his mother's new husband as his father, an economist, distant and consumed by his own pressures. In his entire adult life Harjunpää hadn't met his real father once.

In the back of the police car, on top of his suitcases, sat a slightly stooped, thin old man who at times was clearly in another world. Harjunpää had been overcome by an almost nauseous feeling; he'd wanted to slam the door shut and say to hell with him, but then he'd recognised his own forehead and jaw, and above all his thin fingers and hands striped with blue veins. And on top of everything else the man had looked at him, smiled hesitantly, imploringly almost, and said: 'You must be Timo.'

They already had a Grandad and Papa, so for the girls' sake they'd decided to call this one Grandpa. And Grandpa was only supposed to stay the night, but no care home would take him in and they were faced with the possibility of waiting lists months, years long. A strange contradiction was gnawing away at Harjunpää. If he'd been honest with himself, he'd initially wanted to get rid of Grandpa as quickly as possible, to free himself in some way, to have everything back the way it was before. But on the other hand he was content when it seemed the situation would be prolonged: there was something he wanted to understand, or something he wanted from his father, though he couldn't put his finger on precisely what it was.

'Here come the berry-pickers…'

They could hear speech and footsteps coming from outside, and a strange series of thumps: Pipsa came in hopping on one leg. Her legs were long and thin like a grasshopper's. She was holding Grandpa by the hand and the old man was swaying so much that Harjunpää had to look away.

'You'll be all right with him, won't you?' he asked hastily. It had become a matter of great concern to him, as had the fact that their entire life seemed to have gone off kilter since Grandpa's arrival; more and more often arguments had sprung out of things that would normally have been dealt with in a few words.

'I suppose so… The only thing that worries me is that he puffs away on his pipe during the night, but he'll never learn to go out to the steps. And Pauliina's a bit put out at having to share with the little ones.'

'I know. I'll try again this week…'

The door opened and the house filled in an instant: shoes flew into the hallway cupboard with a clatter and warm air flooded inside — still, August air that foreboded a thunderstorm.

'Grandpa lost his pipe,' Pipsa explained. 'But we found it again.'

'I thought we agreed not to say anything about that.'

'You'll never guess where we found it!'

'Well?'

'You know how it is,' Grandpa interjected. 'These things happen.'

'We went back along the track looking. Then down by that giant spruce tree we saw smoke. The moss was burning.'

'But we stamped the fire out.'

'Good. You've got to be very careful with fire, and you must never smoke in bed.'

Grandpa brushed off the incident with a smile, pulled out a chair and sat down. Elisa started pouring him some coffee, and before long they were chatting away — it came so easily to Elisa, words just bubbled from her mouth — and again Harjunpää felt left out. This was always the way. Grandpa had befriended everybody else; he and Pipsa got on especially well, but whenever he saw Harjunpää he soon slid off somewhere and started forgetting things. As strange as it sounded, there were times when Harjunpää felt that he did this accidentally on purpose: upon seeing him, Grandpa's mind was filled with things he couldn't properly process. Perhaps this was part of the irony: the last time Harjunpää had had a father, he'd been helpless and couldn't quite understand things, but now that he was an adult and wanted to talk things through, it was his father who was helpless and couldn't quite understand things.

'Yes, you're Timo, aren't you?' Grandpa asked suddenly and looked at Harjunpää. His eyes were unsure; it was impossible to play-act such uncertainty.

'Yes.'

'And you're an economist, yes?'

'No. I'm a policeman. We've talked about this before, remember?'

'That's right… But you're not wearing a uniform.'

'I don't have a uniform. I'm at the Criminal Investigations Division. We wear civilian clothes.'

'And did you know that your grandmother's father was a constable in Tampere?'

'Yes, Grandfather Bergman. We've talked about this too.'

'He had a bicycle, you know. Aren't you a constable?'

'I'm a detective sergeant. And I've been at work all night, but now I have to go back again,' he said and began to get up. In a peculiar way he felt almost nostalgic. Through his wistfulness he realised that perhaps Grandpa really did want to get to know him but that, without knowing it, he himself was being standoffish, and he knew that Grandpa could sense this. Perhaps what they really needed was to spend some time together, just the two of them, but there never seemed to be a suitable opportunity.

'Dad,' Valpuri hissed. She'd been standing in the hallway all this time, and as Harjunpää made to leave she darted past him on the stairs and stood there with the rabbit in her arms, her cheeks red with excitement.

'We'll go and get the mesh tomorrow, as soon as I get back from work. Remind me if I go off for a nap or something.'

'No, listen…'

'Yes?'

Valpuri started sniggering the way adults sometimes do, laughter bubbling up inside no matter how much you know you shouldn't laugh, no matter how serious it is.

'Well, when we were in the woods, Grandpa told Pipsa that…'

'Hey, cut it out!'

'I mean, a man his age… He said he thinks the rabbit got in his room during the night and… wet his bed…'

'He says a lot of things…'

'I just went and looked, and his bed's wet, but it's not the rabbit's fault!'

Valpuri started howling, almost paralysed with laughter, and the rabbit panicked and shifted position in her arms.

'Listen, calm down. The thing is, when you get to that age everything seems a bit... Why don't you tell Mum, but make sure Grandpa doesn't overhear you.'

'I know. When will you be back?'

'I'll be back soon. You can be sure of that.'

'Afternoon,' said Harjunpää and stepped into Järvi's office. He leaned over the papers on his desk, as though he didn't want Harjunpää to see them. Harjunpää didn't like the way Järvi was looking at him: slightly perplexed and questioning, almost a continuation of the silence through the corridors of the Violent Crimes department.

'Good afternoon...'

'Well, here I am.'

'Yes... and may I ask why?'

'You had someone call me at home and ask me to come in right away, sir.'

'That's not true,' he replied, almost startled. Perhaps he was worried that Harjunpää would ask to be paid the normal call-out rate. They looked at one another, as if each of them thought the other was insane, and Harjunpää had the surreal sensation that he was still lying beneath the sauna benches, still dreaming. He sat down without asking.

'Well, *somebody* called us...'

'Of course.' Järvi cleared his throat and moved as though he had realised something but still wanted to conceal it. He was a pale man, almost retiral age, and if you'd thought of him as a lake, as his name suggested, you wouldn't have thought of a serene open lake in Saimaa but one of the polluted ponds of southern Finland.

'There's clearly been a misunderstanding. I asked DS Lampinen to call you, but I asked him to tell you to come and see me first thing tomorrow morning.'

'Yes,' Harjunpää groaned, and as he sat there he realised this was precisely what had broken his soul. 'Well, I'm here now.'

'But let's return to this matter in the morning.'

Harjunpää raised his hands and started rubbing his temples. Time passed, the room was stiflingly hot, and eventually he said very calmly and carefully: 'I've been working all night. I've only slept about an hour, and now I'm here again. What's this all about?'

Järvi glanced at the wall, which was covered with an array of medals and honorary diplomas. Eventually he snapped out of the state of mind that Harjunpää's arrival had disturbed, stood up, brusquely folded his arms and glowered at Harjunpää with his chin jutting forwards. Now he was a general on horseback in front of his troops, his sabre raised aloft.

'Very well. To put it bluntly, you have acted in a manner most unsuitable for an officer of your ranking.'

'I see,' Harjunpää had to milk it out of him. Järvi made him remain silent.

'You irresponsibly sent a young, inexperienced officer – by himself – to a location where a suspected rape had taken place.'

'But two calls came in at once. What else could we have done? I'm not the one that's been cutting back our resources… Besides, Suominen said he took care of the matter. It was only an attempted rape. It was somewhere in Töölö: some kid broke into a woman's apartment and touched her up in her sleep. But then she woke up…'

'Some kid,' said Järvi imitating him; he could do it in the most scornful way. *Bastard*, thought Harjunpää. He had no respect for Järvi or for the majority of the High Command in the force. Järvi was an old-timer. He'd started out as a constable back when the selection process hadn't been quite as rigorous, and had gradually climbed up the hierarchical ladder, not because of his ability, but by using his elbows and by his sheer bloody-mindedness. It was still written all over him; he had the mentality of a beat cop and that was why he'd never made it to the top. Working for the police force was like an exciting toy to him; it enabled him to go knocking on the doors of the big boys, while he could freely slap the wrists of those who weren't in a position to do anything about him. And if decisions had to be made, he would always suggest creating a separate task force – then delegate the tasks to everybody else.

'This wasn't just some kid,' Järvi boomed. 'This man holds the values of our society in utter contempt, and if you'd been up to your job you would have known that.'

'How on earth…?'

'Like this,' Järvi snapped, turned to his shelves, located the relevant folder, flicked through it and handed Harjunpää a dog-eared photocopy. It was an internal police bulletin; Harjunpää had seen thousands of them. He quickly glanced over it: the memo asked all officers at Violent Crimes to pay particular attention to cases where a man gained forced entry to a woman's apartment. Harjunpää vaguely remembered people once talking about it in the coffee room. The bulletin was dated over a year ago.

'I remember reading this.'

'Then why didn't you act accordingly?'

'I've already said... Nobody can be expected to remember all these age-old memos,' Harjunpää growled and, though he tried to control himself, his irritation came across loud and clear. He didn't care about Järvi's reprimand – he knew he'd done the best he could – but he was furious that a stupid misunderstanding had cost him an entire day. Something about the incident was out of proportion, and that generally meant it involved something that was very important to someone, and Harjunpää was filled with a desire to find out what that something was.

'These cases haven't even been assigned to a specific officer,' he exclaimed. 'They're just hanging around in everybody's cold-case folder.'

'That is... that is purely a tactical decision. You know very well the risk of information leaking outside this building. In addition to their own cases my boys have been keeping a number of suspects under surveillance, but this kind of sloppiness from your officers could ruin everything.'

Harjunpää stood up as impassively and exhaustedly as he could, and hid an exaggerated yawn behind his hands.

'And where do you think you're going?'

'Home. I'm tired, and I have things to do there too.'

'Just wait a minute. I want you to understand quite what a serious matter this is. I trust your ability to keep this to yourself.'

'Yes.'

'This case involves somebody very high up indeed.'

'Well,' Harjunpää remarked and moved closer to the door.

'Oh, very well, I'll tell you. But I hope you realise what a show of trust this is.'

'I'm sure I do.'

'I take it you are aware of the Right Honourable Mr Kuusimäki,' Järvi began, and an expression came across his face that could only be described as patriotic.

'Honourable indeed.'

'That was inappropriate... But now you understand why this matter must be handled with the utmost discretion. He lives elsewhere and he's married, but naturally he has a temporary apartment in the city. And it's perfectly understandable that... well, loneliness often plagues young men. Well, about six months ago this same kid of yours gained entry to his residence too. Mr Kuusimäki contacted me about it personally. He wants the perpetrator caught and says he can't fathom how investigation standards have slipped since his days in the force.'

Harjunpää felt as though something inside him had smiled; he remembered Kuusimäki only too well. He and Harjunpää had been sergeants together for a while. The man had been full of restless, boundless energy that too often found an outlet in his baton and in talking back to the supers. If Harjunpää remembered correctly, it was to Järvi that Kuusimäki had once blurted out, 'Listen, you're an excellent chief, but you're living in the wrong century,' and that had been the end of Kuusimäki's career in Criminal Investigations. But then he'd gone off and studied somewhere, graduated in record time, moved back to his home town to work as a lawyer and now he was in his second term in the parliament.

'He's done it out of spite,' said Harjunpää.

Järvi didn't seem to understand, but assured him, 'No, this is more serious. How do we know the break-in wasn't politically motivated?'

'Quite,' said Harjunpää. 'Now, good night.'

He didn't leave the building and go out to his car but went instead to the Violent Crimes department, walked listlessly up and down its corridors for a moment, then realised that he could take a short nap on the sofa in the computer room at the Arson Division.

A moment later, however, he found himself outside Onerva's office. He stood in the doorway and smelled her scent in the air: the smell of perfume, of long hair, of things shared and years gone by. Onerva's cardigan was hanging over the back of her chair; Harjunpää stood staring at it. She called it the Heart. It was obvious when you looked at it; its colours were just right, full of pulse, a wonderful flow and vitality. It had all sprung from deep inside Onerva's mind, she had passed it through her hands and along the strands of wool, and there it was: a cardigan that was a heart.

This wasn't the only thing she'd knitted; small boutiques fought amongst themselves to be able to sell her knitwear, and Onerva knew she could make just as good a living from them as she could as a police officer, and that she would be a lot happier too. Harjunpää knew it would only be a matter of days before she tendered her resignation. Onerva wasn't a dreamer: she knew what she was doing.

Harjunpää sat down in Onerva's chair, propped his elbows on the desk and his cheeks in his palms, and sat there thinking about his life. It felt as though crying might have helped a little, but he couldn't think of a reason to do so.

He couldn't comprehend that Elisa wasn't the only woman he loved.

One-Bedroom Apartment

Sari hadn't been able to enjoy her new home for a while now, even though it was exactly what she had wanted: a light one-bedroom apartment, its surfaces coated in a fine off-white, and the furniture suited her tastes — simple, cheerful almost, and the fabric colours were coordinated and soothing. On top of that, the windows caught the afternoon sun and the rumble of the traffic on Runeberginkatu didn't disturb her as the windows were triple-glazed and soundproofed.

Yet a strange Evil had managed to sneak inside.

It hadn't been there a year ago, when she had first moved in, and back then the flat had signified the beginning of a new life. Her husband had died a few months earlier, inexplicably and, with hindsight, almost stupidly, as though life and death had been playing a trick on her. Simo had arrived slightly late for his meeting, had sat down in a hurry, clumsily missed his chair and landed awkwardly on his behind. Everybody had laughed, of course, even Simo, or so she had been told later on. The meeting got underway and an hour later Simo fainted. Two hours later he was dead.

Sari hadn't asked to see the autopsy report, but had accepted things the way the police had explained them: the trauma to the spine had fractured something, the fracture had caused some kind of internal bleeding and the bleeding had shut down something else and that was that. Cause of death and the findings of the health-and-safety officers.

She still wasn't quite over it all. She knew this, and that was something, at least. In addition she was constantly trying to get over it, and moving into a new flat was part of the process; she could feel Simo's presence all too strongly in their former home. But still it always felt as though ridiculous things could bring everything tumbling down, and one of them was the stupid envy of her stupid sister-in-law.

Sari had renovated and decorated the apartment with the money from Simo's life insurance and made it into just the kind of home she had always dreamed about as a girl. But when her sister-in-law had seen the mirrors and tiles in the bathroom, she had commented simply: 'That's just great, cut up your dead husband and plaster him on the wall in a thousand pieces. You'll be lucky if he doesn't turn up one night and demand to know what you think you're doing frittering away his hard-earned cash.'

The Evil presence manifested itself in that Sari was afraid to be alone in the flat in the evenings. Neither was her sense of dread alleviated by the fact that she knew exactly what she was afraid of: she thought she was losing her mind. That being said, she would have been even more paranoid and afraid had she known that her name was Wheatlocks, for she firmly believed her name to be Sari Anneli Luoto. This was her name too, after all, her driver's licence said so, and the plaque on the front door read: LUOTO. And every time she looked in the mirror, Sari Anneli stared right back at her.

That Sunday evening Sari Anneli Wheatlocks was sitting curled up on the sofa with a book. She hadn't read anything for the last quarter of an hour but had been glancing absent-mindedly around her home, at the tassels on the rugs and all the beautiful glassware, at how the darkness had consumed the world behind the windows one bit at a time, and it was the darkness that reminded her once again that perhaps, in some way, she was mentally ill: she was afraid of her dead husband. And because of that she was afraid of herself, and because of herself she was afraid of almost everything.

Rosalyn wasn't going to give in just like that, Sari began reading, almost mechanically. *Her bosom heaving, she sidled up to Carl and looked him defiantly in the eyes...* The book fell once again to her lap. She wasn't prepared to give in either; she only had one life, but she needed help if she was ever going to beat this. There had been plenty of sympathy immediately after Simo's death, but her problems had continued despite moving into the new flat, and once she had cautiously hinted that Simo still visited her at night, even her best friends had started rolling their eyes in exasperation. And now she was even more alone than before.

Her therapist hadn't been much more sympathetic either. 'What's most important is that you try to calm down,' the man had advised her. 'You shouldn't let these notions and dreams frighten you. The human mind is full of unpredictable things. This may mean that you're still grieving. And if we take into consideration that you've been enjoying a regular sex life which has now come to an abrupt end... A friend of mine discovered that becoming widowed reawakened her erotic fantasies of puberty. But they soon settled down once she accepted that they were a natural part of her...'

The worst of it was that he appeared in some way to have decided precisely what was wrong with her, and although she had tried hard to accept this, she simply didn't believe it was true. One benefit was that she had been prescribed a course of Diapam which she truly needed. She was pleased that she'd had the courage to seek professional help in the first place, though what courage did that really take? After all, she would have gone to the doctor's if she'd hurt her hand, too.

'Right, this girl's off for a shower, then straight to bed,' Wheatlocks said out loud; she found this often helped, though this time the words echoed through the silent, cavernous apartment, and she understood more clearly than ever before quite how helpless and alone she was. She decided to flick the radio on. She enjoyed listening to Baroque music, it calmed her thoughts, and, as if to order, the strains of Vivaldi came flowing across the Classic FM radio waves.

She took a few steps towards the bedroom but stopped suddenly and turned back; the bloke downstairs couldn't stand the radio blaring late at night – once he'd even started hammering on the radiators – but if the music were too loud it would drown out any other sounds too, and if the door suddenly opened she wanted to hear it.

She closed the bedroom door and began to undress, and only then did she realise what she'd done: she had closed the door. In her own home, by herself! She scoffed at herself, but didn't open the door and all of a sudden her hands felt as if they belonged to someone else, making unnecessary, jerking movements, and her stomach felt so sore that she might soon need a course of Alsucral. She slipped on her dressing gown – it too felt strange; in the past she had enjoyed walking around the flat naked, nothing but air against her skin – then she made a beeline for the kitchen, took a bottle of Riesling from the fridge, poured herself a glass and downed it in a few gulps.

Wheatlocks closed her eyes. She could already feel the wine warming her stomach, the pain wasn't quite as sharp any more, then the effects of the wine reached her head, softening it, making it feel more woolly; she felt safer and it occurred to her for the umpteenth time that she ought to look for a lodger. At first she thought of Inkeri, but then realised that she'd have to put up with her constant flow of boyfriends. Besides, sometimes not even the best of friendships could survive such intense proximity and she didn't want to lose anybody else.

Thunder rumbled outside; Wheatlocks gave a start. It hadn't started raining yet. The wind rattled the roof slates and whistled through the TV antenna; it all felt somehow stifling. Sweat ran down the length of her back. She poured herself another glass of wine.

A man would have been one option, and there was no doubt that she missed having a man around. But that solution came with the greatest risk of all. She didn't want to discover suddenly that somebody owned her or that being with someone came with certain strings attached; she didn't want to end up in a ridiculous power struggle that would end with her having to compromise herself to make someone else feel good about themselves. She took pity on other people all too easily.

The whole boyfriend question was a problematic one because, without knowing it, the therapist had been right. She couldn't simply go to a nightclub and come home with a man. Of course, she *could*, she had done so in the past, but it never gave her the satisfaction she imagined. She was always revolted afterwards; revolted that snoring beside her lay someone for whom she felt nothing at all, and who in the morning avoided eye contact, who glanced at his watch and who said 'see you around', then left, and who beneath his utter meaninglessness was happy at having simply added another notch to his bedpost.

Besides, she didn't want to repeatedly endanger her health, not to mention her life. This had made her realise something almost amusing: men were afraid of condoms, and she had worked out why. Condoms and AIDS appeared side by side in posters and in virtually every well-meaning public health campaign. They were inextricably linked to one another, to the extent that producing a condom had become a hint: I don't trust you, you might be infected. Or the other way round: beware of me, my love might be deadly. There couldn't be many men who would still want her after that.

The lift jolted into motion, its sound clearly audible inside the flat, and Wheatlocks gave a start. She put down her glass and listened, following the hum and the clunking of the cogs, but it went past and came to a stop on the sixth floor. She found herself thinking that anyone could walk one floor down, and suddenly she didn't want to take a shower after all. She stood there thinking, her head slightly to one side. Maybe it was because you had to walk through the hallway to get there. She hadn't switched the hall lights on, and in the darkness the clothes hanging on the coat rack were like men waiting with their shoulders hunched.

I *will* go to the shower, she told herself and started moving, and as she walked she stared fixedly down at her toes and her red lacquered toenails flashed against the white birch parquet like berries escaped from a basket. But at the edge of the hallway she stopped; she had to. She continued to stare at her toes, but now she was thinking of the chain on the front door and whether she had remembered to secure it. She raised her eyes; the clothes men were still there, but now they seemed almost tame, and the door chain gleamed in the darkness – and of course it was locked.

She slipped into the bathroom, flicked on the lights, took off her dressing gown and began busily washing her face. She didn't enjoy it the way she used to; she couldn't concentrate on the sensation of the water gently brushing against her skin or the soft fragrance of the lather. Instead she scrubbed her cheeks with hard, abrupt fingers and thought about what her sister-in-law had said and whether Simo really did see her somehow. Then the other possibility rose up in her mind.

What if someone really did visit her at night? As horrific as it would be, it would almost be something of a relief. She'd thought about this many times and she knew it was impossible; she'd changed the locks straight after moving in, not even the caretaker had her key, and many mornings she'd checked the chain and it was always locked. And when she'd asked her brother Marko whether she ought to go to the police, he'd remarked: 'They get all kinds of lunatics visiting them. You want them to start looking for an invisible man? Get a security lock, then you can forget about it.' And she'd thought about it, but buying a security lock would have been an admission that she wasn't all there. And what if the visits still continued?

She tried not to think of locks and chains and listened instead to the rush of the water, then all of a sudden her mind was filled with images from *Psycho*, the scene where the woman is standing in the shower; the hand carrying a knife rises up and the water turns red. She could see herself from the outside, bent over the bathtub, her back to the door, naked, her back white and her bottom bare, and all she wanted to do was spin around and shout, shout, shout!

But she told herself that she mustn't do that, that it was very important that she didn't do that; she mustered all the willpower she had and turned the water off, then she slowly stood up and stared ahead, as though there had never been anyone standing behind her. The mirror was there in front of her and she could see her hair. It was like corn. She could see her forehead and her eyes – they were beautiful eyes but she couldn't see that; all she saw was that they were terribly frightened.

She let her gaze wander, glide slowly along the tiles covered in images of seagulls flying with their wings spread open; she saw the clothes horse, all manner of little items hanging from it. Her tights had gone all funny and now they drooped like trolls' ears – then there was the door. It was nothing but a dark, ominous rectangle, like a beast's jaws or an open coffin, empty. Nobody was standing there watching her.

Wheatlocks leaned with both hands on the edge of the sink and took deep, heavy breaths. Her shoulders suddenly began to tremble and she started to cry. She stood there blubbering, inconsolable as a little girl, and that little girl felt so wretched that she was about to collapse. She left everything as it was, didn't brush her teeth, comb her hair or moisturise her face, but huddled her dressing gown in her arms as if to protect herself and ran into the kitchen, her bare feet slapping against the floor.

The dressing gown fell to the floor as she opened the fridge and drank wine straight from the bottle. It dribbled down her chin, and though she knew that alcohol and pills don't mix well she wrenched open the cupboard door, grabbed the box of pills, pressed a Diapam out into her hand and swallowed it. All she wanted was for her torment to end, to be able to put her mind to rest, and she turned the lights out and curled up in a tiny ball on the bed.

She lay there listening to the rain and hoped that she'd soon become drowsy and fall asleep – she couldn't do this sober any longer. She'd become afraid of sleep too, as she didn't know what happened to her while she was asleep, and she couldn't choose her dreams in advance.

She often dreamed of being with Simo again, of making love in a yellowing hayfield full of butterflies. Once she'd woken in the night but her dream had continued nonetheless: Simo had been kneeling beside the bed caressing her thighs, she'd called his name and he had replied: 'Sleep, my love. Everything will be fine.' And it had made her feel so happy that she'd dreamed she could fly and they'd kissed each other high up in the air. But the following morning she'd begun to question it all; parts of the dream had seemed too real and she'd checked through the flat, but everything was just as it had been and the chain on the door was locked.

Wheatlocks lay motionless and let the wine take effect, its warmth like a lullaby humming quietly inside her. The lamp crackled as it cooled and the floor seemed alive; the boards creaked a few times as though the Sandman had come to send her to sleep.

Open, Sesame

The stairwell was dark, as though the night's soul had stepped inside. Only the light switches glowed red.

But on the fifth floor shone a barely perceptible light, and oddly this one was on the floor: a strip of light twenty or so centimetres long, gleaming like a worm that had swallowed a ray of sunshine.

The worm came from Sparkle Eye. It was a narrow penlight, its bulb covered almost entirely in duct tape and with small indentations in its tin covering at the other end, the kind of marks left by someone nervously chewing a pencil. They were teeth marks: Tweety often held the torch in his mouth, especially when he was just getting to know a lock. But now he was already hard at work and the torch lay on the floor. From this point onwards he needed no light whatsoever.

He was on his knees in front of a dark wooden door and working away, his hands raised up. More than anything he was listening, following the lock's melody: a soft, three-voice humming accompanied every now and then by a tambourine. And he wasn't only listening with his ears, he was listening with his hands too. His fingers moved like feelers, holding a piece of brass barely the size of a matchbox and turning a tiny screw at one end first to the left, then to the right, then back again. A small pipe stuck out at the other end and from inside that a steel pin thinner than a crochet needle moved inside the lock.

More such needles lay on the floor in Sparkle Eye's light, each with a different hook on the end or a carefully cut iron tooth. The needles weren't envious of each other as they all had their own function that no other needle could perform. The pouch lay there too, empty this time, and a collection of tiny pieces of steel; a layman would only have guessed that they were part of some machine or other.

Tweety had already gone through the pins a few times and would have been able to open the door if number five hadn't been giving him trouble. It was caught somehow, almost like a maggot that didn't want to be pronged on a fishing hook, but Tweety remained unfazed. He didn't force it; you had to be gentle with locks, otherwise they could turn difficult and could easily seize up with something resembling angina. Talking to them often helped – you didn't even have to speak out loud. *You're a beautiful, wonderful lock*, he thought and let the words flow through his fingers, along the needle and into the keyhole. *And you know me well. It's Tweety, and you've always opened up for me before…*

Then everything was in place. Tweety could feel it somehow, or else the lock quietly whispered it to him. He unscrewed the steel needle, gently pressed the stump of piping with the flattened end into the keyhole, and turned. The lock creaked, the catch moved, and then the door was ajar.

Tweety froze and sniffed the air. From inside the apartment came the smell of night and woman, like a sensuous, gaseous ointment, and nothing indicated that anyone had reacted to the creak. Not even the Ghost had moved. He listened to the stairwell, but nothing spoke of impending danger; a car hummed past the front door. He picked a plug-like key from the collection on the floor and straightened out the inside of the lock, packed his things into the pouch, checked that the button and safety pin fastening his back pocket were still in place and finally switched off Sparkle Eye.

The world slowly began to appear before him; a gram or two of light always seeped in from somewhere. At first it consisted mostly of darkness in all its various densities. You had to listen to them with your face and understand them with your soul. Where a shoe had stood during the daytime, there was now a stone covered in moss or an angel's feather, and a hinge wasn't necessarily always a hinge, it might be a laughing skeleton. The edge of the door stood out, a slightly lighter strip in the middle of the darkness. Tweety took hold of it and pulled. The door moved an inch, then there came a dull clink and the movement stopped. The security chain was on.

Tweety's lips rose in a faint smile. He reached into his pocket, pulled out a small tube and a piece of twisted steel wire, then rolled up his jacket sleeve. His cuff was loose, as if it had been stretched before, and rose up to his armpit with ease. He squeezed odourless white Vaseline from the tube on to his forearm, rubbed it into his skin, then untwisted the steel wire. At one end of the wire was a small loop, as small as a doll's ring, and he pressed it against the tip of his index finger. He pulled the rest of the wire until it was straight, letting it run across the palm of his hand and along the inside of his forearm down towards the elbow.

He pressed his chest flat against the wall and began wiggling his arm in through the chink in the door. In it went with surprising ease, swimming inside the apartment, as slippery as a snake, his fingers groping all the while first for the groove, the chain, and finally the nub. The next stage was delicate – his tongue came out of his mouth to sneak a look at what was happening. With his left hand he slowly moved the wire, then he removed the hoop from the tip of his finger and successfully slipped it around the nub of the chain at the first attempt. He then brought his hand back out, pushed the door almost shut, pulled sharply on the wire and lowered the chain, leaving it dangling limply towards the floor. He knew how to close the chain again too; this was slightly more complicated but it was worth doing in places he visited often.

He remained on his haunches and slipped inside, held the lock and closed the door silently behind him, then crouched down on the doormat and listened. First he made out the hum of the fridge, then the ticking of a clock – probably one of those old-fashioned ones that you had to wind up with a key, he'd thought on previous visits – then finally he heard the sound of breathing, a slow, low-pitched rumble that betrayed her deep sleep and considerable drunkenness. There was only one snorer in the apartment though, he knew that already.

But one thing was missing; Tweety crouched there waiting. Then he heard it, a comforting pat, no louder than if a pillow had fallen to the floor. A few seconds passed, then the Ghost was there in front of him: Soot Rose's cat. On his first visit the cat had almost scared him to death. It had started playing with his hand while he was trying to undo the chain, but now it was used to him and only came to say hello once he was inside. He reached out his fingers; the Ghost nuzzled them, then went into the kitchen and waited.

Tweety began to undress, his clothes still damp from the rain, and listened to himself, but he wasn't happy with what he heard. It was something murky, like a blood-red fog, but it didn't seem to be warning him of any immediate danger. Perhaps it was a kind of apathy, the same apathy he had felt earlier that evening. The feeling had been so powerful that he'd sat caressing the pouch for a full three hours, listening to *Carmina Burana* over and over before he'd been able to sense the Power surge within him. There was something else inside him too, almost a desire to do something bad, smash things, tear things up, but he suppressed it immediately – there was something so frightening about it, like a bad-tempered black dog that had almost gnawed through its leash.

Tweety was already naked, he'd only been wearing trousers, shoes and his jacket. He turned Pessi and Moses to face the door, placed his trousers in one pile and his jacket in another. That was good, it would be easy to get dressed again as he left, and if necessary he would be able to scoop everything up in a single swipe of the hand. The previous night he'd had to get dressed in the stairwell. Only once had he been forced to run out into the street with nothing on; it had been earlier in the spring, the nights were turning dangerously light and the Pig in question had chased him round the block brandishing a bread knife.

He moved but hesitated at the last moment and took the Flame, his knife, from his jacket pocket. Just in case, he thought and moved inside without thinking what 'just in case' meant. Soot Rose was a harmless woman; he knew that.

Every Sunday she drank herself into oblivion and it wasn't uncommon to find her asleep on the sofa with only half her clothes on. Once he'd found her lying fully clothed on the floor in the hallway. She rarely brought men home with her – perhaps she was so drunk that no one would have her. The most amusing thing about Soot Rose was that she always let Tweety into the building – she must have thought he was a neighbour – then all he had to do was go down to the basement and wait for her to get home.

Soot Rose hadn't pulled the curtains, and the darkness in the living room was a deep-blue dusk; it was like being in an aquarium filled with ink. Tweety stopped amidst the ink and made sure that Soot Rose was in bed, then he continued towards the kitchen. He walked strangely, though he moved with ease: he remained in a crouching position, his hands resting on top of his thighs, and it seemed as though his legs only moved from the ankles, rolling like wheels beneath him. But by walking like this he was always hidden behind the furniture and he wouldn't be given away by anyone turning in bed and glancing around the room, and when he stopped still, in the darkness he blended in with the furniture so well that a drunken sleepwalker going to fetch a glass of water could walk right past him without noticing a thing.

Tweety closed the kitchen door behind him, he couldn't open the fridge and allow the light to shine into the bedroom. The Ghost was waiting for him next to his bowl; he was a chunky, grey-striped cat, and now he was so happy that he came up to Tweety and nudged against his bare shins. There was a tin of Kitekat in the fridge. It was the fish-flavoured one. The Ghost preferred the chicken-flavoured one, but continued to gobble it up, purring contentedly. Tweety flattened the surface of the remaining food in the tin, replaced it and walked out of the kitchen. He didn't feed the Ghost out of a deep affection for animals, but for the simple reason that, if he didn't do it, the cat would start rubbing himself up against him, and the evening would all come to nothing.

Just before the bed he stepped on Soot Rose's clothes that lay strewn across the floor. The first item he found was her bra. He fingered it for a moment, but to his surprise it didn't awaken the same feelings in him as before. He found himself thinking how strange it was that certain parts of the body are trussed into cups that are then fastened over the shoulders. But next he found her nylon tights.

He slipped his hand in through the top and spread his fingers so that the fabric stretched, then ran it along his cheek. But this didn't arouse him either. His hand slumped down. He didn't know what had got into him – perhaps it was the black dog growling again. Regardless, he hastily pressed the Flame's blade against the tights at the point where the fabric was at its most taut. The nylon gave way, but he pressed harder still. There came a quiet hiss and the tights tore.

Tweety remained perfectly still, breathing with his lips slightly apart. Finally he shook his head as if to wake himself up, let go of the tights, clambered towards the bed and knelt down beside it. Soot Rose was asleep on her back. She had shoved the duvet to one side – it must have felt too hot before the storm – and now she was lying there naked, her breasts rising heavily, and her hair gave off the sharp smell of the bar and of tobacco. There she lay and didn't know anything about him. There she lay entirely at his mercy.

He breathed in Soot Rose's different scents and tried to imagine what her life was like, and decided that she probably did a boring job that she secretly hated; and when the weekend came she would take a bath and start to put on her make-up, she'd say something to the cat, because there was nobody else to talk to and her telephone probably didn't ring all that often, then she'd pull on her tights and her nicest clothes, take a bottle of perfume from the bathroom cupboard and spray some of it behind her ears, then finally she'd sit in a nightclub all by herself and nobody would try to pick her up, she'd become more depressed and order more to drink, then stagger home drunk and collapse, her body heavy with inebriation. It was a miserable life and she'd have been happier dead.

Tweety felt almost sorry for her, and he sat up and kissed her gently on the forehead. She didn't react in the slightest. He sat back down, the taste of Soot Rose's make-up and sweat in his mouth, and he didn't know what had come over him, but somehow he didn't want to touch her anymore.

Perhaps he did know what it was after all: he missed Wheatlocks. It was her that he had wanted to visit, but he couldn't visit her too often as she might start to sense something and he didn't want to lose her. For he loved her. Of all women, she was the sweetest. All the others, Soot Rose, Silkybum, Little Faun, they were all substitutes. It was true and he knew it.

Sometimes they almost disgusted him, as Soot Rose had done, her snoring or her breath. Tweety's nostrils began to twitch. Soot Rose was nothing more than a lump of meat, and if she'd been his wife she'd probably have nagged him constantly and cooked horrible food, and she'd never want to sleep with him because she'd always have a headache.

'Vile slut,' his lips moved. He knelt up, and he almost wished that she would wake up. He wanted to see the look of fright, how the terror would twist her face and make it even uglier, how spit would fly from her mouth as she screamed – this he truly wanted to see. She would have screamed and screamed and there would have been nothing left of the lady she had been as she'd swaggered into the nightclub, her tits packed into her lace bra and her pussy smirking to itself inside her silk panties.

He raised the Flame and turned it slowly in the air. There was just enough light shining in from outside: an electric blue flash ran the length of its blade. He lowered the knife so that it was almost touching Soot

Rose's chest, at the spot where he thought the heart must lie, and held it there, barely a millimetre away from her white skin. *Wake up*, he thought, *sit bolt upright!* He wondered what it would feel like as the knife sank into a person: would you be able to feel their heartbeat? Would it feel different once they were dead? And if so, what would that feel like − like holding your bare foot on a frog thrashing in the grass?

Station

'So this morning I finally did it.'

'You did... Sorry, what did you do?'

'Just like you said. And you should have seen him. He just clammed up and tried to shuffle his way further left, but he couldn't move an inch because there was another man sitting there who looked like a pilot.'

'Really?' Harjunpää gasped, and now he really was interested. In a way he was always interested in Maija's stories. She was a nice woman, freckled and energetic, and it seemed as if she was always holding back a smile because she knew something funny that nobody else did. She was the departmental secretary, and for years she and Harjunpää had walked together from Pasila to the police station each morning.

'So when we stopped at Leppävaara he came up with something. He stood up and pretended to get off, but he only went into the next carriage, I saw him as I got off. I'd love to follow him into town one day and see where he works... He looks like such a gentleman, like a judge or something.'

'So what did you do to him?'

'Well, this time he was sitting opposite me. Whenever he sits next to me he starts touching his hand against my thigh, but when he sits opposite he slides down in the seat until his leg is between mine, then he rubs it up and down with the motion of the train. Well, bloody hell, I thought! I just kept on reading the paper, slipped my shoe off and stuck my toes up his trouser leg and started curling them up!'

'Good for you!'

'He went all red and grabbed his briefcase so hard I thought the handle might snap... What's eating you?'

'Grandpa,' Harjunpää sighed and felt as though he'd been caught out and spoiled someone else's happiness. It was embarrassing that Maija could read him so well.

'Anything in particular?'

'Just the whole situation,' he lied. They walked along the wall of the police station and the building rose up above them like a castle full of misery. Grandpa had been in a lot of pain that morning, hacking into his pipe and popping nitrate tablets one after the other. It had only just come to light that he'd had two heart attacks previously and that his medication could have been anywhere. Elisa had promised to contact the doctor. Harjunpää had seen a lot of old people in his work, and though it was hard to think about it he somehow knew that Grandpa didn't have much time left, that it could only be a matter of months, less even. And he'd seen in Grandpa's eyes that he knew this too; they both knew it. And they knew he didn't want to go into a home.

'You're pretty worried about him.'

'You could say that,' Harjunpää agreed and he felt as though everything was closing in on him, but he didn't want to talk about it, he couldn't talk about it. At times he felt an inexplicable resentment towards Grandpa, something approaching hatred, and yet it seemed unreasonable and wrong, especially given that the other person's life was hanging so precariously; it felt shameful, as though people would have despised him if they'd known. Even the sense that behind it all was the same feeling of being stranded and lonely he had experienced as a child and throughout his youth didn't put his mind at rest. He wondered why his father had never contacted him, not even when he'd got married. Then it finally occurred to him that, after all these years, the one person in the world whom his father had sought out had been him.

The entrance hall smelled of waiting and the misery of the previous night. He and Maija wished each other a good day; Harjunpää stepped into the lift and the unavoidable chores ahead began to suck him in. First up was the autopsy for the nameless torso he had found in the sea. He hadn't been able to find anything on the body that might have given a clue to its identity or anything that might be considered a distinguishing feature. He thought of how he would have to make sure X-rays were taken of the body before it went into the autopsy in case any bones had been broken in the past. With regard to missing persons files, it would be a great help if the coroner could establish how long the body had been in the sea. He estimated around three or four years.

A young woman with short, cropped hair was sitting in the waiting room on the fourth floor. She looked very frightened – Harjunpää thought of a butterfly fluttering against the window – but he didn't take a closer look at her. Everybody they dealt with was unhappy, and he didn't have any interviews scheduled for that day. On top of that, the door into the corridor was open and, further off he could hear the sound of an intense exchange.

'…doesn't matter, just so long as things get sorted out.'

'There's no way Haapanen can do it. The Näkinpuisto homicide is still open and his squad are already doing overtime because of it.'

'But come on,' said Lampinen. 'Can't the boys on day shift take care of that bird?'

'What's one bird here or there? There's much more at stake in this case,' someone snapped; Harjunpää thought it must have been Järvi. 'But let's get to the point: these incidents should be concentrated with one officer. It's tactical madness to have them spread through the department, one case in one officer's file and another in someone else's…'

'What we should be doing is setting up a separate task force. Three officers from your team, two from ours.'

Harjunpää approached the office; he could make out the voices more clearly and he harboured an awkward hope that the bird Lampinen had referred to wasn't the butterfly woman sitting in the foyer. Onerva was far away at the other end of the corridor where the Robbery Division began. She was waiting for the lift, holding her key card – perhaps she was going down for breakfast – and when she saw Harjunpää she started waving both her hands at him. He realised this wasn't a normal greeting, that there was more to it than that, but he couldn't work out what, waved back and stepped into the office.

The room was full of people in grey suits. Tupala, who ran the office, was sitting at his desk, a pained look on his face, and speaking on the telephone, his free hand plugging his other ear. The Fraud Division's phone was ringing incessantly. Tupala was supposed to answer that one too, and nobody had thought to answer it for him.

'Morning,' said Harjunpää and made for his pigeonhole. Only then did he notice that the discussion had suddenly stopped. Then he realised what Onerva's waves had meant, clear as day: *Whatever you do, don't stick your nose in there!*

'Morning,' everyone in the room replied almost in unison; at least that's what the mutter that filled the room sounded like. He turned slowly and suddenly felt very self-conscious: everyone in the room was staring at him with a look of revelation. In addition to Järvi there was Lampinen and his almost inseparable partner Juslin, and standing opposite them was Ahomäki, head of the Violent Crimes unit, DCI Hyttynen from the Arson Squad, and Nuutinen, the head of the Investigations Division. Only Järvi was staring at the floor; he was almost entirely bald, the light shone on the top of his head and his taut face was almost the shape of a wrench.

'What's your current situation, Harjunpää?' asked Ahomäki. He said it almost as if asking for help. He was a quiet, thoughtful man with a firm sense of justice. Harjunpää understood quite how deeply Ahomäki had been affected by the shouting match in the office, and if anyone else had asked him this question he might have said anything at all, but now all he could do was shrug his shoulders. The previous night's homicide had gone to Suominen's team – Harjunpää had taken care of the paperwork – and an autopsy and one unidentified drowning victim were all part of his everyday routine. Replying that he needed some time in peace to take care of his father would have been out of the question.

'In fact,' Järvi cleared his throat. 'DS Harjunpää is already acquainted with the matter, and perhaps it would be for the best that certain classified information remains within as small a group as possible.'

'And I know who was behind it too,' said Lampinen matter-of-factly, Juslin added something and Nuutinen started explaining what all this was about, then Hyttinen tried to better him, and soon everyone was talking at once, the whole office hummed and people started flicking through papers and Tupala, who for years had mastered the art of keeping cool, stood up sharply and shouted:

'Quiet!' He looked around, somewhat bewildered, and when he realised who was standing in the room he became even more embarrassed and rubbed his nose. 'I mean… sorry. I can't hear what the person on the phone is trying to tell me…'

'Why don't we go into your office?' said Ahomäki and looked first at Harjunpää then up at the ceiling, at a spot high up where someone must have been handing out mercy. They began to shuffle out into the corridor. Onerva was there; she had come back once she'd realised what had happened, but there was no disparagement in her eyes, just something approaching sympathy. She brushed against Harjunpää's hand as she walked past, and her fingers were warm and good.

Lampinen stopped momentarily by the waiting room, reached out his hand and curled his little finger.

'Right, girlie. Let's see what we can do about all those bad old men.'

The woman stood up, or rather she jumped to her feet, and for a moment it looked as though she wanted to apologise and make for the lift, but she gripped her handbag against her chest as if to protect herself and began walking down the corridor.

It was only now that Harjunpää noticed the full oddity of the woman's appearance: her hair resembled a hedgehog's bristles, its shortness highlighting her thin neck and the shape of her head. Her eyes were large and blue, and her hands small like a little girl's, and there was something strangely austere about her, perhaps because she wasn't wearing any jewellery or make-up, or because her clothes were so simple, almost masculine. Harjunpää liked her instinctively; perhaps it was because she was so afraid, and this awakened a desire to protect and help her.

'You interview her,' he whispered to Onerva. 'Sit her down in the consultation room with a cup of coffee.'

He felt suddenly annoyed at Lampinen's behaviour, though he knew the man wasn't being tactless out of mere spite. There was a puzzling contradiction about Lampinen. On the one hand he felt a burning desire to be the boss – he served as some sort of aide to Järvi and was often seen sitting with the supers in the cafeteria. His own path to becoming a detective inspector had run aground time and again at the entrance exams for the leading officers' course. On the other, he wanted to be a clown, or at least funny, and to that end he had started quoting and copying the gestures and catchphrases of countless TV comedians. Only a few of the sergeants actually knew what he was talking about, and thus most people considered him a jovial jack-the-lad; maybe even the supers needed a court jester.

Eventually Harjunpää realised what was bugging him and he strode off after Lampinen.

'Listen, Lempi…'

But Lampinen didn't hear, didn't want to hear, and only then did Harjunpää understand why: it was probably not a good idea to use Lampinen's age-old nickname. Originally he'd been Lempinen, so Lempi – sweetheart – had come from that, but after getting married he'd taken his wife's surname, and thus Lempinen had become Lampinen. Despite this, the spectre of 'Lempi, darling' hadn't gone away, and those who knew him better claimed it bothered him more than anything.

'Hey, Lampinen.'

'Is someone addressing me or is that just the creak of shoes I can hear?'

'What did you say to Valpuri yesterday afternoon?'

'What did *I* say? I don't think I know anyone by that name.'

'I came all the way out here for nothing. Valpuri said I'd been ordered to come back immediately.'

'For goodness' sake… I said you were to come here presently – at the start of office hours. As far as I know, office hours in all state departments start on a Monday morning, not Sunday.'

'Well, that's very funny.'

Lampinen didn't respond; Harjunpää, too, held his silence. And although the two of them had never exactly been friends, what there had been was now gone. The others spoke for them as they filled the corridor, a herd of clattering shoes, and made their way towards Harjunpää's office. Imppola came towards him, a charred rubber boot in his hand, pressed himself against the wall and remarked: 'I don't know what's going on, but I'm not the least unhappy about it.'

At half past nine Onerva came back into Harjunpää's office and the newly formed task force was assembled once again. Lampinen and Juslin were already there and the air was thick with cigar smoke: Lampinen chain-smoked Café Crèmes, and Harjunpää was sick of the sight of the cigars bobbing up and down at the edge of his mouth whenever he spoke. To head the force was an inspector from the Third Division called Valkama. He was relatively new to the force and was widely considered competent, if rather indecisive, when it came to making big decisions. He was also a member of countless other task forces and spent the majority of his time somewhere other than the station in Pasila.

'Poor woman,' said Onerva; her voice was mute and the spark so often in her eyes had disappeared. 'She's spent two weeks wondering whether to come in or not. And though she didn't say as much, she's even contemplated...'

'You don't think she's a dyke, do you?' Juslin said reflectively, and his eyes lit up with interest. 'She seemed a bit odd.'

Onerva said nothing but stared at Juslin, her head to one side. He remained unperturbed and tapped his thighs.

'Come on, darling.'

Juslin was a big burly man who undeniably looked more like a guerrilla or a burglar than a policeman. He had short, spiky hair and a few days' worth of stubble on his cheeks, and he wore a pair of hunting trousers, tightly laced commando boots and, despite the heat, a thick woollen jumper. At a fair distance his clothes smelled as though they hadn't been washed for a long time, and if ever anyone commented on this he proudly replied: 'Real men smell of shit and petrol, that's the way it is.' He didn't smell of petrol, but he enjoyed teasing women, placing his hand on their hips, looking them in the eyes and asking imploringly: 'How about it, sweetheart?' He took care of his work well enough, obtaining clues and tip-offs from the underworld; many a case had been solved with information he had provided.

'What's her story?' asked Harjunpää, but Onerva gently squinted her eyes, which meant that she'd tell him later and that she wanted the other two to leave.

'How about Onerva and I go through this material first, then you go through it, then we have a meeting and see what we've come up with. OK?'

'Oh aye,' scoffed Lampinen with what was perhaps the most common of his famous television allusions. 'But I want one thing to be clear from the start: we maintain two parallel lines of approach. You take care of yours, we'll take care of ours. And just so you know, this won't be a very long case. It's Klaus Nikander. Nobody picks locks better than he can, and he's quite the pervert to boot. Well, his luck's run out...'

'You're going to have him watched?'

'Him and a couple of others, yes,' said Lampinen mysteriously and stood up. Juslin followed his example, and when they stood next to one another you could see quite what an odd couple they were: Lampinen was of average height and gangly, while Juslin was over six foot and stocky, and his movements were somehow exaggeratedly intense, tight and almost bear-like. His belt gave off a dull clunk as, in addition to his revolver, virtually everything that could be used as a weapon dangled around his waist.

'Onerva,' he growled. 'How about it?'

'Right away, sir,' she replied and without further ado reached out and put her hand on Juslin's flies. He gave a start, backed off and disappeared into the corridor. Harjunpää could see that his neck was bright red.

'Dear oh dear,' said Harjunpää quietly as he looked out of the window, and a sense of dejectedness began to fill his mind. The basis for the investigation couldn't have been worse. He didn't like Lampinen; Lampinen probably didn't like him either; Onerva was sure to have problems with Juslin – or rather he would have a problem with her. On top of this, supervising everything was Järvi, and Harjunpää felt that Järvi had handed him this case as some form of punishment for the events of the previous day, when he had apparently been incapable of showing due respect.

'It was a mistake calling him Lempi.'

'Come on, it just came out.'

'I know someone who works with his wife. The whole idea of changing his name was to stop people calling him Lempi. He can't stand it because it's a woman's name, and you know he's a bit...'

'How was I supposed to know that?'

'That's why he's so pally with Juslin, he wants to look as macho as him. Poor man doesn't know how wrong he is.'

'What d'you mean?'

'Well... You don't seem that interested in this case.'

'Not really. But we can get off with admin if Lampinen catches this Nikander in the act.'

'Don't get your hopes up. You know Nikander, he's a bit on the chubby side. But this woman Pirjo described the intruder as almost scrawny. She said he reminded her of a chaffinch. Besides, Lampinen's been a bit obsessed with Nikander for a while now. He's been watching him for goodness knows how long, but after that job in Herttoniemi he hasn't managed to catch him red-handed. But it was the toilet incident that really got his back up.'

'The *what*?'

'He was in a pub following Nikander, and when he went to the loo two blokes grabbed hold of him, held his head in the toilet bowl and flushed it, saying "Greetings from Klaus". You know he'd never forgive anyone for humiliating him like that. But Timo…'

'Yes?'

'Let's crack this one because… who knows, it might be our last case together.'

'We'll do that,' said Harjunpää, but he couldn't look at Onerva. Instead he looked down at the papers Ahomäki had just brought them, and he didn't have the faintest notion of how he was going to keep that promise.

Bogey Man

Chief Inspector Kontio certainly lived up to his name: like a bear he was short, stocky and had a round face. His hands crowned it all: they were covered in hair, like paws with short, stubby fingers. Kontio didn't know anything about his parents, but they'd undoubtedly had a roguish sense of humour as his first name was Otso – another of the epithets for the great bear of Finnish mythology. And if a man's full name is Otso Kontio, you'd expect him to have a nickname anything from Teddy to Grizzly, but everyone referred to him as the Bogey Man.

And there was something decidedly bearish about him too. He was stubborn, a man of few words, but when he opened his mouth the words sounded at once friendly but so sharp that people listened to him immediately. He never raised his voice, but his subordinates were still afraid of him – and with good reason. He was filled with a deep sense of ambition and power and had a possessive nature, and perhaps this was why life and work were like games to him, games that didn't involve people but playing pieces ready to make a move. And woe betide the unlucky fellow to whom, after losing one of his games, the Bogey Man said: 'Listen, your career just took a sharp turn. A turn for the worse.'

Just then Chief Inspector Kontio was sitting in his dingy office and talking on the telephone, or rather he was listening, punctuating the caller's words every now and then with a mumbled 'yes'. The caller clearly wasn't just anybody; Kontio had stopped fidgeting with his paperclip and there was something approaching respect in his expression. He definitely wasn't a yes-man, despite the fact that, like Järvi, he was an old-timer with minimal education and had friends in extremely high places.

He didn't need to suck up to anyone; other people sucked up to him. All kinds of people were always being picked up on minor offences: an MP's son is found in possession of cannabis; a small-town police officer's wife walks out of the department store wearing a pair of shoes she hasn't paid for; a prostitute cleans out a bank manager in a hotel somewhere. These things happened despite the goodness of people's hearts, and at times like that it was nice to know there was someone you could call. What was even nicer was when that someone called back a few days later and said: 'Don't worry. You can rest assured the press won't find out about it...' Even more wonderful than that was when the voice said: 'Forget about it. I've had a word with the officer in charge of the investigation and he assured me there are no grounds to take the matter any further. I think he's typing up the final report as we speak...'

The conversation in which Kontio was now engaged was clearly coming to an end; the elbow of the hand holding the receiver rose from the table as he added, 'You can rely on me. As I said, it's a matter for the Violent Crimes unit, but in practice that doesn't really matter. Let's leave it a while yet. Do give Helen my regards...'

Kontio replaced the receiver, tightly pursed his lips, took a deep sigh and was clearly thinking things over, gathering the different parts ready to make his next move, and if a person's brain really did consist of little cogs and wheels, the room would have been filled with an almighty humming and whirring. The telephone warbled again and interrupted him.

'Kontio.'

'Hi, Vaarala here.'

'How's tricks? Haven't heard from you in a while.'

'Well, you know what a circus this place can be.'

'Suppose we should be grateful there's enough money to put bread on the table.'

'I suppose so. Gets a bit much sometimes, but can't complain, eh... Actually, I wonder if I could have a word with you about a potential problem.'

'I'll pop by your place; I was just leaving.'

'It'll only take a few minutes. I'd...'

'I'll pop by.'

'OK. Let's say in half an hour? Pull up next to the office block and I'll come out.'

'Fine. Half past eleven on the forecourt.'

Kontio ended the call, and for a brief moment he was able to forget about the depressing thoughts that had plagued him for months. He smiled, and it was a shame there was nobody there to see it, because when he smiled he was just like any other old man, and it wasn't hard to imagine happy grandchildren in his arms. Kontio didn't have any family; his marriage had been childless and his wife had died over ten years ago. Soon he wouldn't have anything left: his department was being closed down, the Property Theft unit was already being transferred to the Public Order Division and his subordinates were disappearing by the day in compulsory transfers to other departments.

It had been hard for Kontio to swallow. At first he hadn't believed it would really happen, and when he finally accepted what was going on he thought that behind it all there must be a faction bent on crushing him. He'd used all his contacts and made frequent visits to the ministry – but to no avail. His only faint comfort was that he would have to be a depart-mentless head of department for just four months, then retirement awaited him. But still, what was a pensioner? A frayed woollen sock that nobody respected.

Kontio dialled an internal extension and someone answered immediately.

'It's me,' he growled. 'Get me a car. I'll be in the parking bay in five minutes.'

He stood up, pulled a set of keys out of his pocket and walked towards the filing cabinet. He unlocked one of the doors and slid it to one side. The upper shelf was full of neatly folded plastic bags, hundreds of them. He selected two of them, with firm fingers folded them smaller and pushed them into his trouser pocket. Finally he locked the cabinet, took his jacket from the back of his chair and stopped at the door to look behind him, as though he suspected that someone might come into the office and snoop around, but he couldn't think of anything that others might have noticed and stepped out into the corridor.

Hämäläinen was driving with Kontio in the passenger seat. The men sat in silence: Kontio because he was thinking and Hämäläinen because he'd learned to be quiet – he knew how to read his boss and his expressions.

Hämäläinen was a slightly older senior constable who knew that this was as far as his career in the police force would go, and perhaps Kontio's company fascinated him as it felt good even being close to power and everything that he himself had never achieved. He knew a lot about Kontio, things that many people would have paid to find out, but he was unflinchingly loyal to his superior, though he didn't always understand why.

'What kind of man is Harjunpää?' Kontio asked out of the blue.

'Just… part of the furniture, really.'

'Does he drink?'

'I've seen him have one or two in the sauna, but he's never passed out or anything like that. I did hear that once he was apparently so drunk that Mäki managed to slip a pair of Ulla's knickers into his pockets, and as he reached for his wallet on the train, they fell out and he was…'

'I mean – if someone claimed he'd been on night shift and had one or two to drink, would anyone believe it?'

'Absolutely not.'

'What's he like otherwise?'

'Well… he used to be a bit uptight, but he's changed. Stenu said he'd heard his wife had joined the church. Maybe that could've affected him.'

'Drive in there, then park by that window with the blinds half shut. Wait in the car.'

Hämäläinen steered the Lada through the gate and into the terminal area, skilfully driving between the lorries, and parked where he'd been instructed. Kontio got out of the car and Hämäläinen stayed where he was. The air was thick with the stink of diesel oil and exhaust fumes; the lorries' motors roared and pneumatic brakes hissed. Cars came and went, and it occurred to him that millions of marks' worth of freight must pass through this area every year and that losses were probably considerable, at least twenty million marks a year. Things disappeared as packages fell apart, address labels came off, parcels were sent to the wrong recipients and left lying around here and there. That's how it must happen, in little droplets.

The matter was once considered so significant that a separate division for harbour and freight crimes had been established and Hämäläinen had worked there in the past. But with all the other upheavals that had racked the force, that too had been discontinued, and this had been the only time he had felt a certain contempt towards Kontio: the incident was the first time Kontio had supported the closure of a unit under his direct supervision.

Kontio strode towards the door, his hands on his backside, thoughts racing through his mind. He felt a comforting sense of expectation, like a child on Christmas Eve, and he was enjoying it so much that he almost hoped Vaarala would be slightly late. But he hadn't even made it to the door when Vaarala dashed outside. The man was in his forties, thin and carefully groomed. He was wearing red, expensive-looking shoes, which he'd probably bought on his last trip to Italy, and on his little finger there was a white-gold ring with a small, gleaming diamond. Kontio's sense of contentedness was suddenly gone.

'How's it going?'

'All right. You know how it is, trucks in and out, freight moving from place to place.'

'That's the way it is. Sorry, I've got to be at a meeting in fifteen minutes. Fancy lunch later in the week?'

'OK. The Fisher's Croft Hotel is a decent place. Thursday at one?'

'Fine. Let's take a walk over there. Let me get straight to the point: my sister popped round yesterday. She's having a spot of bother with you lot.'

Kontio murmured something indistinct and didn't look at the other man. He merely stared at the ground in front of him so that Vaarala couldn't read his expressions but could only see how concentrated he was on the matter in hand. Out of the corner of his eye he could see that Vaarala seemed rather ill at ease.

'Who's leading the investigation?'

'There is no investigation – really. They're keeping an eye on her bloke. She mentioned someone called Lampinen. His name's Reino Leinonen. He did over a couple of deposit boxes a few years back apparently, but he was never convicted. He's been clean for a while now, but this Lampinen's still on his tail.'

'Then he's up to something.'

'But my sister comes here in tears and swears he isn't. Reino and his brother have got themselves jobs as subcontractors for a firm that does up old digging machines before shipping them to Russia and the Baltics. It's small-time stuff, but he's trying to keep on the straight and narrow... And he's worried he'll lose credibility if the police are always hanging around him.'

'And you're sure there's nothing else going on?' Kontio asked and looked up suddenly, and the look in his eyes made Vaarala start.

'No… why would I cover for him? It's my sister I'm trying to help here, she's had to put up with enough as it is.'

They stopped by an empty truck. Kontio put his foot on the step, and now he was no longer a guest – he was the lord of the manor. Vaarala rummaged for his cigarettes.

'Smoke?'

'Nope. You see, this is a tricky business,' he said slowly and he wasn't lying. It was particularly tricky for him as he wasn't really on speaking terms with Järvi – or Lampinen, for that matter. He and Järvi had started out together and had ended up fighting for the same supervisor vacancies, but it had been too much for Järvi when Kontio was appointed departmental chief inspector. By way of compensation, the Special Unit had been tailored for Järvi, back in the days before people knew anything about profit responsibility, but now it seemed as though Järvi had once again drawn the short straw. And wasn't Kontio the one behind it all in the first place?

'It's a tricky business.'

'On a different subject… I hear you'll be retiring in the not-too-distant future. There's been some talk round here of establishing a small Security unit to help train our drivers going to Italy and the east. And I'm sure we'll need to consult an expert every now and then…'

'I'm retiring in April next year. But let me have a think about this business with your sister.'

'Excellent. I knew I could rely on you.'

'What's this?' Kontio exclaimed, his voice mockingly playful, and pulled the carrier bags out of his back pocket. 'I wonder what these empty bags can be doing in my pocket.'

'Hmm,' Vaarala chuckled conspiratorially, but a look of disdain flashed across his eyes. 'They're clever bags, you see. They don't feel very well because their stomachs are empty. Maybe they had a hunch they might find something to remedy that around here.'

'Well, I've never heard of such a thing.'

'Why don't we go and have a look in my car. I thought I heard something jingling in the boot when I drove into work this morning…'

They came to a stop behind Vaarala's Volvo. Kontio glanced around vigilantly; he'd done so every now and then throughout their conversation, but now he was particularly careful. Everything was fine; nobody was staring at them and Hämäläinen looked as though he was reading something in the car.

Then he looked into the boot of Vaarala's car and his satisfaction returned, stronger than before, and his mouth watered as though he had stepped up to a table laden with treats. The boot was full of treats too, cartons of cigarettes piled up, bottles of Chivas Regal in discreet packages, boxes of chocolates and bottles of perfume, dark strings of salami and small tins of preserves, foie gras, all manner of things. Kontio let out a faint sigh and took hold of the side of the boot.

Vaarala hastily filled the bags and finally weighed them as if to say 'that'll keep you going', but Kontio cleared his throat and said quietly: 'Another carton of cigarettes. The red ones.'

'You don't even smoke…'

'For the boy in the car. He's a good officer.'

'Very well,' Vaarala snorted, stuffed another carton of Pall Malls into one of the bags and handed them back to Kontio. After this they didn't look at one another again; it was a rule of sorts. Vaarala was already thinking of his upcoming meeting and Kontio of his home and of emptying the bags. And above the roar of engines and the smell of exhaust fumes he felt suddenly happy and almost excited, just like the time when, as a little boy, Old Vähä-Hinkka's farm girl had lifted up her blouse in the barn and placed his hand on her bare breasts.

His home was his castle – not one other police officer had even set foot inside it. Perhaps it would have been more correct to call it his warehouse: he had sold off some of his furniture and replaced it with shelves reaching up to the ceiling. He even had three fridges, and each of them was full. He kept a meticulous log of everything he acquired, though even without this he would have been able to list that he had seventy-nine bottles of whisky, sixty-five bottles of Cognac and exactly forty bottles of gin; then there were the cured sausages and rounds of cheese, stacks of preserves and cans of beer, washing powders and toothpastes. It might have been easier to list the things that were not in his flat – babies' nappies were missing from the collection.

All this was the result of years of hard work and saving. He felt this same joy almost every day upon coming home. More than anything, it made him feel that life hadn't been wasted after all, and now he was untouchable. And the feeling became stronger every time he took out his bankbooks and looked at his balance, and no one who knew him would have believed that he was the happy owner of a fortune just shy of six-hundred-thousand marks.

Kontio walked up to the Lada, put the bags in the rear foot space so that Hämäläinen couldn't see them properly, though Hämäläinen had learned years ago not to snoop, then he sat down in the passenger seat and sighed heavily as though he'd just brought difficult negotiations to an end.

'It's a good job you don't smoke either,' said Kontio once they were back on the road. 'There's nothing worse than getting into a car full of smoke. But let's go via Paloheinä on our way back to the department. I've got to stop in at the house for a moment.'

'OK.'

'So what did Harjunpää do when the knickers fell out of his pocket?'

'He was so embarrassed that he got off at the next stop.'

'I see,' said Kontio, not in passing, but weightily, as though something had just fallen into place.

Queen of Angels

'Should take about five minutes,' Tweety lied, because he knew it would take at least ten. But he wanted her to stay, he wanted to mend her shoes. He loved mending ladies' shoes.

He couldn't bring himself to look her in the eye; he couldn't look anyone in the eye. He was afraid that people's eyes would betray that they knew what he was and that they wanted to blow the whistle on him. He'd always been afraid of this, even as a little boy when he was supposed to go to school, so he looked at the counter instead. Beneath the glass stood bottles of polish; they were clearly male and at night they doubtless crept up to the second floor and kissed the mannequin wearing the three-hundred-mark lace corset.

'Well, that isn't long at all.'

'Excuse me?'

'That'll be fine. I'll wait.'

'OK,' Tweety mumbled and glanced up at the woman; she had delicate, feline features and in his mind he christened her Pussycat. Another reason he couldn't look at her was that her hair was almost the same colour as Wheatlocks' hair, and he missed Wheatlocks, yearned for her, and his yearning wasn't merely the taste of mint in his mouth but a throbbing in his neck and joints, and at once he knew where to go for his lunch break.

'Do sit down,' he said, and the woman smiled: she was already sitting down. He had her shoes. It was the greatest flirt he was capable of with women who were still awake. He'd never kissed anyone or danced with anyone. And whenever he wished to try, he'd been consumed by a crushing fear that he might die or that the woman might die – but he didn't want to think about that now, his curse. For that was what it was: a curse.

The shoes were brown suede loafers decorated with small, green leaves and black silk roses in the middle. He thought of Soot Rose, but immediately slammed the door on the fourth deck of his mind, shutting Soot Rose inside, and it served her right. He turned back to his workbench and slid his hand inside one of the shoes, and it was warm with women's warmth and slightly damp, and he thought of how her foot grew into a slender shin, then came the knee, which curved into a firm thigh; he gently rubbed his shoulder and imagined that his fingers were beneath Pussycat's skirt and spread out across her soft skin.

'Is there something else?'

'What?' Tweety gave a start; his heart was pounding, kicking spitefully. The woman looked at him inquiringly; Weckman looked up from his work but didn't say anything.

'Is there anything else wrong with them?'

'No… well, the inner is a bit frayed in this one, but there's no need to change it right now,' Tweety replied, his voice like plastic warped in the sunshine, and he got to work, removed the worn heeltaps, started up the cutter and smoothed the surfaces, took out a pair of harder heeltaps – he always put those on women's shoes, he wanted to hear the clip-clop as they walked – spread the glue in place, quickly put them in the press and tidied up the edges, and with that he was finished. He was quick. He was very quick and did good work, that's why Weckman kept him on, though he would have preferred a chattier assistant.

'Quite a cutie,' Weckman remarked once the woman had left. Tweety nodded and wandered round the back of the counter pretending to be lost in thought, and through the shop window he could see her again: there she was, skipping across the Railway Station towards the underground, her almond-coloured thighs flashing and her hips swinging. Tweety put his hand on the stool where she had been sitting and it was warm, and the warmth had radiated from her bottom, and there it swished in front of him, and it felt as though his hand were almost touching it.

'Would it be all right if I took my lunch break now?'

'It's pretty quiet at the moment.'

'There'll be a rush on in the afternoon…'

'Go on then. But fix those boots when you get back. The lining's come loose on both of them.'

'It won't take long,' said Tweety and took off his red overalls, and although he wiped his hands they were still covered in glue, as though they were afflicted by a terrible blotchy disease, and he wondered how Wheatlocks would be wearing her hair that day. He hoped she had it in a French plait as this always left little wisps of hair falling across her ears like curls of light.

He made his way round the front. In his haste he hit his hip on the corner of the counter and almost fell over, but somehow managed to keep his balance and staggered to the door. Weckman shouted after him. Sometimes he could be really mean, almost let you go to lunch, then call you back while he went off instead.

'Yes?'

'You must be pretty damn hungry.'

'No... I mean, yes.'

'Well, enjoy your break, eh?'

'Thanks...'

Outside it was the height of summer: the air shimmered above the tarmac, and although Tweety could have gone through the underground passage to Aleksanterinkatu, he decided to walk along Mannerheimintie instead. He enjoyed summer. Everywhere you looked there were only beautiful things: brown, tanned legs and thighs, miniskirts and buxom tops and see-through jumpers, but when autumn came raincoats appeared like jellyfish, sucking everything inside themselves, making even the most beautiful women seem ugly; fog came in from the sea and engulfed the city, and the darkness was desperately long.

He rushed through the square by the University Pharmacy, then he could see the big clock above the entrance to Stockmann's department store in front of him. Tweety slowed his step; he was almost there. Again he thought of Wheatlocks and how she often slept: rolled up with the pillow in her arms, like a little child, and his mind was suddenly filled with memories of when he was very young and they all still lived in Kallio. The walls of the courtyard had been covered with long-legged spiders. His pet spider was called Hissu and his friend Pekka's was Hessu. One day Pekka got angry at Hessu and squashed him, and that same autumn his mother had died.

Tweety stopped hesitantly beneath the clock with a group of people standing waiting. He should never have thought about Hissu and Hessu, or rather Asko shouldn't have done so, because already the thought was digging something out of him. That was it: Mother Gold was in danger that very minute. Tweety moved restlessly. Was her cottage on fire? Apparently so. She was inside and couldn't find her way out because of the smoke, flames grabbed at her hair and crackled wickedly, she started to scream but her clothes were already ablaze, then she slumped to the floor and lay there in a black heap. And all the while Reino and Lasse had been in the workshop and hadn't noticed a thing.

'Is something the matter?'

'What?'

'Can I help you at all?'

'No,' Tweety rebuffed the man; it was the Salvation Army man who was always standing there holding a collection tin and a handful of leaflets, and now his eyes were like balls wide with concern, his mouth set in a smile. Tweety didn't like being looked at like that so he pushed the door open and stopped inside the entrance hall. There he slowly began to calm down. This happened every time he visited Stockmann's; it was as though Mother Gold were trying to stop him going in there. The first time it had happened he'd been so afraid that he'd had to call the house and Reino had wondered whether he was high on something.

He remained in the entrance hall and dried his face, and the scent of wealth and good people came wafting from inside. He slowly began to feel normal again, and he turned and pushed open the glass doors, and there in front of him lay a marvellous and wonderful world and the opening bars of *Carmina Burana* began to ring distantly in his mind.

He was in the cosmetics department. Tweety held his breath and he simply couldn't understand how it was possible to build something so beautiful: the surfaces were all rose pink or light shades of wood, and in between them stood mirrors and glass panels and pictures glowing with inner light, and in those pictures were dark, painted lips and stiff, jutting lipsticks, and the counters weren't arranged conventionally in a row, but formed small fortresses and together the fortresses made up a town that filled the entire ground floor, and through the streets of that town people could wander bathed in a shadowless light shining from all around and yet from nowhere. And above it all a column of light rose into the air, high up above where there must have been a heaven and a God who blessed with his beauty all those who bought something from this cherry-blossom paradise.

But it was the sales assistants who crowned it all. They were angels: young and dainty and pretty-faced with hair that looked as though it had been touched by the hands of the most skilled hairdressers. It didn't matter that deep down he knew they probably had to sit in front of the mirror for hours every morning in order to recreate themselves again and again. They were all indescribably beautiful, stunning women, and the fairest of them all was Wheatlocks. Among the others, she was the queen.

She was there now, under a sign reading *Rubinstein*. She was standing alone, her hands relaxed on the countertop, and staring into the distance, her head tilted to one side. She didn't have a French plait after all, she was wearing a thin, black velvet Alice band that perfectly set off the soft corn tinge of her hair, and Tweety was filled with a strange hallucination. He was standing outside on a mossy tussock, it was early summer and every-thing was still light green and fragrant; the grass was dotted with yellow stars and swallows piped through the air. Then he was back inside the department store and he felt a profound tenderness and love for Wheatlocks and wanted her to become his wife.

She needed a good man. And he needed a good woman. She was the only one of his women whose workplace he had visited and whose home he'd visited during the daytime. He'd been compelled to find out every-thing about her: he knew she was a widow and that her late husband was called Simo. And he realised that, although in her sleep she seemed to love her dead husband, it was him she really loved in the form of her husband. It was him she hugged with a pillow in her arms, his hand she fumbled for, and if her sleep ever became restless she calmed down in a few moments if he whistled to her, and this too proved that she loved him.

Tweety could feel the temptation drawing nearer, the almost irresistible temptation to walk up to Wheatlocks and say: 'It's me, my love. I'm the one you love at night.' And he was certain that, if he did it, she would reach out her delicate hands and place them on his neck and lean closer, a single intoxicating scent, and they would have kissed.

Tweety sighed. Then he took a decisive step, then another, but Wheatlocks had a customer. It was a man, of course, a swanky-looking foreigner, swaggering about, boastfully speaking English, and Wheatlocks melted into a single, broad smile and it made Tweety feel bad; he turned his back to her and a black dog started howling within him.

He was both shocked and moved at the thought that occurred to him, but it was true nonetheless: if Wheatlocks didn't care for him, or if she fell in love with someone else, he would never be able to let her go. Never. He would marry them himself. And he knew exactly how he would do it: he'd marry them with Lasse's revolver – he could see it now as if it were on film! He'd come in wearing his small-checked suit, walk right up to Wheatlocks and hand her a bunch of purple roses and say: 'I love you...' Then he'd fire, without a moment's hesitation, and she'd die happy, her last memory being the roses and the knowledge that somebody loved her, then he'd shoot himself and fall down next to her and one of her colleagues would come over and join their hands and scatter the roses over them, and somewhere in the distance would come the sound of sirens approaching.

Tweety gave a sigh, his shoulders shuddering, and he turned to leave but his eyes were so full of tears that he couldn't go anywhere, and all the while he repeated to himself that he would have done it out of love, of *love*; someone like Soot Rose he could have killed out of hatred or disgust if she'd woken up, but not Wheatlocks, for he loved her.

Answering Machine

It was just before four in the afternoon, but Harjunpää decided to give it one more go; he tried to suppress the murky feeling that had nested in his mind that he was up against an insurmountable mystical force. He dialled the number, and after a few rings the tape cut in: *You have reached the answering machine for senior citizens' officer Kaisa Salin at the Department of Social Services. I will be unavailable today. In urgent matters, please contact my colleague, officer Timo Väänänen, on extension...* Harjunpää had already written down the number and he knew what was going to happen, but he dialled the extension nonetheless and it went straight on to the tape: *You have reached the answering machine for senior citizens' officer Timo Väänänen at the Department of Social Services. I will be unable to answer the telephone today. In urgent matters, please contact my colleague, officer Kaisa Salin, on extension number...*

He put the receiver back in place and looked out of the window; far behind the horizon lay Kirkkonummi, Elisa, the girls and Grandpa.

'Same again?' asked Onerva, her knitting needles clacking. Harjunpää nodded; he didn't know whether to be disappointed or relieved. He'd managed to get hold of Ms Salin last week and they'd almost ended up having an argument: as she saw it, Grandpa wasn't a lonely old man without a home or a carer and therefore his case wasn't considered urgent, and her opinion remained unchanged despite Harjunpää's explanation of why things were the way they were. On top of that there had been something in her tone of voice that had made Harjunpää feel like the villain of the piece and he wasn't sure he even wanted to contact her again. He didn't know what to do. He felt caught in one of life's mysterious traps.

'I've had an idea. It's pretty simple, but it's good,' said Onerva. She was sitting in front of a map, knitting; it looked so down-to-earth and made him think of autumn. Harjunpää was used to seeing Onerva at work with a pair of knitting needles in her hands and he'd learned that from the point of view of their ongoing investigations it could only mean good. When Onerva was knitting she was connected to a power concealed within her and, as strange as it sounded, it was at these moments that her mind brought fresh ideas to the problems at hand.

'Yes?'

'It seems from the interview transcripts that all these women had spent the evening in a bar somewhere, but only Meriläinen's report mentioned where she'd been: the Hotel Inter.'

'OK,' Harjunpää mumbled and didn't quite follow; he was still thinking about Salin and what old people must feel like every time they reach her answering machine.

'So tomorrow we'll call all these women and ask them where they'd spent the evening. And I bet we're talking about no more than maybe three locations.'

'Right,' said Harjunpää, suddenly smiling: it seemed so simple and yet so utterly sensible. 'And we'll visit these places and ask them if they've got a regular customer that looks like a chaffinch.'

'Or whether anybody's seen somebody matching the description on the street. In one of the doorways opposite, perhaps.'

They had gone through all the reports and transcripts several times (there were now twenty-six separate incident reports and as many red pins on Harjunpää's map, most of them in the Töölö area) and they all followed the same basic pattern: the victim had left a bar fairly drunk and come home, often with a man they had only met that same evening, and woken up in the early hours as the man had started caressing her again, only to discover that there was a third person in the apartment. The intruder had then fled immediately and no one had been able to give a detailed description of him due to the darkness, let alone identify him from photographs. Many had stated that the bathroom light was switched on. None of the victims had claimed to have been sexually assaulted by the intruder, and the medical examiner's reports had remained inconclusive because each woman had already engaged in intercourse with the man she had brought home.

'What do you think?' Onerva asked. 'We'll let Lampinen and Juslin concentrate on Nikander as much as they want to, yes?'

'I was thinking along the same lines… Now I understand the whole thing with the bathroom light: he switches it on so that enough light seeps through the doorway for him to see properly and to escape if necessary. And both people who live in the flat think the other forgot to turn the light off.'

'That could well be it. And I was thinking: if we now have twenty-six reported incidents, there'll probably be just as many who have noticed something but haven't reported it. And how many women haven't noticed anything at all?'

The telephone rang.

'Harjunpää.'

'Hi, it's me,' said Elisa, and Harjunpää knew from her voice that something was wrong. 'Timo, I'd arranged a doctor's appointment for four o'clock, and Grandpa knew about it, but now I've been looking for him for half an hour and I can't find him anywhere.'

Harjunpää drew a breath; Grandpa had gone missing several times before.

'Did you go down to the phone box?'

'That's where I went first. They haven't seen him at the shop either.'

'What about the girls?'

'They're all at home. Ari said he'd seen an old man standing up on the hillside about an hour ago…'

Harjunpää rubbed his forehead. There were a number of paths leading down the hill, the majority of which led to other clusters of houses, but those on the left went first to the meadows then on to the swamp, and after that there was nothing but forest for about ten kilometres.

'Should we call the police?'

'Not yet. I'll be there in an hour, let's see if we can find him first,' Harjunpää tried to keep her calm, though he felt so worked up himself that he wondered whether or not to go down to the parking bay, take one of the police cars and speed back home.

'Timo… I think he's trying to avoid the doctor. And his nitrate tablets are still on the hall table.'

'Have another look for him. Look through the neighbours' gardens. And I'll be there in an hour…'

Onerva looked at him quizzically.

'Grandpa's gone missing,' he said, went over to the wardrobe and picked up his jacket. 'Sometimes he just can't seem to find his way home.'

'Good day, one and all,' said Lampinen who had appeared at the door with Juslin lurking behind him. 'What kind of blooding sewing group do you call this? In case you're interested, Nikander's been hanging around the city centre all afternoon. In Töölö, to be specific. It's as if he's casing the area in advance so he can have his way at night.'

'And he's one hell of a letch,' growled Juslin. 'You should see his head spin whenever a woman walks past him. I can see him there in the dark: some sweetheart lying there virtually unconscious, legs akimbo, naked as the day she was born. And he puts his hand down on her thigh, gives her a little squeeze… Breasts like foxes' muzzles, he has a little suckle… and… and his fingers start stroking her bush and he's… He's probably got a different woman every night. What a fucking pig!'

'But we're going to get him. We'll set him a trap he can't…'

'Is it all right if we talk about this tomorrow? I've got to go.'

'Well! I suppose it'll have to be all right,' Lampinen said, then nodded at Onerva's knitting. 'I hear people actually pay you for those things, those… let's call them rags.'

'That's right. I get the money brought round in a wheelbarrow twice a week.'

'Get away,' Lampinen scoffed, his interest growing, and a glimmer of envy flashed across his face. 'Well, when I've been out round town with the missus I've seen people pay over 600 marks for those things… And when you make them on duty, and add that on to your police salary, I bet you make a nice healthy profit.'

'Goodness, you think just the same way I do.'

'I take it you've got a secondary occupation licence for that?' he asked, apparently in jest. 'I used to do a few shifts as a doorman, and you could even say that's related to police work, the things you hear… But one day they demanded to see a licence and the squad didn't grant me one. You can imagine what it's like trying to pay off the mortgage on this wage.'

'I'm off. Onerva, will you lock the door?' said Harjunpää and left the room, though even in the corridor he could hear Onerva laughing.

'Buy some needles and get knitting. We could set up shop together.'
Harjunpää strode along the pavement towards Pasila train station. Holding
it by his finger, his jacket dangled over his shoulder and sand crunched
beneath his feet, and he kept telling himself that in all probability Grandpa
had already returned home. But like some kind of life jacket he thought
that, if Grandpa were still in the woods, the most obvious place for him to
go was Pilvikallio; Grandpa had been very taken with the place when they'd
been out picking mushrooms. His third thought sent a shudder through
him, though he knew that Grandpa didn't want to end up in an institution.

'Who's that walking so fast? Whoever it is, you can tell by his steps that
he's superintendent material.'

Harjunpää turned around; he'd heard quickening footsteps behind him
a moment earlier. The Bogey Man was standing behind him. He hadn't
noticed where the chief had sprung from; he certainly wasn't among the
commuter regulars.

'Afternoon.'

'Quite the Indian summer,' said Kontio, and Harjunpää slowed his step
a little though he didn't want to – perhaps he did it out of politeness or
surprise, as Kontio was never seen talking to people from other units.

'Can't complain, I suppose...'

'I've got a spot of business over at the eastern building. I hear you're
pretty busy down at Violent Crimes.'

'We're never short of cases.'

'What was it I heard today – was it in the canteen? Apparently you've
got a case so big you're coordinating a Combat unit.'

'Well, we're just liaising really.'

'You see, Harjunpää,' Kontio lowered his voice and glanced behind
him as if to make sure nobody was listening in. 'To be honest, we're on
similar ground, you and me, and it's all a bit delicate.'

'Yes?'

'My boys are still looking into the Finnair deposit-box job. And
between you and me they're pretty sure who did it. You might know him,
one Reino Leinonen.'

'Can't say I do, sir.'

'Be that as it may, my boys are keeping an eye on him. But what with
your case, Lampinen's watching him too now. My lads are worried it's
going to blow the whole operation.'

'There must be some misunderstanding... Our suspect doesn't officially have a name yet. One rather weak suggestion is Klaus Nikander. Lampinen's been following him.'

'Listen, Harjunpää,' said Kontio firmly, like someone who knows better. He stopped by the entrance to the underpass and Harjunpää stopped too; he had no choice. 'You know I'm not on good terms with Järvi and his team. They'll make things hard for me out of pure spite. Make sure this Leinonen isn't watched any more.'

'But how can I...?'

'Make sure he isn't watched, or it could cause the investigation a whole range of problems if there are too many people sniffing around him.'

Kontio gave him a curt wave and turned, and he was soon halfway along the tunnel and his dark, stout back seemed to be repeating: *Make sure he isn't watched.*

Harjunpää walked up to the platform. He felt clammy and dirty, as though his soul needed a shower, then he remembered the autopsy and the smell of the pathology lab: after all these years of routine he'd started to feel nauseous. What was that all about? And as for the water body, he was still none the wiser. There was still nobody he could visit, nobody he could tell, 'We've found your husband. Your father'.

Connections

Night was burgeoning; stars shone clearly above the birches. Tweety was on watch in the hayfield outside the workshop. He didn't like it, and he didn't like the fact that Reino was so nervous. Everything seemed like proof that an unknown danger was threatening them, that the Chancellor was just as evil as his powers, turning God into an angry old man with eyes of fire, his hands already fingering the enormous boulder he was about to cast down upon them.

He crouched down by the front wheel of a broken bulldozer, as small and invisible as he could, just outside the light shining out from behind the workshop door, and watched Lasse's cottage. The lights were on. The women were all in there, even Mother Gold. Reino had rented some videos and bought them a bottle of wine and told Bamse to keep everyone there. Tweety was keeping watch on the path and that's what he was most afraid of, because if anything bad arrived, that's where it would come from and its name would be Police. Without noticing it, he was staring more at the cottage.

The city lights glowed on the horizon; the traffic on Suurmetsäntie made a constant humming noise and a train juddered along the railway tracks. The path remained deserted and the cottage was quiet.

'Come on, Lasse, make it work,' Tweety beseeched for the umpteenth time, and for Lasse's sake he truly hoped it would work – Lasse was pissed off that everything was always down to him – but also for the sake of the Chancellor and all the good it would bring them, and because he was consumed once again by the Power and it was being wasted as he crouched there. Besides, it hindered his job. He saw and heard far too much, how worms writhed in the mud, how moths called to one another and how fairies flew down from the hedgerow and made love with the pinecones.

In addition to this he was able to make out the night's real messages. They were similar to those given off by deserted houses and aspen forests, but these messages emanated from the city centre, and before them he was powerless when he shut his eyes. He could just make out the clip-clop of high heels and bright laughter – and all of a sudden his face was transformed into a blonde woman's breasts and his eyes were her nipples, staring unflinchingly in order to see, though through the lace and the jumper everything looked like it was behind a cloud of curtains. But this woman through whom he looked out at the world was just then in a restaurant toilet; someone came out of the cubicle and adjusted her clothes and a very dark-haired woman was putting on more rouge, her lips almost touching the mirror, and her movements were unbelievably soft and dainty – she could be herself when men weren't watching her.

Tweety opened his eyes and fidgeted, and the night sucked at him so hard that his lips were sore. He tilted his head and tried to follow what was happening in the workshop. Reino was listing everything Lasse would be able to buy his wife and kids after they'd finished with the Chancellor. This showed just how stupid he was: Reino didn't understand that Lasse was thin because he had bird-bones and that was why it was no use shouting at him. Lasse had to be left in peace by himself to get on with things.

'Will you shut the fuck up?' he snapped, to which Reino replied, 'Well, is it going to work or not?'

'Not with you jabbering on all the time. Anyway, it's nearly there. If only I could work out what that symbol means. Should I put the black in there or the red?'

'Let's have a look. If it's red, it'll link the whole damned circuit back round there.'

'No it won't, because I broke the connection over there.'

'Well, switch the power on and we'll have a look.'

Tweety tasted the sound of Lasse's voice when he said it was nearly there, and immediately he wanted to see what was going on. He cast a quick glance at the path and the cottage windows, convinced himself that nobody was going to come out, jogged silently to the workshop door and knocked so that they knew it was him and there was no immediate danger. They looked at him as if he'd disturbed them, and Lasse took his hand back out from under the table. He'd screwed a plastic case beneath the table and kept his Smith & Wesson there whenever he was working, its handle always within reach.

'That seems to work,' said Tweety by way of an explanation and twisted the wooden latch shut. The workshed was full of half-stripped motors and small machines – he could barely tell what most of them had once been used for. Cogs and belts and tools hung on the walls, and rickety shelves groaned with the weight of battered canisters and pots. At one end of the workbench was a selection of welding equipment and a blowtorch. The air smelled of oil and rust and rotting wood. A single lamp dangled from the ceiling above a desk that had seen better days.

Wires and switches and meters had been rigged up to the table. Tweety didn't understand the first thing about them. He'd always been afraid of electricity; it existed, yet at the same time it didn't exist. But he recognised the oscilloscope and the small, gleaming metal cylinder the size of a plate almost hidden amidst everything else: it was the alarm system for the door to the bank's vault. Originally it had belonged to the Valkeakoski Savings Bank; Reino had picked it up after a job there, and it had been a smart move. The only problem was that Lasse had been lumbered with having to learn all about electronics and God knows what else, and they'd had quite a job finding another bank that still used the same security system.

The cylinder was still open, the inside looked like an animal's spilled guts. Lasse started screwing the lid back on, then stood up and bit his lip in thought. After a moment he looked at Reino; Reino nodded in reply and Lasse flicked a number of switches. A light bulb wired up to a small black box lit up and the needles on the ammeter waved back and forth before finally settling next to one another.

'This one's like the police's alarm system,' said Lasse, his voice strained with excitement. 'And that's the one they use in security firms or what have you, bank managers, caretakers. And now, lads, once we're inside we'll start...'

He picked up the alarm, banged it on the tabletop so that it rattled, but this time the needles remained in position and the light bulb didn't start to flicker. The edge of Lasse's mouth twitched grotesquely before an almost beatified smile spread across his face.

'It's working, lads,' he said quietly. 'It didn't go off...' A moment later they were all huddled in a cluster around Lasse and the table, like ice hockey players after scoring a goal, and the workshop was filled with a joy and success that tasted like soft, almond chocolate, and although none of them said it aloud, it was on everybody's mind: soon they would be able to say goodbye to Tapanila, its cold water pipes and nosy neighbours, to final demands and bailiffs and the taxman, and for a fleeting moment Tweety saw himself in a small one-bedroom flat: it was in Alppila or Kallio; everything was painted white and it had its own shower and cupboards that didn't smell of mould.

'Fuck me, lads, it works!'

'We've still got to test it though…'

'Of course we've got to test it. We've got to measure it too.'

Everyone was talking at once, their words like glass wheels whirring around the already packed shed. Reino was particularly excited. It seemed as though he too secretly wanted to share the limelight, and he motioned everybody over to the workbench. On top he spread out a plan of the ground floor of the bank. Its proportions weren't exact but it showed all the features that they would need to know. Beside this was a small pile of photographs they had taken on their preliminary visits to the site, and Reino had used a felt-tipped pen to show how he planned to cut into a number of the safes. It only required very small cuts, just as long as they were in the right places, and if anyone knew exactly where to cut, it was Reino. He knew about safes: it wasn't for nothing he'd been on good terms with a bloke called Mäkinen who used to work in a factory that manufactured them.

'There you go, boys,' said Reino, jabbing a stubby finger at the map. 'That's where you can see along the stairwell up to the first floor and the window that looks out on to Museokatu. But I've worked out how we can take care of that. There. See the lower banister? We'll tape a sheet of one-and-a-half by two tarred cardboard up there, so there's no way anyone will see the flame.'

'Bloody hell… but what about the smoke?'

'There are no smoke alarms in there,' said Reino and flicked through the photographs until he found what he was looking for. 'See that switchboard? One of those must be the switch for the central ventilation system. The smoke will rise up to the ceiling and disappear into thin air and no one'll smell a thing…'

They were all filled with a quiet enthusiasm, even Tweety, and it felt comforting to think that the mystery and, at times, desperation surrounding the whole Chancellor job had now come to an end. His brothers radiated that same sense of relief too, and a moment later they were eagerly going through the job phase by phase. They started with how they were going to check the area around the bank before the job and finished with how and where to dispose of the equipment and clothes they had used during the operation itself. It was perfection, like a symphony.

'And lads,' Reino winked, his expression at once cunning and vaguely childish. Then he began whistling and moving clutter lying on the floor in front of the workbench. He cleared a space on the floor and knelt down, scratched at something for a moment then lifted one of the floorboards out of the way. The smell of earth wafted up from beneath the floor. In a hole about twenty centimetres deep lay ten metre-long lengths of copper piping, welded shut at one end and with a tightly fitting brass plug at the other.

Reino had made them. These were his 'treasure chests'. After each job he'd divided the loot into these pipes and buried each one in a different place, leaving only one of them easily accessible at any given time while they lived on its contents. Working like this there was no need to worry that the whole lot would disappear at once, no matter how thoroughly the police searched the premises.

Reino knelt down, groaned, reached his hand far beneath the floorboards and pulled out a copper pipe. It was clearly older than the others; the metal had darkened and it was covered in something that looked like green mould. Reino's firm hands twisted the plug out of the end and moved over to the workbench, placed the pipe on the floor plan and tipped it up. Something yellow started flowing slowly out of the pipe, and only when the light of the single lamp settled on it could they see that it was gold. It seemed as though the flow from the pipe would never end; it was filled with heavy signet rings and intricate brooches, tie clips and necklaces and small, clean-cast ingots, and amongst it all dozens of different coloured stones sparkled, red and white and pure green. There were hundreds of items of jewellery; there must have been several kilos of gold on the floor plan.

They stood in silence. It seemed as though they were all breathing together, slowly and heavily, and perhaps each of them was searching the depths of their minds for a fragment of a book they'd read as children in which the hero manages to prise open the pirates' treasure chest, while deeper down still a strong sense of power stirred within them, the knowledge of something better, of surviving, of winning.

Before them lay their emergency supplies: the jewellery taken from safety deposit boxes on their two most recent jobs. Reino hadn't wanted to sell them, and he'd been right: they had survived until then on cash alone, and they needed so many middlemen to sell off their stuff that the risk of being grassed up was too big.

'Just to remind you what's at stake here, lads,' Reino said eventually, his voice hoarse. 'Soon we'll be shovelling more of this by the sackload. Cash too. People keep loads of money in deposit boxes nowadays. That way the bank could go bust twice over and they'd still get their money back, but if they'd had it in a normal account…' Reino's hands moved stiffly; he was holding a wad of banknotes. He swallowed. Lasse picked up a fistful of jewellery and let it trickle back on to the table, giving off a soft jangle the colour of sunshine as it fell.

There was a knock at the door. They jumped as though they were already in the bank and the police had started flooding into the room; it was as though they had suddenly awoken or something had snapped. Reino grabbed the sack and threw it over the gold and the floor plan; Lasse ripped the alarm from its sockets, slipped it into a plastic bag and stuffed the bag on the floor between two dismantled chainsaws. Tweety didn't move a muscle.

'Tweety? Are you in there?'

'It's Sisko,' said Tweety and realised how stupid it sounded – the others had heard her too – and opened the latch hoping that nobody would notice how much his hands were trembling. Their sister stood in the doorway. Sisko was almost forty, a lonely, strangely introverted woman, maybe even slightly masculine: her hair was short and almost entirely grey, and like an American farmer she only ever wore checked shirts and dungarees, but she was a good person and Tweety wasn't as close to anyone as he was to her.

'Bamse says you've got piles of laundry to be done,' she said, her voice metallic. 'I'm going to put mine in to soak overnight and wash them tomorrow. I could do yours too…' She didn't even try to peer inside, but Reino and Lasse continued talking to one another, pretending to work on an electric mangle missing its lid.

Sisko leaned closer to Tweety and whispered: 'The women will be over in a minute. Ritu and Mum have been whispering about something all night. She's worried sick that our Lasse'll get himself banged up again.' Then she was gone, striding like a shadow towards the trailer where she lived all year round and read – she was always reading – and Tweety realised that she'd come to warn them, and she wouldn't have done so unless she'd known they were up to something.

'Mother Gold is coming,' Tweety hissed and turned around, and he was suddenly overcome with nausea, like the time when Lasse had kicked him in the groin. The others snapped to it: Reino put the floorboard back in place and moved all manner of junk on top of the sack on the workbench, and Lasse dismantled the rest of the alarm in only a few swift movements. Already they could hear voices outside, then the door was flung open and Mother Gold and Ritu were standing there with Bamse, who skulked behind them looking oddly guilty.

'Mother Gold started having one of her turns,' explained Ritu, a pale, humourless woman who always kept a jealous eye on Lasse. 'We thought we'd have a little rest here on the way back.'

'Haven't you got your nitrates?' asked Reino. 'I'll get Asko to fetch them.'

'Oh, it's nothing really.' Mother Gold tried to play it down, but her head hung in sorrowful resignation.

She stepped inside and sat down in Lasse's chair. Tweety slowly backed off. He loved Mother Gold just as everyone loves their mother, perhaps more so, as he was always filled with a childish sense of helpless anxiety whenever something was the matter with her. That's how he felt now, but there was something else, too, and it frightened him, made him feel ashamed and guilty. There was somebody else inside him, somebody whose thoughts were cold and sharp: *Of course she was having a turn because she knows we're up to something. She always has a turn when she feels left out and wants to punish us.*

'No matter,' she sighed. 'I suppose I'd better be off. Don't want to trouble you any more than...'

'Mum,' said Lasse abruptly. 'Don't start that again, eh.'

'It's the truth. I tell you, I've always hoped I'd see the day you lot did something worthwhile with yourselves.' *Now she's starting to scold us, the way she always does. She knows it works, especially with Reino. Maybe she wants him to speak up for himself and, in doing so, accidentally let the cat out of the bag. Soon she'll start on about how good things were when Dad was around – and that'll make Reino even angrier.*

'Oh, come on,' Reino tried to placate her, his voice still harsh. 'We've tried all sorts of things, but with the bank and the taxman on our backs all the time there's nothing we can do... We've got one or two projects on the go. Who knows, we could soon be exporting these machines to Estonia.'

'Oh Reino, Reino,' sighed Mother Gold, and now her voice was full of loving sympathy. 'I know all about your wheeling and dealing. There it is, rusted junk littered all over the place. A thousand things on the go at once and none of them ever come to any good. You can say what you like, but your father was a decent man. We didn't have to eke out a living back then...'

She's so good at that... Her voice is like honey but her words are full of poison.

'Here we go,' Reino growled, his thick neck bright red. He made as if to leave the room but growled again and stayed where he was. Mother Gold had a strange power over them all.

A thin sweat covered Tweety's brow. He wiped it discreetly and hoped that the wicked voice within him would fall silent, and he looked at Mother Gold and tried to see her simply as his mother. She was the same as she'd always been: tall, somewhat dry and arthritic. Her nose was disproportionately large, like a lump of lifeless wax, and her eyes were very dark and didn't really suit her. Rather, they seemed out of character given her chest pains as, ever vigilant, they scanned the room looking for something to latch on to.

Tweety gulped. He knew the thought that had just occurred to him was impossible, but still he expected her to go over to the bench at any moment, wrench the sack away, and once she'd seen everything to calmly take out her mobile phone and remark: 'Now Mum's going to have to call the police.'

'And you can believe it or not,' she began. 'But I've got a strange feeling that something terrible is about to happen. Very soon. Something really terrible. Lasse, you haven't got yourself into any more... difficulties, have you? I had such a terrifying dream. You went to prison for what someone else had done.'

'Not bloody likely,' Lasse muttered and fidgeted awkwardly before looking almost helplessly at Reino. 'It's this August weather that's made you...'

'No. I know it. Just like I knew the time your father went off on that fishing trip. I tried to stop him, you know...'

Tweety held his hand in front of his mouth as though he were about to throw up. He remembered all too well what had happened. The previous week, after fixing the Paavolas' plumbing, their father had been lounging on the sofa drinking lager and Mother Gold had nagged him all day that she wanted some fish, salmon, and that Dad was supposed to go down to the market to get some. Later that afternoon, as if it had been prearranged, Heikki Ahola had turned up, Dad started getting his fishing gear on, then she'd shouted: 'Don't think you're going anywhere tonight.'

'I think I can decide that for myself.'

'But I've said you're not going anywhere.'

'And I've said I am,' he'd replied and left – he'd had no choice, what with Ahola listening to the whole exchange. In Tweety's mind, Mother Gold had in effect killed him that night.

'And what about you, Asko?' she said suddenly and looked at Tweety. 'You haven't got a weak bladder, have you? Always creeping out to the yard at the strangest hours of the night… You'll fall off that ladder one day and spend the rest of your life a cripple.'

'Oh… it's nothing…'

'Come on, Mum,' said Bamse. She'd finally come inside after seeing Reino gesticulating at her frantically in the doorway. 'Let's get back to the cottage and you can take your tablets. Then it's off to bed.'

Mother Gold stood up, looked at them all once again and left. A moment later came the sound of Ritu talking with her about something.

The workshop fell silent. The brothers all tried to avoid looking at one another. It was as though something had been killed. Lasse stirred, took his revolver out from under the table, opened the barrel, then shut it again, opened it, shut it… He sometimes did this for half an hour at a time.

'Stop bloody fidgeting,' Reino eventually snapped. He was full of ill humour and anger and looked at Tweety, his expression taut. 'Where *do* you go at night? We all noticed ages ago how you sneak off all the time. We hear the scooter all right.'

'I don't really… I can't get to sleep up there sometimes, with the heat and that.'

'Just mind you don't do anything that'll land you in the nick. And let me tell you, lads: we might be brothers, but if anyone fucks up the Chancellor, I'll personally beat the living shit out of them.'

Tweety went outside; the wind had brought in clouds and he could no longer see the stars.

He understood all too well that he shouldn't go anywhere that night, but knew nonetheless that he would.

Ogre

The slaughterman had shown Raija twice before but she couldn't for the life of her remember how to do it. Her fingers wouldn't obey her; she couldn't make them into an O shape, and she had to do so in order to tear the ears off the ogres, and she had to tear their ears off to make them relent and retreat back beneath the moss. They enjoyed eating all the soft parts of the body: the breasts, thighs and face. The path suddenly began to subside, even though it had been asphalted, and it was only then that she realised she was naked. She felt even more unsafe and wanted to turn back, but there were far too many crows behind her and all she could do was start running – then something grabbed at her thigh. The hand was hard and knobbly, full of something rough, covered in gnarls or scales that oozed burning glue on to her skin. She quickly made an O shape and bent down. The ogre was a man with blue skin, who resembled a chimpanzee; he was completely bald and she managed to grab hold of his ears. But they weren't normal ears; they were pointed like a pig's and extraordinarily slippery – holding them was like trying to extract a bream caught in a fishing net – but still they cracked easily like crispbread and the hand disappeared from her thigh. A car drove past; its light painted a twisting triangle on the ceiling, and gradually she returned to where she was, on her back on her familiar bed. The alarm clock ticked beside her.

She lay there and stared up at the chandelier. In the dark it looked like an angel, her skirt billowing beneath her. She was afraid her dream would continue if she fell asleep straight away. She knew where ogres came from; she'd found an old book at her grandparents' summer cottage and read it through again. As a child she'd loved this story because it scared her so. Ogres lived beneath the ground. Raija had looked just like the little girl in the story. But even as a girl she'd been annoyed that the girl in the story could be so silly. A scientist had arrived in a time machine, and as a present she had given him a beautiful white flower. The flower had shone with light – there were lots of them growing along the edge of the path – and although she knew it was dangerous to venture into the woods, she wanted one of these flowers as she thought it would protect her. She stepped on to the moss and reached out her hand, but then the birds started squawking once again, she heard the sound of flapping wings, and at that moment the purulent hand of another ogre grabbed her thigh.

Raija started but, comfortingly, the chandelier angel was still where it had been. She lay perfectly still and listened: she sensed that something was not as it ought to be. She felt a sudden chill – maybe it was because of the dream; that's why she'd slept so fitfully – and realised she had kicked the sheet into a crumpled ball at the end of the bed. She sat up just enough to pull it back over herself and glanced at the clock: it was already five past three. It didn't matter, because they both had the next day off and she didn't even feel drunk any more, not that she'd drunk much that evening anyway.

She stared again at the angel and listened to Juha's breathing; she could barely hear it though he was lying right next to her and that fact suddenly made her remember everything else. Their relationship was coming to an end, and the sadness she felt at this thought was like a pool of cloudy water in which she only just managed to stay afloat.

The worst of it was that, once again, she felt that it was somehow all her fault, though she realised that the truth of the matter couldn't be so black-and-white. She rolled on to her side, keeping her back to Juha – at that moment she couldn't bear to look at him – and their home lay around her, full of dark furniture-shadows, and only then did she work out what was bothering her: a faint light was shining in from the hallway. The bathroom door stood ajar. Juha must have got up and left the light on.

She considered whether to get up and switch it off but decided to leave it. Perhaps the ogres were still lurking in the back of her mind, and she was still thinking about Juha. His behaviour had begun to change just as Markku's had before. At first he'd been head-over-heels in love with her. Men seemed to fall in love with her easily; sometimes she felt like

Camille Oaks in *The Wayward Bus*. He hadn't once noted her initial reservation, but after two months of dating he'd all but insisted that she sell her flat and move in with him. And when she'd refused, he'd taken offence.

After that he'd started gradually wearing her down. It was at its most obvious whenever they had sex: all the tenderness had disappeared, all the slow foreplay and gentle build-up – precisely what made her feel alive – until there was nothing but the act which in itself was often so brutal that it made her feel kicked to the ground every time. And naturally it was always her fault that it brought neither of them any satisfaction: she was so frigid that nothing could warm her up.

The bathroom light was still tormenting her. It was like a white pillar amidst the darkness. Still she didn't get up, she couldn't be bothered, and in any case it might just have been one of Juha's mind games: deliberately leaving the light on so that she'd have to get up and switch it off. Other similar things happened all the time: Juha would always leave the morning paper sprawled all over the table and never rinsed his shaving foam down the sink. At the beginning everything had been different; he'd taken care of her, even washed up and made the beds.

That evening something had finally snapped. They'd booked a table at Lehtovaara and had spent the evening talking in mock politeness about the weather. When they got into the lift back home Juha had started groping her and she'd frozen. She'd tried to talk things through with him but he just sulked, drank half a bottle of whisky in the space of an hour before almost passing out, and she couldn't bring herself to throw him out in that state. But in the morning when he woke up, it would be *Adios*! Of that, she was suddenly dead certain.

She gave a sigh, pulled the sheet away, swung her feet on to the floor and walked towards the hallway. She just couldn't leave the light on, it annoyed her so much. Her bare feet pattered on the cork flooring and she thought of what one of her bosses, who had been after her for a long time, had once said: 'The fact of the matter is you're just too stunning. And you're sure of yourself. Men are afraid of you. Deep down they're convinced they don't have a chance of being with you, and when one way or another this is confirmed, the only way to regain their self-esteem is to put you down.'

She switched the light off and turned back. Maybe her boss had been right. It was just so hard to believe, especially as she knew only too well quite how unsure of herself she was, how the most ridiculous things frightened her, dreams and imaginary creatures, ogres. She was afraid of them now too, and made sure not to touch anything so as not to brush against their bald heads. Was she really stunning? She was beautiful, she knew that, but there were obvious wrinkles on her face and her bottom was getting flabbier, and if she forgot to hold her head and neck straight the beginnings of a double chin were there for everyone to see.

Raija lay down on her back. She knew straight away that she wouldn't get to sleep but decided to try all the same. Slow, peaceful breaths; she'd read somewhere that this calms the body as well as the mind. And because she'd been so certain that she wouldn't fall asleep, the lamp angel began to appear hazier, the hem of its skirt shimmered, and a moment later she was queuing in front of the candyfloss stall and a willow warbler chirped... But she didn't get further than this before waking again.

She woke to the feel of Juha's hand on her upper thigh. She lay motionless and tried to continue breathing as though she hadn't noticed a thing. *He's up to his old tricks*, she thought. *If he'd really wanted something he'd have moved up close to her first and started kissing her, but now all he wanted was a fuck.*

She raised her hand purposefully and placed it on the back of Juha's hand; he clearly gave a start but didn't make to pull his paw away, and all of a sudden Raija's thoughts stopped dead. Her entire body stopped. In a surreal way, she felt as though she were a colossal combined eye and ear straining to see and hear. Juha lay breathing on her left, snoring away, but the hand on her bare thigh and which she was now holding wasn't coming from Juha's side of the bed. It came from the right. Where there was nobody. Where there was nothing but darkness.

She gulped quickly, again and again, and tried to convince herself that she was asleep, yet all the while she knew it wasn't true, just as she knew ogres weren't real – and yet at that moment she was holding one by the hand. She yanked her hand away and rolled over, almost on top of Juha, and screamed, and through her screams came the sound of rustling from the floor. It wasn't human, it was so short – it was like an enormous tarantula or a chimpanzee. It even moved like a monkey, hobbling on its hands and feet before disappearing into the hallway.

'What the...?' Juha snapped and pulled back the blankets. He was still fairly drunk and his face gleamed with sweat.

'It went into the hallway! Juha, the hallway!'

'What went into the hallway? And don't steal the...'

'An ogre!'

'What...? What are you on about? Have you been drinking?'

From the hall came the sound of the lock clicking shut and Juha fell silent. A moment later he was filled with energy: he threw off the remaining blankets and staggered naked to the floor, hesitated for a moment then grabbed the bedside lamp and pulled it hard, ripping the cable out of it. A moment later he was running towards the hallway like a black ghost.

'Don't go out there!' shouted Raija. 'It'll kill you! It'll bite!'

She crouched on her knees, her whole body shaking and her lips moving as if in prayer. She heard the door open and Juha angrily hiss something, there came a clatter from the stairwell, then suddenly everything was quiet, and only the door stood ajar.

Raija repeated to herself that she had to get up, get up and see what had happened, switch the lights on at least, and somehow she managed to muster the courage to wrap the sheet around herself and tiptoe over to the switch and turn the lights on.

Just then the outside door rattled again and Raija froze to the spot. She had no way of knowing which one of them was coming in, so for safety's sake she lowered her eyes and stared at the skirting board, but then she heard Juha calling her, and the sense of relief was so powerful that she felt almost faint. Only then did she notice that Juha's voice sounded strange, nothing but a moan.

'Raija...'

She went into the hallway. Juha was leaning against the doorpost. The lamp in his hands was cracked and twisted. He was holding his other hand up to his face. Blood trickled like red porridge between his fingers, and ran in shining snakes down his chest and darker smudges on his arms.

'Oh my God, what happened?' Raija asked, though she already knew the answer: the ogre had bitten him, it had tried to eat him! Then she began repeating to herself, over and over: What's the emergency number? What's the emergency number? I mustn't say anything about the ogres!

'The cable,' Juha stammered. 'I tripped on it... fell down half a flight of stairs on my stomach and slammed my face into the wall. Drunk as well... Help me.'

Brownie

The pile of post came halfway up his shin, tightly packed around the door, and Tweety kicked it frantically to one side. He was still full of the night's events. It had been so close – and something had got into him. He'd stopped on the second-floor landing, turned and held the Flame ready in his hand, and if the man had gone for him he would have got the blade in his stomach right up to the hilt. But judging by the crash he'd stumbled on the floor above, and that misfortune had saved them both.

He managed to move the papers out of the way and close the door. The darkness was stifling; a strange, pungent smell hung in the air, at once acrid and sweet like that given off by gases or cheeses, the kind riddled with mould and swarming with mites that English lords might pick from their silver platters and discuss whether its taste was angularly backward or subtly foreboding.

But Tweety drew his hand up to cover his mouth and nostrils; the smell made him feel ill straight away, it was all around him, thick like the darkness, so thick that he could almost lean into it. All he had to do was overcome his nausea and stay firmly put. After a moment or so he opened his fingers slightly and took a deep breath, for there was something about the smell that fascinated him.

Perhaps it was because it affected him with such force, set his imagination loose, rattled its hatches, driving his ghosts into their corners, and when he allowed this to happen he was filled with an almost unfathomable, dreamlike calm and he felt as though he had conquered something. He wasn't afraid anymore. Nothing frightened him, not even thinking about the Power, and a desire to paint surged within him, his mind filled with visions and images and colours, and even now he was thinking how he might paint his inner calm and the smell of the air. How can you paint a smell?

Excitedly, he pulled out Sparkle Eye, switched it on and walked further inside. Brownie's flat was the only one in which he kept his clothes on and walked upright. He paraded around like a king, his back straight and with firm steps, and the thin strip of light wiped across the floor in front of him; it was an old, dark-oak parquet, hardwood, not just an imitation covered with veneer, and although the rugs were slightly worn they were obviously genuine, the kind that must have cost an arm and a leg. And as he slowly tilted the lamp upwards he could see the countless paintings that covered the walls, and upon looking at them even a layman would feel a quiet sense of amazement and melancholy, a yearning for beauty, and at once he would know that these were the works of true masters.

Tweety walked onwards. Heavy picture frames glinted on the walls and silver on the tables; the layers of darkness were deep and it felt almost as though he weren't in a real flat at all but in Sleeping Beauty's castle while everyone was asleep for a hundred years. He stopped where the parquet creaked and raised the lamp: a great crystal chandelier glittered with blazing sparks, and as he moved Sparkle Eye the sparks shifted and changed colour and glowed like the stones in Reino's treasure chests. Immediately he began to wonder whether he could paint it, and the more he thought about it, the more he knew the answer was yes.

It was a large flat. There were five rooms in all – the floor space must have been almost two hundred square metres – and it was clearly the home of someone old and very wealthy. Tweety had first visited this flat by accident: he'd gone to the wrong floor. One floor below lived a chubby redhead he had meant to visit, but little by little this place had taken on a special significance for him. There was something solemn about it, like being in church, and he came here whenever he needed to calm down, particularly when something had gone wrong.

He paced further into the flat and the smell became stronger, as though there were a hole in the floor and in that hole a spring sending fumes into the air. At last he came to what must have been a great hall, its walls covered with bookcases reaching up to the ceiling, and in amongst the thick leather-bound volumes on the shelves Sparkle Eye's wedge of light fell on sculptures of bronze and marble and crystal vases like huge chunks of ice. In the middle of the room was a long mahogany table, draped with a lace tablecloth, and six high-backed chairs around it. The flowers in the vase had surely once been fresh, but now they were brown, nothing but kindling that rustled and disintegrated when you touched it.

Tweety's calm was mixed with a strange excitement. He walked up to the record player, switched on the bluish current and started playing the record: *Carmina Burana* began quietly, then fully – this was where he'd first heard it – and he walked towards the bay window and the two large, leather-covered chaises longues that stood there. He approached them, turned Sparkle Eye off and made sure not to look at the floor – he didn't want to look down there just yet, he wasn't ready – and sat down in the right-hand chair. It surrounded him like a miniature fortress and he felt safe.

He felt all the more that the curse which had plagued him was finally gone. It always disappeared when he was in Brownie's flat and returned when he left, and he felt a profound sadness that one day he would inevitably lose everything, that someone would eventually notice what had been going on. But now was not that moment. Now was the moment when he sat on his throne, and he was filled with colours and shapes and thoughts of Wheatlocks, and he knew he could paint her just the way she was in the cherry-blossom world, and he thought of her and loved her – he felt he could almost paint love itself.

He moved suddenly, as though he were trying to keep out a sorrowful chord barging its way into his head, but it was no use. He knew that he *couldn't* paint and that he *would* have been able to paint if only his life had been different, if he hadn't been born into the Leinonen family, if he'd got a place at art school, and if… he didn't know what, but that's how he felt. And it was painful because he faintly understood something but didn't quite understand *what* he understood. It was as though he were trying to squeeze through a small hole but didn't quite fit, or as though his soul were covered with an eyelid made of layer after layer of elephant hide, so thick that every time he tried to wrench it open it slammed shut again.

It must have had something to do with the fact that there were two of him: Asko and Tweety. Together they could have been… something greater. And now when he thought of it, he brought his hands up to his eyes and wept, rough and tearless, grieving for something so much while all the time hoping. He hoped with all his heart that the Chancellor would be a success and that he'd finally have some kind of chance, and he knew that if he were given that chance he would change and finish with everything, even the night-time visits.

Some ten minutes later Tweety came to. He felt as though he were filled with heavy metal plates frozen into the earth, and with this came the knowledge that he hadn't been born like this. Something had made him like this, and it was a crime for which he had the right to seek revenge. He just didn't know whom to punish. He would have dearly loved to know. He thought and sighed, then quickly flicked Sparkle Eye's switch and without a moment's hesitation aimed its beam of light at the floor in front of him.

The source of the smell lay there. Suddenly it looked like nothing but a dark heap on the floor, a rolled-up bearskin.

But it was a human body nonetheless.

She was lying on her front. Her legs were straight and pointed towards the other chair as though she had just stood up when death finally arrived. Her left hand was twisted in front of her face as though her last act on earth was to blow her nose.

She had grey, permed hair. And her face was completely black. A black skull-face: the flesh had slid away and the skin had dried to the bone, though you could still make out the wrinkles on her brow, the contours of the cheeks and even the sparse silvery hairs on her upper lip. Her teeth showed, her lips tight as though she were grimacing with horror at what she had become, and where her eyes had once been there were only two holes lined with mould and filled with darkness.

It was the body of an old woman – a granny, a crone, a biddy, a hag.

The strip of light began moving shakily across the body's face and Tweety held his breath. His terror was about to awaken; it was like an avalanche deciding whether or not to unleash its powers. He gripped the arm of the chair more tightly and hesitantly wet his lips, and his fear retreated and froze into a lifeless mass.

He moved the light. The body's skin was a brown-black colour, like cardboard and just as hard – he'd tried tapping it with a spoon – and its fingers and toes had shrivelled oddly; they were like brown bottle-glass, and through the glass something lighter could just be made out, presumably joints and bones.

Beneath the body a puddle had formed on the floor, though that too had dried a long time ago. Still, it was best to avoid stepping in it as his shoes would stick to everything and crackle wickedly with every step.

Tweety looked at Brownie with his head tilted to one side – he had christened her Brownie – and he could still bear the sight of her fairly well. The first time he'd seen her he'd run headlong out of the flat and vomited on the street, but a few days later he'd felt compelled to go back. After that he'd returned again and again, each time daring to come closer to her, gradually overcoming his initial horror. It was as though he was compelled by a profound need deep inside him, one far more powerful than his own will. And when he looked at her now a strange sense of satisfaction glowed within him, a mysterious feeling of fulfilment and victory. Never before had he experienced anything like it.

He moved Sparkle Eye back to Brownie's face. It looked just as horrific every time. When he moved his hand the lights and shadows moved too, as if her expression were constantly changing, and all of a sudden Tweety knelt down closer: was her grimace somehow different? Was there mockery in it? Something knowing?

Tweety's mind seemed to shimmer. He suddenly found himself thinking of precisely what under normal circumstances he consciously tried to avoid ever thinking of: he had never slept with a woman, properly, had actual intercourse. He hadn't even done it with Soot Rose. He'd tried it with her many times, but every time the same thing happened: at the critical moment he was always flaccid, and Brownie grinned there on the floor as though she knew. Tweety jumped edgily to his feet, panting, his hands clenched into jagged fists.

Finally he spat on Brownie's back. The spittle shone like a white blotch and she couldn't do anything about it; she just lay there with no eyes, her guts and heart rotting away, dried to a crisp, and she would never get up from there again and would never tell anyone what she knew or what he had done to her.

Tweety turned around, switched off the record player and left the room and its stench; the narrow strip of light flashed in front of him, the silverware glinted, the floorboards creaked. In the living room he stopped still and raised the lamp. He aimed the light at the gable wall, and lit from such a distance they stood out well: dozens of different weapons. The wall was covered with them. Most of them were old revolvers but among them there were a few pistols, an old Mauser M1916 and about ten bayonets and three swords. He knew that there were cartridges for two of the pistols; he'd found them in the lower drawer of the glass cabinet. He'd loaded the guns once, but now he let them be. Somehow he was too agitated.

He continued towards the bedroom and thought of Brownie's real name: Helga Anna-Liisa Kivimäki. She'd died in March; the oldest newspaper in the pile of post was dated 2 March, and nobody had missed her. Nobody had loved her enough to actually miss her, and perhaps now Brownie wished that her heirs might love her money enough that they'd finally come and lay her to rest. She'd spent long stretches of time abroad – he'd examined the entire flat and knew almost everything about her life – and perhaps people who knew her thought she was just sunning herself somewhere. But they were wrong. Though she was certainly brown enough.

Tweety paused by the dressing table, let the light slide across the porcelain pots and the comb with the silver handle, and stopped when he reached a small photograph. In the picture was a woman of about thirty; Tweety guessed it was Helga Anna-Liisa, her clothes and the style of the photograph were so dated, like something hundreds of years old. The woman was beautiful. Her neck was long and magnificent, her cheeks full and rosy; she had a pretty, pursed mouth and, judging by the picture, large and very dark eyes. Their expression was gentle, accepting. It made you want to answer her – and Tweety was suddenly struck by how much he missed Toby and wished he could have held him and stroked him.

He held the photograph closer to his face. Helga Anna-Liisa had little dimples, too, and wild curls of hair behind her ears. He began to sense that she was a good person after all, or that she once had been, and if she had been there in the room, either how she was in the picture or how she had been just before her death, she would surely have clasped him in her arms and stroked his neck and his hair, caressed his ears and his mouth. She would have lulled him like a child without demanding anything from him. She would have loved him.

Pet Shop

Harjunpää sat on the steps at the back of the house with the night around him and the rabbit in his arms. He gently scratched Viljami's neck. The rabbit's jaws munched, stopped every now and then, then started munching again, and each time the rabbit finished eating its dandelion leaf Harjunpää quietly apologised and fetched him a fresh one growing by the wall.

On the horizon he could see that morning was almost upon them; the darkness was fractionally bluer. It was almost four o'clock. He'd woken up around three and hadn't been able to get back to sleep. Instead he sat there breathing in the fragrant night; he would have liked to think about the pet shop, but this time he found he couldn't.

It was just a thought he'd had, a daydream that would have involved buying a slightly older house somewhere further away. There was a suitable house for sale in Veklahti and it even had a garage big enough; he'd already been to look at it. Then the whole family could start raising rabbits and guinea pigs and mice and everything in between, they could grow their own hay too, then they'd rent a little place in the centre of Kirkkonummi and open a shop that Elisa could run. There wasn't a single pet shop in Kirkkonummi, but there were plenty of children and teenagers.

And somewhere deeper down another thought began to crystallise: if the business were successful he could do the same as Onerva. But he couldn't mention it out loud; he knew all about unemployment, bankruptcy and the recession, and those who didn't understand that all this was just a game knew to their cost far more than he did. It was as though the recession had claimed people's very idea of happiness, too.

111

He was so overwhelmingly tired of death. He was overwhelmingly tired of bodies, but new ones were always waiting for him somewhere, still warm, almost human, or changed somehow, black monsters, rotten and stuck on the floor. He was tired of murderers and arsonists and rapists, tired of the fact that behind even the most horrific acts there was always someone crippled, someone crushed by human stupidity or the sheer lack of love. Therapy was of no use to these battered souls, far less being crushed with the full force of the law.

He was tired of serving as a sticking plaster; he was tired of trying to solve a problem to which there was no solution.

And he was tired of the police force and its personnel policy, which wasn't a policy at all but a means of demeaning and breaking people. The latest officer to be broken for good was Osmo Salonen.

Osmo's name had appeared on an advance list of those to be transferred to the Public Order Police. The list consisted primarily of officers who'd had problems in the past or who didn't know how to keep their mouths shut or bow down low enough to the powers that be. The Public Order Division then quickly produced another list of officers they weren't prepared to take under any circumstances, and Osmo's name had been first on the list. Two weeks later he was pulled over for drink-driving and booted out of the force, but his gun was finally taken away one bullet too late.

Harjunpää started wondering when his own name would appear on a list – nowadays it was on everyone's mind – though, on the other hand, wouldn't it ultimately be something of a relief?

Grandpa had been sitting in the woods at the foot of a great spruce tree and there had been nothing wrong with him. In fact, he'd been exceptionally lucid. He'd looked Harjunpää in the eyes and said, almost apologetically: 'I just had such a strong feeling that… it was time. And I figured, better out here than in front of the children… I've always loved the woods. And when I was younger and pressed my hand into the side of a tree, I could feel it breathing, it was alive…'

Harjunpää propped his elbow on his knee and pinched his fingers tightly along the side of his nose.

Out in the woods a strange bird chirped.

Viljami started whimpering as he finished his dandelion leaf.

Tuesday Morning

It was often like this: at first everything was like a vague, opaque mush that nobody wanted to touch, and when they did every thread seemed to lead to a dead end, then amidst it all the telephone would ring or someone would walk in and from that moment on the case seemed electric, so many sensible tasks to take care of that you didn't know where to start, and each check, in one way or another, led you another step forwards, and more importantly the mood changed, the spirit, and it was suddenly clear that the case was about to wind itself up, that the perpetrator would be caught in a matter of days if not hours.

Harjunpää felt just like this; he sat in his chair impatiently, doodling small birds on the cover of the telephone directory – they oddly resembled chaffinches – but officially he was waiting for the man sitting opposite him to read through his interview statement. The man was being agonisingly thorough, occasionally flicking back to the previous page and thinking about something, his head tilted to one side, then he would scroll down the page with his finger until he found the relevant place and continue reading. He might have been feeling unwell and his bandage may have hampered his reading: one side of his face was swollen and partially covered in plasters, and around his forehead was a bandage that covered one of his eyes almost entirely.

The man was one Juha Backman. In her own office, Onerva was interviewing a Raija Somebody-or-Other; Harjunpää couldn't remember her surname. Backman had dashed into the stairwell after an intruder, switched on the lights and was close enough to get a relatively good look at the man for about ten seconds. The description was included in his statement, and Harjunpää had realised while he was writing it down that it wouldn't be too difficult to find potential suspects that fitted the description from their online photofit database.

'That sounds fine. Of course, the height's only approximate – I was looking at him from above and he was all hunched up.'

'It's close enough for me. These descriptions are always approximate. I'd just like to double-check what you said about his feet…'

'He was barefoot, I'm absolutely certain. He was carrying all his clothes crumpled up in a ball with his shoes dangling at the front, a pair of light brown trainers.'

'And he wasn't wearing any socks?'

'I think I would have noticed, especially as he was completely naked. What does it matter? I'm sure he's wearing some now.'

'The soles of your feet have the same kind of friction ridges as your fingers… If you'd like to wait outside for a moment, I'll fetch a witness, we can sign your statement and go to the flat together.'

Harjunpää glanced into the corridor but Onerva's door was still shut. There wasn't the faintest sign of Lampinen or Juslin, and with a sense of relief he returned to his desk and dialled the Forensics office.

'Thurman.'

'Harjunpää here. I need someone to come with me to a scene in about twenty minutes. Dagmarinkatu 10.'

'A body?'

'No. An apartment fresh from our mystery intruder.'

'And?'

'We'll bring the lock back here, take it apart and photograph it, so bring a spare latch with you. Most importantly we're looking for prints. Fingerprints. Primarily from the door but also from all around the flat below waist level: he moves around on his haunches and might have steadied himself against something. And the bed apparently has wide, painted boarding around the edges, so they might give us something.'

'OK. But you know it'll take longer than a quarter of an hour.'

'I know. And we have to start off by looking for footprints. Our man was barefoot and the place is covered in smooth vinyl flooring. Then we'll look for any fibres, at least in the hallway – it would be logical for him to leave his gear there.'

'Not a problem. We'll take care of it.'

'Thanks. I'll ring when we're ready to go.'

From the corridor came the joyful clip-clop of high heels, and without even looking up Harjunpää could see how Onerva's skirt fluttered around her legs and clung to her thighs... A moment later she was at his door. She was smiling about something. They had conducted the initial interviews together and both knew the particulars of the case, and now there was a glimmer of happiness in her eyes once again, the same happiness that shone out of her knitting, and even now her hands moved nimbly as though she were holding her knitting needles, tying the whole case together just as she did everything else. And again Harjunpää wanted to touch her.

'Timo, I think only one of us should go to the Dagmarinkatu flat. The other should stay here and call through the list of other plaintiffs.'

'Maybe it would be best just to have a quick look around then leave Thurman to get on with it. I'm itching to see what the photofit database will come up with.'

'Excuse me...'

Kauranen had appeared at the door. He'd been on night shift and you could tell. His face was a pallid grey and his eyes seemed distracted, as though they were caught up in the past, and everybody knew with what: blood and guts, tears and sorrow. In his hand he had a printout and a plastic bag containing a number of bottles of pills.

'I think you can wind up one of your cases,' he yawned. Harjunpää and Onerva were silent. 'I've just got back from the scene. At first I thought it was suicide, pills and alcohol, but there was nothing to back it up, no note, nothing organised. These don't look out of the ordinary and there were even some pills left. Judging by the number of bottles, I'd say the victim was only a moderate drinker. But both of them together... Vomited in her sleep then choked to death. It'll probably be recorded as accidental death. It's just that I found your card at the scene and there was a note in the case folder.'

'Who is it?'

'It's... hang on a minute.' Kauranen fumbled around. There were so many things running through his head after his shift that he had to consult his papers. 'Pirjo. Pirjo Marjaana Lehmusto. Worked in telesales.'

Onerva turned her back to the others; it looked as though she brought her hands up to her face.

Harjunpää made to stand up and groped at the air for a moment, as though reaching for a handbrake that didn't exist. Was it only yesterday morning she'd been here?

Pirjo had been sitting in the foyer like a startled butterfly; her hair was very short, the shape of her head was beautiful, her neck slender with an endearing furrow running down the middle. He'd wanted to protect her, help her — she was so frightened — and her whole body had seemed to ask forgiveness simply for existing.

Watchman Elf

Tweety needed surprisingly little sleep. It puzzled him; it must have been because he could escape every now and then, doze off for thirty seconds at a time throughout the day, though nobody ever noticed.

Just as he did now: he was sitting on his stool behind the counter waiting for customers, looking at the people moving in a mass of clothed flesh on the other side of the window, listening to the wail of the vacuum as Weckman got rid of the dust beneath his goggles. And all the while... In front of him was a chair made of glass, every bit of it, right down to the seat and the delicate ribs of its back, and if there were any screws, they too were made of glass – that's why he couldn't see them – and behind the chair was a dark-red velvet curtain, and from the folds of the curtain there suddenly appeared a naked woman, the spitting image of Annie Lennox. She sat down on the chair, winked at him and smiled seductively, urging him to get down on all fours and crawl under the chair to marvel at the splendour of her pussy. He dearly wanted to comply, but he was terrified – what if it was a trap? What if the chair suddenly shattered and the shards rained down on him tearing open his veins?

'Have you finished those Eccos yet?'

'Yes... But you need to tell her not to leave them to dry in warm places. She's got them wet somewhere.'

'They'll never learn,' Weckman muttered. The vacuum wailed again and Tweety jumped: stepping out of the curtain was Reino. He was fully clothed, at least, and had Lasse with him. Tweety rubbed his eyes and brow. Reino and Lasse were standing outside the shop window. They were

117

trying to look in without Weckman noticing and Reino was gesticulating as if to say he was coming into the shop and that he had something important to say. Tweety sat there motionless. They'd never come to his workplace before and they were both clearly worked up. Reino was moving his hands anxiously and Lasse kept looking behind them. Lasse's jumper bulged beneath the left arm: he was carrying his Smith & Wesson.

'Hey, Weckman,' said Tweety, his mouth dry, and didn't quite know how to continue. But Reino had more power over him than Weckman. Their father had been able to get him to do anything just by looking at him. 'Is it all right if I take last week's overtime now?'

'What, all of it? Don't be daft.'

'Well, an hour then… It's a bit of an emergency. My mum is… I mean, I've got to run a few errands for her.'

'Running errands for your mum,' said Weckman and stared at him weighing up the situation and prolonging the silence. Tweety tried to think why Reino and Lasse had suddenly turned up at the shop and he had a nagging suspicion that they'd come to warn him of something. Maybe the police were on to him after what had happened that night and come round the house asking for him, causing Mother Gold to have a heart attack – she'd said that something terrible was about to happen. Maybe Reino wanted to hide him – or kill him; he'd said as much. Tweety could feel the edge of his mouth twitching. Lasse had even brought his gun.

'On you go.'

'Thanks…'

Tweety walked around the counter; Reino and Lasse noticed and started sauntering towards the post office. Common sense told Tweety they hadn't come to bump him off – without him they wouldn't be able to see the Chancellor through. He snuck out into the street but didn't feel any sense of relief. The air was tinged with blue, foreboding and poisonous; even the sound of the traffic seemed abnormally piercing, as though that very afternoon a horrific accident might occur.

They were waiting for him at the corner. He hadn't been mistaken, Lasse was more agitated than usual, constantly peering around and checking beneath his arm, and there was something twitching at the edge of his eye, like a little mouse wagging its tail.

'Let's walk that way like we're minding our own business,' said Reino and nodded somewhere in front of them, then whispered to Tweety so that Lasse couldn't hear. 'He thought he saw Lampinen again this morning, at the shopping centre in Malmi. I didn't notice anything. I think he's losing it.'

'But what if they're on to something?'

'They're not... don't you start,' Reino snapped, and the fact that he snapped meant that he could have been thinking anything. 'The point is we've got to switch the alarms tonight.'

'We've just been there,' Lasse butted in, the way people do when all they have is bad news. 'Pretended we were customers. There was a van from a security firm parked outside and one of their guys in the building, walking around talking to some manager bloke. They were talking about updating the security system...'

'They were probably talking about the cameras,' said Reino trying to sound certain. 'But it made me think they might decide to change the alarms too, they're that old. But we're not waiting for that to happen. We're going to get the Chancellor on the road and we can start by switching the alarms tonight. So don't go sneaking off anywhere this evening.'

Tweety didn't dare look at Reino. His voice was so firm and every bit as domineering as their father's. He didn't want them to go that evening; the air was such a strange colour and he'd been plagued with bad luck many times in a row.

'I won't... though we agreed we'd do it at the weekend.'

'And now we're agreeing to do it tonight. A week night might be better, there won't be as many police cars on patrol.'

They crossed the street and passed Poste Restante. Reino's car was parked behind the railway station and they walked towards it, each of them lost in thought. Switching the alarms was probably the most uncertain and most dangerous phase of the whole operation because they had to deliberately set off the alarm and they would have no way of knowing how close a police car might be at the moment the alarm was registered. It was annoying not being able to listen in to the police radio any longer; you needed a computer nowadays and Lasse's attempts at building one had been hopeless.

'We could try and put them off the scent,' Lasse suggested, his voice dry as sandpaper; he too was scared to death.

'How?'

'By making a few phone calls… We could say there's a man running about with a rifle shooting people, or a bomb's going to go off somewhere. Then they'll send all their cars elsewhere.'

'Like hell they will. They'll soon see there's no man with a rifle, then they'll be even more on the lookout. There's nothing else for it, at the end of the day it's all down to luck. With bad luck there'll be a squad car just round the corner taking a couple of drunks down to the nick, and you can be sure the drunks will have to wait nicely in the car if the bank's security alarm goes off.'

'What if we put someone on watch outside?' Lasse persisted – perhaps Ritu had put the wind up him. 'We could borrow those mobiles from Nordberg.'

'Look, for fuck's sake… It's no use putting anyone on watch or working out intricate warning systems. It all comes down to speed.'

Reino stopped and looked around to make sure nobody was listening, and struggled to sound cheerful and convincing.

'Think about it. The police get a call about an alarm going off. A light flashes and a buzzer starts beeping somewhere, but they haven't got a location on it yet. The bloke sitting at the call desk pulls out his reference book and starts looking for the address. You can bet that'll take at least thirty seconds, and if he's in the middle of something else it could be two minutes. Then he feeds the information into his computer or wherever it is he has to log it in and starts asking around for a free squad car. That's four minutes already. How long did it take when we practised?'

'Two minutes to do the switch, then another minute when we imagined getting out of the building.'

'There, you see? And remember, when the police car accepts the job, one of them might be queuing for a hotdog. He's been standing there for a while and he's just about to be served. They won't get going right away, and when they do they'll go to the street address first. And what'll they do when they get there? They'll look through the window into an empty bank and wait for a member of staff to come and unlock the door. And all that time we've been one floor further down and we leave through the back. We'll be home before they even get inside. They won't find anything and they'll think it was just a false alarm…'

Reino managed a laugh – maybe it was a genuine laugh, maybe he was so relieved at finally starting to believe in the whole thing – and it had the desired effect: Lasse's face relaxed and he gave a small chuckle.

They stood there looking at one another. The matter was settled and there was no need for them to get into Reino's car. Even in the car Lasse was afraid to talk as he thought Lampinen might have planted a microphone somewhere; maybe he'd been reading up on his electronics a bit too much.

'And remember, Asko,' said Reino abruptly and poked him in the chest. 'Tonight's the night.'

'I won't forget,' said Tweety – there was nothing else he could say. He could never say no to Reino, just like he'd never been able to say no to his father, and yet now he felt all the more strongly that this was the wrong day. He could have explained why, too, but Reino wouldn't have believed him. In fact, he would have believed him even less; he was born that way, he just didn't understand. He couldn't possibly understand what it meant when, his knuckles white with exertion, the watchman elf on the upper deck of Tweety's mind started banging his warning drum.

Bangers and Mash

After the initial formalities the conversation had dried up and the men ate in silence. Järvi greedily shovelled watery mashed potatoes into his mouth. Kontio occasionally watched him out of the corner of his eye and felt very pleased with himself, pleased that he'd finally taken the bull by the horns. It had required a fair amount of effort on his part, but now he didn't regret it in the least. He was pleased too that he'd chosen the perfect venue almost intuitively.

They were in a run-of-the-mill lunch spot on Mäkelänkatu, the kind of place that smells of stale lager and cold cigarette ash. The place brought back fond memories for Kontio. It reminded him of the time when he still had the strength to fight his way up tooth and nail, relentlessly, and he'd been right: Järvi had clearly felt the same, he'd ordered bangers and mash without a moment's hesitation – perhaps it had been a relief not to have to sit at the table wondering what words like Chateaubriand actually meant – and now he was eating contentedly, probably reminiscing about the time when they were true partners.

Kontio knew perfectly well why Järvi had accepted his invitation: he had heard from a source very high up that Special Branch was also on the Criminal Police's list of units to be discontinued. It was understandable: Special Branch had originally been tailor-made for Järvi by separating various specialised groups from their own departments to create an office that needed a DCI to run it. Järvi had kept personal tabs on all the vacancies under his authority; he if anyone knew how to pull the right strings.

But now it was of no help to him. The need for results had bulldoz-ered its way over any string-pulling, and Järvi had heard the rumours that were going around – one of Kontio's 'eyes-and-ears' had confirmed it to him that morning – though understandably he was careful not to let anything slip, because nothing had yet been made official. But something was gnawing away at him, Kontio could see it clearly, he knew the symptoms all too well from his own recent experiences: Järvi had come to the chilling realisation that he was nothing, that for all his stripes and medals and chairmanships he was such a mediocre man that he wasn't even going to be replaced when he retired and that his office was no longer needed.

Kontio knew what it felt like and he knew the kind of loneliness that crept into a man's mind, the desperation, the distrust of everyone else, then there was the need to find an ally, someone who understood – and who better to fill that position than someone who had been through it all before?

· But Kontio wasn't feeding Järvi with sympathy. He knew from bitter experience that things he had once taken for granted could be lost in a heartbeat, and he didn't want to lose Vaarala's friendship at any cost; he didn't want to lose his position as a security consultant; he didn't want to lose the thought that, even once he retired, he would still be *somebody*.

He'd spent a sleepless night because of this. He felt he couldn't trust Harjunpää alone in the matter, and that had awoken a feeling of annoyance, a mixture of disappointment and fear that, for all his insignificance, Harjunpää might pose him a significant threat. On top of that, his annoy-ance had grown once he'd realised that, ultimately, all he wanted to do was break somebody because he himself had been broken. But by morning he'd had confirmation of quite how dire a state Järvi's affairs were in, and this had calmed him down. A back-up plan had begun forming in his mind.

'I don't know,' Kontio sighed, pushed his plate to one side and drained his glass of soured milk. 'I'll tell you, the decision to close down the department fair took away my fighting spirit. It makes you think, is this the way they repay you for years of slogging away? But now that I've got over it… you realise it's just other people's greed, their thirst for power.'

Järvi gave him a quick look; apparently, for the first time, he'd thought the very same thing.

'And to be perfectly honest, I feel as though I want to show them what's what just one more time.'

'I reckon the Criminal Police have seen all they want to see,' Järvi replied and forgot that he wasn't yet supposed to sound so bitter.

'Tanttu is a waste of space... He's given in to all the chief commander's demands without saying a word. And these demands haven't even come directly from the chief; it's Hongisto that's behind it, he's the one really running things. Talk about a bloody Napoleon complex.'

'When our units are shut down and officers are being reassigned to the Public Order Police, they end up working under Hongisto. His power increases with every move. I've heard rumours that he's asked for even more units to be closed...'

'And what do you want out of all this?'

They looked at each other silently. Each of them knew that this was a game and that they both had their reasons for playing it. Kontio hauled his chair closer to the table, glanced around and almost leaned over Järvi's plate.

'To be honest, I'd really like to teach Hongisto a little lesson.'

'He's set himself up for a fall pretty nicely.'

'You hear a thing or two down at the ministry...'

'Such as?'

'But I can't do this by myself. I haven't got enough men.'

'A full-blown operation, then?'

'They've been planning it out at the ministry and the regional council, and Hongisto is supposed to spearhead the whole thing. The mayor apparently said that medals will be awarded on Independence Day...'

Kontio had guessed this would work; Järvi was now looking at him far more intently. Järvi was filled with a burning desire to be recognised, to be in the public eye. These two desires often coexisted in awkward conflict in the line of duty. Particularly when it came to security arrangements, he was over the moon at being able to run things from the background, but couldn't resist the temptation to rush in front of the cameras so that the whole world could see him babbling into his walkie-talkie: 'Seagull One to Eagle Two. Do you copy?'

'So what's this project then?'

'It sounds like small fry, but it isn't. It's to do with graffiti.'

'What?'

'You know, daubs on walls and that sort of thing.'

'Right?'

'There's been a thorough, region-wide investigation into these daubs, concentrating primarily on the Helsinki area. Get this, in the city alone getting rid of graffiti costs the council over five million marks a year...'

'Hell of a sum...'

'And apparently that's not even near the correct figure. What's more, most of the spray paints are stolen, so retailers are making a loss too.'

'OK.'

'At the end of the day it's a fairly small group of people behind this. Catching them will raise the profile of the city council – and of the police force in the eyes of the general public. Of course, with Hongisto's resources there'll be nothing to it...'

Järvi picked up a toothpick, carefully unwrapped it and starting sucking it thoughtfully; a fly appeared and started feeding at the sauce left on Järvi's plate.

'My field officers could take care of it no problem,' he said finally as though he could have come up with the idea himself. 'They could keep an eye on the shops and see who's taking the stuff. And if I could temporarily have the use of a couple of dozen extra officers, all it'll take is a few nights' concentrated effort.'

'Precisely. And you'd be able to demonstrate that Special Branch will always be Special Branch and Hongisto won't get yet another feather in his cap,' Kontio began enthusing, but then his face turned serious and he rested his hands limply on the table. 'But I don't know if it'll work. Your men are tied up with God knows how many other cases. I heard someone in the canteen saying they've got some DS from Violent Crimes ordering them about.'

'You mean Harjunpää? Lampinen and Juslin are helping him out. It's the same case we talked about in the board meeting recently.'

'The one Kuusimäki contacted me about? Well, if Harjunpää cracks that one he'll be getting accolades from much higher up.'

'I'm the one that got things moving with that case. Without me it would be buried in a file somewhere.'

'That's how it goes – other people swipe the medals from under your nose.'

'And skim the cream from the cake,' said Järvi as though he knew what thread the other was tugging and wanted to tug it back. 'They say Onerva Nykänen's fair rolling in money. She knits sweaters while she's on

duty and makes tens of thousands of marks every month selling them...
Anyway, thanks, I'd better be off again.'

The men stood up and more flies appeared. They were in for a
banquet with the treats to be found on Kontio's plate too.

'We could call it Operation Spray,' said Järvi once they were outside.
'It's businesslike, gives you a clue as to what it's all about but doesn't give
anything away.'

'True. If you bring it up in a board meeting I'll second it. We can argue
it's to do with shoplifting. But we need to be quick about it so Hongisto
hasn't got a chance to present the motion somewhere higher up... So
Onerva Nykänen's made a mint, has she?'

'So they say. Well, she says it's not as if she's bringing money in by the
wheelbarrow... Some shops downtown sell her jumpers. Apparently a
trial batch sold out in a couple of weeks in Stockholm.'

'And I'll bet she hasn't got a secondary occupation licence for it.'

'Apparently not. Bangers and mash, eh? You can't beat plain nosh.'

'Nope, especially with lots of ketchup.'

Broken Cog

'But you're not even sure about it. You can't just keep an eye on other people. And what's this Reino Leinonen got to do with the case anyway?'

'Bloody hell, nothing. I never said he was involved. In any case we're not officially tailing him. That bloke's got at least four deposit-box jobs to his name, but he's only done time for one of them. Straight up, I go round there every so often just to remind him what mortality really is. God it feels good thinking about him fretting afterwards, but more importantly he won't have the guts to get up to his old tricks for a while. It's called preventive action. Look it up in the dictionary.'

'So what about Nikander?'

'Did you get any prints from the Dagmarinkatu flat?'

'No, not complete ones, only a couple of smudged partials. Thurman said he thinks our man's work must involve something that causes a mechanical strain on his fingers; it's as though his fingers are coated in some kind of gunk that's blocking up the ridges.'

'Right, now there's another thing that brings us back to Nikander. You take a look at his prints in the database. They're so faint we had trouble classifying them. It wouldn't be the first time someone had tried it, but Nikander's the only one who almost succeeded. Nobody knows how he does it. I've heard people say he either sands them down or rubs his hands with something that removes any grease and stops him sweating.'

'What else fits the description?'

'Everything, for crying out loud. Compare that sketch to his mugshot.'

Lampinen took a photograph from his jacket pocket and placed it on the table in front of Harjunpää. There was already quite a collection of photographs on the table, each showing a gaunt or otherwise bird-like man from numerous different angles. Next to them was the facial composite drawn up by Forensics on the basis of Juha Backman's description. Harjunpää squinted at them and compared them. Lampinen was partly right: there was something about Nikander's chin and nose that matched the composite.

'What can I say... But the witness didn't pick out Nikander from any of the photographs. What's more, Nikander is chubby, and everybody who's seen this guy – including Juha Backman – has described him as thin. On top of that they've said his hair was thick and messy, but Nikander's bald.'

'Right, but bear in mind what kind of state the witnesses were in when they saw him. You remember the Moisio case? Every description said he was stout and podgy but that's because he was always wearing that damn bomber jacket and all the time he was skinny as a rake.'

'This bloke's been seen naked.'

'Nikander boasts that he can do as he pleases with women,' Juslin joined in. 'That he can have as many as he wants.'

'Well, that could mean anything.'

'He treats Hotel Inter as his headquarters,' said Lampinen. 'And you said yourself that over half of these women had been there on the night in question.'

'Nikander's got a soft spot for blondes, and of all these women we've only got five dark-haired ones and one redhead.'

'And nobody picks a lock better than him. In ten minutes he can open a lock that it would take our boys half an hour to crack. And that's exactly the area he hangs around.'

'And he's a total pervert, believe you me,' Juslin sneered and agitatedly rested his leg on his knee. 'Last year we were searching his house and we found at least a billion porn mags and a rubber twat. Fucking sick... hair and everything... And when we switched it on, it vibrated so much I almost dropped the thing. Yours isn't like that, is it, Onerva?'

Onerva looked out of the window. Harjunpää leaned back in his chair and crossed his hands behind his neck. He didn't like the situation or the tone of the conversation, but he had a strange feeling that he, too, was spoiling for a fight. Perhaps it was because Lampinen and Juslin had abruptly dismissed the plan they'd devised for that evening.

'It seems to me as though you don't want this guy caught,' said Lampinen. 'Too much of a dent to your pride if *we* solve this case?'

'Now listen... your pride... I do this because I've got five mouths to feed. Six.'

'Or does it bug you that this came through Järvi? That this is an important case for him?'

'And just why *is* this so important to him?' asked Onerva. Harjunpää recognised her tone of voice and prayed that someone would change the subject soon.

'Well...'

'Because DCI Järvi's had a little phone call from the Right Honourable Kuusimäki, that's why,' Onerva answered for herself. 'And he wants to be able to call him back, stand to attention and say "Minister, after much hard work, the officers in my team have succeeded in blah blah blah..." It makes me sick. Is he so desperate to have a Member of Parliament come to his retirement do? Don't you get it? One of this intruder's victims has died. And the one we had in here this morning was on the verge of a breakdown. Yes, I want him caught. I want him caught for all those women – but not for Järvi. And I want to catch the real intruder, not Klaus Nikander just because you've got a grudge against him.'

'For Christ's sake, Nykänen... What grudge? And that attitude of yours... You feminists ought to learn that no amount of burning your bras has ever solved these cases in the past and it won't solve this one...'

Onerva threw her head backwards in an exaggerated laugh then walked right up to Lampinen.

'Do you know? A funny thing happened to me this morning. No, I bet you don't... Tanttu asked me to report to him this morning and he told me I needed to apply for a secondary occupation licence to sell my jumpers. Oh, and he said I probably wouldn't be granted one, because I couldn't possibly be considered impartial enough to investigate potential cases involving the retailers in question or the people who purchase my stuff. Funny, eh? We only talked about it yesterday.'

'Oh piss off, Nykänen! There's no point blaming me, you're the one that's screwed up... Come on, Juslin. And stay away from Hotel Inter, got it?'

The two men stood up, their chairs rattling, but Harjunpää raised his hand.

'Lampinen. We are going to Inter.'

'No, you're not! You'll ruin everything. Tell them, Juslin.'

'We're going to set him up. Heiskanen's got a flat on Humalistonkatu and that's our base. Forensics is rigging the place up with infrared cameras as we speak. Susanna from Fraud is going to be our bait. She's got long blonde hair. She's going to stumble back from Inter pretending to be drunk and making sure Nikander sees her. And guess what'll happen later on when he starts groping her? Guess who's going to jump out of the wardrobe and catch him red-handed?'

'Why the hell didn't you tell us?'

'We agreed to maintain two parallel lines of approach. If you go down there asking around with your photographs and composites he'll smell you a mile away.'

'OK,' said Harjunpää slowly, rather hurt. He felt as though he'd been tricked, and on top of that the whole set-up was perverse: they'd never have ended up in this kind of stalemate with other officers from Violent Crimes.

'Let's maintain two lines, but we're going to maintain ours too. We'll leave Inter for tonight and concentrate on Lehtovaara. And if you don't get him tonight, then we'll go to Inter tomorrow night.'

'No, you won't. We're going to see this through however long it takes.'

'And who was it was worried that someone else might catch him?'

Lampinen marched into the corridor without another word but Juslin lingered in the office. He stopped behind Onerva, placed his hand on her buttocks and whispered: 'My God, you're sexy when you get angry.'

'Hands off, eunuch!' she snapped and Juslin removed his hand and disappeared after Lampinen.

'Oh God,' she almost moaned. 'I just can't stop thinking about Pirjo. If only I'd tried talking to her a bit more... And now this whole thing with the secondary occupation licence – as if you can't get through life without a licence.'

'I know...'

'And Juslin... Why can't I keep my big mouth shut?'

'I'm sure it did him the world of good.'

'No, he used to work in a joiner's yard. A cog must have come loose; I bet he's still got a piece of something stuck in his head...'

The Exchange

Tweety tried to keep on imagining that Reino's van was like an elephant. True, it was the wrong colour – it was dark blue – but the headlights were like an elephant's eyes, small and tearful, and he knew it was an elephant because if it had left its droppings on the street it would have left a pile exactly the same as the one he'd seen at the Mission Museum. As a child it had always fascinated him: ELEPHANT EXCREMENT. He'd always wondered how it had been brought back from Africa – in a priest's knapsack?

An elephant – he tried to hold on to the thought, but it had passed and in his head he immediately heard the sharp tata-ta-tum of the watchman elf's drum.

Reino was driving. Tweety sat in the middle and Lasse in the passenger seat; he wanted to sit there so he could look in the wing mirror to see whether they were being tailed. Reino had followed his instructions and driven back and forth through the city centre, pulling over every now and then, but now they were cruising down Museokatu, which spread out in front of them like a dreamy gulf between the houses. The street lights had blue eyes and the cars' sleep was nothing but a tin-covered bluff.

'There's nobody following us.'

'No. And did you notice? Only one police car all this time, and that was back at Hakaniemi.'

'They'll be around here somewhere.'

'Somewhere's fine by me. I'll pull over on Temppelikatu. Check the park to see if there are any drunks hanging about. Doubt it at this hour.'

Tata-ta-tum! went the watchman elf's snare drum, its sound piercing. Tweety jumped as though he'd sat on something sharp. He wanted to grab the steering wheel and shout: *Stop! Let's leave it tonight, let's go back!* But he didn't dare. Lasse would have agreed straight away, he was so wound up that his fingers were twisted with cramp, but Reino wouldn't have given in to them. He was fired up in a happy, mischievous mood and he'd forced them to go through with the plan. Lasse was unable to work under too much pressure. He was supposed to carry out the actual switchover and he'd have bungled it up somehow and that would be the end of things.

There were no people in the park, but there were hidden dwarves, not even knee-high, with fur like moles and green curly hats, burying the toys the children had left lying around deep in the sand. Soon they were on Cygnaeuksenkatu and Tweety peered at the house on the corner: in the bank's window glowed a squirrel fashioned from a blue neon light-strip. Inside the bank it was dark, but from the outside he couldn't tell whether it was good or bad dark. Reino turned the car again and Temppelikatu rose up the hill in front of them. There was an empty parking space further up the hill; Reino steered the elephant into the space, and when he switched the motor off everything fell eerily silent; it was as though the whole world had pricked up its ears to listen.

'Right then, you pricks,' Reino said eventually, the mock cheerfulness in his voice filling the car. 'As soon as we get into the courtyard we'll check the windows in the outer wing of the building. If that woman's there we just walk past the rubbish bins minding our own business, make our way into the neighbouring yard and leave that way. Then we'll come back an hour later. She's hardly likely to be there, though...'

Tata-ta-tum! Tata-tum-tum-tum! Reino was stroking his chin. There was no need to go through the plan again; they all knew what to do. Unless he had to go through it for himself. Tata-ta-tum!

'And if she's not there then we go straight over to the doorway, Asko opens the door, then we go through to the door with the squirrel. Once we're inside the bank we make sure the tarred boards are in place and get the meters ready. Then we switch the alarms. Once we've pulled out the cable, the clock starts ticking... As soon as we're done, we get out. And remember: even if there's someone in the yard or you hear sirens in the distance, walk calmly across the yard and back to the car. Don't run. Don't look around. Calmly, OK?'

He looked at them firmly, his stare forcing its way deep into their minds, and Tweety thought he could almost see the watchman elf marching back and forth banging his drum, about to blame Tweety for not telling them... But Reino hadn't noticed anything; his eyes were like the balls in bottles of deodorant and Tweety decided not to say anything. Then there was the other thing, and at some point he'd have to tell them, but maybe this wasn't the right moment. Reino wouldn't start making a racket once they were inside the bank.

'OK?'

'Yes,' Lasse hissed and Tweety nodded. Lasse's lips were moving as though he was going through the plan to himself once more, the part about walking calmly out of the building, then his expression changed to one of certainty, fragile as a mask of papier-mâché, but even that was better than nothing. He kept his hand by his side, and Tweety wondered what it felt like to touch the handle of a gun – would it be metallic or wooden? Reino had allowed Lasse to bring the revolver. He'd said he wasn't going to use it but that it made him feel safer. Tweety wasn't so sure.

'Let's double-check the equipment,' said Reino. He lifted a thin briefcase from beside his feet and Lasse did the same. They laid the briefcases on their laps and flicked open the locks; Tweety didn't have a briefcase, only the pouch in his pocket, and it made him feel useless and at that moment he wanted nothing more than to be a pigeon sleeping up on the rooftop.

Inside Lasse's briefcase was an alarm with the lid loosened and held on by a piece of brown tape, then there were four different-sized screwdrivers, two slotted and two crosshead, and numerous screws of different thicknesses attached to the inside of the briefcase with a strip of tape. He pointed at each item in turn, occasionally glancing up at Reino, who looked focused and eventually gave a nod.

They then checked Reino's briefcase. It too was sparse – he always carefully planned what they would need and didn't allow them to take anything else, and in that respect he was absolutely right: the more they carried with them, the easier something might be left behind, and an extra screwdriver left lying beside the bank's main vault would let the staff know that something was going on; Reino even claimed that a forgotten roll of tape could be enough evidence to secure a conviction. Tweety didn't look at the contents of the briefcase. He stared at the rear lights of the car parked in front of them and he didn't like them; they were like a pair of diseased eyes watching them. Finally Reino and Lasse nodded at one another, Reino took three pairs of leather gloves from his briefcase and handed them out, then they snapped their cases shut.

'It's half twelve,' said Reino. 'Now listen, lads. By one o'clock this will all be over. Right, let's get going…'

They got out of the car. The night was like black chamois leather and the air was fragrant with the evening rain and the trees in the park. There was also a hint of danger in the air, its smell like a blue thread drawn through the nostrils with a needle. But Reino and Lasse didn't notice it. High above them a bird gave a shrill chirp.

They were on the move, three businessmen; they were wearing suits, white shirts and ties. It had been Reino's idea and in its simplicity it was a good one. The first time they'd come out of the bank at night they'd bumped into a woman taking her rubbish out to the bins in the courtyard, and she'd clearly thought they worked for the bank as she'd said: 'I suppose I should charge you for this, but you can have it for free, as long as you can make the ticket machines give out five-mark coins instead of…'

They turned at the corner. A taxi went down Museokatu and disappeared somewhere, and further off a drunken man staggered along, his shoulders hunched in sorrow. It wasn't far now, only about twenty metres, and for Tweety going to the bank had never felt so agonising. He knew what would happen: the alarm buzzer would go off right in front of some copper's eyes, then it would only be a matter of minutes until blue lights were flashing through the night, and inside the cars there would be stern-faced men with batons and revolvers at the ready. Tweety wet his lips; he was cold, yet strangely he was sweating at the same time and he was doing everything he could to make the blue images in his head disappear.

The worst of it was that he knew he had to do this; the Chancellor depended on him. Lasse had rearranged the wiring inside the alarm: to the people working at the bank it looked as if it worked and everything was fine, but the new alarm no longer reacted to heat or shock waves. And when they came back on Friday night for the final phase of the Chancellor, all they had to do was wrench the door open and make straight for the safety deposit boxes and nobody would know about the robbery until the women at the counter arrived for work on the Monday morning.

They stopped in front of the archway and carefully looked around one more time, but they couldn't see anyone watching them and the court-yard was dark and quiet. Tweety grabbed the handle and pulled on it, and the narrow grille in the gate opened; he'd put a paper egg in place that afternoon, and even if someone had removed it, using Vaseline he would still have been able to slip his hand through the mesh in the gate and open the door that way if necessary.

The grille shut with a clunk and their footsteps echoed in the arched tunnel, raining down upon them from the ceiling. The courtyard was in front of them and they all crouched to look towards the annex at the side: on the second floor lived a grey-haired old woman who spent all day peering out of her window, and the thought of her made them nervous. It was irrational: they all but expected her to smash her windows and start screaming that she'd seen them, but her window was dark. Reino was panting and Lasse groaned, but above it all Tweety heard a third sound: tata-ta-tum! Why was he banging his drum? Though his own premoni-tions often proved wrong, he couldn't remember a single time the watch-man had been wrong.

The air was filled with the smell of the rubbish bins and laundry hung out to dry. A cat darted along the edge of the fence and into the adjoining courtyard. The three brothers turned left, but Reino came to a sudden stop.

'I'll park the car over here,' he whispered and pointed at the spot. 'Bonnet facing the wall. It'll be harder to get away if I've got to turn around and reverse down there. But I'll put the side of the van up here, and if I park diagonally we won't have to carry stuff more than a couple of metres.'

'But the sound of the motor will attract attention,' Lasse whispered, and in his mind Tweety shouted: *Come on! Come on, why are we standing here in full view?*

'We'll just have to take that risk. And don't forget those signs.'

'Unless we bring them out here earlier in the afternoon.'

'Don't be stupid. The whole staff will see them, and they might get suspicious.'

Tweety couldn't stand still any longer, couldn't take any more of their bickering. He walked into the courtyard, went up to the door, took the few descending concrete steps and there was his job: a grey, painted door leading down into the basement. He'd already picked it three times and those three times had been enough. He couldn't stand working with

Reino and Lasse covering him from behind, watching his every move, and he'd been scared to death that someone might appear – at least three doors led out of the corridor right into the yard.

This time he didn't reach for the pouch; from a small pocket in his suit jacket he pulled out a gleaming, brand new key: he'd cut it that afternoon while Weckman had been on his lunch break, and now he prayed he'd remembered the sequence correctly. He worked the key into the lock and turned it; it caught, but only a little bit, the way all new keys do, then the lock gave a click and the door was open. Through the gap came the smell of brick walls and cobwebs.

'Hurry up, will you!' Tweety hissed. Reino and Lasse left the problem of where to park the van for the time being. Tweety wanted to see Reino's expression; it frightened him a little – how would he react? His mouth opened in disbelief, then he closed his lips again because he didn't understand.

'Was it open?'

'No. I opened it.'

'So quickly?'

'Just get inside,' said Tweety anxiously. He couldn't bear it when they stood around without a care in the world; it was as though they were willing something bad to happen. He pulled the door fully open and let them pass, made sure that the door shut properly, and only then did he press the switches and the corridor was filled with flickering light. The corridor stretched out in front of them like a bowel, like a tunnel made of raw meat: the bare bricks gleamed, unplastered, and it was strange to imagine the women at the bank, their lace, their fragrances, walking through here all day.

'Asko, for Christ's sake,' Reino started, but Tweety handed him the key before he could go any further. Reino and Lasse looked at the key then stared at Tweety.

'I cut it today. But you can't get in the other door…'

'But you've known the sequence all along, right?'

'The sequence?'

'For the door! Don't pretend you don't know. You could have done it ages ago, then we wouldn't be…'

'Is it a sequence? To me they're colours. The deepest one is green, that one's light yellow… But with cylinder locks the colours are refracted, so it's impossible to make a bump key.'

'Get a move on!' Lasse hurried them along and Reino realised there was no point carrying on. He gripped the key with a look of content, and Tweety wondered whether he was thinking: *We needn't have brought you along in the first place.* And he had a hunch Reino would try and force him to cut a key for the other door too – but there he would be mistaken.

They walked along the corridor and from behind the wooden doors seeped the smell of roots and juice cartons and skis waiting for the winter, and after about thirty metres they were there. The bank door was massive, made of steel and with thick hinges. A blue squirrel had been painted in the middle. Reino could have broken his way through the door but that would give the game away, and even if he only broke in when it was time to set the Chancellor in motion it would have made far too much noise and would have taken too long, and anyone popping down to the basement would have guessed from the marks left on the door what had been going on.

Tweety took out the pouch, crouched down and emptied its contents on to the floor in front of him. Reino and Lasse had finally learned: they didn't stand around staring at him but kept a few steps back, and there they starting talking in low, hushed voices and it wasn't difficult to guess that they were talking about him and the key and how he'd tricked them.

But Tweety didn't waste time thinking about that. He selected a pick with a tooth like a crescent drawn by a fairy and got to work. The light almost disturbed him – in the dark it was easier to hear the lock's singing – but he concentrated, delicately turning the tiny curve to the left and the right, and the lock started to answer him by either giving way or resisting, and little by little its movements turned to colours and chords, and Tweety was no longer aware of Reino and Lasse's muttering.

'OK,' he said after barely fifteen minutes, sat upright, turned the lock and realigned it staight away. Reino and Lasse marched towards him and just then he could hear it inside him again: Tata-ta-tum! He didn't open the door but held it ajar. Reino and Lasse stopped right beside him.

'What's the matter now?'

'The man from the security company,' Tweety answered, his jaw suddenly stiff. 'What if he's installed a motion detector... Remember, we wondered why there weren't any.'

'Fucking hell.'

'Now you tell us,' said Reino angrily as though this was Tweety's fault.

They stood looking at one another, all thinking the same thing: would an alarm go off the second they stepped inside? Other thoughts came flooding into their minds: what if they were too late, what if all this had been for nothing? What if the Chancellor was never meant to be and they'd be stuck in Tapanila for the rest of their miserable lives? It seemed impossible, as though a truckload of mud had been tipped down their necks without warning.

'Fucking hell!'

'But could he have installed it in a day?' asked Lasse hesitantly, his upper lip gleaming as though it had been sprayed with something. 'They were only making plans. And anyway…' He quickly examined the door frame and glanced further along the wall. 'There'd be a keyhole somewhere for them to switch it on and off.'

'Right, otherwise the employees wouldn't be able to come down here either…'

Suddenly they were all chuckling. It seemed so childish to worry about a motion detector that didn't even exist, and perhaps they were chuckling because they had come so far and everything had gone to plan. Tweety switched off the corridor lights and they stepped inside, and again it smelled different, like an office, the smell of paper, of women, or more specifically that the women's locker room was somewhere close, filled with the smell of their clothes soaked in perfume and deodorant. From the bank's main hall above them came the dim glow of the streetlights.

Tweety flicked life into Sparkle Eye and in its light Reino laid his briefcase on the floor, opened it and took out two torches – their lenses had been taped up too – and handed one of them to Lasse. Aiming the beam of light in front of him, Lasse walked off towards the main vault. He was almost tiptoeing, out of respect for the vibration sensor that was still working, and with good reason: while rewiring their replacement alarm he'd discovered that it was possible to adjust the sensor so that it reacted if someone so much as stamped on the floor or accidentally fell over.

'Asko, over here,' Reino muttered, ordering him around like a dog, and Tweety followed him towards the stairs, all the while trying to listen to what was happening within him: had the watchman settled down? Perhaps he'd been banging his drum because Tweety had been thinking subconsciously about the motion detector all day and had managed to convince himself it was there. But he hadn't stopped altogether; he was marching on the spot, taking steps that didn't lead anywhere, and he wasn't drumming any more but banging his sticks together: clack, clack, clack.

'Hold the light up here, where that bolt is.'

Tweety did as he was told. Reino pulled out his tape measure and held down one end, muttered something to himself, forgot where he had started and had to start all over again, and the sound of urgent bells rang through Tweety's mind, but he still didn't dare say anything; did the cardboard need to be so exact, he thought to himself and wished that they were already with Lasse helping him switch the alarms. What he really wished was for everything to be over and done with, for them to be back in the corridor or out in the street. He decided that he would fill his lungs with the smell of night if he ever managed to get out there again and that once he got back home he would take Toby out of his cage and let him crawl in under his shirt. Reino was so damned slow; he was writing down the measurements in a small notepad in thick, block lettering, carefully and exactly so that he wouldn't mistake them, then measured everything again.

'Right, let's see how far Lasse's got,' said Reino after what seemed like an eternity and they walked off into the darkness towards the beam of light from Lasse's torch. Tweety imagined the bank holding its breath around them, as though the tiny pores of each and every wall were blocked, as though the building itself knew they had no reason to be there, and Tweety prayed that it wouldn't decide to punish them. Then he remembered the rear lights of the car parked in front of them – why had he thought they looked like diseased eyes?

Lasse's briefcase was open on the floor and he'd laid the replacement alarm ready in front of the vault. It was an incredible door, like the casing of a battleship, and right in the middle was an enormous, gleaming wheel like a great crown of antlers. There must have been at least a kilo of steel around the keyhole. The alarm was on the opposite side of the door and its armoured cable ran across the jamb making it impossible to open the door without removing the contact plugs.

'This is a thousand-series door, lads,' Reino said as if giving a lecture. 'And that thing's rigged up so that if someone goes in and makes a dog's dinner of it then *bang!* It'll be so jammed there'll be no way in after that. But as you'll see from the points I marked on the photographs, the most important bit is right there.'

'Let's get cracking.'

'Yes… That's where I'm going to start. Just think about what's on the other side of this door. Jesus Christ, lads, there's boxes one after the other full of money and gold, the bank's cash stores and all their foreign currency. If we're lucky, a few million will soon be like pocket money to us…'

'Let's get cracking!'

'All right, all right.'

They crouched down to pick up what they each needed from the floor, just the way they'd practised back in the workshop, then they stood up and Reino held the new alarm in the air, ready to hand it to Lasse as soon as he'd removed the one attached to the door. Tweety was holding the alarm's gleaming cover and the screw to fasten it in place and he was afraid he'd lose it – through his gloves it felt so tiny, he didn't even know whether it was in his fingers or not. How would Lasse be able to work with gloved fingers? Tata-ta-tum! Tam-tam-tam! Lasse was holding the screwdriver ready; he laid his left hand on the alarm cable and looked up at Reino. Reino gave an audible gulp and panted: 'Now!'

Lasse gave a tug and the cable came loose. Reino looked at his watch. Lasse was already frantically unscrewing the cover. Tweety saw a light flashing and he could hear the buzzer: beep – beep – beep! At that moment a blond, moustached policeman noticed the alarm and stood up from his chair in order to see the code number more clearly, then picked up a red-covered directory and opened it. The screw was out; Lasse prised off the cover and handed it to Tweety; Tweety placed the cover in Lasse's briefcase. Lasse was already working on the insides of the alarm with his screwdriver as the policeman mumbled to himself: 'Ah, Museokatu 18'. Then he pulled his computer keyboard closer and started typing. Tweety was fidgeting anxiously on the spot and Reino suddenly started coughing.

'It's off,' Lasse gasped. He had the alarm in his hand; he didn't give it a second look but bent down and put it in the briefcase, Reino held the new alarm in place and Lasse began screwing it in just as the policeman leaned right over to the microphone and asked: 'Dog patrol, do you copy?' Lasse held out his hand. Tweety gave him first the alarm cover then the screw.

'That's the wrong fucking one!' Lasse hissed. 'The thinner one!'

'Dickhead,' Reino chipped in and Tweety didn't know where the thinner screw was and he was filled with such panic that he could have cried; it was like a whirlwind inside him, getting nearer all the time. Reino snarled something and snatched the correct screw from on top of the briefcase and handed it to Lasse, and the point of the screwdriver glinted in the light from Sparkle Eye, and the policeman said into his microphone: 'Is there a squad car in the Töölö area?' Lasse's hands dropped and the alarm shone proudly just as it had done before; Reino reattached the contact plugs – and there it was. Tata-ta-tum! Tata-ta-tum!

'Two minutes exactly,' Reino gasped. 'No rush. Now get everything back in the briefcases and make sure nothing's left behind. And remember: calmly, don't run, don't look around…'

They grabbed the few things they'd brought, packed them into the briefcases and snapped them shut. The beam of light from Reino's torch was sweeping the floor and there was nothing left lying there, not a single screw or a piece of tape. And their minds pounded with the same thought – *it worked, we did it* – then another thought, almost immediately afterwards: *Let's go!*

They turned together, like one person, and started heading for the door, and though they might have felt like running and shoving they walked calmly.

'No panic, lads,' Reino kept repeating. 'Don't run…'

'Aaw!' Lasse cried out. 'Oh God, oh God…'

They stopped. Tweety aimed the light at Lasse. His briefcase fell from his hand and gave an almighty thud as it hit the floor.

'What the hell's wrong now?'

'I don't know. Burning like… Aw, aaaw!'

'Lasse's face had turned white. His teeth were clenched – just like Brownie's – and there was an expression of sheer agony in his eyes, as though someone were twisting a knife inside him. He slumped to the floor in so much pain that he was howling like an animal.

'Get up!' Reino demanded and grabbed him by the arm. 'We've got to go!'

'I can't… My hip's on fire… and my leg. I can't move.'

'Asko, grab on to him. We'll have to carry him.'

Tweety took hold of Lasse's arm and they tried to lift him up, but Lasse gave an agonised scream and his head drooped as though he'd fainted.

'Jesus, Reino, what are we going to do? The pigs will be here any minute!'

'We've got to carry him. Take him by the legs.'

They tried again, but it was hopeless; they could only take short, staggering steps towards the door and beyond that was thirty-odd metres of corridor, the courtyard and the alleyway back to the gates, and the car itself was miles away on Temppelikatu. On top of that Lasse was still moaning, his voice getting louder and louder. Reino's briefcase slid to the floor and opened up, spilling its contents around him.

Reino let go of Lasse and swore, a flood of curses rattling from his mouth, and Tweety wondered how much it hurt when the police hit you with their batons. Where did they hit you? Surely not in the groin? He felt sick and silver stars began flashing in his eyes just like after he'd given blood. Suddenly Reino seemed calm and his resolve was chilling.

'We'll all have to stay here,' he said. 'We'll hide. Pick him up.'

'No, don't… they'll bring the dogs…'

'There's no other way. Now keep your mouth shut… In the changing room.'

Tweety felt as though the floor was swaying back and forth, but he held on to Lasse's legs and shuffled forwards while Reino panted in front. Reino let go.

'Wait here, I'll go and have a look outside. You pick up those tools. Quickly!'

Reino disappeared into the darkness; there came a thud as he bumped into something, then a tinny creak as he opened the door. Time seemed to pass quickly, as if it didn't exist. Lasse was whimpering on the floor. Tweety went over to him. He'd undone his jacket, taken out his revolver and was gripping it with both hands. It looked huge, gleaming, its barrel was long and the end was so wide you could put your thumb in it.

'You mark my words,' Lasse gasped. 'They're not taking us for free.'

Call-Out

'If we had binoculars we'd be able to see whether they've got fillings or not,' said Onerva after a long silence. Harjunpää nodded. It was almost one o'clock and they'd been on the move for over three hours, searching the areas around potential restaurants and watching people wandering about late at night, they'd gone through the chain of events stage by stage trying to come up with something conclusive, but now they'd reached the point when fatigue was beginning to set into their limbs and somewhere close by lurked the belief that all their efforts that evening had been for nothing.

The restaurant was about twenty metres in front of them. It was on the ground floor with walls made of glass like an aquarium, and despite the tinted panes of glass they had a good view inside through the darkness. Harjunpää had been keeping an eye on a blonde woman sitting with a significantly older man. She wasn't his daughter; Harjunpää knew this already. Perhaps it was her body language, the way she played with her wine glass, occasionally leaning forwards then sitting back and stretching her shoulders. He and Onerva were in the car, but from the park the view would be even clearer. It was easy to imagine their stalker on the prowl, how he loitered in the bushes and selected a suitable couple.

'My mother called just before I left the house. Get this – when she heard Grandpa was still at our place she hung up without saying a word.'

'Have they really never seen one another since the divorce?'

'Not that I know. Last night I started thinking about why I never tried to look him up…'

'And?'

'It's as if I didn't do it out of some kind of loyalty to my mother. And I've got vague recollections of when I was in primary school and we still lived in Kruununhaka and I used to visit him regularly. Whenever I came home, Mother wouldn't speak to me for hours at a time, and she wouldn't leave me any food if I was late for dinner.'

'Oh God. It's the old story: if I don't love him nobody else is allowed to love him. It's revenge. Jaana Karonen did the exact same thing to her daughters. And she talked about Jussi as if he was some kind of monster – their own father. Just imagine, one day they'll want to understand their relationship with him.'

They fell silent. A man in a grey jacket walked past, but he was the wrong build and in a hurry, and Onerva continued: 'Children start to believe these things. It's logical. And it works on adults too. In telling people about the divorce, Jaana slagged Jussi off behind his back to all their friends, and even though they knew what he was like they bought it all hook, line and sinker. Eventually people could barely bring themselves to say hello to him.'

'Museokatu 18,' the radio crackled. 'National Investment Bank, zero-two. Any units in the Töölö area that can take this? This is call one.'

'And after her call I realised she hasn't invited the girls round to see her all this time. And part of what's stressing me out about my father is…'

'Museokatu 18, National Investment Bank. This is call two.'

'Are we far from Museokatu?'

'Not very far. How come?'

'Some bank alarm's gone off.'

'Public Order should have the resources to take care of that.'

'That's just it. According to the initial patrol principle they should register the call immediately, which means they're indoors for at least an hour after every call-out.'

'Museokatu 18. This is call three.'

'Unit 1-5-1 is in Lauttasaari.'

'Is there nobody closer? Any units downtown?'

'Shall we take it?'

'OK,' said Harjunpää, pressed down the clutch and turned the ignition, and the Golf's motor revved up. He was already trying to envisage where Museokatu was and how best to drive there, and he decided to go straight down Topeliuksenkatu then along Runeberginkatu, then it was one of the turnings after Hesperiankatu.

'Control,' Onerva made the call. 'Unit 5-8-3 will take it. We're on Sibeliuksenkatu. We're on our way.'

'Unit 5-8-3, roger that. You'll be coming down to the corner of Cygnaeuksenkatu. I've put the initial call-out down as urgent.'

'Roger,' said Onerva. Harjunpää was already changing into second gear; he swung the Golf round to the right, raised his hand and reached towards a switch with white stripes. He turned it a notch and a bright blue light blazed in the legroom at Onerva's feet, again and again. The flashing light worked just as it should; Onerva rolled down the window, straightened out the cable, grabbed hold of the plastic dome, the size of a child's head, and held it outside. There came a greedy thud as the power-ful magnets sucked the device on to the roof of the car. Blue light began to flap across the trees in the park and the windows of the buildings opposite. Harjunpää turned the switch a notch further and a long moan pealed from the bonnet: *Piuuu!* Then came the repetitive, hammering tones of the siren like a giant leather belt thrashing the air: *woa-woa-woa*!

Harjunpää turned on to Topeliuksenkatu and started gathering speed: it was as though the cars parked along the road had started strangely reversing and before long they were streaming past in a blur of shining metal. He put the car into third, then fourth gear; the tarmac disappeared beneath them and the siren echoed from every wall: *woa-woa-woa*!

'What can it be at this time of night?' he said without taking his eyes off the road. He didn't increase their speed any more. The most important thing was getting there, a few seconds here or there didn't really matter.

'Probably nothing. These alarm systems are often faulty.'

'There could be burglars,' said Harjunpää almost as a joke. It reminded him of the scoundrels in Donald Duck comics: big, stubbly men with floppy ears, a black mask covering their eyes, each carrying a crowbar and a gun.

Onerva picked up her bag and undid the zip. It was always odd seeing her with a heavy Smith & Wesson in her hands. Harjunpää touched his hip and the rubber handle of his gun felt at once familiar and yet strangely comforting in his fingers.

Töölö hospital and all the pain and suffering inside its walls was left behind them. Harjunpää braked a little as they approached the junction and the square.

'Unit 5-8-3 on its way to a call. This is Control.'

'Receiving.'

'I've been liaising with a man called Kauppila. He's an economist, works for the bank. He says it's probably the automatic alarm in the vault; there have been some problems with it before. He lives on Apollonkatu and he's on his way over with the keys.'

'So we won't need the dogs?'

'Not at this stage. Take a look around first. But remember: always be on the safe side.'

'Roger.'

The traffic lights were blinking at orange and Hesperia Park lay ahead of them. Harjunpää glanced to the sides, but as there were no pedestrians he continued over the zebra crossing. After the junction he flicked the switch again and the wail of the siren stopped its lashing. Air whooshed through the open window and the tarmac crunched beneath the wheels. Only the flashing light continued, its blue light licking the traffic lights and the walls.

'Museokatu is at the next turning. Didn't he say the corner of Cygaeuksenkatu? That's almost the other end of the street.'

Harjunpää switched off the flashing light; everything seemed darker, stiller. The Golf was cruising along Museokatu, and Onerva leaned against the window to see the street numbers more clearly, all the while keeping her eyes on the street for anyone running away from the bank. It occurred to Harjunpää that there were two bulletproof vests in the boot of the car, but the idea seemed so over-the-top – or was that how accidents happened, when taking necessary precautions seemed over-the-top? As if to defend himself, he told himself they'd check all the doors and windows first, and if they found anything suspicious they'd take the vests. Or would even that be too late?

'Twenty-four,' said Onerva. 'Twenty-two... Twenty. It's the next building. Pull over by that gateway. We can walk the rest of the way.'

'OK.'

'Control. Unit 5-8-3 is on site.'

'Roger. Take the walkie-talkie with you and report back when you're ready.'

'Will do.'

Harjunpää swung the car into the empty space and switched the engine off while at the same time reaching for his torch and pushing the door open. Outside there was nothing out of the ordinary; nobody fleeing the site, nobody standing in a doorway watching them, no car waiting with the engine running.

They left the car doors ajar so they didn't slam shut and began making their way towards the bank, walking tight in against the wall, one after the other, their shoulders instinctively hunched. Harjunpää went first. In one hand he was carrying a long, black torch – in an emergency it could be used to club someone – and with his other hand he pulled back the front of his jacket and brought out his revolver. Number eighteen was in front of them: it was on the end of the terrace. The bank's walls were covered in pretty decorations; its logo shone blue.

They came to a halt. There were no shards of glass on the street and no noises coming from inside. There were no other sounds either: running footsteps, the roar of an engine, the squeal of tyres. Harjunpää took a deep breath and decided they could probably do without the vests. He gave Onerva a nod, lowered his firearm and walked on. The bank's windows were right there; behind it shone a bright neon squirrel and behind that there was nothing but darkness. He gave the door a sharp tug and it was firmly locked. There were no marks on the lock or around the door frame. They made their way round the corner. The windows on that side of the building were all intact.

Harjunpää switched on his torch, stood on tiptoes and angled the bright white beam of light through the window and into the bank. The furnishings inside were dark; the light glided across the counters and along the floor, but still he couldn't see anything suspicious. The furniture was as it should be, there were no papers strewn across the floor and he could- n't see any light or movement.

'There's nothing here,' he said and slowly relaxed. 'It must be a problem with the alarm.'

'I've heard that even a lorry rumbling past can set these things off.'

'I know. Let's take a look round the back.'

'If we can get in there… The staff probably use a door at the back of the building.'

'We'll see… this is the only gate into the courtyard.'

They walked further along Cygnaeuksenkatu and stopped in front of the gate. It looked heavy and unyielding, and Harjunpää pulled on the handle almost as a formality, but the lock gave a click, the hinges creaked and the gate swung open. It hadn't shut properly after the last person went through; perhaps you had to give it an extra tug. Harjunpää and Onerva glanced up and down the street but still there was nobody in sight. Kauppila was probably still pulling his clothes on.

They stepped through the gate and into the alleyway and their footsteps echoed comfortingly, as though a company of horsemen were galloping through. The courtyard lay ahead, slightly better lit, and the air smelled of childhood, of going down to the jetties by the sea without permission.

'And I can remember,' Harjunpää said suddenly, 'when I was a little bit older my godmother told me how brave I'd been as a child. I didn't understand at the time, but she meant that back then I'd accepted my new father in a matter of weeks. It was only then that I realised that mother had rung round all our relatives telling them how much I worshipped Heikki and how happy I was now that my father was out of the picture.'

'Maybe it was guilt.'

'Maybe,' said Harjunpää and let the beam of light sweep across the yard, paying particular attention to the locks on the doors into the basement, but they too all looked intact and firmly shut.

'I was afraid of him for years. He was a stranger who'd turned up and stolen our home and our life… He brought this old cuckoo clock – and I hated it. Whenever I was at home by myself I'd hold the hatch shut so the cuckoo couldn't come out and tweet. Eventually poor Heikki gave up mending the thing. To this day he still doesn't know that it was me that kept breaking it.'

'That's a pretty normal reaction for a child. You're on good terms now, aren't you?'

'Well… I've only really started to understand him in the last ten years. It's that door over there…'

Harjunpää shone the torch at a grey door a few steps down from the courtyard and began walking towards it. The words National Investment Bank stood on the door in weathered blue lettering; Harjunpää went down the steps, all the while keeping his torch on the lock and the door frame, but still he couldn't see any scratches or cracks.

'Control, this is unit 5-8-3 on the walkie-talkie. Do you copy?'

'Copy.'

'From the outside everything looks in order. All the doors are locked and there are no signs of forced entry. We'll wait for Kauppila and have a quick look inside.'

'Roger that. Records show the alarm has gone off at night twice this past summer and on both occasions it was a false alarm. Just so you know.'

'Copy.'

'What a waste of time,' Harjunpää yawned. 'Can we be bothered to go back to the restaurant?'

'I know... Let's carry on tomorrow. But we should get Forensics down to the park during the day to process the muddy area by the bushes for footprints, especially if they find a spot that's been trampled on.'

The gate clattered and from the alleyway came the sound of quick footsteps and the jingle of keys. Harjunpää got his badge out ready. A shortish man with a round face appeared in the yard; he was wearing a smart raincoat and a pair of loose tracksuit bottoms that flapped comically beneath the coat.

'Crime Squad. Good evening.'

'Risto Kauppila. Do forgive my appearance – call-out in the middle of the night, you know how it is. I'm sorry about all this. As far as I'm concerned you two can get back to your other work and I'll take care of this from here.'

'We're not in any hurry,' said Harjunpää. The man amused him, put him in a better mood – he seemed so jolly and yet so embarrassed at the whole situation. It demonstrated that some things were simply out of our control. He could easily imagine what the man was like during office hours: polite and scrutinising, wearing a hand-tailored suit with a grey silk tie and a tiepin boasting a small pearl.

Kauppila opened the door and the faintly underground smell of the basement wafted towards them. He switched on the lights and started striding briskly along the brick-lined corridor with Harjunpää and Onerva behind him.

'I'm sorry. These security systems are my responsibility. We've been talking about getting the whole system updated for a while now... I'm sure you know how it is these days; it's all about investment...'

Kauppila stopped in front of a heavy steel door. The same squirrel logo that had been shining in the front window had been painted on it. Someone had drawn this one a pair of closed eyes and a tongue drooping from its mouth as though it were ill. It was secured with a cylinder lock; Harjunpää glanced at it instinctively and made sure there were no signs of a break-in, though he didn't have the energy to give this case any more attention than was necessary. On top of that he sensed that Kauppila had taken control of the matter.

Kauppila opened the door and they were met with the smell of banks during the day. A faint rattling sound came from the ceiling, then one by one the fluorescent lights flickered into life. Everything seemed in order and, although Harjunpää had never seen the place before, it looked just as it would after a normal working day.

'It's ironic, I suppose,' said Kauppila, busying himself and hurrying forwards. 'A fitter from the security firm gave us an estimate only this afternoon. We'll start by renewing the cameras and carry on from there. There'll be motion detectors upstairs and down here. It's that shiny box over there...'

Kauppila stopped by what was apparently the main vault.

'It's old, I'll grant you, but it still does its job. The fitter checked it this morning so I hardly think we need to ask him back again because of this. If you'd just wait here a minute I'll go and register the alarm and switch the thing back on.'

Kauppila turned and walked off towards a set of stairs leading upwards and Harjunpää whispered to Onerva: 'Give the main hall the once over just to be sure, then we'll have a clear conscience. I'll have a look down here.'

Harjunpää stood still for a moment. Fatigue was beginning to take its toll on him, that and everything he had thought and understood. He felt himself slipping away somewhere, about to remember something, but managed to shake himself out of the past and stood staring at the door to the vault. It was extremely heavy, but even that wasn't enough to stop some people. He tried to imagine how much it weighed, then he imagined everything that lay behind the door and the image of Scrooge McDuck diving like a mole into his chests full of glinting golden coins sprung hazily to mind.

He yawned again, stepped unenthusiastically towards the nearest door and opened it. Mops and brushes and bottles of detergent stared at him in silent surprise. The next door was open and he switched on the lights. It was clearly a changing room; the walls were lined with the same kind of plate-metal lockers that they had down at the station. The air carried the faint smell of perfume and make-up.

He walked silently up to the row of lockers and opened the first door. Inside the locker was a white cardigan on a clothes hanger and an umbrella. On the floor were two briefcases placed next to one another, one of which had been closed so carelessly that a piece of notepaper with numbers in thick pencil had been caught in the lid. He began wondering whether a person might fit into one of these lockers – it was possible, at least for a short while in an emergency. And though it felt pointless he decided to check them all and took hold of the next door along – and that's when he heard it. He let go of the door and stood perfectly still.

It had been a sound of some sort, but he couldn't hear it any more. The sound of footsteps came from the hall upstairs, Onerva gave a quiet chuckle and Harjunpää told himself that it must have been the tiredness – but there it was again. A very faint sound, like a sniff or a sob. Goosebumps rose on his skin. He wet his lips and tried to swallow, silently so that his throat didn't give a gulp, then moved his hand down to his hip, pulled up the bottom of his jumper, located his holster and undid the popper, gripped the handle and pulled out his revolver. He placed his thumb on the safety catch, but didn't cock the gun just yet.

Again the same sound. A sniff or a sob. And this time he knew where it was coming from: it came from the toilet on the left, its door standing ajar. He wondered whether he should get Onerva's attention or quietly call her over. He guessed he was probably imagining it all and crept towards the toilet on the balls of his feet.

When he reached the door he stopped, using the wall as cover. Through the open door he could see that the room was dark. He tried to guess which side of the wall the light switch was on. He decided to try the left-hand side, switched on his torch, held his gun ready and slid the tip of his shoe into the open door. He gave a sharp kick and the door flew open; he was already on his haunches in the doorway, the torchlight groping through the darkness. His fingers found the light switch and the lights came on. The room was empty.

He stood there, his heart pounding, and he still had the feeling that someone was close by. Then came the sniff again and he realised what it was. He walked into the toilet cubicle and stopped in front of the porcelain bowl. There it was: the surface of the water was shimmering almost imperceptibly at the bottom of the toilet. The flush was somehow stuck leaving water running slowly into the bowl. There it was again: *sniff…*! The mechanism let another drop of water into the bowl. Harjunpää lowered his hand. Suddenly he felt overwhelmed with fatigue.

'Timo,' Onerva called out. 'Let's get going.'

Harjunpää switched off the lights and took a few heavy, dull steps across the locker room. He decided not to mention the incident to anyone. Onerva was carrying a money-box that looked like a miniature cash machine. Perhaps that was what she was laughing at, that she'd found it in the first place; that or the fact that after her resignation she wouldn't have anything to put in it.

'The alarm's back on and everything seems to be in order,' said Kauppila as though he'd just saved the world from a global market collapse. Good, thought Harjunpää, good that everything's in order.

Night

It was half past one; the night was at its darkest. Assistant Chief of Police, Superintendent Olavi Sakarias Tanttu was awake and drinking whisky.

His home lay silent around him; the bedroom was far enough away that he couldn't hear the sound of his wife's breathing. All he could hear was the humming of the fridge and the tick-tock of the clock on the wall. Even the cat had stopped purring. He lay slumped in his arms, a warm ball of fur, dreaming cat-dreams, his mouth twitching like it did when he clawed at the sparrows that had fluttered up into the bushes and sat there mocking him.

Tanttu didn't really know what to think. There was nothing left to think about; he'd already thought about everything, many times over, and the things he'd thought about had formed around him like a dark mass through which it was pointless trying to escape. He knew what it meant. *Night* stretched out in front of him, depression, and he'd learned years ago to accept that it happened once or twice a year. Calling it Night was one of his ways of fighting it: night always eventually ceded to morning.

He shook his glass so that the ice cubes clinked, took a large swig and tried to enjoy the warmth the whisky gave him. But he couldn't. He wanted to understand what it was that triggered his depression. It always seemed to appear in the most illogical situations, and almost without exception at times when he had reason to be happy – like now. After almost three months of hard work he'd managed to complete the second draft of his proposal for an amendment to criminal law, and he knew it was good. He'd found a number of inconsistencies in the first draft that had been overlooked, and he'd heard on the grapevine that his comments were already making an impact. He'd had success in another matter too: both the commander and Hongisto had demanded the transfer of another fifty officers to the Public Order Division, but he had managed to talk them down to twenty and it hadn't been easy. He'd had to go through the statistics for the last three years with a fine-toothed comb and relate the results to the goals set by external officers.

Tanttu took another swig and groaned. Was that it? Facing continual criticism despite all his achievements – and without due cause? He slowly savoured his drink and couldn't really believe it was true. He'd become hardened to this sort of thing years ago.

He laid his hand lightly on Cat's back. A few decades before, he'd had a spaniel called Dog. Cat was probably part of the reason that Night was on its way again. It was his neighbours. And even though he was used to handling the knocks that came with his job, attacks on his private life affected him deeply. He knew very well why. His position required him to be constantly on his guard, to live as an example to others, and yet it was precisely because of that position that some people went out of their way to find reasons to criticise him.

From one year to the next Cat seemed as good a reason as any. A letter lay on his desk, signed 'Local Residents', claiming that Cat was a beast that terrorised the neighbourhood, stripped trees of their bark and brought children within an inch of their lives. Tanttu cleared his throat. Reasonable complaints were one thing, but this was nothing but malice. Cat was a thirteen-year-old, six-kilo castrated male and was so lazy that he only ventured further than their garden to creep under next-door's woodshed, and even then he slept most of the time.

This last letter had ended by saying that the matter would be made public if something wasn't done about it, and his wife had taken the threat so seriously that she'd told him to have Cat put down. He hadn't agreed to it – and now she was giving him the silent treatment.

Tanttu emptied his glass and realised that it was true: alcohol only serves to heighten the mood of the moment. The night ahead now looked even bleaker than before. He sighed heavily, held Cat tighter, stood up and laid the half-asleep animal in the corner of the sofa. Then he picked up his glass and pattered through to the kitchen in his slippers. What bothered him most about this depression was that it always made him more irritable – meaner, his wife would say; nastier, his daughter would say. He knew it himself, and he knew why it happened. It was because even though depression was invisible and hard to keep in check he still tried to control it, and then all his efforts focused on something else, something real.

He put his glass in the kitchen sink and turned off the lights. Back in the living room he opened a drawer in the bureau and pulled out a small black box ready for the morning. In the box was an Alcometer, a breathalyser. He breathed into it every morning before setting off.

He hated drink-drivers even when it was Day.

Loan

The door closed behind Wheatlocks, cutting off the buzz of traffic and the midday heat, and she delicately walked down the corridor towards the lift, stopped suddenly and looked behind her. Nobody was following her; she knew it, but she hadn't trusted her intuition. She tried to counter the matter with a smile, but she could only manage a smile that was one-sided, more of twitch, and it startled her: only crazy people smiled like that, and she suddenly felt as though she were about to cry.

She hastily opened her handbag and rummaged around in it, as if to give herself a reason for stopping. It wasn't the first time she'd checked behind herself, and what bothered her most was that it had started happening at work too. She might stop midway through serving a customer, convinced that someone was staring at her, and the feeling was so strong that she couldn't just be imagining it. At these moments she sensed an imminent danger, as though she was being eaten away or threatened with a gun. The situation wasn't made any better by the fact that lots of men really did look at her, which was perfectly understandable. For a couple of days she'd suspected it was a blonde-haired boy until she found out that he worked in the sports department upstairs and that he had taken a genuine shine to her.

From her handbag she took a small compact and looked at herself in the mirror. Her hair was neatly done in a French plait. She'd tied her hair like this especially because she knew that Marko liked it that way; as a little girl she'd often had her hair in a French plait. She only wore a small amount of make-up, and that too was a carefully thought-out move: now she wasn't an independent woman getting on with her life, she was a lost little girl who needed her big brother's help. She had another motive, too. She wanted to be rid of what she sensed was the root of her nightmare: she wanted to be ugly. Rather, she wanted to be a man because then she felt she would have been able to take care of the situation differently. It wasn't even that simple either: she wanted not to be afraid of being a woman. Whatever the reason, she was plagued by a strange feeling that there was something unhealthily inconsistent about it all.

She slipped the mirror back into her handbag and made her way up the stairs. Her clothes too were part of her tactics: a loose red-and-white checked blouse with slightly baggy jeans and a pair of old plimsolls, shapeless and silent.

Marko's company, or rather the advertising company he worked for, was on the second floor. Wheatlocks stopped outside the door and rang the buzzer, and without any warning she felt suddenly nervous. She felt her heart pounding and her hands seemed almost as though they belonged to someone else. She was worried that if Marko had had second thoughts she would be left every bit as helpless as before; she was worried that her actions might accidentally get Marko into trouble and because, for the first time in her life she was about to do something illegal. And somewhere deep inside her was a seed of doubt: were these the actions of a rational human being?

Her steps approached the door and she tried to suppress the thought, beat it back. All she could think about was that she had to seem calm and level-headed, calm and level-headed, and not like someone who was anxious and desperate and contemplating all kinds of things. A young woman opened the door.

'Hello. I've got an appointment with Marko Heinonen.'

'If you'd like to come this way. You probably know the way. It's the door on the left.'

Wheatlocks smiled in thanks and strode down the corridor feeling almost as though she were swimming in the silence of the office. For the first time the bustle of the department store had started making her agitated. There was a time she'd loved it, but now the continual hubbub was like a flock of birds circling her and pecking at her. Again she reminded herself to appear calm. She knocked cheerily on the door and stepped inside.

Marko was sitting at his desk in shirtsleeves. His head was propped on his hands and he was staring at the oil canister in front of him trying to make it come to life, to transform it into something fresh, and Wheatlocks felt as though she had interrupted him, disturbed something; Marko might get angry just like when they were children and she'd touched his Lego blocks. The anxiety she'd felt a moment before was awakening again.

'Hi,' she said in as happy a voice as she could muster.

'Hi there, take a seat,' said Marko and smiled, though the furrow in his brow betrayed that he hadn't fully relaxed. Wheatlocks thought about how best to proceed: should she begin with some chit-chat, the little pleasantries you had to get out of the way first, or should she get straight to the point. She plumped for the latter.

'I've come to pick it up,' she said, trying not to fidget with the strap of her handbag. Marko swept the hair back from his forehead. There was a note of impatience, almost regret, in the gesture. *Please, God, just make him give it to me*, Wheatlocks repeated to herself.

'Are you absolutely serious about this?'

'You know very well that I am…'

'Right, then why don't you apply for a licence of your own?'

'Oh, surely you understand. They'd never give me a licence. I don't even belong to a club. And anyway, this is only temporary.'

Marko reclined in his chair, rubbed his chin in thought and watched her as though his grey-blue eyes were assessing quite how crazy she was. Wheatlocks leaned her head to one side, her smile fixed, and looked back at her brother imploringly and seriously. Time passed; somewhere a telephone was ringing incessantly. An ambulance sped past outside.

'Tell me honestly,' Marko began and couldn't bring himself to look her in the eyes, choosing instead to concentrate on adjusting the position of the canister on his desk. 'You're not… you're not going to do anything stupid, are you? I'd never forgive myself.'

'Marko, listen,' she said, almost chiding him, and waited a moment before continuing. 'I could never do something like that to you. Or to myself. That's never the answer… Do I seem out of my mind to you?'

'No.'

'And in case you were worried, I'm not about to kill anyone or start robbing banks, OK?' she joked.

'I'd love to see that,' he quipped. He managed a brief smile before turning serious again. 'But surely you realise that all this talk about Simo's visits really worries me.'

'That's exactly why I need it, so I don't need to be afraid of them any more, so I can feel safer. I remember how calm I felt that time you left it at the cottage when I was there by myself.'

'All right,' he said abruptly – he'd always been quick to make decisions once he'd fully understood the matter in hand. 'Shut the door.'

Wheatlocks stood up, and as she touched the door handle she felt the same sensation she'd experienced whenever she'd fired Marko's gun or was alone at the cottage and knew the gun was hidden under the mattress in the spare bed. It was a strange and oddly relaxing sensation, as though she'd been able to channel fierce, forbidden powers hidden within her, as though that power had come to protect her, all the while remaining outside her in the form of a black, iron object that went *bang* when you pulled a small trigger. The very thought was breathtaking.

Marko had lifted his briefcase on to the desk and opened it. Inside it lay the gun, bare on a white sheet of paper. There was something both frightening and fascinating about it. It was like an animal, a tamed beast that people wanted to stroke, even at the risk it might harm them. Marko picked it up, pointed it towards the floor with exaggerated care, pressed a small button and opened the barrel.

'As you can see, it's not loaded. I'm sure you remember: bullets in those holes, then lock this bit shut. And when you fire, either pull the trigger directly or set the safety catch with your thumb like this.'

Marko pulled back the safety catch and the gun made a comforting, sonorous click. Then he aimed the gun at the empty armchair and squinted.

'Imagine it's the Sea Dragon,' he said with a smile. Wheatlocks chuckled – the Sea Dragon was the woman next door who had always told tales on them as children – then Marko squeezed the trigger and the barrel spun round with a sharp click.

'Dead. See her lying there? This is a small calibre firearm, a .22, but it can kill someone just as easily as the next gun.'

Wheatlocks managed not to think about that. She stepped closer, placed her hand on her brother's wrist and looked him in the eyes, and though it only lasted a brief moment they both felt something neither had felt for years: thoughts of how life had been before, how they'd grown up together and taken care of each other, even fought quietly so their mother wouldn't hear. Marko held the gun by the barrel and handed it to her without a word.

Its handle felt firm and calming. She remembered how it shook when it went off, the smell of gunpowder, the cases once they were taken out, still warm, but let it pass. She didn't stand around feeling the gun but quietly slipped it into her bag. After that she didn't once leave her bag on the floor but hung it over her shoulder, keeping it tightly pressed between her side and her elbow.

'Here are the rounds,' said Marko and handed her a small blue-and-red box. 'But maybe it would be for the best if you didn't load it unnecessarily. Besides, don't carry it around with you. Keep it at home and don't talk about it to anyone.'

'Thank you,' she said quietly, held her brother's neck, smelled his scent and kissed him on the cheek as lightly as a butterfly. Then she backed off towards the door and decided to load the gun as soon as she got home.

Pike Teeth

It was no longer evening, but it wasn't fully night yet either. It was the moment when he would have been happy to be an eagle owl, to awake high in the branches of a giant spruce tree, slowly letting his eyes adjust to the light and listening to what was happening in the world below; where a bunny rabbit has gone to eat; where the crows have found shelter for the night. But Tweety wasn't an eagle owl and he wasn't happy. The thought of the locker tormented him. He felt like a train ripped from the tracks, shuddering along the railway sleepers with sand between the runners.

He hadn't been able to stay at home. Restless thoughts had filled his mind like rubber balls bouncing from one wall to the next, and now he felt as though he didn't want to be in town either. He trudged aimlessly north up Mannerheimintie, his Power was gone and now he was just Asko, the world around him nothing but a faded photograph. And there were far more people out and about than usual; cars sped past, their eyes glaring as if they knew something, and a storm was brewing, the wind gathered pace and the air was humid.

It had been the same inside the locker: he'd started sweating profusely. It was like one of those dreams in which you're forced into a coffin alive, then the coffin starts gliding towards the mouth of the crematorium; it was like being *caught*, when evil things happen, when you're killed twice over and threatened with death a third time. If that policeman had continued, his locker would have been next. He could hear the ebb and flow of the man's breathing, like timothy-grass blowing in the wind. Lasse had been in the adjoining locker, and when the policeman had gone into the toilet a soft metallic click had come from behind the tin wall: Lasse had cocked his gun ready. Down at the pit they'd once used a watermelon for target practice, and at the first shot it had exploded like a bomb. Nothing would have been left of that policeman's head except his ears. Would they have dropped down on to his shoulders and lain there like epaulettes?

He walked on and looked at his feet, Pessi and Moses, as they came into view one after the other. They were always faithful to him. His entire life had been like that locker and he wanted out. In fact it was even stranger: he *was* the locker and was unable to escape himself.

He stopped and breathed, his lips slightly parted. He had a strong sense that he had to get away, to run. He walked out into the road without looking to see if any cars were coming. The street shimmered in his eyes; the tramlines lay ahead, like jewellery made of molten steel, but there were no cars. If he were knocked over the seagulls would have pecked at his remains and he would have been able to fly in their stomachs. They had very powerful stomach acids; if their droppings land on a car they always leave a stain.

Lasse had got better all by himself once the police had left. Reino had still forced him to see a doctor, who hadn't been able to find anything wrong with him. An X-ray had revealed a swelling on one of his vertebrae, and that night he might have had a muscular spasm so strong that it pressed against the disc for a while. Once they were alone Reino said he thought the swelling was probably in his head, but nonetheless they'd established a new division of labour with regards to the Chancellor: from now on Lasse wasn't to carry anything heavy.

The Chancellor had started to frighten Tweety. The wind carried a yellow leaf across from the park, and he realised that he really didn't want to die. He wanted to be born first.

Tweety stopped beside a drainpipe. He stopped because Wheatlocks was suddenly in his mind. She appeared from the darkness between the middle decks, came out on to the main deck, lay down on a divan with golden feet and fell asleep in an instant. She looked exactly like she did when she was asleep in her own bed, her hair splayed across the pillow and her lips apart, and when he leaned over her face he could breathe in her breath. Her hand was like a child's but had red, woman's nails. And her thighs were so soft, and her stomach so smooth, and her belly button was just big enough to fit the first joint of his little finger.

He took hold of the drainpipe and it felt like he was keeping the entire house upright. He hadn't stroked Wheatlocks in two weeks; for two whole weeks he hadn't experienced tenderness, hadn't felt love from anyone, and his dreams had often been black-and-white and miserable, dreams about wading across a swamp or being tied up in a cupboard and nobody coming to save him.

Wheatlocks' apartment wasn't far.

Neither was Brownie's apartment for that matter, or the aquarium restaurant. He loved that place. He loved standing outside in the dark watching people eat, the hedge branches brushing against his cheek; at moments like that he was almost an eagle owl. He was an owl preying on rabbits. He'd left his moped in the area too. He would have liked a car but he couldn't afford it and didn't dare ask Reino for a loan: he would have wanted to know where Tweety was going. And though the moped was childish, at least it meant he could get home, as the buses didn't run at the time of night when he most needed them.

He let go of the drainpipe and the house didn't fall down, but he couldn't decide what he wanted or what to do. And though he had pricked his ears and tried to listen to his soul he couldn't hear any music. He stared blankly around, ahead, then he realised that the hotels were close by – he was almost there – and he decided to walk past them and peer in through the windows, and he felt that after that he would know what he wanted.

He enjoyed hotels. Their atmosphere was somehow different, richer than other places, wealthier, and the people around hotels were different too, stunning, glinting like spider's webs, and they smelled of perfumes that were probably only sold abroad. And once in their rooms they slept naked on silk sheets, and their skin was so downy and white that he almost wanted to bite into it.

Tweety set off, now striding decidedly more briskly than at any point that evening, and as if by magic a taxi pulled up in front of the first hotel and the porter hurried to open the door. He must have felt embarrassed; his clothes were so smart he looked like a clown, a silk top hat on his head and a jacket that could have been from an operetta. The crew of a foreign airline stepped out of the taxi; Tweety could tell from their uniforms. One of the stewardesses was particularly beautiful. She looked a bit like Madonna, blonde hair down to her shoulders, and enough of a chest to share around, and he was sure she was about to go to bed with one of the pilots.

Tweety found himself thinking about how strange it was that even a beautiful woman's pussy was in fact a frightfully ugly thing, wrinkly and foreboding, as if deep inside it were hidden layers of teeth, sharp as a pike's; curled, bony hooks, and if they suddenly snapped shut – that was it. There would be nothing left but ripped shreds of flesh. The wind gusted in swirls along the walls, carrying the woman's scent to Tweety's nostrils. It was the smell of a stifling, almost nauseating perfume, like the smell at the fox enclosure at the city zoo. His stomach started churning and he looked elsewhere, up into the sky, high up amongst the first raindrops, and he didn't want to be a locker or a man. He wanted to be a bird.

Storm

It had been raining for a moment or two: heavy, ominous raindrops that drummed dejectedly as they hit the roof of the car. Harjunpää wondered whether to turn on the windscreen wipers, but decided against it; it was good that the windows were hidden behind sheets of water. They could just about see out, but with any luck they wouldn't be spotted from the street. There was, however, another side to this: it was extremely unlikely that their mystery man would voluntarily get himself soaked in the rain or that anyone would willingly leave the restaurant and brave the downpour.

A bolt of lightning flashed; time passed, a moment more, until finally there came a distant rumble, and Harjunpää rested his head against the car window, hoping that the storm would let rip, thrashing the trees back and forth and sending a deluge of water on to the streets; the pavements would be flooded and the air would be thick with white light and a deafening crash. Afterwards everything always felt somehow different.

Despite this, he realised that he would have to create the storm he so needed for himself, and he knew that he would be unable to do so. Or was he only imagining it?

For he knew what was wrong. He knew that it was amateurish and stupid to put only one of their two possible locations under surveillance using only one car, and an easily identifiable one at that. The matter should have been handled differently: both restaurants should have been under simultaneous surveillance every night for several weeks in cars manned by those working on the case. Now, in effect, he and Onerva were struggling to work the case alone, keeping an eye on the place for a few hours during the day and a few hours at night; it was like sticking your hand in the sea and waiting for a fish to swim up to you.

And behind all this stupidity was one glaring, basic stupidity: the investigators had split into two quarrelling camps, each pushing their own agenda. This was no longer cooperation – if, indeed, it ever had been – this was a bitter, childish point-scoring exercise, and Harjunpää was no longer sure quite how they had arrived at this standoff. He felt strangely guilty, as though he himself had played a part in the matter. Valkama, the man appointed temporary chief of investigations, wasn't much help either; he was continually caught up with other pressing cases, and his comments were always offhand and vague: 'Well, these differences of opinion aren't very helpful now, are they?'

On top of this, in the last day the situation had taken a significant turn for the worse: Lampinen had refused to comment on how things had gone with the Nikander case, presumably because they hadn't got a result, and the others on the case had kept their mouths firmly shut, almost as if they'd struck a deal not to talk. The whole case had reached a stalemate, as had the situation at home with his father: Harjunpää still hadn't been able to reach Ms Salin from Social Services. He shifted in his seat and hoped for an exceptionally ferocious storm.

'Onerva,' he said after a while. 'We need to wrap this thing up, somehow.'

'There may just be a very good chance of doing that,' she replied quietly. This was her 'action voice', ever so slightly agitated. Her eyes nothing but a squint, she stared past Harjunpää, through the rain, and into the park in the direction of Mechelininkatu. 'There's somebody standing over there, by that tree, absolutely still. I don't know where they came from all of a sudden... And just by those bushes is the spot where Thurman found the footprints.'

'Where? I can't... There is someone there. A man.'

'And he's staring across the street at the restaurant.'

Harjunpää fidgeted restlessly, as though an electrical current had been plugged into him: he was suddenly wide awake, his thoughts utterly focused as he estimated the distance to the tree and tried to think of any potential escape routes, and the rain – it, at least, had taken note of his wishes and was lashing down in torrents – and beneath his excitement he had the distinct feeling that the solution to the case was close, that this was the right man, this was their stalker, he could feel it just as he had sensed danger back on the shores of Mustikkamaa, and with eager fingers he took hold of Onerva's wrist.

'We can't mess this one up,' he whispered instinctually. 'Let's be on the safe side. We'll call Control and get them to send a plain-clothed patrol to the corner of Mechelininkatu, then we'll split up: one of us will approach him from the front, and the other will go round the park and come up behind him. And if he's not our man, we'll just check his ID and leave it at that.'

'It's him all right. Who else would be standing out there in this weather? Just so you know, all the people who've tried to apprehend him have said he's a hell of a fast runner... Should we ask them to station a dog patrol somewhere near Hesperia hospital?'

'OK.' Onerva picked up the car radio while Harjunpää groped in the door's side pocket for his handcuffs, and didn't take his eyes off the figure for a second. The man had appeared by the tree like a ghost and could disappear just as easily. It was difficult to see him properly: he was standing there perfectly still between the darkness and the sheets of rain, and his clothes were distinctly colourless. He was almost part of the tree, a gnarl or the stump of a broken branch. With his other hand, Harjunpää picked his long, wooden baton up from the floor.

'Patrol 5-8-3, this is Control.'

'We've got a visual on a suspect in Topelius Park, but we need a plain-clothed patrol posted on Mechelininkatu to make sure we get him. Can you sort it out?'

'Hang on a minute,' came the voice from the switchboard. The radio crackled and fell silent, and Harjunpää could almost see the clerk going through the computer screen in front of him. Another flash of lightning cut through the sky, bathing everything in trembling light, followed immediately by a boom as if something above them had ripped open. The man remained standing by the tree trunk. At least for the moment.

'5-8-3, the only plain-clothes unit we've got is currently with Social Services taking some kids into care. They could be another hour or so. Won't uniform do?'

'I'm afraid not, this guy's renowned for doing a runner. What about a dog patrol?'

'No, I'm sorry,' said the clerk, and there was genuine regret in his voice. 'One officer just clocked off for the day and the other is out in Vantaa helping officers there with a search.'

A look of desperation spread across Onerva's face, but she didn't give up: 'Well, are there any Crime Squad officers in the area? What about Lampinen and his lot?'

'They've been on line 23. Why don't you try there?'

'Roger. Over and out.'

Onerva looked imploringly at Harjunpää, then they both glanced out into the park; the man had moved away from the tree, taken a few steps, as though he were wondering whether to run for cover before the rain got any worse, but then started moving restlessly, carelessly, and leaned back against the tree.

'It's worth a shot,' Harjunpää whispered to Onerva. 'The surveillance flat's around here somewhere. There might be someone there.'

'Are Lampinen and Juslin from Crime Squad on the line?'

'Yes,' Juslin replied, his voice as clear as if he were sitting right next to them.

'You're somewhere around Humalistonkatu, right? We've got our eyes on a probable suspect by the edge of Topelius Park opposite the Lehtovaara restaurant and we need some back-up. Can you help?'

'Hang on,' came a voice in the background. It was Lampinen. 'Our suspect'll be on the move any minute. We've got to be ready for him, so nobody's going anywhere, I'm afraid.'

'Roger,' said Onerva as she slammed the microphone back in place and switched off the radio, and her eyes were nothing but a pair of hard furrows. Harjunpää felt the same anger, a mix of anger and weariness with everything, the police force, their case, the whole world, and with it came a desire to leave it all behind him for good, but then he took a deep breath and came back to earth and his anger had suddenly changed form; it had become a kind of bullish determination, focused on the man waiting outside.

'We could always try to make a run for him,' he said, restlessly gripping the handle of his baton. 'But I think he's too far away. He'll have enough time to run off.'

'And running on wet grass isn't easy. Let's try coming at him from both sides.'

'Get out of that door slowly and keep your head down. Don't move in on him until I've reached those bushes. We'll walk up to him calmly – he won't suspect a thing. And when we're right by him, then we take him. OK?'

Onerva nodded, slung her handbag over her shoulder and grabbed the door handle. The rain was coming down like a rippling wall in front of them and the surface of the pavement seemed to bubble with water. Onerva was already outside in the thick of it; Harjunpää clambered over the gearstick and frantically gestured to Onerva to keep down. Onerva didn't react, but instead opened the car door wide and leaned against it as though without it she would have been unable to stand up. Lightning flashed, followed immediately by a tremendous clap of thunder, and the wind shook the trees in a fury.

'We screwed up,' she said, pretending to remain calm, but beneath the act her voice was tense. 'Just get out of the car as though nothing's happened. He noticed the light come on as I opened the door. Now he's on the other side of the tree, you can hardly see him. But I bet he's watching us.'

'Damn it...'

'Forget damning it. We were in the car having a bit of a smooch and now we're still drunk and making our way home...'

'It's pointless.'

'No, it isn't!'

Harjunpää got out of the car; raindrops pounded painfully on his head and face, Onerva opened her arms and wrapped them around his neck and shook him. Harjunpää fumbled and rested his hands on Onerva's slender shoulders. He pulled her closer; her face was right there, almost touching his own, wet from the rain, a lock of hair stuck to her cheek. He could smell her faint scent, feel her warmth; he kissed her nose and chin and then her mouth, and it felt good, it felt overwhelmingly good, forbidden and yet so right. Water lashed down around them and time stopped, then Onerva drew away and peered into the park.

'He's still there,' she said, slightly out of breath. 'What's our plan of action?'

For a fleeting moment Harjunpää wanted to say, *Let's keep on bluffing*, but he didn't want to spoil anything. He had felt Onerva respond to him and yet he knew that the matter could go no further, that neither of them would allow things to develop, it wasn't meant to develop. It had been something that was almost impossible to understand. He slowly moved his baton to his other hand, held Onerva close, pressed his cheek into her wet hair and started walking.

'Let's cross here,' he said in a hushed, low voice. 'Then we'll turn at the corner and walk right up in front of him.'

'He's watching us. He's moving round the tree trunk so he can remain hidden. You can just make out his white face.'

'When you compare him to the tree, he must be pretty scrawny.'

'Yes…'

They crossed the street and continued walking forwards until they were only twenty or so metres away from the man; the rain was so heavy that it was hard to make out any details. Suddenly he felt nervous, excited, as he always did when he was about to apprehend a suspect, thoughts rushing through his mind: what's going to happen; is it the right man and will he make a run for it; what if he has a gun? His body was getting ready, producing a strange, mystical energy.

They came to the corner and turned so that the restaurant was right in front of them; the light coming from inside looked safe and warm. Harjunpää's shoes were already soaked through and his shirt clung to his back like a jellyfish.

'He's slipped behind the tree trunk,' Onerva whispered and slowed her step. Then, all of a sudden, she tore away from Harjunpää's side and broke into a run. 'Timo, he's there in the bushes!'

Immediately Harjunpää was running too; water on the tarmac splashed beneath his feet as he ran, his baton waving in his hand. He ran on to the grass; it was soft and slippery, every step almost tripping him over. The black tree trunk flashed past and a bolt of lightning lit the sky, a long, quivering blue-and-white explosion, and in the momentary light he saw the man, who by now was running in between the trees and up the hill. He ran as nimbly as an animal, a deer perhaps. Maybe it was his deer's instincts that had warned him.

'Stop!' Harjunpää shouted, though he knew it was no use. 'Stop! Police!'

The branches of the bushes whipped against his shins. Onerva ran to one side; she had already kicked off her shoes, then she reached for her handbag. A moment later she was holding her revolver. 'Don't!' Harjunpää tried to shout out, but Onerva wasn't pointing her gun at the man running away. She held the gun to one side, to the ground, and aimed somewhere in the shimmering grass. Again Harjunpää ordered the man to stop, then Onerva fired once, twice; sparks flew in all directions and the air was filled with the smell of gunpowder. The man continued running just as before, perhaps even more furiously. The distance between them was growing and there was nothing they could do about it. He was going to get away.

'In the car!' said Harjunpää, out of breath. 'Onerva, back to the car!'

'No, you go. You've got the keys. I'll go after him and see where he goes. Pick me up on the way.'

Harjunpää handed Onerva his baton, then sprinted in the opposite direction winding back through the park, and suddenly he regretted his decision. It felt dangerous — dangerous for Onerva. What if the man stopped and started to struggle with her? And what if he did have a weapon, a knife even? But there was nothing more Harjunpää could do about it. All he could do was move faster and trust that Onerva knew how to handle herself. And that she certainly did. What's more, she had a gun and a baton, and the man might have been so startled by the gunshots that nothing would make him stop now.

He could see the car in front of him. Water bubbled white on its roof and the bonnet was facing the wrong way, of course. He reached into his pockets for the keys, then a moment later he was at the car, wrenched the door open, his hands trembling with the exertion, and threw himself inside. He grabbed the radio from the dashboard but realised straight away that it was useless; he was too flustered and out of breath, Control wouldn't be able to make out a word he said. He decided to try them in a minute and turned the ignition. The rain looked like reeds dancing in the headlights. He steered the car out of its parking space and accelerated. He realised it would be pointless wasting time trying to turn the car or go through the park where the wheels might have got stuck, so he swung on to Humalistonkatu instead, took the first left, and Mechelininkatu was there in front of him. There was no traffic at all and at first he drove on the wrong side of the road along the edge of the park. The flashlight was too far away for him to reach. Perhaps it was a good thing, the blue flashing lights would have warned the man he was coming.

Trees flashed past, bushes, the park. Harjunpää couldn't see the slightest trace of their man or of Onerva, and it struck him that someone cunning enough would hide in one of the bushes and attack Onerva from behind. A bitter taste suddenly began tickling the back of his throat and he grabbed the car radio.

'Control! This is 5-8-3. Do you copy?'

'Copy.'

'Send immediate assistance to the corner of Topelius Park. Our man's done a runner. He's heading for the city centre.'

'Calm down… Can you give us a description?'

'Short,' Harjunpää gasped. 'Thin. Grey clothes. Fast runner. Onerva Nykänen is in pursuit on foot.'

'Copy that. Is there a patrol car in the Töölö area that could…?'

Harjunpää didn't need to listen to the rest. He was approaching the Sibeliuksenkatu intersection. He still couldn't see anyone along Mechelininkatu, unless the sheeting rain was obscuring the man from view. He made to take a left and braked hard, the car skidded and swung almost sideways across the street; Harjunpää frantically spun the steering wheel and managed to straighten the car just before hitting the kerb. The trees growing on both sides turned the street into a leafy grove and kept a lot of the rain out, though he still couldn't see anyone, only parked cars. Further along the street, almost at the Topeliuksenkatu intersection, a motorbike went past.

Harjunpää stopped and rolled down the window, stared into the park and listened. At least he couldn't hear any shots or cries for help. Somewhere in the distance he heard the faint wail of a siren. He couldn't understand what had happened to Onerva, then all of a sudden came her voice somewhere in the distance: 'Timo!' Harjunpää saw her straight away; she was in the park, a good couple of hundred metres away, urgently pointing in the direction of Topeliuksenkatu. Harjunpää understood instantly: the motorbike! Its lights had been switched off, and for someone to be out in this weather… The man must have parked it ready on Sibeliuksenkatu.

He looked further up the street and could just make out a dark flash disappearing to the left, perhaps into Töölönkatu. Then he looked into the park. Onerva had stopped and was trying to catch her breath, her hands resting on her thighs, and didn't even try to get into the car – she knew it would take too long. Harjunpää scooped the flashlight from the floor, threw it on top of the dashboard, lifted the clutch and pulled away. He groped for the switch, turned it and the car was filled with a glaring whirl of blue light.

Careful, he told himself over and over. Its engine roaring, the Golf sped across Topeliuksenkatu, waves of light flashing all around, and headed onwards. The windscreen wipers were going at full speed but the windows were beginning to steam up on the inside as moisture evaporated from his clothes. Harjunpää put the fan on full blast and hastily wiped a small gap in the condensation behind the windscreen with the back of his hand.

He took a left on to Topeliuksenkatu – and he could see the motorbike! It was probably a moped, it was so small. The man had switched the headlights on – perhaps he thought he'd got away. Harjunpää accelerated and quickly closed the gap between them. The moped-man looked behind and gave a start: the whole bike swayed from side to side. He very nearly fell over but somehow miraculously managed to regain his balance, accelerated and swerved to the left, his foot skimming against the ground. Harjunpää reached for the switch and the siren began to wail: *woa-woa-woa*! It would make the man even more nervous, he knew this from experience and he knew the risks that came with it, but there was practically no traffic and, because of the rain, going too fast on the moped could have been dangerous.

The Linnankoskenkatu intersection lay ahead. The moped-man had taken a right on to Nordenskiöldinkatu and by now there was less than a hundred metres between them. An almost intoxicating sense of victory washed through Harjunpää in warm waves. He tried to suppress the feeling. It was dangerous, it could blind him in all the wrong ways. At this stage anything was still possible: he might be careless and drive the Golf into a lamp post or the moped-man might decide to turn into the narrow side streets and set off by foot – and that would be that.

Dee-daa-dee-daa, came the yell of the siren. Harjunpää shifted into third gear and put his foot on the accelerator, only to release the pressure and brake almost immediately. It was as though the moped-man had read his mind: at the very last moment he swerved across the street and disappeared down a side street to the left. The Golf sped on like a train; because of the rain Harjunpää didn't dare brake as hard as he should have. He passed the intersection and managed to stop the car, slammed the gearstick into reverse and revved the car back down the street, changed gear again and swung the car into the side street. Now that the situation had changed he quickly turned off the lights and the siren.

Another empty crossroads was right in front of him. Harjunpää slowed down until the car was stationary, and looked around. He could see neither the moped nor anyone on foot, and disappointment flooded his mind like a thick liquid. He slumped against the car seat with his full weight. No! He felt the same as when Onerva had first spotted the man in the park and now he was consumed by a pressing need to catch the stalker and to wind up the case. The moped-man couldn't just have disappeared. He had to be somewhere – and so did the moped.

Again Harjunpää instinctively turned left and looked up at the street sign. He was on Messeniuksenkatu and let the car glide slowly on, making sure to look between the parked cars and along the walls. Just as he had almost reached the end of the street he saw it: the moped. It was in front of a grey van and had been parked in a hurry, almost right up against the bumper. Harjunpää pulled over, grabbed his torch and stepped out of the car, pulling his jacket back from around his revolver just in case, and walked up to the moped. It was the right one: its engine was still so hot that the raindrops hissed as they hit it.

He looked at the building in front of him: a brown block of flats, grand in a way that meant the flats inside were probably very large. He made towards the nearest stairwell, walked up the steps and pulled the handle, but the door was shut. He switched on his torch and aimed its beam of light through the thick pane of glass and on to the floor in the stairwell. The floor was dry; he couldn't see any wet footprints. He thought for a moment and decided that it would be best to establish where the man might have gone before any possible footprints could dry out and only then call for assistance if necessary. He moved on to the next door with the same result. A moment later he had come to the corner of the building. It curved round on to Stenbäckinkatu, and on that side of the building there was a gateway.

He strode up to the gate in the thinning rain, raised his torch and illuminated the ground through the iron decorations. He drew a quick breath: on the tarmac were fresh, shining wet footprints leading through the archway and into the courtyard. The gaps between them were so large that they were clearly running steps. Harjunpää pulled feverishly on the gate, but it too was locked. But on the wall he spotted a white buzzer with the word GATE printed beneath it. He pressed it, and a few seconds later the lock gave an electric hiss and he pulled the gate open.

Harjunpää stepped into the archway but stopped immediately: he had a strange, almost superstitious feeling that he was stepping into a trap, that he had crossed into a realm of evil forces. He pulled out his gun and listened, but all he could hear was the sound of water splashing down the gutters and thunder booming somewhere to the north. He crept towards the courtyard, his thumb ready on the safety catch, and just before he reached the end of the tunnel he crouched down to follow the direction of the footprints. It appeared that the man had veered to the right before entering the courtyard. If this were the case, he would probably have gone into the first stairwell on the right. Harjunpää stood up and peered into the courtyard. All he could see was darkness: the stairwell window gleamed black and not a single light was on in the flats above.

Harjunpää instinctively hunched his shoulders and ran through the thinning rain to the first door after the corner and pulled the handle. The lock gave a quiet click and the door opened. He had the odd feeling that he'd done this once before but let the notion pass. He stood and listened to the deep silence inside the building. He pressed the light switch, glowing in the dark like a red eye, and a soft yellow light flickered and filled the stairwell.

First he looked at the floor. The footprints were clear. The man hadn't used the lift but had gone up the stairs. Water had dripped from his clothes, which must have been soaked through, and the small droplets gleamed like silver coins in the light from Harjunpää's torch. He made for the stairs. The man had gone up from the second floor, and the third. As he reached the fourth floor Harjunpää suddenly stopped. He was overcome by a hazy unease, but this time it was different from back in the archway. Now he *knew* something was not quite right.

But how did he know? He couldn't work it out. Was it something he'd heard? He tilted his head to one side and listened – perhaps there was someone on the attic floor above. But no, the silence was just as thick as before. His mouth felt dry and he inadvertently gripped the handle of his revolver, took a deep breath, then another – and there it was. There was something else in the air. He knew that smell; he'd smelled it hundreds of times. It was the bitter, sickly smell of a human body in the advanced stages of decomposition.

Balancing on the balls of his feet Harjunpää silently moved up towards the fifth floor and wondered whether he was imagining it. Drains sometimes gave off a similar smell, which explained why people went for months without realising there was a body in the next-door apartment. He sniffed the air again; the smell seemed even more pungent and he knew he was right: one of the flats on this floor contained a dead body.

He craned his neck to see on to the landing above, but it was as empty as the other floors. Only droplets of water glistened on the stone floor and Harjunpää went back to following them. They led to a door at the far right-hand corner of the gable. There was more water in front of the door than anywhere else, it had collected into a small puddle, and there were indistinct, smudged marks on the floor as though someone had been crouching down there or on their knees.

Harjunpää remained at a distance, allowing the wall to shield him, then he carefully crouched down closer to the door, reached out his hand and opened the letterbox – and the smell of death spilled out like a gas. Helga Kivimäki, read the sign on the door. Harjunpää was at a loss: did their intruder *live* with the body? It was possible, he'd seen it before. He'd even seen people try to feed mummified bodies with gruel. Perhaps the intruder's wife or mother had died, Harjunpää thought, and the man has had some sort of breakdown as a result. Or maybe he'd killed one of his victims and wanted to turn himself in. But whatever the circumstances, he was inside that apartment waiting to be caught, and a look flashed in Harjunpää's eyes that was almost malevolent.

Silently he moved to the other side of the door, crouched down and peered through the jamb at the lock. The gap around the door was so wide that he could see the bolt clearly. He realised it would only take him a minute or so to open the door, he had a pouch full of different hooks in his jacket pocket, and without a moment's hesitation he laid his revolver on the floor and reached for the pouch. He opened the drawstring and the tarnished, glinting steel hooks slipped into his hand – then he froze. After a moment he raised his head slowly as though he were waking up. He was about to do something unforgivably foolish: what if, as the door opened, the man were to point the barrel of a shotgun at his head and pull the trigger?

He swallowed, his throat stiff, backed away from the door, pushed the pouch back into his pocket and replaced the revolver in its holster. His whole body was shaking, he was so angry – at something, at himself. Then he took out his badge, walked up to the door at the other end of the corridor and rang the bell again and again. A minute passed, another, before he heard the sound of steps approaching the door. Finally a sleepy, suspicious male voice asked: 'Who's there?'

'Crime Squad,' Harjunpää replied. 'I need assistance. I need to make a phone call.'

Door

At first the stairwell seemed very quiet, but when Harjunpää listened more closely it was filled with almost imperceptible movement and tiny, barely audible runaway sounds: someone shifted position, handcuffs jangling on someone's belt. Somewhere further off somebody discreetly blew their nose. There were over a dozen police officers in the stairwell and things were almost ready. They were all waiting for the go-ahead.

Still in his damp clothes, Harjunpää leaned against the wall between the fifth and sixth floors. It was so late at night that everything seemed rather surreal, like catching a glimpse of someone else's dream, and with that came a sense of relief: he was no longer solely responsible for matters. The operation was being led by Heikkanen, the acting chief inspector from the Public Order Police, who despite his relative youth was quick and firm in his work and didn't expect people to fawn over him. As long as people did their job well, he was happy.

'Anything else you can tell us?' asked Heikkanen and looked over at Harjunpää, though perhaps only to give himself another few seconds to think. He already had the radio in his hand and looked like he was about to give the order to enter the apartment. Harjunpää shook his head.

'I'm still worried because of what the neighbour said about the weapons in there,' Heikkanen whispered. 'I'm just wondering whether to use tear gas first. Though the dog will serve the same purpose.'

'Right, especially since we haven't heard a sound from inside. And given that we'll probably have to process the place as a murder scene, the tidier we can keep things the better.'

Heikkanen was silent for a moment, as though he was scouring his mind for something but couldn't find it. Finally he gave a chuckle: 'He's probably dangling from the ceiling...'

From his expression you could tell this wasn't simply a statement. It was more a wish, and there was no doubt that, as far as defusing the situation was concerned, this would have been the simplest case scenario.

'Everybody ready,' Heikkanen spoke into the radio, this time without the slightest hint of joking or indecision in his voice. 'Let's get started. Kettunen, open the door.'

Harjunpää pressed back against the side of the lift shaft and through the mesh he had a clear view up on to the fifth-floor landing. Kettunen from Forensics moved along the wall and stopped in front of Kivimäki's door. His hands were raised and he was holding a hook or a needle ready. They hadn't been able to obtain the door key as no one from the housing association was on night duty. He knelt down and began working in silence. Behind him, up against the wall, stood two constables in helmets and bulletproof jackets, one of whom was holding a canister of tear gas at the ready while the other carried a small, toy-like submachine gun.

The seconds passed. Not a sound came from inside the apartment. The lock clicked and the door was ajar. Kettunen leaned back tight against the wall. Everybody waited. For a shot, a scream, anything. But still nothing happened. Kettunen turned and dashed for cover, his shoulders hunched. The smell of death grew stronger.

'Dog,' Heikkanen indicated. A muffled scraping sound came from the stairs leading down from the fifth floor, followed by a few instructions and the dog's excited yelping, then came the sound of claws and the Alsatian bolted towards the door like a dark shadow. It stopped before the door and hesitated, as though the smell from the flat made it feel ill too. The order came again, more forcefully this time, and the dog pawed the door open and slipped into the darkness inside. An avalanche of post spilled out into the stairwell; there must have been several months' worth in the hallway. The man with the tear gas started spluttering and brought a hand up to his mouth. Not a sound came from inside.

'He's strung himself up,' Heikkanen repeated, now clearly relieved, apparently just for the sake of saying something. He looked at his watch; its second hand moved across the clock face in regular twitches, started and completed a new cycle, and only then did a soft scratching sound emanate from the flat. The Alsatian came back into the stairwell and returned obediently to its trainer, whimpering all the while, almost sobbing, as though it was mourning what it had just seen.

'What do you think, Lehto?' Heikkanen said into the radio.

The dog trainer answered immediately: 'There's certainly nobody alive in there.'

'You don't think the smell confused him?'

'A bit, probably, but not that much. We'd have heard barking and screaming, believe me.'

'Copy. You two. Inside.'

Two officers in helmets and jump suits appeared on the floor from the same direction as the dog. Both were carrying powerful halogen lamps and pistols, and though to all intents and purposes it was clear that they were in no immediate danger, they darted inside with their shoulders hunched, keeping tight up against the wall. A moment later the lights came on in the hallway, then somewhere further inside the apartment. The pile of post was enormous. The hallway gave the distinct impression of considerable wealth.

'Faint drops of water on the floor here too,' came a voice from the radio. 'And it stinks in here. The place is huge…'

Then everything went quiet. Harjunpää moved restlessly. He wanted to go inside, but he knew it was impossible. The fewer people that went inside the less physical evidence they would destroy, and the matter of determining the cause of death and investigating a potential homicide fell to the Crime Squad officers on night shift.

Heikkanen's radio crackled, then the same voice spoke again: 'There's a door off the kitchen leading out into the other stairwell. There are still a few drops of water right next to it.'

Meeting

'But now we need extra resources more than ever,' Harjunpää exclaimed in bewilderment. At first he wondered whether he had misheard Järvi or misunderstood him. He looked at the others. Everyone had gathered in the Crime Squad staffroom: Järvi and Valkama, Onerva, Lampinen and Juslin and one of the night-shift boys who'd been with them at the flat, but they all remained silent and looked as though nothing in particular had happened. Only Onerva stared up at the ceiling, exasperated.

'That moped is still out in the street and it needs to be put under surveillance,' Harjunpää tried to reason with them. 'Rummukainen's there now, but he can only do mornings. And the same applies to the flat. Our man could easily go back there; he might not even know we've located it.'

'I imagine he was clever enough to hide somewhere and watch what was going on,' said Järvi dryly without looking at Harjunpää. 'He had enough sense to escape via the back door, didn't he? And it shouldn't have taken much brains to work out that that's what he'd do either. Anyway, what's done is done. My men are off this case with immediate effect.'

Harjunpää ran his fingers through his hair. It seemed that he had no other option but to prolong the situation. Ahomäki had promised to join them but he'd been called away and Harjunpää dearly hoped he'd get back in time. The super would have stuck up for them – Valkama didn't have it in him – either that or he would have edged Järvi into a corner so that he would have had no option but to tell them the reasons for his sudden U-turn.

'And what if this is now a murder investigation?' Harjunpää remarked, but Järvi didn't react in the slightest. In his shiny suit he was like a great aristocratic leader that morning. Though everyone else was sitting he strutted about the office with his hands on his hips, and there was something about his expression that said he bore the great responsibility of always knowing best. He stopped in front of Pesonen, the night-shift officer, and asked: 'What do you make of it?'

'Impossible to say at the moment,' he began and moved awkwardly in his chair. 'I mean, it's impossible to speculate on the cause of death. The coroner didn't have much of an idea either because the body was in such bad shape. But on first inspection there were no signs of external violence... And the location and position of the body are consistent with a fit of some sort. It was as though she stood up from her chair and had a heart attack.'

'And what about the flat?'

'Forensics are still down there. But on the face of it there was nothing out of the ordinary. No signs of a struggle. The surfaces hadn't been wiped down – at least not that anyone noticed. Nothing appears to be missing...'

'And you're still desperate to make this a homicide,' Järvi snapped at Harjunpää. 'Well, whatever it is, it's now the sole responsibility of your office.'

Harjunpää stared down at the tabletop and rubbed his temples. It was half past eight and he hadn't slept a wink. The night had been a long series of failures and disappointments, dotted with recurring glimpses of hope over possible breakthroughs that eventually came to nothing. But for the first time the case had taken a significant step forwards: they had the moped and finding out who owned it might lead them right to the intruder; they had the Kivimäki woman's flat which, according to initial reports, was full of fingerprints and footprints. But perhaps more importantly, after the events of the night before, Lampinen and Juslin had been forced to admit that they were more than likely wrong about Nikander. Harjunpää had been banking on this; he'd hoped that once the sense of competition had died down they would all start trying to locate this chaffinch man.

'Let's wait for the results of the autopsy first,' he said, again trying to stave them off. 'And I think it would be a good idea to hear what Ahomäki has to say too.'

'We're not conducting an opinion poll here,' Järvi scoffed. 'There's no use moaning about it any further. I've been assigned a case of national importance, which will obviously take priority over your bird-man. Gentlemen, I think we're done here.'

He clicked his heels sharply and bowed, then marched out of the room with his head held high. It was a stylish exit that many an actor would have been proud of.

Harjunpää couldn't help himself.

'I wonder what the right honourable Kuusimäki will have to say about that,' he said a fraction too loudly. Järvi stopped in the doorway, turned and glared at him, opened his mouth as if to quip something in response, then pressed his lips into a tight, almost frightening scowl and marched along the corridor, his heels clacking as he went.

For a moment the staffroom was silent save for the hum of an industrial vacuum cleaner.

'Well...' said Valkama, breaking the silence. 'It won't be the first time we've had to handle complicated cases by ourselves.'

'Lampinen,' said Harjunpää. 'What's this all about?'

'Apparently it's none of your business.'

'No, of course not,' said Harjunpää and stood up. His cheeks were tight; the events of the last few days were whirling inside him and he could feel a sense of stifling disappointment and anger beginning to raise its head. He would have liked to scream and shout, to break something.

'You know something, Lempi? If you'd bothered to back us up in that park we could have had him in custody by now. And besides... this whole investigation has been going nowhere because of your personal grudge.'

'That's a lie.'

'You'd better make sure nobody else ever sticks your head down the toilet. Klaus Nikander is going to gnaw away at you for ever and a day.'

'Just like your bird-man,' said Lampinen, stubbed his cigar in the ashtray and stood up. He left the room, his movements full of twitching anger. Visibly calmer, Juslin swaggered off behind him.

'Damn it!' Harjunpää snapped and took a few heavy steps.

He felt strangely stuffy, dirty and embarrassed, and it didn't make him feel any better when Valkama remarked coolly: 'We have to remember that we all fail sometimes. And our failures don't become any smaller if we start blaming other people for them.'

'No, of course not,' Harjunpää sighed and stepped into the corridor. He wanted to be by himself, at least for a while, anywhere. He headed down the corridor towards his office and hoped that not even Onerva would follow him.

He stood in the middle of the office and looked out at the horizon. Very slowly his mind settled and the feeling of embarrassment began to pass. But there was still something, something about the situation as a whole, a sense that somebody had to *do* something. But who? He thought for a moment and realised that the onus was on him. He didn't quite understand where his next thought came from but it was clear to him that he would have to speak to the chief of police. Maybe he had recalled something Tanttu had said in an interview about being a father to whom his subordinates could come like children to discuss family problems. Thinking realistically he knew that, despite his tiredness, he would be able to handle the situation properly. More than that, he knew that Tanttu was in a position to set up a task force that could take care of the case, and with any luck it wouldn't take them too long.

He strode off down the corridor, but the closer he came to Tanttu's office the more uncertain he became. He wondered whether it might be wise to leave it until the following day and to start with Ahomäki, but that would have been giving in and he was tired of giving in to everyone else. He resolutely pressed the buzzer on Tanttu's door and the green light came on immediately.

'Good morning.'

'Good morning,' Tanttu replied, a little coldly, perhaps. 'Word travels fast, I see.'

'Excuse me?'

'Please, sit down.'

Harjunpää sat down in a chair near Tanttu's desk and the strange stiffness Tanttu exuded put him on his guard. At that same moment he realised that Tanttu had in fact been expecting him.

'You have almost twenty years of unblemished service in the police force,' he began and glanced at the papers on his desk. There were two documents: a witness statement and a copy.

'That's right,' Harjunpää mumbled and a chill suddenly washed through him, that same feeling of guilt he'd once had as a child when he'd broken the window in the laundry room and had to go and talk to the caretaker.

'Have you been under any particular stress lately?' asked Tanttu, his voice betraying that this was a phrase he'd learned on some leadership course, but that the matter didn't interest him in the slightest. 'Burn-out?'

'Well, yes I mean… this case we're working on…'

'A police officer must be able to cope with the stress associated with a normal job. Otherwise you ask yourself whether that man is suitable for police work in the first place. And the rules stipulate that any man found to be unsuitable for the job can be relieved of his duties…'

Harjunpää couldn't say anything. The chill inside him deepened and perhaps the strangest thing was that he began to wonder whether he really had done something reprehensible. Was it because of his argument with Järvi or Lampinen? He suspected that he was being made a scapegoat for someone else, but there was still enough of the humble officer in him that he waited patiently for Tanttu to continue. On top of this he realised that he was the only member of his family in full-time employment.

'I'm not sure I understand…'

'I have here a complaint about you and your behaviour.'

'Yes?'

'The statement claims that last Sunday you behaved in an unprofessional and, shall we say, disrespectful manner to a woman who had reported finding a body. Then, in a most demeaning fashion, you proceeded to expose to the woman and her husband… your backside.'

'It wasn't like that…' Harjunpää gasped, his mouth dry. He didn't know quite how to continue and waved his hands in a vague expression of bewilderment. 'How on earth…?'

'That's what I'd like to know. Not least because this statement has been written by a person of considerable public standing.'

'We were out in Mustikkamaa. I almost drowned… But as for exposing my backside… I had to put my clothes on, I was freezing, and my boxer shorts were wet. I did ask them to leave several times.'

'I don't want to hear your explanations right now. I won't pass this on to the supers and the assessment board just yet. Write your own account of events and have it on my desk by Monday.'

'Sir, I really didn't…'

'Here's a copy of the statement.'

'Thank you.'

'Dismissed.'

'Thank you…'

Harjunpää staggered towards the door, his legs numb, and instinctively tried to read the statement straight away. He couldn't make out the text;

it seemed to jump frantically up and down in front of his eyes. He could just about make out one section: *"... in an obscene and indecent manner, with scant regard for even the most basic norms of polite behaviour..."*

He opened the door, stepped out into the corridor and almost walked into Kontio. The Bogey Man appeared to be heading for Tanttu's office, or maybe he had just been standing there by coincidence. In any case, he flicked his hand as if to let the matter pass, then muttered: 'And how is DS Harjunpää?'

'Well... can't complain.'

'Chin up, then.'

Light

Harjunpää sat barechested in the hazy afternoon heat and tried to concentrate on the only thing he could feel: the touch of Elisa's gentle hands, how they massaged his shoulders and neck, how the painful knots stopped aching and disappeared for a moment. His soul was in his shoulders. He breathed in the smell of grass, of the forest and late-summer flowers, and listened as a bumblebee buzzed somewhere nearby. Every now and then he managed to shut everything else out and concentrate on simply being. But then a chasm opened up inside him, a mixture of depression, failure and shame. He gave a deep sigh and his shoulder tensed again.

The worst of it was that it all felt so unfair, a lie masquerading as the truth, twisted so much with sly, carefully chosen words that at times he began to doubt himself. And yet, when he really thought about it, he had done the best he could. He always did. Still, doesn't everybody always think they did their best? He took another deep breath and moved as though he were trying to shake something from his skin.

'Timo,' said Elisa softly, without meaning anything in particular but simply to let him know that there was someone who loved him and cared about him, come what may, for better and for worse. Elisa didn't mean herself; she thought of herself as an intermediary. She meant God. It no longer puzzled Harjunpää. A year ago, when Elisa had found her faith, he had considered it almost an illness and feared that at any moment she might cover her head with a shawl and start preaching door to door.

It was a silly thought. Elisa had simply found an inner happiness, a peace of mind. She hadn't started foisting it on to other people, she simply

193

felt that God was *love*, and that that same love existed in all people, even evil people, that evil itself is merely a mental torment that prevents people from connecting with the immense powers within them.

And now, a year later, Harjunpää noticed that there were times he wished he could do the same as Elisa. He wanted to believe that someone was looking after them at every turn and that everything that happened had its own greater purpose that only revealed itself much later. But he couldn't. A doubt lived within him. Every day he witnessed things that made him doubt even more, and made him feel that everything was fundamentally meaningless and futile, a whimsical joke. But no matter what happened, Elisa's presence calmed him, as it did this time too. For all he knew she might be an instrument of the Lord after all.

'Are you sure you're OK to do this night shift?' she asked, a small nugget of care in her voice. 'Why don't you call Tupala and get someone to cover for you.'

'He went through the rota this morning. I should have realised this yesterday. There's been so much going on, I'd completely forgotten about it. How's Grandpa?'

'He's been fairly with it, actually. It's as though he's telling me things that he wants me to tell you.'

'Such as?'

'Well, what he was telling me yesterday about their separation. This morning was the first time he really talked about you and how difficult your mother made his arranged visits, how she kept to a strict timetable and if something came up and Grandpa couldn't make it then he'd miss the entire visit. She wouldn't let him reschedule for another time and he wasn't allowed to visit you at home.'

'I remember that all too well. Mother made me promise not to let him in the front door. In the winter I stood out in the street freezing waiting for him to turn up.'

'It's understandable that your contact eventually dried up altogether… He told me that at one point he just had to get on with rebuilding his life and he simply couldn't spend all his time at loggerheads with things that reminded him of everything he'd lost.'

'I was still his son…'

'But he said that when you stopped contacting him – you never called or sent a card – he started to believe that you hated him the same way your mother did.'

'Yes… that's probably partly true.'

'And on top of that, some doctor told him that he shouldn't make a spectacle of himself, that at some point children realise what's been going on and make contact of their own accord… Why don't you lie down and have forty winks?'

'I can't. Once I nod off, that's it. I might take that basket and have a walk in the woods, see if any trumpet chanterelles have come up yet.'

Harjunpää wasn't thinking so much of mushrooms as of Pilvikallio. Near the peak of the hillside was a small, mossy hollow where he liked to sit and think about things, and why not to have forty winks too. It was at the foot of Pilvikallio that Elisa had seen the light that she believed to be from Jesus.

Pint

Tweety could barely contain his desire to visit Brownie's apartment. It smouldered inside him, unabated, like a burning ember high in the decks of his mind, so sensitive that the flow of air as he walked made it glow, and that's why he was sitting in the evening darkness, perfectly still, on a bench next to a fountain.

He felt that he simply had to find out whether the police had found Brownie and his moped, whether he had lost them too or whether they had saved him, for he had gone there deliberately in an attempt to lose the police. When he'd seen the police lights behind him he'd heard a sudden shout; it was Brownie's voice and that's what had given him the idea. Perhaps she had wanted to make amends.

Thinking about it afterwards, there was more to his act than that: he had given up a sacrifice. He had relinquished something important to him, something that comforted him. He'd sacrificed her to the police, and through the police to God, because they were all on the same side just like priests and teachers. And he'd done it because he wanted forgiveness, for a short while at least, for as many days as it took to take care of the Chancellor, because he'd suddenly realised that it was no coincidence that the police had started chasing him: they'd been out hunting for him.

It was a frightening thought, though not as frightening as it had been. He'd gradually become used to the idea, he realised that he'd lived his entire life in the same situation. In the past he hadn't been sure of it, but now he was certain. It came almost as a relief: he knew there had to be a reason why he was so afraid. And because of this he knew he had to be on his guard. He'd always been afraid of the police, though he'd never had anything to do with them. He remembered how, as a child, the mere sight of a police car was enough to make him wet his trousers, which always meant a lashing with the belt when he got home. Over time he learned to sit in the stairwell for hours until his clothes had dried.

Tweety placed his hand on the bench and tried to sense whether a woman had been sitting there, whether her buttocks had been pressed against the surface of the wood, but he couldn't concentrate, and turned and glanced behind him. He could see nothing but trees and ragged darkness and streetlights further in the distance. Nobody was spying on him, because nobody would think to look for him here. He'd never started following anyone out of Kaisaniemi Park, though there was a restaurant there too, situated at the far end of the park. He thought of how he had lost the aquarium restaurant for good; he'd never be able to loiter outside it again – or Hotel Inter, for that matter.

He moved as though compelled by an inner force, picked up a stone and cast it into the fountain with a plop. He thought of his moped. It was strange; he'd always hated the thing, so much so that he hadn't even given it a name, but now that he didn't dare go and see whether it was still there he suddenly missed it. Reino had put it together from various parts salvaged from older mopeds and Lasse had sorted him out with a tax disc, and although he'd never told Tweety where he'd got his hands on it, he knew it was stolen. It had obviously been attached to something else before.

Tweety stood up but sat down again almost immediately, as though the force of the bench were greater than his own resolve. He guiltily rubbed his chin and cautiously began examining his thoughts and tried to open up the doors to the main deck – he wanted to see whether the glass chair and the velvet curtain were still there – but he couldn't find the hatch, the floor was nothing but solid wood. This had happened to him before, many times, and he didn't let it unduly worry him. He was worried for another reason: the woman that looked like Annie Lennox could have helped him, saved him because, as contradictory as it sounded given his current situation, although he yearned to be with Brownie, a desire to do something was gnawing away at him, a desire that he tried in vain to push beneath the surface but that kept bobbing up again like a polystyrene board.

He knew exactly what he wanted to do. He wanted to touch a woman, caress her bare skin or even just her hair, then inhale the sweet

smell on his fingers. He felt dizzy just thinking about it and started breathing more quickly like a chaffinch as it flies into a window, and all of a
sudden he thought of how tidy Wheatlocks' flat was, of how as a little boy
he'd had a teddy bear called Oskar, and how he used to draw his finger
through a candle flame, slower every time, and slow down even after his
finger had squealed in pain.

But he didn't want to ruin the Chancellor, and he'd been close to
doing just that. Reino was right, of course: he didn't want to lose his
chance for change, to screw up perhaps the only chance he'd ever had, and
though it took a considerable amount of willpower he pressed his slender
fingers together and prayed: *Dear God in Heaven. See us through the
Chancellor; please, let it be a success. Don't let us screw it up. Amen.*

He ran his hands through his hair in dismay. Just maybe his prayer had
ended up on a great answering machine in the sky that God would listen
to after his evening nap. He'd recognise Tweety's voice, of course, and
think, there's no point in bothering, just wait for your day of judgement
like everyone else. At least he'd tried. He'd tried in other ways too,
prepared himself, and in that he trusted himself rather more than God. He
had left the pouch at home. Without it he couldn't go anywhere, could-
n't get himself into any sticky situations.

And it wasn't only because of the Chancellor that his desires worried
him, but because he'd had an exceptionally long run of bad luck. It was as
though his luck were exhausted from working so hard and now it needed
a rest and wanted to lie low for a while. But still his desires kept rearing
their head, and he tried to hide from himself the fact that, despite everything, he was still planning on making an excursion somewhere that
night. It was completely nonsensical, as though a part of him wanted to
be caught, as crazy as it seemed. But when he stopped to think about it
that's not what it was about. He didn't want to get caught, but in some
way he wanted to experience the same as Kariluoto in *The Unknown
Soldier* after being hit by a bullet: *It's over now. Never again.* He'd read that
same passage many times, and each time it moved him just the same; they
were the most beautiful words ever written. *It's over now. Never again.*

He stood up again, and this time he wasn't held back by the force of
the bench but set off with brisk steps along the edge of the fountain. He
walked towards the theatre and continued along the alley at the side of the
building. He was thinking of beer and Alice. Despite her name, Alice

wasn't a woman. She might have been, but he'd never given the matter any thought. Once inside it was hard to tell which sex a building was. There might have been a drainage pipe running along the edge of the roof, and that made him suspect the bar was male, but it could just as easily have been a blood vessel, as buildings' veins were often on the outside, on the surface, and only as he was leaving and touched the door handle did he realise that it was clearly the touch of a woman's hand.

Tweety came out on to the Station Square and there were no police cars in sight. The fragmented jazz of the late-evening traffic rumbled past; a handful of people, runaway musical notes, were wandering around, and though he didn't like large open spaces he began striding across the deserted square, and it occurred to him that although his whole life he'd considered himself something of a coward, he was actually far from it. He was often afraid, but he wasn't a coward. It had something to do with the candle flame, and although he didn't fully comprehend the line of thought, he felt that he was doing the same thing, every moment of every day, and that one day he'd realise that the flame doesn't burn you after all. He felt that someone had been lying to him, lying to him, telling him that life is all about death.

He turned on to Keskuskatu, walked past the entrance to the underground, and the pillars stood right in front of him, holding up the entire building like a giant castle rising up into the sky. He was nervous, just enough, because he knew he was about to do something, though at the same time he wasn't; this he repeated to himself with every step. He was only going to have one pint.

He opened Alice's door and climbed the stairs up into the bar. The buzz of chatter hit him like a hail shower; cigarette smoke floated in the air and he could hear the babble of a television somewhere further off. Glasses clinked and somebody laughed. He approached the counter and tried to glance around casually: lots of women, all with soft thighs and round buttocks hidden beneath their clothes. One woman with pouting lips had hair that was stylishly ruffled. If only he could touch it, it would have been like eating candyfloss.

He waited for his turn. He didn't visits pubs very often because he always felt that everyone was staring at him or that he didn't know how to behave properly, that he'd knock his glass over. He managed to pick it up firmly and slunk further into the bar. He knew precisely where he wanted to sit; the space was generally free, as it was on this occasion too. Other people must have thought it an unpleasant place to sit: the toilets were right behind the table and right in the line of sight. They were next to one another, the women's toilet and the men's toilet, and neither of them had a proper door, only a curtain of beads. There were doors in each of the cubicles, but that was different.

Tweety sat on a high bar stool, shifted to make himself more comfortable and took a sip of beer. It tasted good, cold, the milk of the hop fields. This was another reason he didn't visit pubs very often: little amounts of alcohol made him drunk, sometimes all it took was one pint. And when he was drunk he felt that same falsified sense of safety, as though he wasn't Asko Leinonen after all, as though the entire Leinonen family didn't exist. At times like that he could have plucked up the courage to think and plan anything, and that was dangerous, because in that state of mind it was too easy to be careless.

A dark-haired woman in a red jumper walked into the toilets right in front of Tweety's nose. Her body was brimming with all the elements of womanhood he so admired: a white neck, bouncy little tits and a soft, swinging behind. A tantalising trail of her scent hung in the air and her high heels clip-clopped provocatively against the tiled floor behind the bead curtain.

Tweety knew that there were three cubicles in the women's toilet.

He took another sip from his pint. With his free hand he slowly caressed the smooth surface of the table.

Points of Origin

Harjunpää's clothes were heavy with the acrid smell of smoke. It wasn't the smell of a campfire or the aroma of a lakeside sauna. There was nothing good about this smell and that's why it troubled him; that and the fact that the same smell hung in the air in the coroner's lab downstairs. What troubled him even more was the fact that the fire had had two separate points of origin.

The first and seemingly primary point of origin was between an armchair and a bookcase where the victim had apparently been dozing and smoking his last cigarette, but the other was against the opposite wall, on the floor at the foot of the bed. What could explain this? Harjunpää hadn't noticed anything else that might indicate foul play and he'd been exceptionally thorough, firstly because his partner on this case was Virta, a young rookie at the first house-fire of his career, but also, entirely subconsciously, because of Luukkanen's formal complaint against him. He still had to come up with some kind of response.

He sighed and placed his bag of equipment on the grey stone floor, turned up the volume on his police radio and lay that on the floor too. He was always half-listening to the radio, expecting another job to come in or something else to happen at any moment. The coroner's men had done as they were told; they hadn't wheeled the body into cold storage yet, but had left him on the slab waiting for their return. He was lying on a gleaming steel stretcher, wrapped inside a plastic body bag. That's where the smell of the fire was coming from. Harjunpää pulled on a pair of disposable latex gloves and began to unzip the bag – and then he realised.

'It was the bookcase,' he said to Virta and almost gave a smile. 'The firemen said it had been knocked over when they arrived. And think about the fire pattern on the wall...'

'It went right up to the ceiling...'

'Exactly. And the side of the bookcase was charred right the way along. And the taps were running in the bathroom. And the body was lying by the front door.'

'He'd been trying to extinguish the fire and knocked over the bookcase in all the confusion.'

'Right, and the papers on the top shelf created the second point of origin. The fire pattern at that end was smaller because the fire started later. And as he was trying to put out the fire he was rushing around breathing in carbon monoxide all the while, which is absorbed into the bloodstream hundreds of times faster than oxygen, and that's why he couldn't make it into the stairwell...'

He gripped the body bag and yanked, and the tapes holding it together crackled as they came apart. There lay the body. It felt strange to think that only a few hours ago he was just someone who'd been pottering around all day, blissfully unaware that the world would come to an end that same evening. He wasn't in particularly bad shape – fire victims are often nothing but charred lumps set in a boxing position. He was red with some amount of blistering, and only on his legs, which had been facing the fire, were his muscles visible.

'Why do we need to examine him if...?'

'Let's look for any other injuries,' said Harjunpää, instinctively trying to hold his breath. 'Anything not caused by the fire. And anything that might give us an ID: scars, jewellery, that sort of thing. I'll turn him over. Take a look at his back.'

He took hold of the body by the arm and hip, and as he tilted it towards him something opened deep in its throat and gave out a long wheeze, almost a moan. Virta looked up at Harjunpää then leaned down to look at the victim's back, examined it slowly and finally shook his head. Harjunpää released his grip, laid the body in its original position and suddenly turned towards the radio.

'Did you hear what Control just said?'

'No... I mean, it was nothing for Crime Squad.'

'Wait a minute...'

Harjunpää peeled the gloves from his hands, bounded towards the radio and raised it to his mouth. He wasn't at all sure whether he'd heard what he thought he'd heard, and he was even less sure of the thought that leapt into his mind. It wasn't even really a thought, it was like an unripe apple, a hunch, but nonetheless he pressed down on the keyboard and called Control.

'Crime Squad, go ahead.'

'Just out of curiosity, what was the nature of the job 1-5-5 just took on Keskuskatu?'

'Some Peeping Tom wandered into the women's toilet and groped a customer.'

'What did he do?'

'He was behind a locked door in the middle cubicle. There's a hole in the wall and he'd stuck his hand through and tried to touch up the woman in the next cubicle.'

'Can you give me a description?'

'Not really, but he's in custody. The woman was sober and apparently she does karate. If she decides to press charges it'll be passed on to the bureau of investigations. Do you want his ID?'

'Yes, please,' said Harjunpää and hesitated for a moment. He wanted the suspect taken to a holding cell in Pasila; he wanted to see him for himself. But it all seemed too far-fetched, hope against hope, and he decided to let it pass and ended the call.

He gave Virta a brief explanation of what was going on, pulled on a fresh pair of gloves and began feeling the head beneath clumps of singed hair, but he couldn't find any obvious traumas or bumps, and when he brought his hand away there was no blood on his fingers. He then examined the victim's neck and chest, then continued downwards, but apart from burn injuries all he found were four bruises which, judging by their colour, had been there for some time. In addition to the legs, there were severe burns on his arms, another indication that the man had tried to put out the fire by himself.

'Just photograph him, then we're done,' said Harjunpää. 'General photos, arms and legs in particular. And the face, though nobody will be able to identify him. The Burns unit can come down tomorrow and try to get some fingerprints or a dental profile off him. They'll help make a positive ID.'

Virta took the camera out of his bag. Harjunpää went to the sink and washed his hands. He did this thoroughly, almost too thoroughly, as though there was something other than just talcum powder that needed to be removed from his hands, from himself, his life. He began towelling his hands and heard someone call for him on the radio.

'Crime Squad, this is 1-5-5 at the Alice bar on Keskuskatu. Do you copy?'

'This is Harjunpää. Copy.'

'You wanted a description of the suspect?'

'That's right.'

'About 165 centimetres tall, skinny with sharp facial features. Grey waist-length jacket and dark-grey trousers with a pair of scruffy trainers.'

Harjunpää didn't say anything for a moment. He couldn't say anything. He thought of the man he'd seen in the park and that had been described to him countless times, and he shuddered. Perhaps this was what it felt like when you got seven correct numbers on your lottery coupon and couldn't quite believe it was true.

'Is she going to press charges?' he asked, and his sense of disbelief deepened. It all seemed far too simple.

'Not by the sounds of it. She's a bit shaken up, that's all. There aren't really any grounds to bring a case against him. The cubicles are open at the top and apparently he just tried to stroke her hair.'

'OK. Take him to a holding cell in Pasila, just to verify his ID and as a suspect in one of our cases.'

'Copy that.'

'And just so you know, if it's the guy I'm looking for, he can run pretty fast.'

'I'll bear that in mind. Over and out.'

Harjunpää pulled down his jacket sleeves, and though he knew that there was still a possibility he was wrong, he no longer felt that nagging sense of hesitation. He was almost convinced that he would know the moment he saw the suspect himself; illuminated by flashes of lightning, he'd been able to make out the man's features quite well. He gripped the stretcher's cold handles and pushed the body towards the storage area, opened the door and pushed the trolley into the refrigerated area of the lab, frosty steam billowing from behind the door.

Another call came over the radio. This time it was Virta who answered: 'Crime Squad. Copy.'

'Get going as soon as you can,' came the voice from the clerk at the switchboard. 'There's been a stabbing at a flat at Eerikinkatu 29. Emergency services are on their way. We've already sent units 1-5-7 and 1-5-9.'

'Copy. We're leaving the coroner's lab now.'

'Suppose we'd better get going,' Harjunpää sighed and picked his bag up from the floor. He didn't need another call-out right now; he wanted to go straight back to the station, but it was always like this on shifts. As soon as something started to happen, everything happened at once. The beginning of the evening had been relatively quiet. The fire on Kankaretie had been the first job of the shift.

They stepped outside and the night-time air felt unbelievably good, so pure that you wanted to stand there sniffing it. They strode towards the Lada, Harjunpää threw his bag on the back seat and sat down behind the wheel. A moment later the engine roared into life and the car was on the move and swung down a steep ramp, the glare of its headlights sweeping across the darkness like two enormous, white fists.

'Put on the flashlight,' said Harjunpää. 'And ask Control for some specifics: the condition of the victim, the suspect.'

Virta opened the window and held out the flashlight bulb; Harjunpää flicked the switch and blue light began frantically licking the world around them.

'Control, this is Crime Squad. Have you got any more information on the victim and any possible suspect?'

'According to the emergency services the victim called for help by himself. Male, one stab wound to the side. Suspect unknown and still at large. No description yet. There was a woman in the flat too; she's a friend of the victim.'

'Anything else?'

'Apparently they were asleep, then they woke up as someone else tried to get into the bed. The victim ran after him and got himself stabbed in the stairwell.'

'Copy.'

Harjunpää steered the Lada abruptly on to Mannerheimintie; his stiff fingers gripped the steering wheel and his breath came in short bursts of disbelief. A swarm of curses flooded his mind, and after struggling with them for a moment he forced himself to believe it: their intruder had been at that flat and the man arrested at the Alice bar could have been anyone. It was just their luck that he matched the description of their suspect. The location fitted their man's territory too; so far the most southerly incident reported had been on Lönnrotinkatu.

He reached out his hand and Virta gave him the car radio.

'Control, this is Harjunpää. This incident may be linked to a series of cases we're working on. Give the officers on the scene the following description: male, twenty-five to thirty. Height no more than 170 centimetres; thin, slender build. Angular facial features. Probably wearing grey, colourless clothes. He's very fast on his feet and may be travelling by moped.'

'Got that. All units…'

'Damn it,' said Harjunpää. He switched on the siren and pressed his foot down on the accelerator. The street was almost deserted so he didn't need to drive along the tramlines, but sped along the right-hand lane. The road opened up ahead and the Lada hungrily devoured the tarmac beneath them.

As they were passing the parliament building, Control put out another call for them.

'Crime Squad, go ahead,' Virta yelled above the noise of the sirens.

'An ambulance is taking the victim to the hospital; his condition is stable. Unit 1-5-9 is at the scene and 1-5-7 is searching the surrounding area. And the woman that was there has taken off. Apparently she was a… you know. Maybe you'd be best off going straight to the hospital so you can question the victim before he goes into surgery. His name's Kai Orvo Johannes Retula.'

Virta looked enquiringly at Harjunpää, who nodded and said: 'Tell them to send Forensics down there too. Thurman's on duty, he knows what to do.'

Harjunpää turned off the siren but left the blue lights flashing. They had already reached Erottaja. He steered the car on to the Esplanade and the shop windows lit up with the emergency lights flashing like the beat of a fearful heart. They were almost at the hospital. Harjunpää took a right on to Kasarminkatu and the Lada began the slight incline towards the hospital. An ambulance pulled out of the forecourt; Harjunpää steered the Lada up on to the pavement and parked by the right-hand wall.

'Crime Squad,' Harjunpää said quietly to the medical officer and showed him his badge. There were a couple of people waiting in the lobby: a drunken man holding his bloody face and an old lady sobbing to herself.

'If it's possible, we'd like to talk to the stabbing victim who just arrived from Eerikinkatu... Mr Retula.'

'Oh him,' the man replied, and for a moment his expression was somehow strange, hesitant, as though he wanted to say something but realised that he wasn't supposed to.

Harjunpää had to ask: 'He is still alive?'

'Oh yes. Very much so. Our doctor is over there.' The man clomped down the corridor in his wooden shoes and stopped beside a dark-bearded doctor who was standing reading some papers, muttered a few hushed words, and the doctor looked up at Harjunpää and Virta.

'It's fine to go in there,' he said. 'His little run-in hasn't left him with any life-threatening wounds. There's one stab wound to the lower right costal arch that just managed to puncture the stomach wall. We'll operate to be on the safe side and make sure he hasn't sustained any bleeding or internal injuries. We're prepping him for theatre, so if you could keep it brief.'

'Is there anything else?' Harjunpää asked without really knowing why. Was there something unusual about the doctor's expression, something he was hiding?

'No, nothing out of the ordinary. Have you apprehended the stabber?'

'I'm afraid not. We do have a nameless suspect.'

'I see,' the doctor chuckled dryly and began walking away. Harjunpää didn't understand what was so funny, unless the man was simply mocking their inefficiency.

He didn't stand around thinking about this for long. He proceeded down the corridor; he knew his way around from years of experience. The hospital smell in the air seemed stronger than before, and somewhere nearby he could hear the hum of a machine and a faint beeping. Retula was lying on a bed curtained off from the rest of the ward. The blonde nurse recognised Harjunpää, nodded and moved away from the bed. Harjunpää approached the patient.

Retula's chest was bare and a dressing with a faint trace of blood had been applied to the area the doctor had mentioned. His eyes were closed and his face was pale and gaunt; his chin was dotted with light stubble, and for a brief moment Harjunpää had the distinct impression that he knew the man or that he'd seen him before somewhere. The feeling passed as quickly as it had appeared.

'DS Harjunpää from the Violent Crimes unit. Looks like you've had quite a night. If you could tell us briefly what happened.'

The man didn't respond. He kept his eyes firmly shut but his eyelids were twitching restlessly and his breathing became shallower as though he were afraid of something. The events were so fresh that trying to remember them could set off a panic attack.

'Did you hear me? Was it your apartment?'

'Yes,' the man replied in a weak voice. 'I woke up when the girl started screaming... And then... She said some bloke had been trying to touch her up. I thought I saw someone going towards the hallway. I went after him and... then he turned around and slashed me.'

'Can you describe this man?'

'Not really. It was so dark.'

'Was he tall? Short?'

'I don't know,' he panted as if he were about to burst into tears. 'It all happened so quickly...'

'OK,' Harjunpää sighed. 'So who was this girl you were with?'

'How should I know their names?'

'I don't follow.'

'I picked her up in a bar. She was a tart, if you know what I mean.'

'Which bar were you in?'

'That one in the park next to the parliament building. I can't think anymore...'

'Just bear with me a moment longer. Have you ever seen the woman there before? She must have gone by some name...'

'What was it she called herself...? Veera. I feel a bit faint.'

'All right,' said Harjunpää resignedly. 'I'll be in touch in the next few days. Good luck to you.'

Harjunpää straightened his back and turned around. He felt strangely unsatisfied, disappointed, even though talking to victims in situations like this was often entirely futile. On top of this he had a feeling – not even a feeling, but a vague notion, like a dream that you remember vividly when you wake up in the middle of the night – a hunch that everything was not as it seemed, that somewhere a cog was turning in the wrong direction.

'Let's go back to the flat on Eerikinkatu,' he said flatly.

Favour

Lampinen walked into his office, followed by Juslin, placed his radio on the desk and took off his parka. This, his jeans and his knee-high laced bovver boots were items of clothing he wore only when he was on a job at night; during the daytime he always wore a three-piece suit, a shirt and a loosely knotted tie.

He hung his jacket in the wardrobe, glanced over at his partner and gave a broad smile. He was in a very good mood; he laughed to himself, soft rippling laughter that bubbled from inside him and wouldn't stop. It was catching; Juslin gave a quiet chuckle, then a series of chuckles, but his expression remained more serious than Lampinen's.

'Quite a prank,' said Lampinen once he'd sat down, almost to reawaken his laughter. It didn't develop further than a smile. He took out his box of Café Crèmes, carefully licked one of the cigars and lit it. It tasted slightly bitter; it was still the middle of the night. They had been out keeping an eye on key locations in preparation for the following night's hit as part of Operation Spray, though so far this had yielded only meagre results. They hadn't yet caught a single culprit. Still, this hadn't been their top priority in the first place, they had merely wanted to go over the stake-out locations and check that there would be enough light.

Lampinen put his feet up on the table and sat there looking at his shoes. Society was full of people like him, men and women, accepted, intelligent, often successful and popular in their own circles. On the surface they were good people, like everyone else, like almost everyone. But there was something else about them too, or rather something was missing, something big. They lacked the ability to feel guilt, true attachment and empathy, the ability to understand how other people feel. To them, questions of good and bad were simply matters of expediency: if someone ended up suffering, all too often they thought that that person had *deserved it*.

But because this deficiency had nothing to do with intelligence, Lampinen had succeeded in educating himself, taking care of his work and shadier dealings, which had accumulated throughout his career, in such a way that, if anyone had ever cottoned on to what he was up to, he would always have been able to prove his innocence, and if the matter had gone to the magistrates, he would have been the one walking out of court with a hefty damages payment.

In different circumstances he could have become a killer, a member of parliament or even a government minister. With no children of his own he could have picked on families with children, gradually doing away with all the benefits the state shelled out to them, and could have argued his point in such a way that half the nation would have clapped their hands and thought what an upright man Minister Lampinen really was.

But Lampinen wasn't in the government; he was a detective sergeant. His cigar was almost finished and he squashed it in the ashtray. Then he remembered something and clicked his fingers.

'What have we forgotten?'

'To go home.'

'No… the guy they brought in from the bar downtown. We ought to take a look at him.'

'True.'

'We could interview him too. You know, in a preventive sense. Just in case he's planning anything nasty…'

The men looked at one another for a long, significant moment. In a strange, devious way they complemented one another: despite everything, Lampinen needed someone to whose stature he could aspire and whose physical presence and qualities he could assume as his own. What made it even better was that, in his own way, that other person admired him and silently obeyed his every word. Juslin had always wanted to have the gift of the gab, but he could only achieve this in certain situations, and even then he knew that it was only a façade, a bluff, something to mask his pain. Moreover, for some reason he simply enjoyed being Lampinen's partner.

Lampinen clicked his fingers a second time, as though he were knocking a hammer against the table to confirm an auction sale, then he swung his feet to the floor, took his jacket, grabbed his radio from the desk and left. Juslin trudged silently behind him. They walked down to the cells and took the lift to the bottom floor where the reception for those taken into custody was situated together with a number of offices and bleak holding cells used as temporary housing for those brought to the station.

Lampinen marched up to the security guard sitting behind a computer monitor.

'Evening all. I hear you've got a bloke here who was apprehended on Keskuskatu and is waiting for an officer from Violent Crimes. I'd like to see him.'

'Hasn't he been assigned to Harjunpää?'

'Yes, but we're all working the same case.'

'He's in number seven.'

'Vielen Dank.'

Lampinen turned and made his way down the desolate corridor. The air was thick with the smell of people and problems. Lampinen glanced up at the numbers painted on the green steel doors. Eventually he stopped, lifted his finger in front of his mouth and pushed the cover from across the peephole to one side.

He silently pressed himself against the door, closed one eye and squinted inside. He stared at the man for a long time, well over a minute, and as he finally pushed himself away from the door he nodded to Juslin. He only spent a few moments at the peephole, straightened up and looked at Lampinen.

'Small and skinny,' he said quietly. 'Grey clothes. And very scared. He's almost trembling in there.'

'And his face partly resembles the one in the photofit. Particularly the nose – it's sharp as a beak. We don't know for sure that he's the right man...'

'But he's definitely done something pretty bad in his life.'

'Right...'

The men were silent for a moment and stood looking at one another. Then Lampinen asked, 'Just out of interest: if you'd done something, would you rather take a whipping that would be over in a few minutes or rot away for years on the inside?'

'I think I'd go for the whip. And besides, I'd be making amends for my deeds, as the taxpayer wouldn't have to keep me in prison.'

'Exactly,' said Lampinen. He walked down the corridor and round the corner, stopped, brought the radio up to his mouth and pressed the button.

'Crime Squad, Harjunpää, this is Lampinen. Copy.'

'Copy. We're at a stabbing on Eerikinkatu.'

'We were just passing through the holding cells and there's a bit of confusion going on. There's a bloke down here waiting for you and making a hell of a fuss, saying he's been arrested for no good reason. If you want, we can transfer him upstairs on our way if you've got a warrant.'

'No… Just let him go. And tell him I'm sorry. Give him a ride home if you can. Make sure to photograph him just in case.'

'Very magnanimous of you. Where's this sprung from all of a sudden?'

'He really is innocent. Based on the descriptions we've got, I thought he was our intruder, but now we've got a fresh case.'

'Well… As you wish.'

'Thank you.'

'Don't mention it in the least. We'll be happy to do you a favour.'

Lampinen turned down the volume on the radio and glanced at Juslin.

'Let's go through his things first, just to see if he's got any lock-picking equipment on him. Then we'll take him home.'

Winkie

Tweety was sitting in the back of a car and he was afraid. The fear was like a hole in his head, spewing out silent, bright red screams.

The Big Man was sitting next to him. The one driving was smaller, yet he seemed somehow more dangerous. Outside it was dark. Night.

The Big Man sat with his legs apart; he smelled of sweat and unwashed clothes, the way his father used to smell when he came back from work, and didn't speak to Tweety. Whenever they rounded a corner the Big Man leaned closer to him, sometimes shoving him with the length of his wretched side, crushing Tweety's arm painfully against the door.

The Little Man didn't say anything either, but every now and then he looked at Tweety in the mirror – he'd turned it so that he could see him properly – and if Tweety looked back at him the man's eyes were like pipes with the faint glimmer of blood at the other end.

The inside of the car smelled of hotdog wrappers and farts; every so often the Little Man would raise one buttock and let off without trying to hide it in the least. Tweety wanted to open the window but didn't dare.

He couldn't concentrate on anything; what had happened in Alice, what it had felt like being in the police car and put in a cell. His mind was racing with the thought that he might still be caught. He'd given them false details – the details themselves weren't false but they belonged to someone else – but he'd slipped up when they'd said they were taking him home. He realised he'd got away with it and the sense of relief was too great: he'd told them he lived at Joutsentie 3. Reino would be there, Mother Gold too. What if the two men walked him into the house and told them what he'd been up to? He fidgeted anxiously, and more screams started showering out of the hole in his head, but the men didn't pay any attention to them. He surreptitiously wiped the droplets from his legs.

The car slowed noticeably. It swayed as they took a sharp turning, then proceeded at walking pace. The mudguards brushed the ground and hay rattled against the chassis; branches scraped against the sides of the car. He couldn't see the streetlamps any more, but the Little Man had put the headlights on full beam and moths glowed in the light like snowflakes. Tweety didn't have the faintest idea where they were; perhaps the Little Man was taking some kind of shortcut.

They were soon in front of a small hillock at the top of which stood a house. It was pitch dark. Tweety looked more closely at the house and saw that it was just the body of a house, nothing but walls and a roof. Where the windows should have been there were gaping black holes, just like Brownie's eyes, and the front door was missing altogether. The ground was strewn with pieces of wood, dead items of furniture and spiritless bottles. Tweety started to tremble. He couldn't control it; it was as though he were filled with soft springs that had started vibrating by themselves.

The Little Man stopped the car and pulled the handbrake. He produced a long, black torch that looked like a baton, got out of the car and started walking towards the house. Tweety's eyes followed the man as though he were the only thing in the world. He switched on the torch and walked around the building. He spent a long time behind the house, perhaps the path was blocked with bushes or rubble, but then he reappeared, walked up the steps and disappeared inside the black door-opening.

'You're a real pervert, aren't you,' the Big Man said suddenly, his voice like a cracked block of concrete, before shoving him with his elbow so that he knocked against the door. 'Answer me! Are you a pervert?'

'No...'

'You're lying! You know what happens to liars?'

'No. I mean, yes. I'm sorry. I'm sorry.'

'Well, are you a pervert or not?'

'Yes.'

'Fucking hell,' the Big Man almost spat out the words and backed off in disgust. 'I don't even want to touch you...'

The Little Man came out of the house and began walking back towards the car. He'd lit a cigar; its burning end glowed in the darkness like a dragon's eye, and suddenly Tweety was certain he was going to die. He didn't quite understand how he knew this, but the notion filled him with such certainty and his mind was flooded with a wave of unbearable melancholy. He'd experienced something like this before; perhaps it had been in a previous life.

The Little Man stopped beside the back door of the car and opened it.

'Make room, please,' he said. He was being strangely polite and he seemed somehow amused, but his politeness was a lie. It stank of lies, the Little Man was nothing but lies, through and through, and that must have been why Tweety had thought he seemed so dangerous.

He barged his way into the back seat and sat down, forcing Tweety to move closer to the stench of the Big Man who didn't move an inch. There he was, squashed between them. It felt as though a fire was burning inside him. The decks of his mind were all ablaze; sailing boats burned so easily and nobody was ever rescued from the flames.

'Confess to us,' said the Little Man. 'It'll help.'

'What do you want me to…?'

'Tell us what you've been up to,' the Big Man snapped. 'Tell us, pervert!'

'I went into the toilet and… She had such pretty hair, it was like candyfloss…'

'Fuck that. We're not interested in what you get up to in the toilet.'

'Admit what you've been doing for the last few years.'

'Nothing,' Tweety gasped, and in a flash he realised that they knew after all, that he'd been caught. His veins seemed to turn to ice and he started coughing.

'Tell us about your lock-picking.'

'I don't know anything… Honestly.'

'Where's your moped?'

'Moped?'

'Are you a pervert?'

'Yes.'

'You're a fucking pervert and we know what you've been up to.'

'Ever heard of the EC?'

'No… I mean… the European Community?'

'That's right. They use the death penalty, you know. And it came into effect in Finland a month ago.'

'No…'

'Oh yes,' said the Little Man with a chilling certainty and looked him right in the eyes. Then he got out of the car, pulled his jacket to one side to reveal a short-barrelled revolver on his belt. It looked like a rabid black dog.

'Get out,' he ordered Tweety; he no longer sounded polite or amused. It was as though the dragon that had lit up his eyes had disappeared inside him, and now his expression was cruel and somehow content.

'Start walking towards the house. And just you try making a run for it, just you try,' he said tapping his gun. Tweety stepped towards the shell of a house and both men followed behind him. A torn rubber boot and a baby's blue dummy lay on the ground; the light of the torch hovered across the path and several times the shadow of a long baton was cast across the beam of light.

Tweety went up the steps almost in a trance. Shards of glass crackled beneath his feet; the air smelled of mould and timber and wet sawdust. Tweety stopped at the threshold. He didn't want to step inside, it would have been like stepping into his own grave, but someone shoved his back. He stumbled forwards a few metres, regained his balance and turned around.

The men aimed the torch directly at his eyes and he wondered whether they were going to shoot him, whether he would even register the sound of the gunshot, then the Little Man shouted: 'Take off your trousers. Lie down on your stomach over there. Arse this way.'

Tears began to trickle down Tweety's cheeks as he took hold of his belt buckle and began fumbling to undo it.

Tweety walked out into the yard. He was five years old. He was wearing the brown breeches his mother had sewn, one of Lasse's old shirts and the plimsolls he'd got from Uncle Eino. They were beautiful clothes, nobody else had clothes as beautiful as these, and it felt good running in his plimsolls. With them on his feet he could fly. He could fly better than all the children in the yard. He jumped around lightly, but didn't take off. He didn't want to do that just yet.

And he was beautiful. Marjaana had said so. He knew he was a good boy: he had a key round his neck to prove it. It hung from a piece of blue string and it was a real key, but it didn't fit any of the doors. Lasse's key fitted, but he was already seven. When he came home, Tweety had to knock on the door because he couldn't reach the doorbell. If he stood on tiptoes he could only just touch it.

There was no one outside yet. It was too early. It was Sunday morning; he knew that because Mother and Father had stayed in bed and because the morning was Sunday-coloured, it even smelled of Sunday. It smelled of spring too. The trees in the park nearly had leaves on them, but he wasn't allowed to go into the park without permission. He didn't want to go either. There was grass in the yard too; it was growing beside the garage between the wall and the tarmac.

He ruffled his wings and flew across the yard. He flew all the way to the back door of Loviisa's little café and landed on the ground outside. He saw a ladybird. He wanted to pick it up, he wanted to sing it into flight, but it scurried around so fast and was too slippery. And it might wee on his hand. Ladybird wee was bright yellow and it stank.

He hopped over towards the wooden barrels. They were filled with food. Any food left over from the café was brought down to Loviisa's house and she fed it to the pigs. One time, he and Pekka fished pieces of bread out of the barrels and spread them with pigeon poo. But they only pretended to eat them.

The door opened. It was the caretaker's door; it squealed as though someone had hurt it. Pekka lived there. Pekka's father was the caretaker and he was a strong man. Tweety came out from behind the barrels. But it wasn't Pekka: it was Marjaana, and she saw him straight away.

'Hi.'

'Hi.'

'What are you doing in there?'

'There was a rat here a minute ago.'

'No there wasn't.'

'But there was a ladybird.'

'Our dad's already seen a swallow. Lots.'

'So's ours. And so's our mum.'

Marjaana walked up to Tweety. Her hair was almost white and reached down to her shoulders. She was wearing a red checked dress but no shoes whatsoever, and Tweety was a bit disappointed. He wasn't allowed to walk around barefoot in the city, only in the countryside, but even there it always hurt at bit at first. He pretended not to notice that Marjaana wasn't wearing any shoes. He took hold of the string round his neck and started swinging his key back and forth. Marjaana was only four.

'What shall we do?'

219

'Let's be pigeons.'

'I don't like that. Let's play house.'

'No,' said Tweety and started jumping up and down on one foot. He wondered whether Pekka might come out and see him.

'Let's be flying deer,' he suggested.

'I don't know. Do you want me to show you?'

'Show me what?'

'The thing I promised I'd show you.'

Tweety was suddenly so happy that he clapped his hands together.

'Look,' he shouted and ran off towards the garage door, his hands flailing behind him.

'I'll show you my winkie if you want.'

'OK,' said Tweety, and he really did want her to show him. He felt a bit nervous. It felt the same as the time when he and Pekka stole a box of matches from the laundry room.

'What if someone comes out?'

'Let's go in there.'

They ran across the yard and in behind the rubbish bins. It was a good hiding place, though it was sometimes a bit smelly. Marjaana lifted up her dress and pulled down her knickers. Tweety bent down and looked. Marjaana's winkie was a short, vertical slit. It didn't have any hair growing around it. Mother's winkie did, and so did Auntie Liisa's. He'd seen that in the sauna. But it was nice to look at, it made him feel funny. He was a bit embarrassed and his willy felt strange. It was jutting out. It did that sometimes.

Marjaana pulled her dress down and Tweety stood up.

'I want to put something in it,' he said.

'Like what?'

'Don't know.'

'Go on then. That stick?'

Tweety was disappointed; he though Marjaana was stupid, but he couldn't think of anything better and picked the stick up from the ground. It wasn't a wooden stick but a piece from the handle of a broken rug-beater. Marjaana lifted up her dress again and pulled open the top of her knickers. Tweety dropped the stick into her knickers and it stayed there propped up against her stomach.

'Now can we play house?'

'Let's be pigeons.'

'No… It tickles my tummy when I walk. It hurts.'

'Let's take it out.'

'No. I'm going home to tell Mum.'

'Don't do that,' said Tweety and held Marjaana by the hands the way they always did when they played house.

'I'm going home.' Marjaana started to cry, ran up to the door and opened it. Tweety was scared. You weren't supposed to play things like that. He hopped from one foot to the other, but it was no fun. Then he sprinted to the stairwell and hid in the attic doorway.

Victim

'Damn it,' Harjunpää snapped as though after careful consideration. He sat up abruptly, forgetting where he was, and bashed his shoulder against the sauna bench with the full force of his anger, groaned and slumped back on to the mattress. The matter itself hadn't changed a bit; it still plagued him as it had before, a flickering mess somewhere between realisation and disbelief. He lay where he was a moment longer and thought about the bra they'd found in Retula's flat on Eerikinkatu, hanging on the back of a scuffed wooden chair at the foot of the bed as if it had been forgotten after hurriedly undressing and an even more hurried escape. At least, this was what he'd believed at first because it seemed logical and fitted the pattern.

But the bra was so ugly, large, brown and plain, just another item of clothing, the kind that old women wear. No prostitute would have worn anything like that – unless they were paid to do so. And even through his latex gloves he'd been able to feel that the fabric was hard and stiff, and right then he realised, the following morning, that clothes felt like that when you didn't use fabric softener and took them straight from the clothes line.

He got up again and pulled out his earplugs, went into the bathroom, felt the clothes hanging there drying and sniffed the air. The other thing was the perfume. Thinking about it afterwards, the flat had stunk of perfume; normally it was only barely perceptible in the air. Of course, Retula's girl might have sprayed herself with perfume immediately before leaving the flat, but under the circumstances it was hardly likely, what with the man sustaining stab wounds and the police on their way, and given that she was clearly in a hurry to disappear. Agitated, Harjunpää turned on the shower and, though his body was still drained and sleepy after his night shift, began busily scrubbing himself. He couldn't yet make out the whole scenario – he hadn't even tried – but he was no longer in any doubt that something was out of place. Badly.

With only a towel tied around his waist he went downstairs. He wanted to call in without delay. His thoughts were running ahead of him; he was already on his way to Helsinki. To calm himself down he told himself he would only pop in for a few hours, three at most. The downstairs floor was empty. The door to the garden was open, letting the yellow afternoon light and the full scent of summer flood inside. He could hear the clink of coffee cups, Pipsa giggling, and Grandpa's booming voice as he sang her an age-old nursery rhyme.

Harjunpää dialled the number for the Forensics office. To his relief, it was Häyrinen who answered. He was a slightly older officer who specialised in fingerprints and treated every detail with a scientific thoroughness.

'Thurman processed the scene,' Harjunpää explained. 'He wrote up the crime-scene report this morning. I'm particularly interested in any observations he made about the lock.'

'Hang on,' mumbled Häyrinen. Harjunpää heard a thud as the officer laid the folder on the table, followed by the steady flick of pages.

'Here it says that there were no marks on the inside of the lock, so he didn't pick it, but there are a couple of scratches on the bolt that are consistent with some sort of hook. And... here we are, Thurman's left you a note. He says that, as you know, a hook was used on several previous occasions, most notably at the scene at Messeniuksenkatu 10, but that these marks differ in that they're stronger. As he sees it, in all the previous cases the intruder took the time to understand the lock, but this time he almost forced it open...'

'Thank you,' said Harjunpää as he fiddled with the telephone cable, his eyes nothing but slits. 'I'd like us to go back to the scene straight away. Near the window there was a low table with an empty wine bottle and two glasses. I want the fingerprints off them.'

'No problem. We've still got the keys to the flat.'

'And if possible, I want to know whether there are two sets of prints or whether only one person touched them.'

'That's fine. I'll attach a note to the case file.'

'One other thing. There's still a strong smell of perfume in the flat. Now, I'm not entirely sure about this but... I've got a feeling there'll be a bottle of perfume somewhere in the kitchen. If you find one, smell it, and if it's the same as the smell in the flat I want prints off that too.'

'Consider it smelled and printed. Anything else?'

'No, that's all. Thanks in advance.'

The bay window in the surgical hospital waiting room was a nice retreat amidst all the quiet background noise. There was an old white table and wooden chairs in the same style, and what's more, a verdant, leafy palm tree reaching up to the ceiling. But still Harjunpää couldn't relax; the agitation he'd felt earlier had turned into something approaching anger – at least, it made him grind his teeth together almost bullishly – and perhaps he was afraid of where all this might lead. He was nervous too, for he knew he was about to do something illegal, something that could have him up on all sorts of charges.

He gripped his clipboard more tightly. Clipped at the top were the incident report regarding the stabbing and a couple of interview transcripts, but he didn't need them, they were just for show. He stood up again and walked to the corner of the corridor, pretending to glance over his papers, and peered into the reception office. The nurse was still there, the same gangly young girl Harjunpää had asked for Retula's room number. Just as when Harjunpää had checked on her a moment ago, the girl looked like she was just about to leave the office. And that was precisely what he was waiting for.

Harjunpää had examined the door to Retula's room. It was one of the few two-person rooms in the hospital, and at that moment Retula was there by himself. The man in the bed next to him had been wheeled out a few minutes earlier. Harjunpää hoped he'd been taken for an X-ray, anything, so long as he was gone for about the next twenty minutes.

Finally the girl picked up a sheet of paper and left the office. Harjunpää started making his way down the corridor, and quickly slipped past a grey door that had been left ajar. He could hear the nurses' conversation coming from inside, and from that room it would only take them a few seconds to reach the reception office, but he was almost there. He quickly glanced behind him and stepped through the open door into the office. The room was empty.

He walked straight towards the filing cabinets along the left-hand wall. He knew that what he wanted was in there, he'd even seen it on his last visit, and it was still in the same place: right at the end of the top shelf. Without a moment's hesitation he grabbed the folder containing Retula's patient history, which was exceptionally thick and heavy, and began flicking through the papers inside. He wasn't looking for any specific information; all he needed was an overview. Over the years Retula had been the victim of all manner of different accidents.

Claims he fell against a bookcase and the shattered glass slashed... Slipped on the pavement and smashed his right wrist against the curb... Claims an unknown man stabbed him in the thigh just above the left knee... Fell out of bed and landed on a bottle, which as it smashed... Unknown woman waving a breadknife which slashed across the... Harjunpää glanced through the rest of the documents. Retula had claimed to be the victim of an attack on five separate occasions, four of which were suspected stabbings while in the fifth attack he sustained a broken rib after a hammer blow to the chest.

He could hear the clip-clop of footsteps approaching the office. He quickly closed the folder and replaced it in the filing cabinet. Then he stepped towards the desk and leaned over it scratching his head. The tall nurse looked puzzled as she appeared at the door.

'Sorry about this,' said Harjunpää. He didn't even need to pretend to sound surprised. 'Typical – my pen ran out. I wondered whether I could borrow one...'

'I'm sure that can be arranged,' the girl smiled. 'Here. Keep it.'

'Thank you. This is just my luck. The ribbon in my typewriter always runs dry when I'm in the middle of an interview, and if I've got a spare then it's the correction fluid or something else.'

He waved his hand, left the office and hurried off towards Retula's room. He couldn't see any nurses in the corridor wheeling the man's roommate back. Now he understood why both the medical officer and the doctor had behaved so strangely the previous night, as though there was something abnormal about the case that they had noticed but which patient confidentiality prevented them from even hinting at.

And all of a sudden Harjunpää came to a stop; he realised why he'd thought Retula looked so familiar. He had seen the man's photograph. It was years ago, but now he remembered everything clearly and tried to recall the words that had accompanied the image. The photograph had been posted on the bulletin board at the Violent Crimes office and beneath it read the words: "Retula, Kai Orvo Johannes. Thirty-four years of age. Currently of no fixed abode. If this man is the victim of an assault, look for the following…"

Harjunpää stepped inside. Retula was lying in his bed, perfectly still. He looked grey and miserable. His face was turned towards the ceiling and his eyes were closed. An intravenous drip glinted in the air.

'Kai,' said Harjunpää and stopped beside the bed. Retula opened his eyes and looked at him. He clearly recognised Harjunpää and took fright; he shut his eyelids tightly and turned his head to one side as though he had fainted, but Harjunpää wasn't going to be fooled again. He wasn't sure how to proceed; it was clear that the man was ill, that his soul was inhabited by a difficult and complex pain, and Harjunpää didn't want to do anything that might exacerbate it and possibly make the man in front of him clam up for good.

'I see you remember me,' he said softly and pulled a chair up to the side of the bed. 'I'm Harjunpää, the policeman you saw last night. And I want to be completely honest with you: in a way, we already know one another. You've reported being stabbed before, isn't that right?'

He looked at Retula in silence. The man had clearly heard and understood what he'd said. He intuitively licked his lips and the fingers of his hand hanging over the side of the bed were trembling. Harjunpää would have liked to let him think about this a while longer but didn't dare – he knew he wouldn't get anywhere if the others came back. For Retula, the presence of other people would have been too much.

'Let me remind you that the statement you made yesterday makes you a legal claimant and that claimants are under a statutory obligation to tell the truth.'

Again he paused. Retula's legs twitched restlessly.

'I could ask you to go over what you told me last night, but I think that would mean you'd have to lie to me. Kai, I know all about your previous stabbings. I know what's going on…'

The sound of footsteps and someone pushing a trolley came from the corridor, but eventually moved past the door, and Harjunpää took a relieved breath. He remembered that the text on the bulletin board had asked officers to pay particular attention to Retula's clothes because no cuts or tears had ever been found in them, though judging by the position of the wound and the victim's account there ought to have been some damage. Suicidal people almost always undress the area they are about to stab. This time, however, Retula had been naked.

'Harming yourself isn't a crime. Nobody can be punished for it. Now that there's nobody listening, you can tell me, then we don't need to take it any further. Did you stab yourself?'

'Yes,' Retula answered almost inaudibly. Tears ran from his eyes making him look even more miserable. Harjunpää felt oddly hazy, as he had no intention of leaving Retula just yet, and neither had he promised to do so.

'Where's the knife now?'

'I threw it in the bin when I went out to the ambulance.'

'And what about the woman?'

'There was no woman.'

'And no night out?'

'No...'

Harjunpää let him weep. He stared at his hands and wondered what it was that made people harm themselves. The first reason that came to mind was anger, perhaps towards someone else, an anger that erupted from time to time. Either that, or Retula truly hated himself. Harjunpää had heard many cases like that too.

'Maybe what you really need is a little care,' he said finally. 'Treatment. Someone to look after you.'

'Y—yes... If only there was someone... sometimes...'

'Everybody needs love, it's only natural, and not everyone gets it at home. Some have never experienced it at all... Tell me. How did you come up with this story of how it all happened?'

'It was the first thing that came to mind,' Retula answered, and the composure of a moment ago was suddenly gone. He seemed more agitated, and Harjunpää knew he shouldn't force the issue. He realised that if he wanted to get to the bottom of this he'd have to sit with Retula for hours, over a long period of time. And it was clear to him that this was exactly what he would do.

'You see, that's just a bit hard to believe.'

'Or did I read about it in the paper... similar cases, that sort of thing?'

'No, that isn't true,' said Harjunpää. The police hadn't released any statements to the press regarding the case, because if the intruder had read them he would have been on his guard and might have started another spate of break-ins somewhere else.

'You've been in and out of prison before,' he said as though he knew the details of all the cases. He was annoyed at himself for not doing a more thorough background check on Retula beforehand.

'Just petty stuff... Fraud mostly. And I've done my time.'

'Someone's blackmailing you,' Harjunpää exclaimed abruptly. Retula flinched and quickly shook his head, then he swallowed hard, his Adam's apple bulging in his thin neck, and with that Harjunpää was sure of it. He couldn't begin to imagine what kind of hold Lampinen had over the man.

An Irreconcilable Crime

'He's over here,' Bamse hollered from the workshop door to someone standing in the yard. Tweety recognised her voice – nobody else had a voice like hers, only the swans might have done if they'd been able to talk – and he knew she couldn't be referring to him because he didn't really exist. It amused him. So did the fact that he used to be so afraid of death, that the others were still afraid, and yet they'd experienced this same thing too, the feeling of not really existing, the state every human inhabited millions of years before their birth.

'Hey, he's over here. I can see his feet under those rags!' Bamse shouted with her back to him. He was lying on the floor next to the far wall of the workshop, on his side, huddled as small as possible, his body almost the shape of an egg. He'd pulled a pile of old sacks over himself; their smell reminded him of digging for worms round the back of Aunt Suoma's cottage. He felt good lying there, nothing could hurt him. He'd returned home in the early hours. He'd been unable to climb the stairs to the attic and hadn't understood why he needed to go up to bed at all.

He'd pulled the sacks over his face, and when he peered through them the world outside looked as though it was made up of dots like a newspaper photograph. The doorway was the brightest part of all. Bamse was standing in the middle of it, her hair shining like an angel's. When he was very small he'd had a guardian angel, but she had abandoned him because he'd been so bad. Light filtered in through the chinks between the boards like upright plates of sunshine. Dust hung in the light, tiny little planets, an entire universe bobbing up and down.

Outside Reino said something and Lasse answered, then Tweety heard the sound of footsteps, like the beat of a drum. Tweety knew he didn't need to worry about them, that nobody could harm him because he was so small, so small that he didn't even really exist, because he'd been so good that he'd sacrificed himself. He felt as though he were sheltered between the palms of two hands.

The world was flooded with more bright dots as Reino wrenched the door wide open, then the floorboards began to tremble. Tweety could feel the tremors beneath him. But the movement wasn't really coming from the floorboards; it was the motion of Wheatlocks' arms as she rocked him so that all his pain disappeared. She held him in her arms and stroked his forehead, and he filled his lungs with the warm, intoxicating scent of her skin.

'Christ, man, we've been looking for you!' said Reino. He was angry, but beneath his anger there was a sense of relief. 'We're supposed to be shaking hands with the Chancellor tonight and then you go missing. Your bed's empty and your moped's gone.'

'We were starting to think the worst,' said Lasse. 'We've rung round all the bloody hospitals and God knows what.'

'On your feet! Fast!'

Reino stamped his foot on the floor and Tweety's bottom hurt but he didn't worry about this, the thump or the pain, because although he was under the sacks, he was really in Wheatlocks' belly, and in there it was warm and safe. Wheatlocks was stroking the bump in her stomach with both her hands, her nails painted red; she didn't want to give birth to him yet, just to make sure nobody could harm him.

'Enough of this nonsense,' Reino snapped and ripped open Wheatlocks' stomach, and Tweety burst into tears. Nobody was allowed to hurt Wheatlocks! He wept inconsolably, trembling, sobbing. Now that the sacks had been taken away he suddenly started shivering, as the world outside was so cold.

'He's sick,' said Bamse. 'He's got a fever. People don't shiver like that for nothing, you know.'

'I'll soon make him better,' said Reino and grabbed Tweety's arms. Reino's fists were like clamps and hauled him to his feet. Tweety yelled. He was in so much pain, his bottom was like an enormous open wound that continued up his back and through his legs right the way down to his knees.

'Jesus!' screamed Bamse. 'His trousers are covered in blood.'

'What in the name… What happened to you?'

'Were you in a crash? Where's your moped?'

'What if he fell down the stairs…?'

Suddenly they were all over him, holding him, examining him. He didn't have the energy to stand up, he didn't dare stand up or straighten his back; just trying to move was painful enough. He didn't understand why they were doing this to him, poking and prodding him. All he wanted to do was shrink away inside Wheatlocks' belly, becoming smaller and smaller until he disappeared altogether.

'Bring the lamp over here… Hold it up…'

'Lasse. Bring the bench over to the door.'

'Mother Gold's not coming, is she?'

'Bamse, pick up those sacks.'

'Asko,' said Reino leaning over him. Tweety had never seen an expression like this on Reino's face before. He looked scared; his cheeks were quivering and tears welled in his eyes.

'Asko. You can still open the door, can't you? Can't you? Asko, the lock. The door with the squirrel. You will be able to open it, right?'

Tweety and Lasse were in the park. Lasse had got permission. And anyway, it was better going there with Lasse than going by yourself. There were so many other children there, from different backyards too. And Lasse was allowed to cross the road; he didn't need to ask an adult to help him.

Tweety was on his knees in the sandpit digging a hole. He was digging with his hands because Lasse had taken the spade; he was digging a pirate's cave. Tweety enjoyed digging with his hands. He was a digger, and his scooper had already reached the wet sand further down. He lifted it out and handed it to Lasse.

'Not here. Put it over there.'

But he couldn't answer. His mouth gave off the sound of a motor engine: brrm, brrm! There was sand in his hair too, but it was dry sand, like sugar. Lasse had put it there; he wanted to pick it out when they went to bed. That always made them laugh.

'Mum's coming!' Tweety exclaimed. He was pleased that he'd noticed first, beaten Lasse to it. Tweety jumped up and ran towards her. He took long, bounding strides, jumping high into the air; he wanted his mother to see. The hem of her jacket was flapping behind her like a pair of wings. Mum was like a bird and he was her fledgling. He opened his arms ready, he wanted to run right into her arms and hold her tightly. He loved Mother and she loved him.

'Mum!' he panted. He was so happy; he had the best mum in the whole wide world. He threw himself into her arms, but his mother didn't embrace him. She moved awkwardly to one side and he fell on the floor and grazed his knee. Mum grabbed him by the arm and yanked him to his feet. That hurt him even more, but he was so taken aback that he forgot to cry.

'Mum?' he said, but she didn't reply. She just stared at him, and she was terribly angry. Her forehead was gleaming like butter and her mouth wasn't Mum's mouth, it was Aunt Hildur's mouth. Aunt Hildur was mean and everyone was afraid of her. Mum took Lasse by the arm too, turned and started dragging them home. They panicked: 'Mum, we forgot the toys! We've left the tipper truck behind!'

'You won't be playing with toys when you're at the borstal,' she said and marched onwards. Tweety had to run to keep up. He suddenly started whimpering and he heard Lasse sniffling to himself. They knew what a borstal was. Mum had told them. All naughty little boys were sent there, and very bad boys had their willies cut off.

Mum sat them down on the bench in the lift.

'What a wicked thing you've done!' she shouted, even though you weren't supposed to shout in the stairwell. 'At the borstal children sleep in wooden boxes on the floor, did you know that? With no mattress and no blankets. And the only food there is gruel that you have to lap from a stone bowl on the floor like a cat!'

'Mum, don't send us there!' Lasse cried. 'Please let us stay at home.'

'Mum!' Tweety wept and held tightly to her skirt. 'Mum!'

'What wicked things you miserable children have done!'

Dad wasn't at home. Dad was in the countryside with Reino and Sisko. The house was empty. Their mother took them into the bedroom. Then she went to fetch the leather dog's leash. At one end there was a handle and at the other end was an iron ring. Mum took hold of the handle.

'Trousers down,' she said. 'Trousers down and lean over the bed.'

They did as they were told. You had to obey Mum. And all of a sudden she was terribly frightening. She was more frightening than the down-and-outs, and Tweety started to feel sick. He looked at the bedspread and concentrated on a picture of a little flower. Then the leather leash slapped him.

'Ouch, ouch! Mum, it hurts!'

'You've raped Marjaana!' she screamed as she thrashed them. 'You've... raped... Marjaana! You've... raped... Marjaana!'

Tweety was in pain. It hurt him, burned him. It hurt, it hurt! He was trembling. The leash hit him again, again, and it stung. He was afraid; he felt broken. His hands had come off and now they were lying on the bed. And his legs felt cold against the floor. He didn't know whether he still had a bottom or a head. He could hear somebody crying, he just didn't know who it was. He was afraid that she would kill them, she was so angry. And Mum could do that because Mum was Mum. She never did anything wrong.

'Get up,' she commanded them, out of breath. 'Pull up your trousers.'

Tweety stood up. Through his teary eyes he could see that Lasse's bottom was bright red. It was covered with something like sausages, except they were blue. There were iron-ring marks on his bottom too, lots of them. Tweety pulled up his trousers. It stung, and again he heard someone crying. A lamp had fallen from the chest of drawers and broken. A piece of its globe was missing. The gap was the same size as the end of the leash.

'Right, we're going,' Mum said and took them by the wrists.

'Mum, no!' shouted Lasse. 'I didn't do anything to Marjaana!'

'Don't lie! Asko is too little. He wouldn't have come up with that by himself. Do you know what happens to boys who lie? Where's the belt?'

'Mum, no! I won't lie any more. Please let us stay at home. Mum, please!'

'Mum, let us stay here! Let us stay here!'

'We'll decide that later. You two are going to apologise to Marjaana and her mother.'

There were lots of children out in the yard. The big Volanen boys were there too. Kari had a skateboard. Their shouts and laughter echoed. A wagtail sat on the roof of the garage. Pekka ran up to them.

'Can Tweety stay out and play?'

'No,' said Mum. 'Asko may very well be going to the borstal tonight. He's committed a crime; Asko has raped Marjaana.'

Tweety couldn't look at Pekka. He stared down at his feet; the lace on one of his plimsolls had come undone. He was ashamed, ashamed because he'd been so bad. He'd been bad and raped Marjaana. He didn't understand what it meant, but it must have been very bad, because even Mum had stopped loving him. Mum wanted to hurt him; she wanted to send him away from home. She wanted him to disappear. His face felt pinched like it did in the winter cold.

Marjaana's house smelled different from theirs. Marjaana was playing with the doll's house her father had built for her. He was a carpenter. Tweety couldn't look at Marjaana. He couldn't look at her mother either. She ordered him to look her in the eyes, but he couldn't.

'Marjaana has been examined by a doctor,' her mother explained. 'Thankfully she didn't sustain any serious injuries, though that stick was so big. I hope you boys learn your lesson: don't put anything in other people's private areas. Ever.'

Lasse said he wouldn't and so did Tweety. Then they both apologised. Tweety didn't know if they would ever be forgiven. Nobody said anything. Only once they were out in the corridor did he dare look at Marjaana. She smirked at him. His eyes filled with tears once again.

Out in the yard the other children had stopped their games. They stood in front of the caretaker's door and stared at them. The wagtail was gone.

'Asko's a raper,' said the eldest of the Volanen boys. Tweety lowered his head. Mum marched them across the yard. All the other children followed them. 'Asko's a raper! Spasko's a raper!'

The house scared Tweety. It had changed; it was suddenly unfamiliar. Everything seemed sharp. Mum picked up the leather leash again. Tweety's bottom was burning. He started to cry, then so did Lasse.

'Trousers down and lean over the bed.'

'Mum, please, no more! Please!'

'Please, not the leash!'

'You've committed an irreconcilable crime. Almighty God is angry too, and he'll never forgive you... Trousers down and lean over the bed.'

They obeyed her.

'Will you ever do anything like this again?' shouted Mum as she lashed them. 'Will you... ever... do... anything... like this... again?'

'No! Mum, please!'

'Never!'

Mum put the leash back on top of the chest of drawers. Then she went and sat down by the hall table. She picked up the telephone and started dialling a number.

'Mum, who are you calling?' said Lasse in distress.

'The borstal,' she snapped. 'The police will come and take you there. Stand by the window and look out for the police car.'

Tweety didn't go to the window. His legs were dancing all by themselves. He didn't want to leave home! He didn't want to be sent away to live with the bad boys! He didn't want them to cut off his willy! He ran up to his mother.

'Mum, please, don't call the borstal!' he begged. 'Let us stay here, please!'

He stroked his mother's hand and leg and her dress. He tried to climb into her arms. He wanted to give her a kiss, to kiss her back to being his mother again.

Mum put down the receiver. She stood up and looked much bigger than before. Then she brought her hands up to her face and went over to the bed. She sat down and cried. Tweety's whimpers soon turned to tears.

'Huh,' she wept. 'Do you hear your own mother crying? Mother feels terrible because you're such naughty boys. Don't you love your mother any more? Is that why you do things like that?'

'We do love you!' they shouted. 'We love you, Mum!'

They ran up to her and huddled against her. Lasse hugged her leg.

'Huh. I don't believe you. My heart hurts, and it's all because of you. Ow, ow...'

Mum fell back on the bed and lay there holding her hand to her chest. She must have been in a lot of pain. She was in pain because they'd been so bad.

'I'm dying. I'll die because of the crimes you've committed...'

Mum's eyes closed. She stopped moving.

Lasse started shouting. He shouted so much that he wasn't saying anything; his mouth was open and he was making shrill squealing sounds. Then he grabbed hold of Mum's dress and started pulling at her.

'Mum, Mum!' he cried. 'Please stay alive!'

Tweety's entire body felt pinched. A moment later he was on his knees on the floor. He didn't know how he got there. He wanted to crawl under the bed and die.

But before he could move, Mum sat up on the bed.

'Now will you believe me?' she said. 'And remember this: if you're naughty ever again, if you do anything wicked, then I really will send you to the borstal. And anyone who sees you doing something bad can call them. Marjaana's mother, Pekka's mother. Do you understand?'

They said that they understood.

Sisko

'Who did it? Who beat you up?'

'Mum…'

'Don't talk shite, man,' said Reino, but he wasn't angry any more. He hadn't been angry for a while; he was more agitated, resigned, and his voice sounded like a cat squashed on the road, run over by dozens of cars. Tweety felt sorry for him, for the first time ever, and was glad he couldn't see his expression.

'Who was it? Asko, I promise you his backside will be redder than yours by the time I've finished with him. Just tell us. Who beat you up?'

'Mother Gold… Mum beat me up, even though I loved her. Then she invited all the women from the village round so she could tell them… I had to open the door for them. So I could confront my shame, she said. I opened the door, then I ran away and hid under the bed.'

'For Christ's sake,' Reino growled quietly and stood up from the bench, took a few steps towards Lasse, who was standing further away, and said: 'He's lost it… our own brother. Someone's knocked the sense out of him. For good…'

Tweety didn't care. He lay on his stomach on the bench and smiled. He didn't understand why he was smiling, because he was profoundly sad, so upset that he cried through his smiles. Tears flowed from his eyes and the bench beneath his face was wet. But at least sorrow was better than the fear, which constantly lurked beneath the surface, raising its head every now and then as if to test the water, and when it did that sweat tingled on his forehead and his stomach started churning. The worst of it was when he felt that the world was shrinking around him, that everything was flying towards him, that he was like a black hole in space that sucks everything inside itself. It didn't help, no matter how much he tried to beat the world further away, it just kept coming, and even if he could have run away, it would have been no use: even then the world would still be there to greet him.

'Fuck, fuck, fuck!' Reino shouted somewhere in the distance. 'How can we have such bad luck? Over six months' preparation and on the very day we're supposed to...'

'Let's cut our way through the bloody door.'

'In the basement of the bank? That building's got wooden joists in the floor. The smoke will seep up through every flat above the bank and they'll have the fire brigade out before we even get inside.'

'True.... And what if someone turns up?'

'Why the hell didn't I make him cut a new key?'

'He wouldn't have been able to get his hands on a blank for a grooved Abloy like that.'

'You don't need a blank! You get a piece of thick brass pipe, cut off a chunk and Bob's your uncle.'

'What if he can remember the sequence? If he could tell us...'

'He just wittered on about colours... and whenever I talk to him about the lock or the door he starts blubbing, his face is gleaming with sweat and he starts thrashing like he's swiping flies away.'

'Let's postpone the whole thing. By a week.'

'You heard what the bank manager said. They're about to change the security system and install motion detectors and everything...'

'Are we going to give up then?'

'Are we going to give up...' said Reino in a strange, almost sullen voice. There came a rustling sound as he walked off through the long grass, then everything was quiet for a long time. Only the hum of the traffic in the distance and the sound of an aeroplane taking off from the nearby airfield could be heard. Then came a deluge of curses, followed by the sound of wood splintering and glass shattering. An old set of windows was piled up behind the digger; they were taken from the house that had once stood there. Reino smashed them to pieces – and he'd said he would beat the living daylights out of anyone who ruined the Chancellor. Tweety felt as though ants were running across his face. He tried to wipe them away but he couldn't keep hold of them, and the ants began burrowing through his cheeks and into his flesh. What if they laid their eggs in there, built a nest? He tried to cry out, but couldn't make a sound, leaving only spittle spluttering from his lips.

Tweety squeezed his eyes firmly shut and started breathing heavily. Time passed and he began to feel as though he were sleeping. He dreamt that chunks of flesh came away from his body and landed on the ground with a thud, allowing his soul to flow out through the holes. His soul was like light-blue putty, and he tried to stop it escaping by pressing his hands over the holes, only to discover that new pieces of flesh had started coming away.

'Where the bloody hell's Bamse got to now?' said Reino, and now his voice sounded the same as it did when he had a hangover.

'The chemist's in Malmi?'

'Yes, but we're still taking him to the quack. We'll ask him to prescribe some pills and get him ready for tomorrow. That's only Saturday; we'll still have just enough time. And if he's not back on his feet by evening, then we'll call it off.'

'Call what off?' someone asked. It was Sisko.

'Oh, nothing special... Just something we're working on.'

'What in the name of...? What's going on?'

'Don't go over there.'

'I will too!'

Tweety could hear the sound of sandals approaching. It stopped and there came a strange hissing sound as Sisko drew a sharp intake of breath between her teeth. She went up to him, quickly crouched down, lay her hand on his neck and started stroking him. Her hand was hard from all her chores, but still soft and full of warmth. Tweety felt better almost immediately; he felt safer, just like as a child when his guardian angel had lulled him to sleep. Sisko's clothes smelled of the vegetable patch. Tweety began to cry, he felt so relieved.

'Tweety,' said Sisko, her voice quivering. 'We're going to get you taken care of. We're taking you to the doctor.'

'They were policemen,' Tweety sobbed. Now he had the courage to remember everything.

'Policemen?' said Reino in bewilderment. 'Get away... Were they in uniform?'

'No, they were from the Crime Squad. A big smelly man and a little one.'

'A big one and a… Was the small one kind of smarmy?'

'No, he was too polite, fake,' said Tweety, and it suddenly felt a relief to get it all out. The words felt like tent pegs; they kept him firmly on the ground. 'He was sort of jokey.'

'Lampinen,' said Reino, his voice shuddering. 'And the big one's Juslin. They're on to something. Right, lads, we're calling it off. But he'll fucking pay for this. Dearly!'

Sand crunched beneath Reino's feet; he must have been marching back and forth. Sisko patted Tweety firmly on the shoulders and stood up.

'What are you calling off? The Chancellor?'

'Yes… How the hell do you…?'

'How the hell do I know!' she mimicked them. 'I know about it because you've all been talking about it in the workshop for months. You're like a right witches' coven.'

'You've been listening in on us…'

Reino spluttered and had a sudden coughing fit. He cleared his throat, spat on the floor, then came the sound of rustling as he pulled out his tobacco and cigarette papers.

'Give me a cut,' said Sisko. Lasse kept absolutely quiet.

'Well, there's been a significant change in our situation,' Reino said eventually. It sounded as though he was staring at his feet. His voice had never sounded this humble. 'Asko's not up to carrying out his part of the plan, so we can't go ahead. And if it really was Lampinen who beat him up, that means he's on to something. He wants to stop us at any cost, because he knows his case might not stand up in court. He's done things like this before. This bloke I knew once had a run-in with him…'

The dirt crackled as Sisko stamped out her cigarette. Then she laid her hand back on Tweety's neck and it felt just as good as before. With her other hand she held his fingers.

'Tweety,' she said. 'Did they pick you up for nothing? For no reason whatsoever?'

'No…'

'So you'd done something? It doesn't matter what you did… Is that what happened?'

'Yes. I mean… Maybe they thought I was somebody else and that's why they took me back to the station. But then they let me go. They said they were going to take me home, but then on the way back they…'

'Did they say anything about the Chancellor? Did they try to get anything out of you?'

'No. I wouldn't have said anything…'

'Do they know Reino's your brother? Or did they work out who you are?'

'I gave them false details…'

Sisko stood up. Tweety's hand felt suddenly empty.

'There, you see?' she said to the others. 'Lampinen doesn't know a thing.'

'Still, it's probably wise to let it go. We'll never get the door open…'

'We're not giving up!' snapped Sisko. 'You've been planning it for almost six months and you'll never get another opportunity like this again. We've got to take the chance if we're ever going to get out of this dump. I'm not thinking of you, I'm thinking of myself. Have I ever been able to have a life of my own? I've spent years being a free servant, first to Mum and Dad, and then to you lot. Every time I've tried to date someone, Mum gets sick. She gets so sick I have to take everything to her in bed and she starts wetting herself.'

For a good while they were all silent. There came the sound of a car rolling up the lane: Bamse was back from the chemist's.

'Once you've taken care of the Chancellor you're planning on moving away, right?' Sisko asked quickly. 'Right?'

'Right. We've been to look at a house up in Mäntsälä.'

'And we'll get something for this place too?'

'Well, the bank will take their share. You'll be lucky to get enough for a bedsit.'

'But that'll be plenty for me. I'd buy a bedsit in the middle of nowhere as long as I can get away from that bitch.'

Reino coughed and Tweety fidgeted restlessly. Nobody had ever called their mother a bitch before; she was Mother Gold, because the whole world knew that she was just a golden old woman who wished everybody well.

'Go and see Bamse,' said Sisko. Reino and Lasse did as they were told without saying a word. The path crunched beneath their feet. Sisko's sandals pattered against the floor. She came up to him, took his hands and held his shoulders. He felt the goodness of her touch, how she caressed him softly, how she breathed. He wasn't even sure she was speaking to him, but it sounded as though she said: 'Help me, Tweety. Help us all. I'll help you, I'll come with you, I'll be right next to you all the way. All you have to do is pick one little lock. And you can do it, you're so good at it. You're the best. And after that it's all over. We can have our own flat, our own life, and nobody will ever be able to take it away from us.'

'Tweety,' she said softly, and Tweety thought he could hear her weeping.

Briefing Session

Harjunpää had thought he'd be able to take the car back to the station, leave his papers on his desk and start making his way home. It was already well into the afternoon and Elisa had said they'd eat around four o'clock out on the patio because the weather was still so nice. Still, he'd simply had to check the police records to see what kind of a file they had on Retula.

He'd drawn a complete blank. There was no file on Retula, even though the IT people had said he'd been registered in Helsinki. Harjunpää called up to Mäki, who had compiled the original notice on Retula, and Mäki swore that the man *did* have a file down at the records office and that he had personally updated it.

Harjunpää went through the filing cabinet once again. Between two other files alphabetically either side of the name Retula, he'd found a small piece of cardboard hanging from one of the metal fixture rails, the kind of fragment undoubtedly left when someone rips a file from its clip. From that moment he was in no doubt that this was precisely what had happened to Retula's file.

On top of that he'd been down to the holding cells, then back to the records office, and now as he walked along the corridor in the basement floor of the station he looked bitterly at the file in his hand. He turned the corner into the training wing, bounded through the coffee room and stood for a moment listening behind the wide door on the other side. This had to be the right seminar room; he could make out Järvi's voice. He opened the door without knocking and stepped inside.

'Last year, the total expenses incurred by the national rail network were in the region of 1,300,000 marks,' Järvi lectured to those assembled. He was standing on a rostrum in front of the others and indicating items on the overhead projector with a pointer. 'Overall we're talking about four or five million marks in damages per year. Now, say somebody robbed that amount of money from a bank... Well, gentlemen, as you know they'd get their names in the history books. Just to be clear, the reason I bring up this example is to...'

Harjunpää walked up the aisle. There were about thirty men in the room, quite a crowd, considering that profit responsibility targets meant that thousands of crimes were never investigated beyond their initial registration. But the men sitting there could do nothing about it. They'd been drafted in from numerous different forces, though the majority were from the Violent Crimes unit. Lampinen was sitting in the third row and behind him were a couple of empty seats, as though they had been saved especially for Harjunpää.

'... rather, in broader terms, the operation had a great preventive significance not only for certain national companies but for society at large. It's clear that the people behind this graffiti are likely involved in all manner of other crimes. Again, I'd like to...'

Harjunpää sat down behind Lampinen, and as he looked at the man's thinning, sandy hair and his checked jacket he felt a visceral hatred well up inside him. Perhaps this feeling was all the stronger because he was, in a way, utterly powerless: though he wanted nothing more, he couldn't think of a way to catch Lampinen out.

He was well aware that, if he made this issue official, it would all come down to Retula; he'd known this the moment he left the hospital. The man was so afraid that he probably couldn't even bring himself to utter Lampinen's name. And would anyone believe him – a self-harmer who had filed countless false police reports? And as for Harjunpää? His rancorous relationship with Lampinen was public knowledge, and Harjunpää suspected people might just put everything down to a personal grudge. And now even civilians were making complaints about him.

'I'll be personally overseeing Operation Spray,' said Järvi. 'Every night, starting tonight and ending on Sunday. And I won't be hiding away in an ivory tower somewhere; I'll be with you in the field. I've secured the use of the commander's vehicle, which is equipped with the latest in communications technology. My codename will be Seagull One. Seagull Two will be…'

There were two matters he wanted to address, and Harjunpää decided to start with the easier, though he knew exactly what to expect. He opened up the folder he'd brought with him to reveal a photograph showing frontal and profile images of a thickset man about two metres tall with a beer belly and a dark moustache. He tapped Lampinen on the shoulder. Lampinen leaned backwards as if he already knew who was there, which could have been possible seeing as most people had turned around when Harjunpää had entered the room.

'Thanks for letting that bloke go last night,' he whispered. 'I couldn't find the photograph in my locker though.'

'What?'

'I asked you to photograph him as a precaution.'

'Really? I don't remember anything about that… Well, you might have asked, but we probably forgot about it what with all that was going on. Sorry, mate.'

'Damn it, man,' said Harjunpää and thrust the folder in front of Lampinen. 'This was him, right?'

'Absolutely not! This guy looked like a sparrow or something.'

'The information he gave us is for this man. Didn't you think to check out his story?'

'Why would we have done that? We didn't even process him.'

'Oh, pardon me. Just thought you might be your usual nit-picking self. You took him home though, didn't you?'

'So?'

'What's his address?'

'His address… He just told us to drop him off in Pukinmäki… It looked like he walked off towards the flats behind the station. Still, if he has done something, the Lord punishes all crooks sooner or later. Who knows, he might have hit the scoundrel over the head with a hammer already…'

'Oh, I'm sure he will. Thanks a lot.'

Lampinen shook his shoulders for a moment and adjusted his jacket, and Harjunpää leaned back into his seat. He was breathing in shallow, furious breaths. If he'd had the courage he would have grabbed hold of Lampinen's jacket, clenched it in his fist, pinned him hard against the back of the seat and said: 'You're a lying, conniving bastard – and I'm going to prove it.' Perhaps it wasn't so much to do with courage. He could easily have done it, especially given how tired he was, but it would have been foolish and he didn't want to lower himself to that level.

'... an operation that may prove to have a pioneering significance for the entire police force. By that I mean that other countries have already treated this matter with the seriousness it requires. By way of an example, allow me to mention that the Copenhagen police have established a separate Graffiti unit, which focuses its resources exclusively on...'

Harjunpää tapped Lampinen on the shoulder a second time.

'Well?' the latter replied without turning around.

'I said the incident on Eerikinkatu might be linked to our intruder...'

'Yes?' said Lampinen, now leaning back very keenly in his chair.

'It turns out it wasn't the same perpetrator. And the victim's on his way to a full recovery. I have every faith we'll get the right man before long.'

Lampinen turned around, his mouth open in astonishment, and looked at Harjunpää.

'Really?' he said finally. 'But last night, you said that....'

'Excuse me,' Järvi raised his voice. 'Might I ask the reason for this constant disturbance?'

'Sorry,' said Harjunpää as he stood up and moved towards the corridor. 'Crow Three is flying off home.'

Departure

At the front entrance to the central police station in Pasila were two large doors which folded in the middle. These were the main doors to the parking lot: the right-hand door leading in and the left-hand door leading out. This, however, was only for police vehicles that could fit through the doors; it hadn't occurred to anyone designing the building that some vehicles were taller than the average squad car. But as everybody knows, to err is human, to forgive is divine – particularly when men who have spent their entire working lives in the police force are suddenly told they are architects and asked to design a police station.

That Friday evening, just after eleven o'clock, the left-hand door mechanism hissed as someone entered the security code from inside the parking lot. The door slowly began to slide open. Glaring fluorescent light poured out into the night darkness, then a car appeared: a white VW van with an observation platform and a folding ladder on the roof. The vehicle belonged to the Arson unit; a small laboratory and base on wheels, the largest vehicle that would actually fit inside the parking lot, and even then it could only be parked right by the door. But this time the car wasn't being used by the Violent Crimes officers.

An officer from the Drug Squad sat behind the steering wheel. He had been assigned the case, and he and his colleagues had been allocated this vehicle because, at first glance, it couldn't be recognised as a police unit and because the windows were lined with mirror glass. This meant that they could park the car almost anywhere and follow what was going on in the world outside without the risk of anyone seeing.

The car belched diesel exhaust fumes into the night air, crossed the pavement and turned on to Radiokatu. Another car appeared, a dark-blue Golf, followed quickly by a light-coloured Samara. From inside the parking lot came the echo of words, the slam of car doors and the revving of engines starting up, and it wasn't hard to guess that another ten or so police cars were about to speed out into the night, that something out of the ordinary was in the offing, that on that night anyone thinking of getting up to mischief would be better off staying at home quietly sipping their lager.

Cars started appearing, another seven. One after the other they rumbled over the pavement, accelerated down the street and headed off towards the city centre. Last of all came a majestic black Volvo, gleaming and waxed, with numerous antennae attached to its roof. Seagull One glided out into the night.

Operation Spray was underway.

Another Departure

Reino had parked the elephant right in front of the workshop and Tweety could see it clearly through the open door. He was on his knees on the oil-stained floor, leaning against a bench, and he was laughing because Lasse had attached large, yellow stickers on to the elephant's side that read Helsinki Emergency Plumbing Services Ltd. The signs even gave a telephone number and an address at Vaasankatu 5. That was the funny part; if somebody's pipes sprung a leak and they tried to call this company for help, the phone would ring and ring and nobody would ever pick up, and if they went to the address on Vaasankatu they'd find themselves in a clothes shop. Water would be pouring everywhere and the crack in the pipes would just get worse.

The fact that the elephant had another car's registration number made him laugh too. Apart from bluffing for them, in a few hours' time the elephant would help them carry home sackloads of money and gold and diamonds. He was especially amused at the realisation that Mother Gold was really a witch. She was a wicked witch who had laid a curse on him, magicked him in two, Tweety and Asko, and turned his life into a meat grinder from which she wouldn't let him escape.

The thought of the corridor in the bank's basement was suddenly in his mind. Its walls were like flesh, red meat caught on the surface of the grinder, and something moved in his stomach and a thin trace of sweat tickled his upper lip.

Outside Reino said something to Sisko. Night had fallen, enveloping the world in soft folds of cloth. Tweety's sniggers made Reino nervous, and every now and then he sent Sisko to keep an eye on him. Reino was nervous anyway; his voice sounded like frayed barbed wire. He shouldn't have been like that; someone should have said something to him. Because when someone is nervous, he attracts failure like a magnet. Sisko understood his giggles; she'd explained that laughter is fear's backside, and when it turned to face you, fear itself was looking elsewhere and didn't notice you.

Sisko came indoors; she was wearing the same clothes she always wore and could easily be mistaken for a plumber. She'd been helping Reino and Lasse carry the tools and gas cylinders outside, and on Reino's orders she'd been keeping a checklist, the kind that pilots keep, making a tick beside each item as they loaded it into the van. She was going with them, specifically to help Tweety. She helped him by holding her hand on his neck; she was his guardian angel, and with her hand on his neck he wasn't afraid of the pouch or the picks or the locks. They'd done it all before. They'd even practised; he'd been able to open every lock Reino had given him, though none of those had been a grooved Abloy lock.

'Tweety,' said Sisko and looked at him, her head to one side. 'Are you all right?'

'Yes,' he replied. He looked down at his hands and his voice seemed to thicken. 'Yes…'

'And you're still thinking about the lock on the squirrel door?'

'Yes. It's singing very quietly, and I can see lots of shades of brown.'

'Good… We're nearly ready to go.'

Reino and Lasse walked in, bringing with them the smell of tobacco and sweat and nervousness. The night had left tiny messages on Lasse's clothes, so small that he hadn't noticed them. Tweety inhaled them deep into his lungs and tried to read them, but stopped immediately; they were bad messages. They were shining with a trembling, blue light that licked through his brain, through the city, through the whole world even, and he began to feel as though he'd been out in the rain and his clothes were soaking wet. He started to giggle; he had to. Giggling was a tent peg too, just as words had been earlier that day.

'Right,' said Reino and looked at the others, and with that the Chancellor came to life, it was real: Museokatu was somewhere in the distance, sleepy cars parked along the street, and the bank with the blue squirrel glowing in its window. The gate leading through to the yard was real, the flesh-coloured corridor and the squirrel door. Then inside the bank they were met by the smell of paper, the smell of plate-metal lockers and the toilet that hissed to itself; then there was the alarm that couldn't raise the alarm and the thick door that Reino would have to cut through. Minutes going past agonisingly slowly, the fear that somebody might come, that they'd be caught. But then there was the money, the gold, the diamonds.

'Or what?' he added. He shouldn't have. Those words and his expression meant: shall we postpone it until tomorrow, or shall we call the whole thing off? It made everyone uneasy; they shuffled their feet, and perhaps it occurred to them that this might be the last time they'd all be together like this for years. What would it feel like to be cross-examined, put in a cell, sent to prison? Lasse held his hand to his waist and kept it there, his fingers touching the thick handle of his Smith & Wesson, and in a moment his lips had turned white.

'What are we standing around here yacking for?' said Sisko as though someone had tooted a horn. 'Let's get in the van and get going.'

'Right,' Lasse muttered, his voice hoarse. 'The sooner we get going…'

'I still wish we had that bloody police radio. At least then we'd know how many patrols there are in the area, and whether they're planning a raid, so we don't walk right into a trap.'

'But we haven't got it,' said Sisko. 'We'll be fine without it.'

'And you're sure Mum's asleep?'

'Yes. She won't wake up until tomorrow morning now.'

'And you've packed Asko's…?'

'Let's go.'

'Right, let's go…'

Sisko came round to Tweety's left and Lasse to his right. They held him under the arms and helped him stand up. From there he made his own way to the van, stiffly, as though he were learning to walk for the first time, and now all sense of nostalgia was gone; they were filled with action and a sense of assurance. It was in their every movement, encouraging one another: we can do it! And very slowly they began to believe in it themselves, they had no choice, and as that belief set in so the night smelled suddenly much better. It smelled of magic, of a life that was about to take a turn for the better.

Oversight

'There you go,' said Harjunpää, his voice strangely taut, and laid the papers on the desk in front of Tanttu. He looked only at Tanttu and tried to pretend there weren't other people in the room; Kontio was sitting to one side with his legs crossed and a sour expression on his face, and Järvi was standing by the window with his back to them, looking outside.

Harjunpää's statement was two pages long. He had tried to stick to short, laconic sentences: '*I pointed out that the body was about to sink beneath the surface. For this reason I could see no option but to fetch it myself. Because I was alone, I took off my clothes except for my underpants...*' He had attached a copy of the original report, which gave a good all-round picture of events, and a copy of Koponen's post-mortem report, which he'd written up in record time. There was an element of mischief to it all, but Harjunpää hoped that the turgid, official text of an objective second party would make Tanttu understand that the matter was being taken out of all proportion.

But Tanttu didn't touch the papers; he didn't even glance at them. He looked right at Harjunpää, and his eyes were decidedly hard and abrupt.

'That's not why I summoned you.'

'OK...'

'This is a different matter, the repercussions of which are far more serious.'

'And yet it's always the same officer, isn't it?' said Järvi without turning around. 'I wonder what that tells us.'

Harjunpää quickly wet his lips. Tanttu hadn't even asked him to take a seat.

'Last Tuesday night you were on patrol in unit 5-8-3.'

'Yes…?'

'And what happened?'

Harjunpää didn't understand. He remembered the moped-man and visiting the flat on Messeniuksenkatu, but that had all happened the following night. He shrugged his shoulders.

'Control gave you an assignment.'

'That's right,' he remembered. 'It was around one a.m. Control called…'

'It was at 00.49,' Tanttu corrected him as though this was of great significance. He was holding a piece of paper from which he read the time that the call had gone out. Harjunpää shifted his feet awkwardly.

'And what was that assignment?'

'The alarm had gone off at the National Investment Bank on Museokatu. We were relatively close to the scene and…'

'That would be Museokatu 18.'

'Yes… but it was a false alarm. There was a…'

'How do you know it was a false alarm?'

'The alarm attached to the main vault in the basement had gone off. Nobody had broken in: the windows were all intact and there were no signs of forced entry on the doors. Additionally, a man who worked at the bank turned up and he…'

'Mr Kauppila.'

'Yes,' Harjunpää spluttered, and now he really started to worry, though he couldn't understand why. 'We entered the building with him and everything was as it should be. He even showed us the door to the vault and the alarm itself. He told us that the alarm had gone off several times in the past because of a problem with the wiring. These alarms are so sensitive that they can be set off by a lorry going past…'

'I don't need a lesson on the workings of alarm systems. I'm quite aware of how they work. What action did you take?'

Harjunpää looked past Järvi and out of the window. What actions *had* he taken?

'We quickly checked the interior of the bank, just to be on the safe side, and reported back to Control that everything had been taken care of.'

'And after that?'

'Regarding what?'

'To my understanding we're not talking about a bicycle theft here.'

'I didn't do anything else.'

'But you should have,' Järvi almost yelled, and now he turned around, and in his hand he was holding a piece of paper folded in two.

'This is an order, signed by me, requiring officers to report all – I repeat, *all* – incidents involving a bank alarm going off at night to my team.'

'I… What year is that from?'

'Don't be smart! That won't help us now. The fact of the matter is that you have disobeyed a direct order from your superior. In writing.'

'It wasn't a false alarm,' said Tanttu. 'It was set off on purpose. The alarm in question was swapped for another one that didn't work. And as a result, this weekend these same people carried out their plan: they cut through the vault door with a blowtorch.'

'This was a highly skilled, professional job.'

'The vaults happened to be holding an exceptionally large amount of money. Initial estimates put the sum at just under three million marks. The vault also contained the bank's reserves of foreign currency; we still don't know how much that amounted to. On top of that, safety deposit boxes belonging to private clients were all emptied. At this stage we can only imagine what they might have contained: cash, jewellery, gold ingots…'

Harjunpää stared at the floor and forced himself to take deep, calm breaths. When he thought back, he knew they couldn't have done any more than they did. Neither could anybody else.

'To my mind, there's nothing I can do about this,' he said finally, as it seemed they were waiting for him to comment on his actions. 'Nothing whatsoever.'

'But this incident could have been prevented if you had taken care to notify the relevant people,' said Tanttu. Arguing the point clearly annoyed him; he stood up and leaned his hands against the desk. 'If you had acted in a manner befitting your training and your experience, this might never have happened. Our officers might at least have valuable information to help them with their investigation.'

'So there's nothing to go on?'

'That's right,' Kontio growled. 'They didn't leave a calling card.'

Again Harjunpää looked down at the floor. It all began to make sense: Kontio's officers were in difficulty, or at the very least they were at a loss, and that was perfectly understandable because the investigation was in its early stages, but it still irritated Kontio profoundly. Harjunpää recalled how Kontio had taken on the Finnair deposit-box job as his own personal mission. What's more, this might well be the last big case in Kontio's long career, and naturally he wanted it brought to a swift conclusion.

As for Järvi, his responsibilities included making sure professional criminals were under constant surveillance, keeping the investigation team up to speed with what they might expect to uncover, and after the fact to collect reliable intelligence on what had happened. But this time it hadn't worked. In addition, while the bank job was underway, Järvi was himself out on patrol with an exceptionally large number of officers, and rumours the next morning had it that absolutely nothing had come of Operation Spray. And the icing on the cake was that over the weekend at least a hundred gravestones had been overturned and smashed at the cemetery in Hietaniemi and the police had no information regarding the perpetrators. Indeed, one of the tabloids had led with the mocking headline: POLICE WATCH TURNIP PATCH – FENCE STOLEN!

And what was now going on was a procedure typical in the force: looking for a suitable scapegoat. There was always someone to pin the blame on, and they usually came from the lower ranks of the force. Harjunpää also understood perfectly well that there was probably nothing personal in this; he had simply happened to be in the wrong place at the wrong time.

'If I might say something…' he said, clearing his throat. 'It seems rather senseless to me to…'

'Are you calling your superior senseless?' snapped Järvi. 'Are you calling the chief of police *senseless*? In front of two board members?'

'No… But as far as I can see I don't…'

'There's no point making a fuss now that you've screwed up,' Kontio snapped. 'It would be a damn sight more useful for you to go into the woods for a while, sit down in the grass and think about things.'

'Dismissed,' Tanttu scoffed, his eyes hard as ever.

'Thank you, sir.'

'But when we take all this into consideration,' he added pointing to Harjunpää's incident statement. 'It's no secret that the Public Order Police have requested twenty officers to be transferred to their team. Fourteen of them have still to be named. That was earlier this morning. Now there are only thirteen.'

Monday Afternoon

The weekend had seemed to crawl past. They had spent most of the time indoors and hadn't really spoken to one another, which was in itself quite out of the ordinary. Tweety had imagined things differently; he imagined they'd be laughing and singing, dancing across the yard and hugging each other with joy. But they didn't.

In an almost subdued mood, they had seen the Chancellor through. They collected up the tools and equipment they'd used, even their clothes – Reino had insisted; he'd learned this in jail – and now he and Lasse were at the dump destroying everything. Bamse was out in town with Mother Gold and Ritu and the kids, which had given them a moment to catch their breath.

'You know what, Tweety?' said Sisko with a note of astonishment. 'We did it…'

Tweety didn't say anything; he knew Sisko wasn't expecting an answer. She was just thinking out loud, trying to accept the fact that she too was now a criminal. She'd decided to join them so suddenly. Still, she'd known about the Chancellor for a long time and had come to accept what they were doing. It was a good job she was there, too, and the best of it was that, as they were leaving, she'd taken a mop and a bucket from the cleaning cupboard and scrubbed the floor cleaner than it had ever been before. Only the vault door stood open, smirking right in the middle.

Sisko picked up a piece of hay from the ground and started chewing it. They were lying on the grass in front of the cottage. Tweety turned so he could see her better. They looked at one another and smiled. It was as though a hatch had been opened somewhere, letting laughter pour in, and though it felt good it startled them and they averted their eyes.

Tweety stared at the ground, a clover leaf, an ant, and thought of Wheatlocks. He was in her arms, he could fly, and he thought of how she caressed his hand in her sleep, how she held her pillow and dreamt of him, how tidy she kept her flat. If she didn't want to please him, the place would have been a mess. He thought of how beautifully she dressed every day, and he knew that she did it all for him.

He had talked to Sisko about Wheatlocks and told her that there was somebody he loved, and he was glad he'd done so. As soon as he'd mentioned her, Wheatlocks had ceased to be a forbidden secret and his feelings towards her had ceased to seem so bad. Sisko hadn't said anything, she'd just looked at him, but he could tell from her eyes that she'd understood. It had felt so good. It still did.

Because of this he'd felt much better in general. He wasn't so afraid anymore, and the world only seemed to creak whenever he saw Mother Gold or heard her voice, even when he remembered that she existed and lived close to him. Of course, he was relieved that the Chancellor was finally over and done with, and though the thought of punishment popped into his mind every now and then, somewhere deep down he had faith that they wouldn't get caught. It helped that they were all in it together, that there was someone to look out for him.

Sisko stood up and Tweety remained lying on the grass. He lay with his face towards the smell of the earth and inhaled deeply, and he felt as though a curtain were lifting inside him. It was made of heavy, green velvet and was infinitely high, and a soft, beautiful light flooded out from behind it, glittering in thousands of colours, then a symphony orchestra began to play and a choir started to sing. He didn't recognise the music, but it was the most wonderful thing he'd ever heard.

'I love that woman so much,' he said, or maybe he only thought it. 'And I'm going to tell her. Today. I'll ask Reino for some money and I'll buy myself some new clothes, some roses and chocolates. And I'll get a haircut, then I'll walk right up to her and tell her.'

He felt suddenly impatient. He wanted to run, to hurry to her. He wanted to be in the city centre, he wanted to sit in the barber's chair, watching what he looked like in the mirror. He rose to his knees, then Sisko shouted somewhere in the distance: 'Tweety! They're here!'

The van rumbled into view from behind the hedgerow and turned into the drive. Now it looked the same as it had before; Reino had reattached the original number plates first thing on Saturday morning, and Lasse had removed the stickers and washed off any remaining glue with petrol. Everything seemed fine: Reino waved his hand at them cheerfully and Lasse was laughing heartily. Tweety followed Sisko as she left the workshop and went to meet them.

'Greetings from the big wide world!' Reino cried as he jumped out of the van. He was holding a half-empty bottle of whisky and a copy of one of the tabloids, and he was brimming with excitement, just like Lasse. Their movements seemed somehow exaggerated, as if their arms and legs were laughing too. Reino let out a series of unashamed yells and Lasse shook his carrier bags so that their contents made a full, heavy jingling sound.

'Have a drink, you've earned it!' said Reino, thrusting the bottle at Sisko and waving his newspaper. 'It was a bloody good thing we didn't have the police radio after all. We'd never have gone through with it. The city was swarming with patrols out on a vandalism operation. And there we were right in the middle of it all...'

'It felt damned good getting out of here for a while,' said Lasse. 'It reminds you that the world's still going round just like it did before. You should go into town instead of sitting here waiting for...'

'Is there anything in the paper about the Chancellor?'

'Oh yes,' Reino laughed. 'But they're talking about a bloke called the Chancellor of the Exchequer. Does anyone know his name? Hah! But we still don't know anything about a chancellor that lives on Museokatu, got it?'

Sisko handed the bottle to Tweety. He closed his eyes and drank; the whisky tasted bitter and warmed his throat and chest, and he took another swig. He wanted to share in their carefree spirit; he wanted to be able to laugh. He wanted to be able to join them. Reino's good cheer was like permission to the others to laugh, to celebrate the Chancellor and the fact that they had succeeded.

'We did it... just like that...'

'Maybe we're not just a bunch of idiots after all.'

'And Sisko too, I'll be damned! Mopping the floors and everything. I half expected her to clean the toilet bowl too.'

'But now we've got to be careful. And keep our mouths shut. This happened all the time when I was inside; the blokes there were always bragging about what they'd done... and somebody always blows the whistle. We can brag to each other, as much as we like...'

'And we don't go flashing our money around either.'

'No. We'll gradually start moving out of this place. But I want to give Mother Gold that one ring, the one with the enormous red stone in it. Just to show her. She's always moaning about how we're a bunch of good-for-nothings and how back when Dad was alive he...'

They slowly walked back towards the cottage, noisily sipping from the bottle of whisky. Everybody had something to say, it was as though someone had taken a cork out of a bottle, and they were all laughing, though nobody had said anything especially funny.

It seemed to Tweety that they'd been there for hours, sitting and lounging on the grass eating ready-roast chicken and other small delicacies. He'd been drinking with the rest of them, more than he'd drunk in a long time, and by now he was fairly drunk; the ground occasionally swung beneath him, and he imagined he was drunk with thoughts of Wheatlocks. He was nervous about visiting her again, even though he loved her. Perhaps that was the reason.

'But Christ I was scared when the blowtorch wouldn't light,' Reino exclaimed. He was drunk too; they all were. 'For a moment I was convinced I'd packed the empty cylinders.'

'But it didn't half light up when you turned the blinking tap on!'

'I was just so bloody nervous.'

'But everybody pulled their weight. Even Asko, sore arse and all...'

'You mark my words, Asko: that Lampinen's got it coming to him. And once we're finished with him, he won't be able to walk for a fortnight.'

'Don't do anything stupid, eh?' said Sisko. 'What goes around comes around. He'll just beat somebody else up, then somebody else...'

'But he's not getting away with it.'

'We have to think of another way of getting him, try and make him take the rap for what he did to Tweety. Something to get him kicked out of the police, so he won't be able to treat people however he pleases.'

'No... I'm not pressing charges against him. How would we prove anything? It's just our word against his. And there's two of them...'

'What if we could get him to do something else...?'

'Listen to yourselves, for Christ's sake,' Lasse snapped, lowered his voice and started explaining something, but Tweety couldn't be bothered listening. He didn't want to think about it. He wanted to forget about all the beatings, everything. Even the grass seemed to pull him away; he lay down and decided he would propose to Wheatlocks tomorrow. He'd been given a week off work and he decided he'd pop into the shop, too, just to show Weckman he wasn't pulling a sickie.

A moment later and he was dreaming. He had a nest made of twigs and he was a bird with the body of a human. His fledglings weren't real; they were bottles corks with glass-headed pins stuck into them for feathers. Still, they were alive and he fed them with milk which they suckled from his fingertips. Somewhere down on the ground he could hear human voices; Bamse said something and Lasse's daughters giggled, then Ritu started nagging him for drinking in the middle of the day, then Reino and Sisko started talking. All of a sudden Mother Gold was there too.

'What's going on here?' she snapped. 'How could you? You're just as bad as your father…'

Sisko said something, then Lasse replied, both of them trying to worm their way out of trouble, and Reino laughed. Tweety laid his hands around his nest; he didn't want Mother Gold to know that he had fledglings up there – she might kill them, stuff them into the tops of juice bottles as stoppers. But despite this he suddenly felt safe; his nest was so high up in the trees, and Mother Gold couldn't fly. She couldn't do anything about it. She couldn't harm him ever again.

'And what about Asko? Good God, he's drunk so much he's passed out!'

'Go on inside with Bamse. Put on some coffee and come and drink it out here. Have some cognac. Think of it as heart medicine.'

'Oh, oh, my stomach's churning,' groaned Mother Gold. Bamse said something to her, then their footsteps began fading into the distance. Mother Gold muttered all the way indoors, nothing but a hissing through her nostrils. Tweety was afraid of that sound; it always meant something bad. When she made that sound, she was planning something. She used to hiss like that every time she went to fetch the leash.

He carried on feeding his fledglings, but he'd only managed to give milk to the first two before a door was flung wide open with a crash, and Mother Gold squawked anxiously: 'A rat! On the steps upstairs. A rat! But look, I clocked it one!'

Ritual

'He's on annual leave, I'm afraid. Somewhere in the Mediterranean, I think. Can I take a message?'

'No,' said Wheatlocks. 'Thanks anyway. I'll call back later.'

She replaced the receiver in disappointment. Only then did she realise that she'd forgotten to ask when Jani would be back from his holiday and her mind was suddenly filled with a faint sense of annoyance. She flicked her flowing locks of hair and quickly walked towards the bedroom. At least she'd called him, never mind that she'd been putting it off and it was nearly five o'clock in the afternoon. She'd been putting it off because she was worried that, after so many years, Jani might find her request strange, some kind of excuse.

She stopped beside her bed, bent down and opened the top drawer of the dressing table. The drawer contained her knickers, but that wasn't what she was looking for. She moved the undergarments to one side to reveal Marko's gun, dark and silent amidst everything so delicate and frilly, and its barrel was loaded with six lead bullets. The gun was the reason she'd wanted to contact Jani in the first place; she'd been thinking about him constantly for days. They'd dated before she had met Simo. Back then she'd thought of Jani as some sort of gun freak. Perhaps she'd even been ever so slightly afraid of him, and that might have been why the relationship ended.

She picked up the revolver, turned so that she was holding it above the bed, clicked open the barrel and pressed the sprung lever. The round of bullets dropped silently on to the white lace bedspread. She held up the gun and looked at it against the light. The barrel really was empty and she clicked it shut again. Now she saw Jani's enthusiasm for guns in a different light. It wasn't necessarily a latent desire to kill masked as an acceptable hobby or a need to see through the war games he'd played as a child. That's what she'd thought at first. It had clearly been a way for Jani to accept himself, to stop being afraid of himself, his power, his masculinity.

Wheatlocks wound a curl of hair behind her ear. As strange as it sounded, she had found that power in herself too. Rather, she sensed that she was on the verge of finding it, that it existed within her, that it slumbered somewhere deep down like a dark mass that, subconsciously, she knew frightened her. Still, she realised that there were no grounds for her fear. The mass was nothing but fuel, her very own gasoline. All she had to do was find the courage to use it.

Until then she had only been using a motor that had chugged along whenever she remembered to give it a little helping hand, but it never really got started. And perhaps this was why she had been happy living life the way she had: she'd been happy watching her life flow past, as though she were sitting on a shelf, standing to one side or behind the shop counter, as was normally the case. She was happy being beautiful. But she'd left her studies unfinished, and after Simo died she'd left practically everything else too. Now she felt that she was finally waking up again.

And when she thought of her power, she had the astonishing realisation that men and women were fundamentally the same, that perhaps both were made of the same elements, the same powers, but that both were forced to suppress the other half of themselves and to live up to others' expectations and examples in order to become accepted, even if it meant paralysing yourself in the process.

After thinking about this for a while, she'd noticed one of Simo's old jumpers and a couple of his pairs of jeans. She used to wear them all the time simply because she felt more comfortable in them, and gradually they had become her favourite clothes. But whenever anyone had commented on this, she'd started wondering whether there was something wrong with her, that perhaps she wanted to be a man or that she was a lesbian, but thinking like this was pointless. These clothes had simply represented her strength, something which only men are allowed to show on the outside. To her, Simo's clothes were like guns to Jani.

She lowered the barrel of the gun towards the floor, walked with silent, bare feet into the living room and stopped at the spot where she had the best view of the hallway. She wanted to see the clothesmen hanging in the hall cupboard, the front door and the shining security chain. She took hold of the gun with both hands, cocked it with her thumb, held her arms straight out in front of her, squinted and calmly squeezed her fist – and click! The first clothesman would have slumped to the floor. She cocked the gun again – and click! The second would be on the ground, and again – click! The third would have fallen.

She took a deep breath. She hadn't noticed that she was using the words 'slumped' and 'fallen', but not 'dead'. She couldn't imagine herself actually killing anybody. Once, when she'd run over a hare but it hadn't quite died, she couldn't bring herself to put it out of its misery, but had to stop another car, whose driver calmly reversed over the animal's head.

Despite this she still wanted a chance to shoot for real, and that's why she'd tried to contact Jani. She knew he would have taught her and explained all the various details and tricks. For now she'd have to make do with the books she'd borrowed from the library. The problem with these was that she often didn't understand them, or rather she didn't understand the terminology that enthusiasts took for granted. But at least it was a start.

She tried some more instinct shooting – that was one term she had learned. She suddenly flung her hands up in front of her, crouched down slightly, looked towards the lock on the door without aiming and pulled the trigger three times in quick succession without fully cocking the gun: click, click, click! She let the hand with the gun slump to her side and walked back into the bedroom. She had performed this ritual every night, usually just before going to bed and after checking that the chain was securely fastened, and though at first it had frightened her, now it felt relaxing. It was like playing with water as a child, splashing about in the shower was a ritual that had calmed her down before going to sleep.

And because of the revolver, or rather because of her understanding of her 'forbidden' strength, she wasn't so afraid any more. Things didn't seem quite as senseless; she hadn't once had to leave her evening chores and she'd stopped listening out for the lift. She still hadn't given up on the combination of wine and Diapams, and she was ashamed of that, but she felt certain that she would be able to give them up soon. Maybe she was expecting too much of herself, imagining that she'd recover from everything all at once, as if it were simply a matter of flicking a switch when it was in fact a long and slow process. She knew that. And though it might take her years, at least she'd taken the first steps.

She stopped beside the bed, opened the barrel of the revolver and picked up the bullets lying on the bedspread. They felt pleasant to the touch, so smooth and innocent, and one by one she put them back in their place. By now she was sure that, if someone really was visiting her at night, it wasn't Simo; she'd come to accept this. That was merely superstition on her part. More and more she wondered whether she'd just imagined the whole thing, just like her therapist had said. Accepting this no longer seemed out of the question. But imaginary or not, she now had a gun and that helped her. And if necessary, she knew how to defend herself.

She opened the top drawer again, put the revolver back in its place and covered it with her white, lace knickers as if she were putting a doll to sleep, then she pushed the drawer firmly shut.

Perhaps she viewed the gun too much as a purely metaphorical power. The possibility hadn't occurred to her that that power might turn her into a killer.

Onerva

'You do understand?'

'I think so,' said Harjunpää, his head to one side. 'I think I understand perfectly well.'

'No, really,' said Noponen. He moved awkwardly, suddenly, as though to indicate that he wanted to be left alone. There was no denying it was a bad moment: further down the corridor a meeting was underway, and from the comments he heard Harjunpää could well imagine they'd soon be arguing over whether to replace the old police Ladas with Opels or Toyotas – somebody preferred Fords, apparently – and whether they couldn't order food with plenty of garlic for lunch meetings instead of the same old Wiener schnitzels.

'We have to think of these compulsory transfers as part of a larger plan,' Noponen explained. 'You have to think of them as a whole, which the union will object to, of course. But you understand it's impossible to react in every individual case.'

'That may be, but when you are the individual case you can't help reacting,' said Harjunpää. Now he regretted bringing it up in the first place and not trusting what Aho had told him earlier.

'It's pointless,' Aho had said. 'The unions are powerless to do anything. They can give speeches on the super's birthday and award each other ribbons and medals and write critical articles under a pseudonym in their own magazines, but that's it. Like Noponen said, the reason they backed out of the night-shift issue is because they're fed up disagreeing with the supers…'

'I know it's hard on you personally,' Noponen tried to console him. 'And believe me, I've heard these same things from many an officer before...'

'Sorry, I don't mean to be a pain... Thanks.'

'And just so you know, almost everybody thinks there's a personal grudge behind these things, when what's really at stake is... Well, we're living in the age of change.'

'I certainly am,' said Harjunpää, unable to do anything about the bitter note in his voice.

He waved his hand and walked back down the corridor, and so that he didn't think badly of Noponen he tried to think why it was that police officers never stood up for themselves in these matters. As someone in the coffee room had once said: 'If somebody came up with a new directive saying that all officers on duty had to go about barefoot throughout the winter, we'd do it, and maybe at a sauna evening you might hear somebody comment that it wasn't very nice.' Still, he'd seen that same subordinate humility in himself. Twice. And both times it had been in front of Tanttu.

He pressed the button and waited for the lift. Was it perhaps because he and the other officers all related to a glorified idea of the police force, of the institution itself, and forgot that they were simply employees working for a particular employer? Of course, it didn't make any sense grumbling to yourself. Or was that it? When it's your job to ensure that people follow rules and regulations, how can you oppose the decisions of your superiors?

Whatever the cause, these grudges always manifested themselves as bickering between the different factions of the police force. There were almost ten separate unions within the force, and when the representatives of these unions went around whispering things to the supers in secret, the powers that be realised quite how fragmented the officers were, and the end result was generally that everybody was left licking their wounds.

Harjunpää got out on the fourth floor and walked reluctantly towards his office. The worst of it was that he didn't know whether Tanttu was serious or not. Ultimately, he hadn't said anything concrete. The chief had been happy simply making insinuations and intimidating him.

Ahomäki, the chief of the Violent Crimes unit, thought the idea of Harjunpää's transfer was a joke. He had pointed out that, thus far, nobody had been transferred out of Violent Crimes; on the contrary, the number of officers had been increased over time, which was the result of instructions from above to consolidate and improve the number of those with the most experience of running cases of particular violence against individual persons.

But when he thought of the look on Tanttu's face, Harjunpää was sure the man was deadly serious. He'd even begun getting used to the idea, saying his goodbyes to the little things around him. That Tuesday afternoon was perhaps the first time in his career when he hadn't felt the least interested in the cases on his desk. Perhaps deep down he was relieved. At least he'd be rid of the constant presence of death and the feeling of helplessness that had started lurking at the back of his mind all the more often.

He opened his door. The room in front of him was familiar and smelled the same as it had thousands of times before. His shoulders slumped. This was the hardest thing. There in front of him was his world: the Violent Crimes office. There was Onerva and Tupala and Base, Arska and Grönde and Jami and Luukko who played his harmonica in his dark office whenever he was feeling sad. There were all their shared morning coffee breaks, office parties with the squad's darts club, and all his exhausting cases, the failures and the successes. His entire world was there, and the thought of losing it was agony. It was as though a part of him was being wrenched away. At least there would soon be something to replace it, he thought.

'Harjunpää,' he said as he answered the telephone. It had clearly been ringing for some time. In her own office, Onerva was gesturing for him to answer it.

'I'm sorry, who?'

'Juha Backman. Remember? You interviewed me about the...'

'That's right. You ran after our intruder.'

'He's here! I saw him just a minute ago. If you can get down here quickly...'

'Where is he?' Harjunpää gasped and grabbed a pen. Naturally, it had run out of ink. He threw it away and rummaged through his drawers for another one. 'Where are you calling from?'

'A phone box.'

'Yes, but where? Where is the phone box?'

'In the Sokos shopping centre. The bloke's downstairs, in a locksmith's shop on the ground floor. He was talking to the man working in there as though they knew each other well.'

'But you can't see him any more?'

'No. This phone is on a different floor. But I'm convinced it's the same man. He looks smarter… Looks like he's wearing a suit.'

'What kind of suit?'

'A light jacket and red trousers.'

'OK. I'll send a patrol car down there. Go outside and point this guy out to the officers when they arrive. And if he leaves, try to see where he's going. Whatever you do, don't try to apprehend him by yourself. Don't try and be a hero.'

'All right. And you'll be here in a few minutes, yes?'

'The nearest patrol car will be; they won't be long.' Harjunpää ended the call, gesticulated frantically to Onerva and began dialling the internal emergency number.

'Emergency services.'

'It's Harjunpää from Violent Crimes. I need assistance to apprehend a suspect – quickly! There's a man in Sokos that we've been looking for in connection with a series of break-ins. Can you send a patrol down there on the double?'

'That shouldn't be a problem. Sokos, you said?'

'That's right. The suspect is on the ground floor in a locksmith's shop near the railway station. There'll be a man called Juha Backman waiting for you on the street. He'll point you to the suspect.' Harjunpää quickly reeled off a description of the bird-man. Then he waited, fiddled with the telephone cable and waited, listened to the sound of the duty officer typing at his computer at the other end. Finally the voice came back on the line: 'I'll have to put it in the queue for a while. There's been a nasty car accident in Kaisaniemi, so a couple of patrols are tied up there… But you're third in the queue, just as soon as we can free up a car.'

'Couldn't… Couldn't you bump us up the queue? Just this once?'

'There's very little I can do… We've got a house alarm that's already been waiting for fifteen minutes. Then the fire brigade has asked for assistance at…'

'Fine. Leave it in the queue. How long do you think it'll take?'

'Anything from fifteen minutes to half an hour. Sorry.'

'OK, leave it there. I'll take a car there myself and we'll cancel the request if we get there first.'

'Understood. Over and out.'

Harjunpää dialled the number for the Transport unit while trying to unlock his desk with his other hand. He pulled open the top drawer and there lay his weapon, loaded and in its holster. He grabbed it and attached the holster's clip to his belt. The metallic clang of the wardrobe door came from Onerva's office – she kept her revolver on the top shelf behind her hairbrushes and combs – and a moment later she was standing at his door and gave a nod.

'Transport, Seppälä.'

'It's Harjunpää. We need a car. Pronto! Can you sort us out?'

'Samara or Lada?'

'Doesn't matter.'

'You can have a Golf.'

Harjunpää slammed his door shut then ran off behind Onerva down the corridor. Doors flashed past them and sounds seemed to stretch oddly, even the incessant clicking of a typewriter: click-click-clunk… Onerva had thrown the Heart cardigan over her arm. It seemed to glow in different shades of red, covering her revolver, and its sleeves dangled like tails. Her skirt fluttered, her legs occasionally flashing beneath it, and her shoes tapped the floor: clipetty-clop!

They spun round the corner. Somebody was walking towards them, moved out of their way and said something about a fire. It was a joke. Onerva wrenched open the door to the stairwell and they ran down the stairs. The corners were tight. Harjunpää's palm burned as it chafed against the banister; sounds echoed like dull thuds all around them. A moment later and they could already make out the smell of exhaust fumes coming from the car lot.

They sprinted towards the Transport unit's office. Seppälä looked at them with worried surprise. Harjunpää didn't have time to explain what was going on but grabbed the keys from his hand. The car was unit 5-8-3, the same one they'd used before. Harjunpää wished it could have been a different car.

'Drive carefully, for God's sake!' Seppälä shouted after them.

'Let's go along the tram tracks,' said Harjunpää. 'We'll be there in five minutes.'

'Just be careful around the stops. People aren't expecting a car to…'

'I know. I know.'

Onerva heaved the garage door open. The smell of petrol became stronger. They could hear the sounds of driving, an engine revving. They ran past the lifts. Somebody was reversing into the aisle in front of them. Whoever was driving was reversing recklessly, or else he and Onerva were blocking the driver's view. A brown Lada appeared from the right. Harjunpää stopped in his tracks and tried to back away, but Onerva tried to reach the other side of the aisle in time. The brown Lada's wheels screeched as it braked and tried to avoid hitting them and the car reversing. Harjunpää didn't really know what happened next. He heard a thud, the strange sound of plate metal against stone. The Lada had hit a concrete pillar, and suddenly Onerva was shouting in an unfamiliar, high-pitched voice. 'Help! Oh good God! Timo! Timo!'

Harjunpää darted between the cars and crossed the aisle. Onerva was leaning against the pillar with her left hand. Her face was absolutely white, her eyelids were twitching irregularly and she slowly began to slump to the ground. She held her right arm to one side as though she didn't want to see it, as though she wanted to be rid of it.

Harjunpää gritted his teeth and stepped behind her. He grabbed her under the arms and held her tightly, squeezed her in his arms, held her like a child. Car doors slammed; everybody was asking questions. Harjunpää looked down at Onerva's hand. Her palm was covered in blood, lots of it, pouring out in a steady stream and splashing as it dripped on the floor. He could see the bone, sharp and jagged, and her index finger was drooping limply towards the palm of her hand.

'Show me, Timo,' she said faintly.

'No... It's best that you don't see it. Just shut your eyes.'

'Ambulance!' someone shouted. 'Somebody call an ambulance!'

Onerva suddenly started to shake. Harjunpää held her tighter still and could feel her trembling through his body, then she went limp. Harjunpää took a few steps backwards and laid her carefully on the floor. He knelt next to her and cradled her head in his arms. Somebody held her arm up while somebody else pressed the artery shut. There came the sound of running footsteps.

Harjunpää's hands were shaking. He stroked Onerva's face and hair and gently touched her eyebrows. A single thought throbbed through his mind: this can't be happening, this can't be happening to Onerva, to us, to me... These things only happen to other people.

'I couldn't avoid her,' he heard somebody explaining in horror. 'The other car was reversing so quickly, then you two came running out of nowhere.'

'She's been caught between the pillar and mudguard...'

'Will somebody get the bloody first-aid bag?'

'It wasn't my fault either, you know, what with you two running about blocking my view...'

Somebody opened the first-aid bag. Bandages whirled in the air. Harjunpää didn't want to see Onerva's hand any more.

'Scissors... Get me the scissors.'

'Hold it tighter. And undo those buttons.'

'Out of the way. Somebody go and flag down the ambulance.'

'I wasn't even going that fast...'

'Looks like her knitting days are over...'

'Lay her head down. Put that cardigan underneath...'

Far away came the rising and falling wails of a siren. Harjunpää remained on his knees. He held Onerva's head right next to his own, touched her hair and caressed her cheeks and nose and forehead.

'Oh my darling,' he whispered. 'My love, my love... Why...?'

All of a sudden he started to cry, heavily and violently, and he didn't care that the others could see him. He cried for Onerva's sake and for the sake of all the wickedness he'd seen, because he didn't know who was to blame. He cried for all the woes of his life.

Proposal

The traffic on Runeberginkatu rumbled past just the way it did every afternoon, as though it were tired and slightly agitated after a day's work. Tweety stood at a tram stop in the middle of it all, and he too was agitated. Or perhaps he was just nervous, and that was different. When you were nervous your whole body resounded like a shrill violin, but when you were agitated it felt like eating porridge made from shards of glass.

He glanced around and behind, then he looked at the people actually waiting for the tram, but nobody appeared to be looking at him. Something had unnerved him while he was at Weckman's. A frantic-looking man had been staring at him through the window. When he noticed the man, he took the escalator up to the ground level and it looked as though the man had gone inside Weckman's shop. He didn't hang around to see why but walked right out on to Mannerheimintie. He hadn't seen the man since then, and now he wondered whether he'd just been imagining things. But the incident had made him more vigilant than usual.

He took a tighter grip around the string holding his bouquet of flowers and his carrier bag and tried to forget about the man – and the other thing on his mind. That was more difficult; thinking about Wheatlocks was so easy. She was at home: he knew that. He'd visited her counter at Stockmann's but another woman was standing there, Rosefinch, and when he'd called the house Wheatlocks had answered in her singsong voice, 'Sari...' He hadn't been able to say anything, not even sorry. And when he thought of her voice now, it was like a fairy's, the way it flowed out between her beautiful lips, and when he handed her the roses he would kiss those lips. What joy! He took a deep sigh. What joy!

He raised his eyes, tilted his head to one side and looked up at Wheatlocks' windows, one next to the other, the golden afternoon sun shining in through them. To see these windows was the only reason he was standing at the tram stop. He would have liked to catch a glimpse of Wheatlocks too, but the windows were too high up. He lowered his eyes, checked there were no cars coming and crossed the road. He headed straight towards the door into Wheatlocks' stairwell, walking briskly and purposefully, but a few metres before he reached the door it happened again, for the fourth time. His steps began to slow all by themselves, then he came to a halt, turned his back to the door and groaned: he couldn't decide how to approach her!

Of course, the easiest thing to do would be to ring the doorbell, but that would have been plain and rather silly, as if he were a vacuum sales-man or someone come to read the electricity meter. He didn't want it to be like that; he wanted to surprise her! And how surprised she'd be if he opened the door himself, as quietly as he possibly could, then he'd tiptoe along the hall and stop at the living-room door... There she'd be sitting, there on the pink sofa, reading a woman's magazine. She'd raise her eyes and recognise him instantly. She'd know who he was, her very own beloved, and she'd stand up and walk towards him. 'My love. I've been waiting for you.'

Tweety sobbed quietly, his shoulders trembling. There was something so beautiful about it, something symbolic: he would show her that he was able to open the door that separated them, to break down the wall that stood in the path of their love, that he had a key to Wheatlocks' home, a key to her heart. He gave another sob, but this time for something else, something he tried not to think about. Toby.

Mother Gold had killed him, murdered him.

As soon as he thought about this, the area around his mouth began to feel cold and he didn't like the sensation. He knew what it meant: soon the world would start to creak, and he didn't want it to creak. He was in the city now, and moreover, he was on his way to propose to Wheatlocks.

He set off again. He walked briskly, almost at a run, because he wanted to escape the thought of Toby. What he really wanted to escape was the black dog sitting on the upper deck of his mind. It was sitting with its muzzle towards the sky and howling ominously, howling for Toby's death, the death of his only true friend. But the black dog was howling for another death too, and that scared him. It was howling for Mother Gold's death. The dog was willing it to happen, and though Tweety had tried to silence it, scolded it and said that you shouldn't wish for things like that, it just howled and howled regardless. It was a wicked, disobedient dog.

He stopped in his tracks, panting, and wiped his brow with quivering fingers. The howling wasn't as loud any more and he plucked up the courage to think of the funeral they'd held for Toby. Lasse had made a small coffin out of plywood and they'd buried him behind Sisko's vegetable patch near the hedgerow and Lasse's daughters had read out *Now I lay me down to sleep.*

Thinking of this made him feel better and he didn't feel as strongly that he had betrayed Toby by swapping him for Wheatlocks. Besides, he was sure that, up in rat heaven, Toby would be able to eat as many chocolate drops as he pleased.

He turned and looked almost shyly at his reflection in a shop window. He couldn't quite believe that he was looking at himself. The man in the window was wearing a white dinner jacket with small shoulder pads, a cream-coloured open-necked shirt and loose, wine-red trousers, and when he stooped to look at his feet he saw a pair of braided shoes with small leather tassels. He gently shook his head and his hair moved; it felt springy and remained fixed in its new style. He'd had it cut in layers, for the very first time. Until then he'd been happy to let Bamse lop it off in the kitchen with a pair of scissors.

All at once his hesitation was gone. Now he realised that he hadn't been worried about how to enter the flat but about whether he was good enough for Wheatlocks. But now that he'd seen himself in the window he knew that he had no reason to worry. He knew he could open the door without his guardian angel simply because his will was so great.

He strode back the way he had come, headed straight for Wheatlocks' door, put his hand on the handle and stopped for a moment, but this time it was for a different reason. He looked around at the cars and the people flowing past, taking in the whole world, and in a way bidding it farewell, for he knew that everything would look different the next time he laid eyes upon it. He pulled the door open and stepped inside.

The stairwell smelled good, of Wheatlocks' closeness. The darkness inside was calming, and the red rug in the entrance hall crunched comfortingly beneath Tweety's feet just as it had done countless times before. And when he listened to it more carefully, it wasn't simply the crunch of the rug but a barely audible whisper: *My love, my love.*

The lift was on the ground floor. Tweety walked past it and took the stairs. He usually took the stairs; this gave him time to listen to the house, to think of what it was trying to tell him. Not because he was doing something wrong or because he was afraid of being caught. The house was telling him good things: the joy in her surprised eyes, the softness of her lips as they kissed, the quiet music, the touch of her hands. It was telling him all about Wheatlocks, about his true love.

He came to the second floor, then the third and continued up to the fourth at the same pace. Wheatlocks lived on the fifth floor, and as he began walking up the last flight of stairs he hesitantly felt his breast pocket. The pouch was there, and it jangled melodiously as he touched it. He thought of the flowers and whether he should take them out of the wrapping paper or not. He couldn't decide: he'd never brought a woman flowers before. If he removed the wrapping he would spoil the thrill of opening up the package, and he would look silly standing there with a mass of crumpled paper in his hands.

He stopped at Wheatlocks' door and waited for his breathing to steady. His mind filled with a peculiar fondness. He raised his hand and gently caressed the wooden door and the name plate. Luoto, it read. He wondered whether Wheatlocks would start using a double-barrelled surname, Sari Anneli Luoto-Leinonen. It was like poetry, like the sound of a wagtail flying through the air. It would be a good name indeed.

He lightly pressed his ear against the door. Wheatlocks was still at home. At least, he could hear music coming from inside. It must have been Vivaldi; the music seemed to bubble peacefully, at once joyous and melancholy. Tweety felt moved that Wheatlocks liked classical music too, and he was sure she would come to like *Carmina Burana* as well.

He laid the bouquet of flowers and his plastic bag on the floor, dug the pouch out of his pocket and crouched down. He didn't dare kneel; it was the middle of the afternoon and somebody could appear in the stairwell at any moment. From a crouching position it was easier to stand up and continue on his way. Still, people didn't just *appear* in the stairwell; first they rattled about in their hallway for a moment, and even an idiot would have been able to listen out for that.

Tweety knew Wheatlocks' door off by heart: red, red, beige, turquoise, red, light blue, blue then orange. He turned his small brass pick in the lock, from left to right, and the lock responded to him. It started humming softly and beautifully, for it recognised his touch, and though he didn't once look at his watch, he knew it had taken him less than eight minutes to pick the lock.

He turned the lock very slowly and quietly. The door was ajar, just enough that he could see that the chain wasn't attached. The strains of Vivaldi grew stronger, a flute singing out its melody, and the air was filled with the scent of Wheatlocks and her home. It smelled of fresh laundry. Tweety quickly wiped the corner of his eye. He felt like he was coming home.

He ran his fingers through his hair, picked up the flowers and his plastic bag – which contained a box of Wiener nougat chocolates and a bottle of white wine, Riesling, he knew she liked that – then he opened the door and stepped across the threshold. The hallway was dark, but the dazzling afternoon sunshine was streaming in from the living room, and somebody was standing right amid the brightness.

At first he could only make out a dark figure, but as his eyes grew accustomed to the light he could see better: her thighs and hips and breasts, her hair shining like a golden halo, and he knew it was Wheatlocks. He quietly cleared his throat and stepped closer.

'Don't move!' she shouted suddenly, her voice shrill with fear. 'Don't move! I'll shoot!'

'Wheatlocks?' he exclaimed, but she didn't answer. She just stared at him, terrified. Her mouth wasn't Wheatlocks' mouth; it belonged to someone else. Her arms were raised in front of her and she was pointing at him. He stepped closer so that she would recognise him.

'Wheatlocks…'

'Stop! Go away!'

'But it's me… You love me… And I…'

Tweety heard the shot, heard the bullet lodge somewhere high up in the wall behind him and, frozen to the spot, he waited for another shot to ring out. But suddenly he felt a searing pain in his head, then it felt as though he were on his back, flying through the air. He found himself staring at the ceiling, and he realised that things weren't over, that this wasn't the end. *Don't kill me! Let me live!*

Talisman

Pipsa wasn't Pipsa any more. She was Talisman. Talisman was a pony. He was the pony Pauliina looked after at the stables in Masala, and he was dappled brown-and-white like an Indian horse.

Pipsa was dappled too. She had a flowing, fair mane and a long, whisking tail, and now that she'd escaped from the stall in the back garden and ran cantering across the meadow they billowed as the wind whistled through them.

'Oy! Talisman doesn't run away all the time!' Pipsa pretended not to hear Valpuri's cries. She just tossed her head back and forth and beat her hooves into the ground, trampling the flowers in her path.

'Come on, I don't like him running away all the time.'

'Neigh! Neigh!'

'I mean it… I'm not playing if you're going to run away all the time.'

That sounded more serious. Pipsa stopped in her tracks and turned to look back at her sisters in the garden. Valpuri's lower lip was jutting out, and that meant she was serious.

'But sometimes he just wants to run away.'

'But not all the time. If we're going to take him to a show, we'll have to plait his mane and polish his hooves. He usually gets some pieces of crispbread too…'

'But this pony would rather eat sugar.'

'Your teeth can't take sugar,' said Pauliina, but Pipsa didn't care. Pauliina was only pretending to be all grown up because Mum wasn't at home. She hadn't even come to play with them; she was just sunning herself and reading a book.

'I'll get you some,' said Valpuri. 'But only two sugar cubes, OK?'

Pipsa trotted towards the garden. When she reached the white willow tree she turned and looked back up the hill. An old man was doddering towards the forest. He looked almost like Grandpa, but he was walking with great difficulty as though he was in a lot of pain, and he wasn't wearing his waistcoat. Grandpa always wore his waistcoat because he kept his watch in the pocket. It was a pocket watch. And besides, Grandpa was having a nap upstairs and he wouldn't have gone off into the woods without her.

The man disappeared in amongst the trees and Valpuri appeared at the gate with sugar cubes in her hands. Pipsa galloped away and gently bounded across the shallow ditch that ran between the garden and the meadow.

Wild Animal

'Harjunpää!' somebody shouted down the corridor. Harjunpää heard it even though he had shut his office door, but he didn't react to it. Perhaps it didn't register that somebody was looking for him.

His sat by his desk, his face buried in his hands, and thought of Onerva who was still in theatre, lying under the dazzling lights, covered with green sheets, people silently working all around her. Harjunpää was hoping for a miracle. He prayed for one, prayed that the surgeons would be able to fix her hand, to attach her torn finger, to do everything they could so that nothing needed to be amputated. He knew it was possible; he remembered reading that with the help of microsurgery surgeons could even reattach severed limbs.

'Harjunpää! Has anyone seen Harjunpää?'

Every time he let his thoughts drift from Onerva, he found himself reliving the moment in the car lot again. He dashed through the door and ran after Onerva; he sensed the smell and the sounds, saw both cars; he recalled the screech of brakes and the clatter of metal against concrete, and after that... damn it, damn it, damn it.

He moved in anguish, shuffled his feet. What could he have done differently? He might not have rushed her. Perhaps. But after all the problems with the investigation, the unexpected lead had felt so exhilarating... Thinking about it afterwards, it wasn't just about catching the intruder. Deep down it was about winning, beating all the Tanttus and Järvis and Lampinens of the world. Was that wrong? Was that why he was being punished like this?

'Harjunpää! Any sign of Harjunpää?'

He rested his face on his arms, took a few deep breaths and inhaled Onerva's smell. He was wearing the Heart cardigan. He'd picked it up off the floor along with Onerva's gun once the ambulance crew had left. The cardigan's sleeves were a little too short for him but that didn't matter. The important thing was that he was wearing the cardigan. That way he would be with her every step of the way, holding her hand.

'Harjunpää!'

Kauranen flung the door open and stood in the doorway, out of breath, an investigation bag in his hand and his legs full of impetus.

'Henrikson and I are responding to a call-out. A man's been shot on Runeberginkatu. I think you should come with us... There's a Public Order Squad down there already, and initial information suggests the shooting victim might be your intruder.'

'Is he dead?'

'Not yet, at any rate. An ambulance has taken him to Töölö hospital. A single bullet wound to the head.'

'How did it happen?' Harjunpää asked and made to stand up.

'Apparently he'd picked the lock and entered the flat – in the middle of the day... The woman seems to have suspected that someone was breaking in for a while now and she'd got a gun to protect herself.'

Harjunpää brushed the hair from his forehead; he didn't want to leave. In a way, he was broken. He knew he couldn't be as vigilant as he needed to be, that he'd just wander about and get in everybody's way, and to his surprise he realised that he couldn't care less about what had happened. On top of that, he was waiting for a call from Onerva's son, Mikko, who had promised to let him know how the operation had gone.

'Well... Why don't you take a separate car and go straight to the hospital?' Kauranen suggested. Somehow he understood the situation. 'The gun was only a .22 calibre. He could be all right if the bullet didn't hit him too badly. He might already be conscious... You remember the bloke that escaped from a shooting a while back and sat in the hospital waiting-room with a bullet through his head...'

'Let's do that,' said Harjunpää. 'But take Thurman from Forensics with you. He knows our man's handiwork from before.'

Harjunpää steered the Lada into Töölönkatu and continued towards the hospital. He'd driven the entire journey amongst the other traffic and hadn't hurried – he'd had enough of rushing about – and it occurred to him that less than a week ago he had driven down this same street in pursuit of the same man. And just when he'd come to accept that he would probably never set eyes on the chaffinch man, now they were finally about to meet.

He rolled the car up on to the pavement and placed his parking certificate in the window, got out of the car and walked up to the door, and he was suddenly overcome by a faint sense of melancholy. He'd walked through this door dozens if not hundreds of times, and this might be the last time he did so on official business. Inside the air was pleasantly cool and smelled of treatment and pain; out of sight he could hear what sounded like a heated conversation. He produced his badge and stopped at the registrar's desk.

'A man was brought in from Runberginkatu with a gunshot wound to the head...'

'That's right. The little blighter... You'd better come with me.'

The man walked round the counter and made his way down the corridor. Harjunpää followed him and didn't even try to guess what the man had meant. In his own mind, he was prepared for anything.

The registrar stopped beside the open door of a treatment room. This was the room the sound of conversation had been coming from. There were four nurses and a doctor in the room. A curly-haired, frightened-looking nurse was having her arm swabbed with a bitter-smelling liquid.

'This man's from the Crime Squad. He's here about the man we...'

'You're a bit too late,' said the doctor, a serious-looking woman with a tight, thin mouth. 'He upped and left a minute ago.'

'Meaning?'

'According to the ambulance crew that brought him in, he must have come to in the ambulance but lain still, kept his eyes shut and didn't respond to any questions... When we'd got him in here he sat up and tried to leave. Of course, we can't force patients to have treatment. It's highly possible that he was in shock from what happened, the nurses tried to restrain him but...'

'He started thrashing about and scratching like some wild animal,' said the curly-haired nurse and showed Harjunpää her arm. It was streaked with red scratches, like the claw marks of a large cat. 'That's the thanks we get...'

Harjunpää sighed and leaned his shoulder against the doorpost.

'How serious were his injuries?'

'According to the paramedics the bullet caught him here,' said the doctor running a finger along the side of her temple. 'It's left a wound about five centimetres long in his scalp. We wanted to make sure he hadn't sustained any greater damage to the skull.'

'So... it's not life-threatening?'

'Not as far as we know. But, as I said, assuming that there are no other wounds to the skull. Still, it must have been quite a knock to the head, which would explain why he was unconscious when the paramedics carried him into the ambulance. Additionally he might have sustained some concussion when he fell. That's another reason it would have been a good idea to take some X-rays.'

Harjunpää stood up straight. 'I'm sure I can guess, but I'll ask anyway: you don't happen to have his details, do you?'

'I'm afraid not. He wasn't carrying any ID, just some loose change and a small bag that jangled...'

'Of course...'

'And to be perfectly frank, he wasn't in a very stable frame of mind. Even his eyes were... somehow like a panicked animal. And then he started thrashing about and scratching. It's in everyone's best interests to locate this man quickly.'

'Indeed. Thank you.'

'What a lovely cardigan...'

'Thank you.'

Harjunpää returned to the car. He sat still for a few moments, his hands folded limply in his lap, and couldn't concentrate on anything. Finally he blew his nose and reached for the car radio.

'Violent Crimes, Kauranen and Henrikson. Do you copy?'

'This is Kauranen. Copy.'

'The shooter can't hear you, can she?'

'No, she's inside. I'm out in the stairwell. We're taking the lock apart.'

'The victim only sustained a five-centimetre wound to the temple. He did a runner from the hospital before they could examine him.'

'Damn it... That information certainly won't comfort our lady here. She's in shock, I think, but not too badly. She's worried she might have killed him. Her story makes sense though: for about a year she's suspected that someone was coming into her flat at night.'

'Tell her that may very well be the case.'

'Will do. Are you on your way over here?'

'No, I'm going back to the station.'

Harjunpää turned the ignition and steered the car out into the flow of traffic, but he had barely driven a hundred metres before he heard Control calling him over the radio. He sighed wearily, and imagining all sorts of terrible things he pulled over at the first available gateway.

'Harjunpää. Over.'

'You put in a request a couple of hours ago for a patrol car to apprehend a suspect at Sokos.'

'Yes, and I happen to know they didn't get him.'

'Unfortunately not. But the officers spoke to this Backman guy and the old man that worked in the locksmith's. It turns out the bloke you're looking for works there too. His name's Leinonen, Asko Leinonen. We've got his details and an address if you want to stop by and pick them up.'

'Thank you,' said Harjunpää, then replaced the radio for the second time. 'Thank you.'

Snout

'Lampinen... I see... Tuula, you said your name is? And does Tuula have a surname?'

'You don't need that, do you? Over the phone?'

'Depends what you're calling about.'

'Well, because I know... I mean... I read about that bank robbery in the paper this morning. They got away with millions, right?'

'Carry on,' Lampinen exclaimed. His expression had changed in an instant and he swung his feet to the floor. Ash from his cigar fell on the desk and with his free hand he switched on a small tape recorder attached to the telephone. 'So that's what this is all about... There was such an incident.'

'The paper said something about a reward...'

'Correct,' said Lampinen and tried to remember whether there was a Tuula among his regular snouts. He couldn't think of anyone by that name, but it was no surprise that the woman had thought to call him; Lampinen was well known in the underworld. There was no doubt that Tuula belonged to that world, too. There was something slow and rough about her voice, probably from the drink or from sleeping around. Lampinen knew never to underestimate the skills of these people as sources of information; people whispered the strangest things in the bedroom.

'But, but... Don't you think it would be easier to talk about something like this face to face? To be honest with you, I don't much trust phones either...'

'Yes,' the woman hesitated. 'But first I want to know I'll get that reward.'

'The reward is for information leading to a conviction.'

'Well, what if I said I know who did it?'

'I'm sure that would do it,' said Lampinen trying to sound as nonchalant as he could, which was difficult as his mind was racing. The case was completely dark. None of the officers working on it had the faintest idea who was behind the robbery. The same went for Lampinen's sources: nobody in the underworld had been bragging about carrying out the job, nobody had been flashing money about or asking around for assistance in the weeks leading up to the heist – which was rare, particularly because this was clearly a highly professional job. They'd even mopped the floor before making their getaway. And now all of a sudden there was Tuula, the first ray of light they'd had, and a very promising one at that. Lampinen wanted to find out what she knew. He wanted to be the one to solve the case, and when he wanted something he generally got it.

'I don't want to meet you where someone might be watching…'

'How about I stop by your house?' Lampinen suggested. 'I don't even wear a uniform.'

'You won't be in a police car, will you?'

'You can trust me. I'll come in my own car. It's a green Saab, your average civilian run-around.'

'Don't bring anyone else. And I want to be sure you won't be… recording anything.'

'Now, now… Nothing like that. Now tell me where to meet you.'

The woman gave an address and briefly described the house, and Lampinen recalled the area instantly: it was an area to the north of the city with lots of detached houses. He'd been up there a few years back doing surveillance on a group of illegal fur traders, and eventually he'd managed to wrap that case up pretty quickly. Puistola was full of good luck. That is, it would be for him, if not for the bank robbers.

'Well,' the woman began for the third time after much procrastination, and Lampinen was sure this was it. There was something about the way she was staring at the floor and nervously biting her lip; he'd seen the same body language before. People behaved like this just before finally confessing to a life of crime.

'I know them well. I know one of them far too well… You probably know him too. It's… Oh God!'

Again she hesitated. Lampinen shifted impatiently on the sofa but managed to keep his expression calm. That was the second time the woman had said she knew one of them too well, and that meant he was probably a former husband or boyfriend. What was driving her was perhaps not so much the reward as the desire to give payback for the knocks she'd taken during the break-up.

Lampinen glanced out of the window. The house was situated on a quiet, remote plot of land surrounded by thick birch trees. It hadn't been taken very good care of and even the inside wasn't as clean as he had imagined. Everything was bare. But the biggest surprise of all was Tuula herself. She was actually quite attractive: dyed red hair, a pleasant, oval face, slim legs and breasts as pert as a pig's backside. She lived on the edge of society; she wasn't a whore or a crook, but she clearly wasn't an upstanding taxpayer either.

'What are you so worried about?' Lampinen chuckled as though she were a child afraid of the bogey man. 'All you have to do is give me one name and, abracadabra, the fifty grand is yours. The bank has given me their word. Fifty thousand... You could go to the Med a dozen times with that kind of money. Or the US of A.'

'But if only you knew... If he finds out it was me that told you, you might as well keep the money for my funeral.'

'Listen. That's just talk. It's easy to control people if you can keep them scared. Fear is a great tool if you know how to use it...'

'And you promise my name won't be mentioned?'

'I already said so,' Lampinen sighed and took a swig of beer. He'd been forced to accept her offer of a drink as she might have felt uncomfortable drinking by herself. But Lampinen knew all the old tricks. He just wet his lips with froth every now and then and didn't really drink at all.

Though then again... There was another option, and as he looked at Tuula's nervous expression he decided to take it. He knew that he would always be able to get someone from the station to come and pick him up and take the car, or if one thing led to another he could leave the following morning. Tuula was a nice-looking woman and he had a packet of condoms in his jacket pocket.

'God it's been a rough day,' he sighed, stretched and emptied his glass in a single gulp. 'I'd dearly love to clock off... Sorry for being so blunt. Have you got anything other than beer?'

'But you're driving.'

'I'll sort that out when the time comes.'

They looked at one another. Lampinen saw straight away that the woman understood. That's what she'd been waiting for all along, the slut. She licked her lips provocatively, stood up and swung her way towards the kitchen. She quite literally swung, showing off her body as she went. She had magnificent hips and buttocks. He could make out the contours of her panties beneath her skirt, and they weren't any old underwear either, but a tiny little thong. It aroused him and amused him at the same time. He was amused at the thought of people asking how he had obtained the information, to which he would reply, 'Fucking around'. And if he was awarded a police medal and people asked him how he had got it, he would say exactly the same thing.

An hour later Lampinen glanced at his watch and squinted his eyes with pleasure. Things were going well. They'd both drunk three whiskies in quick succession, held each other by the hand and talked about the difficulties of life and love, and gradually they'd started kissing and fondling one another, and now as he looked at his watch Tuula was taking her top off. She was wearing a beautiful, satin underwired bra and she had a magnificent chest. With one hand she was playing with his flies, and he truly hoped something would start happening down there soon; he couldn't always perform with strange women.

But he knew how to proceed: he would keep Tuula on a high heat and bring her almost to climax, then he would pretend to turn cold, and if she asked him what was wrong he'd sigh and say something to the effect that he was upset that she didn't trust him enough to give him the name – and he was sure that at that moment she'd lean over and whisper it in his ear.

He slipped his hand beneath Tuula's soft armpits and began fumbling with her bra strap. It was a strange law of nature that bra straps were always different from what you expected: you had to pull the clip when you'd thought you had to push it, but he managed to undo it eventually. Tuula gave a light sigh, lay further back on the sofa and began to undo her zip. Lampinen took off his shirt and let it fall to the floor, undid his belt and his flies – and gave a sudden start.

'What was that?'

'Oh my God… The door!'

Lampinen jumped to his feet. The sound of someone wiping their shoes on the doormat could be heard from the hallway. Then came a dull cough.

'For Christ's sake... so you don't live by yourself? Who is it?'

'My husband,' said Tuula, her voice suddenly frail. She crouched down and covered her breasts. 'He wasn't supposed to be back until the day after tomorrow. He's... He's terrible when he gets angry. He could kill you!'

'Just get fucking dressed,' Lampinen hissed. His head felt suddenly swollen; the whisky and the bitter taste of stomach acid rose up in his throat. He struggled to get his shirt on but it was useless; the damn sleeves were inside out and the fabric caught everywhere. 'Fuck it, fuck it...'

'Tuula, I managed to put up the...'

The man's sentence was left hanging. He just stood there with his mouth open looking, staring at them as though he couldn't believe what he was seeing. And he was built like a truck, rugged and muscular with angry, spiky hair and a lopsided face, as though it had been beaten that way in countless brawls.

'Easy... Just take it easy,' Lampinen managed to say, and he barely recognised his own voice. 'I can explain...'

'I doubt it,' the man growled between clenched teeth and stepped closer. The floor creaked under his weight. 'Your explanations aren't good enough for me.'

'Wait! This isn't what it looks like,' said Lampinen as he grabbed his wallet, flicked it open and showed the man his badge. 'Police!'

'All the more reason to rip your head off,' said the man, suddenly so full of rage that his head was trembling. He stormed past the table, stopped by a cupboard in the corner and wrenched the door open. The cupboard was full of weapons, rifles and shotguns, and that was enough for Lampinen.

Tuula ran shrieking into the back room. Lampinen grabbed the rest of his clothes and dashed towards the hallway. He quickly glanced behind him and saw the man brandishing a bluish black shotgun. There was a click as he opened the barrel. Lampinen shoved open the door; he feared for his life and the fear had almost paralysed him. His thighs suddenly felt stiff and he almost tripped and fell on his front. He gave a faint cry and bounded down the steps.

He ran across the yard as fast as he could, expecting to hear a shot at any moment, to feel the impact of the pellets. The man was at such close range that the pellets wouldn't have time to separate; they'd take his head off. He hunched his shoulders and ran towards his car, all the while grappling in his pocket for the keys. They wouldn't penetrate the body of the car, he knew that, unless the bloke got so close that he managed to shoot him in the neck through the windows.

Lampinen pulled out the keys. One of his shoes fell from under his arm; he left it behind, all he wanted was to get out in one piece, nothing else mattered! He pushed the key into the lock and fumbled, fumbled, finally managed to yank the door open, and looked behind him. The man had only reached the steps. He'd dropped the cartridges and was rummaging for them on the floor – either out of rage or agitation – and this gave Lampinen a few extra seconds.

Lampinen all but jumped inside the car, felt around for the ignition – it was on the wrong side, he'd forgotten he wasn't in a police car – found it eventually, managed to get the key in and turn it. The engine roared into life. He looked behind: the man had raised the shotgun to his cheek and was aiming at the car. He crouched down as far as he could, released the clutch and the car bolted forwards, hitting the post box as it went. Still there was no shot. Lampinen swerved on to the road. Gravel crunched beneath him; it was all he could do to keep control of the car.

Tuula was standing by the living-room window. She had taken a small mobile phone from her handbag and was now nimbly pressing its buttons.

'Police. Emergency services,' came the voice at the other end.

'Good evening, this is Kirsi Suhonen. I'm calling from Puistola, near the Nurkkatie junction. There's a car been careering up and down the road for a while now; I think it must be a drink-driver. It's a green Saab, and it looks as though he's gone off down Puistolantie towards the city centre.'

'Did you get the registration number?' she was asked. She did have the registration number; she dictated it into the phone and was asked to hold for a moment. She could hear the man putting out a call over the police radio: 'That's the third report about the green Saab. For all patrols in the area, the registration number is…'

Tuula sighed with satisfaction and ended the call. She then took a quick swig from the bottle of whisky and started to get dressed. Mara came in holding the shotgun.

'Jesus Christ, Jatta, he was driving fast. I was afraid he was going to run the car into the ditch, then I'd have had to beat him up for real.'

'I really hope they catch him. He was such a nasty piece of work...'

'There are always patrols on the move. I already called them twice.'

'Leave five hundred in the kitchen for the rent and let's go.'

Mara went into the kitchen. Jatta buttoned up her blouse. She didn't have the faintest idea who she had done this favour for – the plan had come through so many different people – but she suspected it had something to do with drugs. All she needed to know was that she and Mara had just earned themselves two thousand marks each.

Shot

'How did it go?' asked Kauranen. He was driving and Henrikson was in the passenger seat. Harjunpää was by himself in the back of the car. He liked sitting there, at a distance from the others.

'Timo! How did it go?'

'What?'

'Onerva's operation. Weren't you just talking to her son when we arrived?'

'Yes… she's still in recovery. That's why it took so long; they had to stitch her finger back on. Then they pulled the…'

Harjunpää fell silent. Onerva's hand, her lively, warm hand… It was hard to think of it crushed, something to be put back together like a broken vase. It was difficult to talk about it the way they talked about other victims' injuries.

'But the operation was a success, right?'

'Yes. It'll be a few days before they know for sure. You know, whether there'll be any… whether everything will work. And they told Mikko that this was only an emergency procedure and that they'll carry out a follow-up operation later on.'

'Great. Bloody good news. Who knows, her best cardigans might be yet to come.'

'True.'

Harjunpää leaned back and shut his eyes; he didn't want to talk about it any longer. He wanted to be sitting at the top of Pilvikallio thinking about things in peace and quiet. He wanted to let the sense of relief wash over him, little by little, just as night filled the woods. But instead he was reclining in the backseat of a Lada on his way to Joutsentie to arrest Asko Leinonen. The chief had said it would be best to make the arrest immediately and Ahomäki had agreed, and when he thought of what they'd told him at the hospital, it was in Leinonen's best interests to be apprehended sooner rather than later.

Henrikson leaned over and turned up the volume on the police radio. An agitated voice was calling Control: 'Can you tell the fire brigade to send a patrol down here, please?'

'What's your situation?' asked the duty officer.

'He won't come down. At this rate he'll sit there for a week and be stone cold sober by the time we get a breathalyser in his mouth. The car smells of drink and shit.'

'Have you been able to make contact?'

'Yes, but it's no use. He just maintains he was acting in an emergency.'

'Isn't that what every drink-driver says?' somebody interjected. 'They had no choice but to drive under the influence.'

'He's claiming someone came after him with a shotgun and all sorts. There are no gunfire marks on the car, and the bonnet got fairly mangled when he wrapped it around the pillar.'

'Very well,' the duty officer said dryly. 'If it really was an emergency, he should have stopped when he saw your patrol.'

'Right, but we were in pursuit for at least three kilometres. And he was doing 110 in a fifty limit. And what with him being a colleague and that...'

'OK. Tell him he's got exactly one minute to come down by himself and after that the fire brigade will turn the hose on him. If that doesn't work we'll cut down the tree. I'm sure we'll hear some rustling up in the branches once the chainsaws start cutting into the trunk.'

'Understood.'

Henrikson turned the volume down and fidgeted awkwardly. If one officer was bent, it disgraced the entire police force. It shook your belief in yourself.

'That's another position open...'

'And in record time if it's one of our lot,' said Kauranen. 'Tanttu loves drink-drivers.'

He turned the car into Tasankotie. Harjunpää tapped him lightly on the shoulders. It was as though he had suddenly come to, and he had a nagging feeling that there was something important he should have understood. He was puzzled, and illogically he found himself thinking of two doors, which should have been locked, but which opened when he pulled the handle.

'Pull over for a minute,' said Harjunpää. Kauranen slowed down and steered the car on to a small gravelled area at the beginning of the road. 'What is it?'

'Just wait a minute,' said Harjunpää and began once again going through the pile of papers in his lap. They contained all available information on Asko Leinonen. He had no criminal record, but their computer system had come up with a few pieces of information. They also had copies of documents pertaining to the property.

He took out the piece of paper about the property and glanced through it. It had a list of everyone that lived at Joutsentie 3, and they were quite a colourful bunch: nine persons altogether and, judging by their names, all members of the same family. Harjunpää went through the list of names one last time. He stopped for a second at the name Lasse Leinonen, then slightly longer at the names Reino and Sisko Leinonen. But no, he didn't understand; a light bulb didn't suddenly switch on in his mind. Perhaps Leinonen was such a common name that he was confusing matters. And it was no wonder; he was far from being on top form.

'You've got something?' Kauranen asked and turned around. Henrikson looked back, too, and Harjunpää moved uncomfortably. He couldn't understand the hunch he'd had a moment ago; it somehow kept changing form, but still he had a vague suspicion that something wasn't quite right. There was something threatening about that hunch; he felt that something terrible was about to happen. He almost jumped as he realised the fundamental nature of his fear: he was afraid that someone was going to die.

'Timo. Can we, erm…?'

'No. I mean… I don't know… I'm just wondering whether it's wise to go in there when there are so few of us.'

'Few?' Henrikson smiled. 'There are three of us.'

'He's not a murderer,' Kauranen added. 'And there's nothing to indicate that he might be armed. Anyway, every time we get anywhere near him he runs away.'

'Of course,' Harjunpää mumbled hesitantly. 'I'm sorry lads. I've never believed in superstitions, but... I've got a rotten feeling about this.'

Kauranen leaned closer and looked at him pointedly.

'Don't take offence, OK?' he said. 'It could be to do with Onerva. I read a memo from the ministry saying that everyone involved should receive some sort of support or therapy when their partner is injured or... Think about it. You and Onerva were going to pick up this same guy, and look what happened. And now you're in the same situation again. On the same day, too. It's no wonder those fears start to raise their heads...'

'I know,' Harjunpää sighed and didn't know whether Kauranen was right or not, but still a small warning bell continued to ring inside him.

'We can take care of this, if you want to stay in the car,' said Kauranen. 'That's absolutely fine.'

'No, I'm coming with you,' said Harjunpää, embarrassed that he'd even brought it up. 'Maybe meeting him will make this feeling go away.'

'We could call for back-up, just to be on the safe side.'

'Let's do that. It certainly won't do any harm.'

'OK,' said Henrikson, and perhaps he, too, was relieved at the decision. He called Control and the duty officer made almost immediate contact with unit 3-5-7, a patrol only five minutes away in Malmi.

'And 5-8-8,' came the voice through the radio. 'Is Harjunpää there with you?'

'Yes. He's in the back. He can hear you.'

'Harjunpää, call home when you get a chance.'

Harjunpää felt suddenly ill at ease – was that what had been worrying him? He took the microphone from Henrikson.

'Do you have anything more specific?'

'Your eldest daughter just called in. If I understood right, their grandfather's gone walkabout.'

'Copy that. I'll call her as soon as I get a chance. If she calls back, tell her I should be home in about an hour and a half.'

'Will do.'

Harjunpää sighed heavily and lay back in the seat. That was all he needed... Pauliina was probably worried sick because, despite her difficult age, she was a very responsible girl and Elisa was out in town. She'd gone out that afternoon to help a friend finish moving house and they were planning on going out somewhere that evening to relax a little. Of course,

Harjunpää couldn't have predicted that yet again he'd still be at work long after his shift had ended. And when he thought about Grandpa, he was sure he would be sitting beneath the giant spruce or at the foot of Pilvikallio where there was a boulder to sit on and the remnants of a campfire.

The Transit van from Malmi appeared at the end of the road and pulled in next to them on the gravel. They talked briefly about what to do, agreed to check out the area first and only then to decide who was to do what. They got back into their respective cars, drove a hundred metres up the road and parked the vehicles on the cycle path at the side of Tasankotie.

'There shouldn't be anything out of the ordinary here,' said Harjunpää to the constables from the other patrol car; one of them was Lundberg and the other a young girl with blonde plaits who was clearly wearing a bullet-proof vest beneath her uniform. 'But there are a lot of people in there and we're not entirely sure of the layout of the property. What's more, this Asko is one for running away. But let's go and take a look…'

They quietly stepped across the cycle path and on towards Joutsentie. It was a narrow dirt track, just wide enough for a car, with thick patches of grass growing sporadically down the middle. Tall birch trees grew along one side of the path. They sloped across the path making it like a vault, and the evening dusk suddenly turned to almost total darkness. To the right was a black row of thick spruces rising up towards the sky. It smelled of raspberries and a stream rippling close by. In the distance a train rattled past.

'This must be it,' said Harjunpää in nothing but a whisper and stopped by an opening in the spruces. They came to a halt and the crunch of gravel suddenly stopped; the silence felt almost puzzling.

'There are just so many buildings,' Harjunpää added as his eyes scanned the yard. The area looked wild. There were four buildings, or cottages, all in pretty bad shape. In front of a building that looked like a workshop stood a digger and a number of old cars, of which only a blue van looked like it was still roadworthy. A large antenna jutted up from the roof of the cottage to the side and there was light in the windows. The lights were on in the middle building too, an odd-looking, two-part cabin. They could hear voices coming from inside; it sounded as though the inhabitants might be having a party.

'Let's go straight for the middle cottage and ask,' said Harjunpää. 'You two stay here so you can keep an eye on the other house. From here you should be able to see anyone making a run for it.'

Lundberg and the girl nodded, and Harjunpää, Kauranen and Henrikson started moving. They each subconsciously checked their holsters, and a pair of handcuffs jangled softly on Henrikson's belt.

'I don't like our chances of finding him if we have to go through this whole area.'

'We can't do that without the dogs or we'll never get home.'

'I'm not sure there's any point starting a search this evening,' said Harjunpää. 'Let's see what this lot have got to say. And if he's not at home, he might just have popped out somewhere.'

'Right. We shouldn't have any problems now we've got his name and address. We'll put out a search notice and he'll be in custody within a fortnight.'

'Unless he's got shed-loads of money. Then he could hide somewhere or leave the country. Still, I doubt it judging by this place...'

They stopped. The front door of the cottage was ajar. A strip of light shone out, cutting through the thickening darkness like a wedge of yellow. They could hear music and high-spirited conversation. Harjunpää stepped to one side, pushing willowherb and chrysanthemum weed out of the way, and the closer he got to the window the more clearly he could make out the conversation.

'... still might turn up at any moment...'

'... pointless... don't torture yourself... just relax...'

Then an elderly woman asked something in a bitter voice, as though she were hard of hearing or didn't understand what the others were talking about.

Harjunpää stood up on tiptoes, peered through the window and gave a start; sitting right in front of the window was a blonde-haired woman, barely half a metre away from him. Further back in the room was a table with two men, one stocky and one thin. The thin one wasn't necessarily the one they were looking for though; even sitting down he looked rather too tall. Someone else was moving to one side. Harjunpää moved away from the wall.

'There are at least four or five people in there,' he said. 'Two women, one of whom is much older. She must be their mother. Probably nothing... I couldn't see our intruder. But there's a window on the other side. Henrikson, go round there just in case.'

Henrikson went around the house while Harjunpää and Kauranen walked up the steps and held their badges ready. Harjunpää slipped his hand beneath his jacket and undid the popper holding his revolver in place.

They peered through the open door into a porch. It was full of junk and old newspapers. To the left was a steep set of stairs leading up to the loft. To the back was an open door, behind that what looked like a combined kitchen and dining area where the residents were sitting. The men and a woman dressed in blue dungarees were playing cards; this wasn't the same woman Harjunpää had seen through the window. The table was covered with bottles and glasses. Sitting on a bed placed along the far wall was a silver-haired, elderly woman holding a glass of cognac.

'This is it,' said Harjunpää and looked at Kauranen. He rapped his knuckles loudly against the door; a moment later they were in the porch, surrounded by the smell of rotten wood, and at the open living-room door. Everybody inside looked at them in horror.

'Evening,' said Harjunpää. 'We're with the Crime Squad. We're looking for a...'

His sentence remained unfinished. The thinner of the two men disappeared behind the table like a stoat, to hide, to grab something. A moment later he stood up again holding an enormous, shining revolver: a huge magnum. The barrel was still pointed at the floor, then the man began to raise his hands. Harjunpää crouched to one side and reached for his holster. Kauranen shouted something. The stocky man grabbed the barrel of the gun and wrenched it towards the ceiling. All of a sudden the woman in dungarees was involved too, all three of them struggling and yelling, their hands flailing, sending bottles flying all around them.

Then a shot rang out.

In the small, enclosed space it sounded like an explosion. Their ears snapped shut. Wood splinters and sawdust rained from the ceiling and the smell of gunpowder filled the air. The back window smashed as it was struck by a falling plank, and Henrikson was there in the gaping window, his hands outstretched, his weapon aimed inside.

'Nobody move!' he shouted. 'Police!'

But the shot had stunned everyone. The struggle had ended; the men and the woman stood perfectly still, their hands frozen in the air like a statue. Kauranen took their revolver and Harjunpää lowered his gun. The sound of running footsteps could be heard from outside and a moment later the Malmi officers were in the porch, panting, their guns raised.

'What wickedness!' came the old woman's shrill voice as she stood up. Her cognac glass had fallen to the floor and she held both hands up to the area around her heart. 'You devil! Shooting a gun in front of your mother. I tried so hard, but spare the rod and…'

The woman doubled over across her hands. A wheezing sound escaped from her mouth, almost like a sigh. Harjunpää bolted towards her, but it was too late: the woman collapsed on to the floor. There was a crack as her head struck the leg of a chair. Harjunpää knelt down and tried to turn the woman over, but she had gone limp.

'Can anyone do CPR?' he gasped. 'Someone call an ambulance! Get the paramedics on the line. Tell him we've got an elderly woman with a suspected heart attack.'

He sensed that it was all futile, too late, but he had to try at least, always, for anyone. He felt the woman's neck and wrists for a pulse, but couldn't find any signs of life. Around the middle finger of her limp hand the woman was wearing a large golden ring with a dazzling ruby set in the middle. It couldn't possibly be real, he thought, looking around him, and it was somehow too showy. It must have been junk. He stood up.

The young policewoman darted towards them, knelt down and began opening the woman's clothes in rapid, self-assured movements.

'Lundberg! You do the compressions,' she shouted. 'I'll breathe.'

They got to work. Harjunpää drew further back; he suddenly felt rather weak. The dungaree-woman moved away from the others. She approached them, stopped and stood staring at the woman lying on the floor. Then she raised her eyes and looked at Harjunpää. They were the eyes of someone who had grieved for much. The corner of her mouth began to twitch and all of a sudden she burst into hysterical laughter. Harjunpää wondered whether he was mistaken; perhaps she was crying. Either way, her cheeks were wet with tears.

Eagle Owl

The spruce trees in the hedge surrounding the house at Joutsentie 3 were old, thick resinous giants. Their lower branches swept across the ground like the hem of a long skirt, and sheltered beneath that hem lay countless metres of spruce tunnels. The ground in these tunnels was covered in a thick, brown mattress of years of pine needles.

About halfway along the middle section of the hedgerow, right behind the red cottage, grew a larger, grander spruce like the mother or father of all the others. Perhaps whoever planted this hedge had taken inspiration from this very tree.

The pieces of branch scattered around the base of the Mother Spruce's trunk betrayed the fact that someone in the tunnel had been busy with a saw. If anyone were to stand tight against trunk and look upwards, they would notice that certain branches had been cut away to create a small shaft, just big enough for someone skinny, leading straight up into the sky, with supporting branches left at regular intervals to form something almost like a ladder.

About halfway up the spruce, high above the cottages and ramshackle roofs, in the thickening evening darkness, sat an eagle owl. It was a rare bird in southern Finland – particularly in the city, right in the middle of an area of detached houses. What made this eagle owl even rarer was the fact that it had the body of a human.

The owl clearly considered this something of a deficiency, a shortcoming, but the Creator had made up for this deficiency by giving him a human mind, in addition to a bird's mind, and the power of thought. Or something thereabouts.

At that moment the eagle owl was thinking for the umpteenth time that it had been a wise decision to cease being a human and to become a bird. He had done this because he was afraid of what humans called love, something that represented the greatest deceit in the world.

Humans said love was good, worth striving for, the most beautiful thing in the world. But they kept their mouths shut about the fact that those who had been blessed with love seemed to have a clandestine entitlement to destroy those who begged for love in return.

The eagle owl sitting in the tall spruce at Joutsentie 3 knew this very well. The first love in his life, the source of his former human life, every human's role model, his own mother, had tried to kill him. In doing so she had struck an ineffaceable fear into the owl's soul, a fear which, from that moment forth, had dictated his every decision and which his mother had used to control him throughout his life thus far.

The eagle owl had loved his sister, perhaps he'd loved her the most after his mother, and his sister had said she loved him back, even in the last few days, but she too secretly wanted to destroy the owl and that's why she had deliberately given him the wrong advice and forced him into a trap. And as for the deliriously beautiful, blonde-haired woman for whose love the owl would have crawled on the ground... The eagle owl removed one of his hands from the resinous branch and felt the side of his head. The wound had stopped bleeding and the blood had dried to form a plug across it. Even this woman had tried to kill the owl, and still all he had wanted to do was give her love and to accept the love she offered him in return. It had been the first time in the eagle owl's life that he had dared even to attempt such a thing.

The eagle owl leaned his head to one side and smiled the almost sinister smile of a bird of prey. He would never be trapped again. He wouldn't beg for love from anybody ever again, wouldn't offer his own love. He no longer had anything to offer; what he'd once had, had died along with the human being the eagle owl had once been. Best of all was that the owl had finally killed his human form himself, and had done it very skilfully.

After he'd escaped from the clutches of the people dressed in white, he had flown to Joutsentie and climbed up the ladder into his former nest without anyone seeing. There he had taken off his old clothes, his human clothes, and put on his shadow-grey coat of feathers that smelled of his new self.

He'd taken his wallet, stuffed it in the pocket of his red trousers and packed the trousers and the jacket, the shirt and the tasselled shoes into a carrier bag. Then he'd picked up the map in the telephone directory, selected a page with lots of sea and written on it the words 'You'll find me here', and left the directory open on his bed. Then the owl had flown into the city, down to Mustikkamaa and emptied out the contents of the bag on the rocks by the shore.

The eagle owl was a wise bird. Of course he understood that there would be times when he would have to interact with humans, for the world belonged to humans, and was therefore a bad world. He knew that sometimes he would have to pretend to be human, and that's why he had soared across the skies to Good Johansson's place. Good Johansson had promised to make him a new human identity. The eagle owl had chosen the name *Huuhkaja*.

The eagle owl turned his head, listened to the night and looked down at the cottages beneath him. Things had slowly calmed down. He had been sitting up in the spruce when all the commotion had started; he'd seen the police arrive and peer through the windows, then came the shot that had made him tremble and keep his eyes closed for a moment – he remembered how he too had been shot – and that's when the commotion had really started.

Blue lights had started flashing; men and cars came and went. The last to arrive was a white van into which they had carried a human body covered in a blanket. The eagle owl knew who it was: it was the witch. He had seen all the others in the yard, but not her.

And now she no longer existed. She had ceased to be. The eagle owl was puzzled that, though he thought about it time after time, he felt nothing, neither joy nor sorrow. Nothing at all. Perhaps he didn't feel anything because the dead person wasn't his mother: she was a witch.

Lasse had shot the witch. He was the only one the police had taken with them. And because they hadn't taken Sisko or Reino that meant they couldn't know that they were the ones that had paid a visit to the bank. And of course, Lasse had only shot the witch because he loved her. He'd always sworn he loved her, even as a little boy, crying, his backside raw.

His bird's instinct told the eagle owl that it was time to set off. He released his grip on the tree and clambered down the ladder of branches to the tunnel with the pine-needle carpet. He stood for a moment staring at the yard through the branches sweeping the ground, then flew towards the workshop gable, his wings beating silently.

He stood there for a moment and listened, grey and unnoticed, by the front wheel of the crippled digger. There was no movement, and no sounds came from inside, and he darted nimbly beneath the digger. It was like a bear, a real dead bear, a fresh corpse, and the eagle owl wanted to eat its flesh. He ran his hands along the underside of the digger's frame until he found what he was looking for: a hole just big enough to fit your hand through. He worked his fingers inside the gap, groped further inside and found them: a number of tightly sealed copper tubes. There were three of them in the hole, and the eagle owl took all of them.

The eagle owl knew that there was nothing but Finnish marks in the tubes, but that suited him perfectly well – eagle owls weren't migratory birds. He didn't know how much money was in the tubes. No doubt it would be less than his share of the loot, but it would be enough to see him through the next few years. Perhaps there'd even be enough to buy a small nest with white walls somewhere far away.

And when the money eventually ran out, the eagle owl would start to hunt again. He'd hunt the way he should have hunted when he was still a human: he would scavenge for money, only money, the flesh of life, and if a human were to take him by surprise, he wouldn't fly away again. He would fight back. He would strike Flame, his razor-sharp beak, right into that human's chest.

The eagle owl stuck the tubes under his arm, listened for a moment, and when the coast was clear he fluttered into the air, flew towards the gap in the hedge, skimming the tall grass as he went, and made his way through to the path. Then he disappeared somewhere to the left.

Father

Harjunpää climbed up the staircase, instinctively rushing, though rationally he knew that he wouldn't find anything in Grandpa's room that might put his mind at rest, and deep down he had a feeling that the time for rushing was already gone.

He stepped across the threshold and was met by the lingering smell of old pipe smoke. He stopped by the desk. It was exactly as Pauliina had said: Grandpa had left behind his nitrate pills and his hearing aid, and even his pocket watch. He'd never done that before; he'd kept the watch with him as though it were as important as life itself. Harjunpää's shoulders went limp. He gently touched the thin golden chain, prodded it for a while, and after a moment somewhat hesitantly picked up the watch, wound it up, clasped it in his hand and pressed it against his chest.

'Dad,' said Pauliina. Harjunpää gave a start and almost guiltily put the watch back where it had been. 'There was nothing we could do. He was supposed to be having a nap and we were all out in the garden. That's why we didn't even realise he was missing until dinner was ready… And now I think…'

'Listen,' said Harjunpää and turned around. He was tired and strangely on edge, broken on the inside; it had been such a gruelling day. He knew he mustn't show it, because the girls would take it the wrong way. 'Grandpa's a grown man. He's the one that has to take responsibility for himself and his actions. You weren't supposed to guard him, just to make sure he was OK…'

'But still. What if he's…?'

Harjunpää looked at the desk and ran his fingers through his hair. 'He's probably down at Pilvikallio or sitting under the big spruce tree.'

'But your expression… You don't believe he's there either.'

'But I hope he is.'

'Then let's go and fetch him.'

'I'd rather go by myself.'

'Why?'

'Pauliina,' said Harjunpää and took his eldest daughter by the hand. 'I've got to go by myself. He's my father… You'll understand one day. I have to do this by myself.'

They looked at each other for a moment and Harjunpää could see that Pauliina did understand, at least in some way.

'Thank you.'

'That's a nice cardigan,' said Pauliina blankly. 'The colour… it's as if you're in love.'

'Thanks. It's Onerva's. I'm just borrowing it.'

Harjunpää walked downstairs and went to the cleaning cupboard. The only torch in the house was there. He switched it on and gauged that there should be just enough battery power left.

'You're not taking us with you?' asked Valpuri.

'Not this time. I'm sure you understand… I'll be able to look faster and over a wider area if I'm by myself.'

'I suppose…'

'OK. We'll be back before you know it. But I think it's past Pipsa's bedtime.'

'No it isn't!' his youngest retorted. Harjunpää was about to tell her off – but why do that? He contented himself with tickling Pipsa's head.

'See you in a little while…'

Harjunpää went out the front door and began walking up the grass-covered incline. Crickets chirped; night was already well underway. He chose the path on the left which led past the great spruce tree all the way to Pilvikallio, then on to the meadow and the woods, which stretched out like a wasteland almost all the way to the centre of Kirkkonummi. The path drew him further into the mysterious darkness, but when he looked up the sky shone above him as a lighter strip of blue.

He was no longer thinking of Onerva or of the old woman who had died right in front of him. He tried to block them from his mind. Perhaps he wasn't really thinking of Grandpa either, but rather of the strange notion that had occurred to him several times in Grandpa's company: did he want something from the old man that he didn't quite understand? Was he looking for some sort of answer to all his questions, something that would explain away all the ills of his life? Or was it advice, wisdom, something that Grandpa had realised long ago?

He gingerly crossed the planks laid out across the brook and, ever the policeman, stopped in his tracks and switched on his torch. He lit up the bubbling waters, first higher up the hillside then to the right, but all he could see in the stream were the same gnarled roots that had always been there.

He continued up the hill and suddenly found himself wondering whether the Kirkkonummi police had a dog patrol and that, if not, whether he knew any of the dog trainers from the Helsinki force well enough to call them out in the middle of the night. He felt almost as if he were on duty and only stopped and shook himself once he started thinking where it would be best for the police to park their cars to make their journey through the woods as short as possible.

'Please be with Grandpa,' he said suddenly. 'Let him be OK...' He had reached the great spruce tree, switched on his torch and lit up the trunk. At the base of the tree was a tangle of roots where it was nice to sit, but this time there was nobody there. He held the light to one side, but everything looked just as empty. He walked briskly around the tree and shouted: 'Grandpa! Father!' His cries echoed faintly, but no one answered. He felt a sudden disquiet, a sense of helplessness; the forest was so large.

He turned off the torch and continued along the path towards Pilvikallio. He was more worried than before, his concern edging deeper inside him. He was almost in a panic. Without noticing it he had quickened his pace with every step, and a moment later he was jogging forwards.

'Grandpa!' he hollered. 'Father!'

He ran past Valaskivi and the tree where the woodpeckers were always drumming away, and the woods gradually became thicker; trees encroached on the path and the bushes kept catching on his cardigan making him stop for a moment. It was suddenly much darker. By the time he reached the small pool, the air felt much cooler.

'Father!' he shouted. 'Father, where are you?'

The path began to slope upwards. He was approaching Pilvikallio. He knew it wasn't far now, less than a hundred metres. The air smelled ever mossier. A very small animal took fright and darted into hiding.

'Father!' he shouted. 'It's me! Timo!'

The path became much steeper and he was already out of breath. Suddenly he caught the faint smell of smoke, though it wasn't pipe smoke. It was a bonfire, or at least it had been. Now it was the smell of dying embers from which a barely visible trail of grey smoke rose up into the sky.

He slowed his step to walking pace. He could make out Pilvikallio, a dark mountain against the sky. He couldn't see any light at the foot of the hill. At least not yet. He stepped closer and soon he could see the red glow of the embers. He switched on the torch and aimed it at the boulder they used as a chair.

'Father?' he said softly. Grandpa was sitting there, his elbows propped on his knees, motionless. 'Father?'

'Is that you, Timo?'

'Yes.'

'My shoulders are so sore. They do ache.'

'Let's go home. Then I'll take you to the doctor. You must be freezing.'

'Yes, I am rather. But, Timo...?'

Harjunpää lowered his head. His chest was full of something; it felt as though it was about to burst.

'I... You've never... I've never been able to...'

'But it's true. You are my son and I... very, very much...'

Harjunpää brought his hands up to his face and pretended to rub his forehead. He wanted to tell his father that he loved him, but he couldn't; his lips were trembling so much that he simply couldn't. Later, he thought, maybe once I've got him home, and with that he took off the cardigan, wrapped it around his father's shoulders and took him firmly by the arm.